A RUN YOUR MONEY

BY RICHARD LAWS

For Uncle Jack & Grandad

First published 2020 by Five Furlongs

ISBN 978-1-9164600-6-5

More horseracing stories by Richard Laws:

The Syndicate Manager
Gimcrack
An Old-Fashioned Coup

One

It rained the day Mary buried her husband. She didn't remember the service, but she couldn't forget the rain. She recalled that day frequently and the late July downpour always figured prominently, as did her brother-in-law's words. After all, that was the day he threatened her, again.

She was staring down at the coffin from the graveside when the downpour started. She watched, beguiled by the fat water droplets that plinked noisily onto the oak box and remained sitting proud on its highly polished surface. The shiny brass plate engraved with Henry's name and dates was already sullied by handfuls of soil. The rain soon ensured it became smudged with mud.

Henry had pleaded, and when that hadn't worked, insisted she stayed at home and didn't attend his funeral. Her husband had made a number of nonsensical demands in the last few tortured months of his life, but this was one demand Mary had always intended to ignore. Who cared what people thought?

Her brother-in-law waited until the other mourners hurried down the hill to find cover from the downpour. Then he sidled over to stand by her side, close but not touching, the two of them staring downwards into the oblong hole. And above the hollow sound of the rain thumping onto her husband's coffin lid, Eddie Romano spoke to her for the first time in almost thirty years.

'It's been a long time, Mary. I seriously thought you might have died. Yet here you are, as large as life,' Eddie had murmured gruffly in his heavy North Eastern accent.

She'd almost forgotten how odious Henry's brother could be. There had been threats from him before, in another time, another place. Perhaps this was the reason Henry hadn't wanted her to be with him at his graveside, but she wasn't about to miss her darling husband's farewell.

When she purposely remained silent, Eddie continued, 'I understand you looked after him well. Right up to the end.'

Mary hadn't replied. She had hoped, but not expected to hear such conciliatory words. However she knew Eddie too well and didn't comment.

Eddie's voice hardened, 'Do you remember the warning I gave you all those years ago?'

The sound of the rain filled the void Eddie's words left behind. Mary swallowed back a mixture of anger and fear. She did remember their last meeting. She'd replayed that scene thousands of times; Eddie had threatened to kill her.

Mary continued to fix her stare downwards and in a soft, lilting tone, that in no way reflected the mass of raw emotion she was experiencing, Mary gave her brother-in-law an answer she felt was appropriate.

'Yes, and Henry was always ready for you and I will always be ready for you.'

He let out a barking laugh. Mary gave him a sideways glance. She detected condescension in his eyes and a wave of disgust washed over her.

'I'm sure you will,' he said lightly, 'You've never been the sort to just go quietly. That's what Henry appeared to love about you.'

Eddie paused to turn his head, sidle closer, and look down on Mary - the diminutive woman who had beguiled his brother and caused his family to fracture.

'But Henry's gone now.'

Mary muttered an expletive under her breath when she realised how close Eddie was to her. Feelings of claustrophobia and then revulsion filled her.

She gave him a soft push in his chest. It was a natural reaction to his close proximity. But Eddie wasn't expecting it, and was caught off-balance. His shiny leather soled brogues slipped on the wet grass, forcing him to go down on one knee and steady himself with his hands. Wiping and flicking a combination of rain, mud and grass cuttings from his hands, Eddie stood up and met Mary's determined gaze.

Behind her right shoulder Eddie spotted two men hurrying back toward the grave. He and Mary wouldn't be alone for much longer.

Mary heard the shout, but wasn't tempted to take her eyes off Eddie; he was capable of anything. She watched as he skilfully replaced his indignant anger with a falsely benevolent smile for the benefit of the approaching mourners.

'I'll be sending Vincent to see you shortly,' he hissed, 'Do as he asks, Mary. That way, you might get to live beyond Christmas.'

Two

Less than a week after her husband's funeral, Mary Romano answered her cottage door and signed for a letter. The fifty-three year old felt a buzz of excitement as she inspected the envelope. A small logo in the top left-hand corner indicated the letter was from National Savings and Investments.

A tingle of anticipation ran through her as she retreated from her front door. Her Premium Bonds must have come up. It was the right time of the month for winning cheques to be landing. However, eighteen years as a mathematics teacher helped to dull her initial expectations. The odds of winning a major Premium Bond prize were astronomic, but she had been required to sign for this letter, so the chances of it being a decent sized prize were in her favour.

From her front room bay window, she watched as the postman's van inexpertly executed a five-point turn and disappeared back up her tree-lined country lane. Her cottage, just outside the town of Northallerton in North Yorkshire, was the end terrace in a line of six, after which there was nothing but fields. The terrace of two-up, two-downs had been accommodation for the staff at the long since demolished Yafforth Hall.

Mary was about to give the letter her attention when from over the fence her next door neighbour's head appeared. He too was watching the postman depart, whilst apparently assessing the construction of his garden gate. Mary couldn't help smiling. Bert Heck was a terribly nice chap, and an inveterate busybody. You'd have to be incredibly stealthy to visit any of the houses in the terrace without Bert noticing, and most likely, trying to engage you in conversation.

Mary moved into the hallway, ensuring Bert was out of her line of sight, examining the letter again. She rubbed the envelope between thumb and forefinger, assessing the quality of the paper.

Probability had been one of Mary's favourite lessons to deliver to her pupils. Had it really been four years since she had last taught a class the concepts of dependency and mutual exclusivity?

The subject had been popular with the kids too. Over the years she had honed a series of lessons on the subject and thoroughly enjoyed delivering them. In order to enliven the learning experience, she taught her pupils how to calculate the chances of winning the lottery (forty-five million to one), the Euro Lottery (one-hundred and forty million to one) then demonstrated the poor odds scratch cards provide (nine million to one, for a significantly lesser prize), and finally by assigning each student a role, asked her class to play bookmaker and punters before and during a four-man game of snakes and ladders. The children learned how to create a 'book' and react to the changing fortunes of each player, adjusting their odds accordingly. As a by-product, the kids were taught probability, and one or two even went home and managed to convince their parents to cease their scratch card habits.

Mary had been enraptured by the mechanics of odds compilation and the nuances of betting from a young age, as had Henry, her husband. They both loved horseracing. When attending the races became impossible, she and Henry would often challenge each other to see who could work out the over-rounds from the scrolling odds on the television coverage of horseracing. It was certainly a strange little game, but the two of them had always enjoyed one another's company. Their three decades together had flown by, the two of them in their small cottage, living a secluded, largely uneventful and happy existence.

As far as Mary was concerned, she had lost the man she married three years prior to his passing. She and Henry had been lucky enough to enjoy twenty-nine good years together, followed by a bad year, and two soul-crushing ones. Once she was forced to give up teaching and become her husband's carer, their relationship changed. The pre-diagnosis Henry, *her Henry*, disappeared on a close, sticky day in late August, once the seriousness of his cancer was confirmed. Having been informed his death was simply a matter of time, Henry had dealt with the situation in his normal, quiet, and stoical manner. He hadn't complained. He simply withered away.

An image of Henry upstairs in the spare room, lying in what would become his death bed, frail and with scared eyes, burrowed itself into Mary thoughts and she tried to push them away. He'd been such a large, powerful man, reduced to… She shook her head, squeezing her eyes tight shut.

Henry asked her not to dwell on his slow death, or to become bitter at the years they would no longer spend together. She had promised him she would find another chapter of her life to live. Long before he'd become bedridden she had been determined to remember only the vibrant, loving man he had been in the years prior to the cancer. There would be no further grieving now, only new opportunities. She consciously replaced the image of Henry suffering, with one of the two of them dancing along Scarborough beach on their honeymoon night and allowed a hazy wistfulness to consume her for a short time.

Mary decided to allow the bubble of excitement elicited by the arrival of the white envelope to continue to build. Propping the unopened letter beside a photo of Henry on the mantlepiece, she set off into the kitchen to make herself a mid-morning coffee. As she added milk, she teased herself, imagining what the letter might contain. She considered the possibilities a win of a few thousand pounds could mean to her.

She and Henry had never been blessed with much in the way of spare cash. Their cottage was rented and during his illness their savings had dwindled to barely enough to cover a few more months rent. Mary would be forced out of her home within three months if she didn't find an income soon. Even a tax-free win of a few hundred pounds would be extremely welcome. Enough to tide me over until I can find another teaching post would be wonderful, she told herself.

A sense of heightened anticipation was now oozing around her body. Her father's image entered her mind, as it did frequently, smiling encouragingly at her and causing her to mirror his imagined delight.

Returning to her front room, Mary gazed over at the letter above the fireplace, slowly stirring her coffee as she contemplated. It must surely be a win, she thought. Why else would they insist on asking for a signature; wasn't a proof of delivery reserved for the bigger wins?

Mary had enjoyed a few payouts on her Premium Bonds over the years since her father's death, mostly the minimum value. It was always a high point when a letter from ERNIE fell onto her doormat. This little game of anticipation was well practised, but Mary knew the stakes were higher today.

She'd invested the modest proceeds from her father's estate into Premium Bonds. Mary had been raised alone by her father, Jake. He had been a dreamer and a gambler throughout his life, along with his primary passion, his daughter. As far as Mary was aware, Jake had never shown any inclination to replace her mother. She'd died soon after Mary was born. Instead, he was always searching for that magical betting system that would deliver a life-changing payout for the two of them. His meagre Security Guard wages from his job at a Sunderland shipyard meant Mary had grown up in a house that revolved around Jake's wage packet every Friday.

He enjoyed the odd pint, but drinking wasn't her father's vice. Jake was a regular at the bookies on the high street, although when Mary recollected her childhood days, her father had always been around. He had always taken her to school, ensured a hot meal was on the kitchen table for her at teatime, and a babysitter in situ if he was on night shift.

Mary shared her father's interest in betting, which had spawned her love of numbers and eventually a career in teaching. She would sit with him on an evening, poring over his latest system. He did the lot: spot the ball, fruit machines, bingo, the pools and his greatest passion; horse racing. Mary had adored him.

Since the late eighties her investment in Premium Bonds, care of her father's modest death in service payment, had been her way of allowing the spirit of her father to remain in her life as the two of them continued to wait patiently for their big payday.

Mary had opted for her Premium Bond win notifications and

cheques to be delivered by post, simply to enjoy the thrill of opening a winning letter every now and again. Every win, no matter how small, reminded her of her father. How his eyes would gleam when he picked a winner, his childlike enthusiasm for beating the system thrilling him. She could vividly remember how her father would throw her paper-light twelve-year-old body into the air and catch her after they'd watched one of his selections win on ITV's World of Sport racing coverage.

Mary eyed the Premium Bond letter once more. The anticipation was deliciously invigorating. It reminded her of how she and her father would sit at the battered oak dining table in the back room of their small mid-terrace in Sunderland during the football season. They would wait with bated breath and pencil's ready for the results to be confirmed on the radio at five o'clock every Saturday afternoon.

She decided it was time. Leaving her coffee cooling, Mary whipped the envelope from its perch beside Henry's photo and ripped it open.

Her hands were shaking. She caught herself, feeling foolish, before stifling a laugh. She was being silly. In all likelihood the win was just a hundred pounds, or not even a big win at all, just some administrative mistake, accidentally sending a cheque for the minimum by signed-for post.

Mary removed two sheets of paper from the envelope and wandered to the back of the room, in search of Jake. Her father beamed at her in black and white glory from a sideboard, wearing his flat cap and best shirt; her only photo of him. She remembered precisely when it was taken. They'd had a very successful trip to Redcar races one Saturday in 1976; four winners on the six-race card. Her dad had told her she brought him luck, so he always took her racing with him.

Mary knew all the racetracks in the North of England, she'd visited them all many times, both with her father, and then later with Henry; a day out both of them had enjoyed, as they battled the form guide and the bookies for supremacy.

Jake's winnings had burned a hole in his pocket that day at Redcar and in celebration he'd dragged his daughter in front of a racecourse photographer and asked the chap to take their picture, which is why the photo displayed her father squeezing a very happy ten-year-old to his chest with a winning post and racetrack in the background. The photo had arrived two weeks later, the profits from Redcar having been spent and long forgotten. It had made the thick, glossy picture appear an unnecessary extravagance at the time. The way things had worked out, the photo was now one of Mary's most precious and treasured objects.

Mary tentatively unfolded the contents of the NS&I envelope, her heart rate increasing with every passing moment. Her father's favourite words to his daughter came into her mind and she silently mouthed them as she drew the contents out.

'Life is about labour and luck. Mary my girl, *you* will be lucky!'

Mary's heart drummed as she straightened the thick, creamy paper stamped with the National Savings logo. She cast her gaze down the first page. She skim read it and her heart rate increased further as she registered the words, 'Congratulations, you are a winner…'.

'You've won dad,' she told his image in the photo with a smile tinged with sadness. Then she scanned for an amount and caught sight of a figure written half-way down a block of text. Mary swayed slightly and her hand shot out to grab the bookcase, her knees suddenly wobbly. She checked the number for a second, then a third time, blinking and rolling her eyes, counting the zeros in disbelief. She staggered across the front room and crashed heavily into her favourite armchair.

Mary Romano hadn't screamed properly since Jake had spun her around on a roundabout at the local playing fields at the age of twelve. Now she screamed again like a twelve-year-old. She thrust her arms in the air, pumping them up and down, waving the letter about. She bounced on the sofa and shot her legs straight out. Presently her screams became laughter, which soon developed into gasps for air. Holding a hand to her chest, she caught enough breath to check the letter once again.

'One hundred thousand pounds,' she said softly, before crashing into another fit of laughter.

It took another thirty seconds for her to calm down enough to notice the face staring at her through her bay window.

Three

Bert Heck leant against the door jam and wheezed a little as he waited impatiently on Mary's doorstep. He had assumed his shapely, newly widowed neighbour was in need of being rescued, given the noise coming from the house. Now he wasn't so sure this was the case. She'd looked decidedly unimpressed with him, standing on the dahlias in her front garden with his nose pushed up against the window pane. He'd also ripped his trousers when he'd swung his legs over the wooden fence, caught them on a nail and stumbled into her small rockery. He tried to nonchalantly wipe the mud from his corduroys as he waited.

The door opened and Mary stepped out, closing it behind her, forcing Bert backwards a pace, onto the path. She stood on her top step, wearing a warm, but expectant gaze which rendered him mute for a few seconds. He'd noticed some subtle differences in her since Henry died; in the clothes she wore, and how her hair was styled, but he'd never seen her wearing make-up… like this. He couldn't help but gape. She'd never looked as… beautiful, when Henry was alive… had she? No, he was sure she hadn't. It certainly served to accentuate her… well, they were very big blue eyes…'

She raised a quizzical eyebrow and waited.

'Er… How are you Mary…' he garbled, switching his eyes to the ground for fear of staring, 'I heard you shout.'

'Oh, I'm absolute fine!' she responded warmly, 'And how about you, Bert?'

'Yes, yes, the same, fine. Seriously, I thought I heard you screaming. Are you sure you're okay?'

Her eyes fell to Bert's trousers and she noted the long smear of rain-softened mud down one leg, and a tear from his pocket, before returning to his upturned face. Bert's heart was in the right place, but his obsession with other people's business and, on occasion, an inability to respect personal space, tended to ensure he was given a wide berth by the residents of the little line of houses.

Henry, a very private man, had little time for him. However Mary had always felt sorry for the retiree and had done her best to foster a friendly relationship, albeit one which meant Bert was perennially halted at the threshold of the cottage in order to ensure Henry's views on their nosy neighbour were never unleashed. Mary feared Bert would have been crushed, certainly verbally, and possibly physically.

'I'm absolutely fine, Bert,' she repeated, a slight impatience entering her tone for the first time.

Her small sigh and a roll of her eyes before her reply was lost on Bert as he inspected Mary, continuing to look for signs that she was in fact in desperate need of his attention. Her neighbour was a stout man of medium height. Standing two steps higher than him, Mary was pleasingly, marginally taller than him, even though she was only a touch over five feet tall.

'It was just… the noises. I thought you were in trouble,' he explained, a pained expression animating his wrinkled features for a second.

'Really, Bert, I promise there's nothing to be worried about,' Mary insisted, knowing full well Bert was desperate to discover the reason for her squeals of joy.'

'Thanks for checking on me, but I really must get on, I have a couple of hundred… things to do.'

She stepped backwards and closed the door smartly, before Bert could make any further enquiries. She hesitated a moment, re-opening her door a second or two later. Bert had turned his back to the door, but made only a little progress up her garden path.

'I think it might be best if you use the front gate this time,' she called after him. He swung round, a sheepish grin on his face and comically tugged an imaginary forelock.

'Certainly, Madam,' he smiled back, before setting off up her garden path.

Mary returned to her living room and reflected on how, since Henry's death, Bert seemed to pop up every day. He would be in his front garden when she left, when she got back, or when a visitor called, ready to share a few words. Perhaps the sixty-year-old was simply lonely. Even so, suddenly appearing at her front window and pressing his nose against the glass was a new and slightly worrying development. He must have vaulted over the bordering fence! The thought of Bert struggling over the five foot obstacle amused Mary. Once he'd become ill, Henry had insisted on improving the security of their house in order to maintain his privacy. Mary had assumed the real purpose of the fence was to discourage their new neighbour.

Mary made a mental note to be more direct with Bert if he repeated his leap into her garden. However, she was admittedly a little impressed that he'd been able to make it over. You had to give the retiree some credit for that.

It took an hour for Mary to calm down and read the entire two pages of her letter properly. She did so by setting the photo of her father on the kitchen table and chain-drinking several cups of coffee. The letter confirmed one of her Bonds had won a hundred thousand pounds and her winner's cheque would be arriving by signed-for post in about seven working days. Every now and again, she would stop and speak quietly to his photo.

'This is what you dreamed of dad. The big one. The one which is *so* big, we can't possibly lose it again.'

The two of them had often talked about what they would do if they hit the jackpot. Before the classified football results were announced by James Alexander Gordon on Saturday afternoons, she and dad would imagine what they would do with a thousand pounds, with ten thousand pounds… or even more. Even at the age of fourteen, it seemed such a lot of money and therefore a rich man's lifestyle was still within their reach. After Mr Gordon's wonderfully deep voice had finished bouncing off the woodchip walls around the back room, her father would flick off the old radio and together they would tot up their points for each draw and away result on every permutation he had entered that week, looking for that magical number of points to get into the dividends.

'Well, we did it Dad,' Mary told the photo, 'It's finally happened. Our line has come up.'

And Jake replied. Mary was a girl again, grinning at her dad after he'd told her his latest plan to spend his fortune, which always included houses, cars and racehorses. They were in the back room of their small terrace on Brick Lane in Sunderland in 1980 and everything was right with the world.

'Remember this pet,' Jake said earnestly, locking eyes with his daughter and patting her hand, 'Winning is wonderful. But the work you put in to achieve the win is where the fun comes from.'

Fourteen-year-old Mary had nodded furiously in agreement. It had been a decade later, and two years into her first teaching job, when Mary had discovered the true wisdom of her father's words.

Sitting alone at her cottage kitchen table, the fifty-three-year-old widow gazed without focus out of the back window to her garden and out over the back fence to the huge field of grazing sheep beyond. Imperceptibly, she began to nod. Perhaps the universe had a way of putting things right, of levelling out the luck. On the whole her father had been a happy, but unlucky man. The one thing he craved, beating the bookies or the pools companies with a huge win, never happened for him. He had died in 1987 from a heart attack whilst at work, aged only forty-eight. She had been nineteen, and due to get married to Henry two days later.

Mary resolved she would make sure she enjoyed her windfall, not just for herself, but also for dad.

She snapped back from her daydream, blinked and found her father's face grinning at her from the photo on the kitchen table. His smile was radiating happiness. His moment of joy from getting his ten bob treble up at Redcar. She even remembered the exact amount; four-hundred and seven pounds, twenty-five pence. It was about seven weeks wages for dad

11

and he'd counted it out in front of her on the back-room table. She'd never seen so much money. Once he'd finished, Jake had pushed the seven pounds and change over to his daughter.

'Your share,' he had told her happily, 'You spend it on whatever you want.'

In her small two-bedroomed end terrace outside Northallerton, Mary replied to her father across the years.

'Dad, I'm going to do something we've always wanted to do,' Mary said, touching the frame of his photo lightly with her index finger, 'I'm going to buy us a racehorse.'

Four

Two days after she'd banked her Premium Bond cheque, Mary was up and out of the cottage early. She backed her ancient Volvo estate out of the drive and reversed into the lane, feeling slightly self-conscious.

Mary had made some changes since Henry's death six weeks previously. She caught her reflection in her rear view mirror and found herself critiquing her new hairdo. Her shoulder-length mousey-coloured hair had transformed into a startling blonde bob, thanks to an expensive, but completely enjoyable session at a city centre hair salon in York.

Attending Henry's funeral against his wishes had kick-started her thirst for change. After making that decision, a rash of smaller changes quickly followed as Mary began to relish her change of circumstances. Henry had been a kind, thoughtful husband, but he had held some strong views, some of which impacted on Mary. Henry had liked her to wear her hair long, preferred her to use the lightest touch of make-up, and hated her wearing jeans. Her first and only pair of Levi's had been consigned to the clothes recycling bin at the local supermarket after only one outing in public. Mary hadn't complained. She had acquiesced to Henry's many, sometimes odd preferences, viewing them as only a minor irritation. After all, she loved him, and they had bumped along happily for thirty years without any major arguments.

However Mary now felt ten years younger with this new hairstyle. She rolled her eyes at herself in the car's nearside mirror, admonishing herself for being so vain, but loving how she looked all the same. She was wearing designer blue jeans, and a pair of black leather ankle boots with a two inch heel and was amazed at how comfortable and how much taller they made her feel.

And she definitely wasn't going to continue to be a recluse. Three years of focusing on the constant care of Henry had meant she had lost contact with many, but not all of her friends in the town. Henry's friends, exclusively from work, stopped visiting quite quickly, apart from Adam East. He'd been Henry's friend since childhood, and also his boss. Adam had offered Henry a job in his fledgling company and he had stayed with Adam's company his entire working life. Once Henry became too ill to work, Adam had visited his friend at the cottage once or twice a month.

Mary felt Adam treated Henry as an equal, rather than an employee. He and a dozen more of Henry's colleagues from work had attended his funeral, along with large number of his clients Mary had never met before.

Her own social life had slowly melted away, or rather, condensed to a few very good friends, as the chance to get away from the cottage had diminished during Henry's confinement. Mary was still very close to three female friends who lived in or around Northallerton. She had met Audrey, Maisie, and Sarah through her time working at school and the four of them had lived in and out of each others pockets since their late twenties. However, catching up with her friends was a quest for another day. Today she was going to add life to the cottage.

This was the second, and until her newfound wealth, the most important thing on her list of things to do once Henry was gone. The first had been to install a new computer and given her remote location, a wireless mobile router that she had been informed, would give her a high quality broadband signal. Mary had always used computers and the internet at school but never at home, and decided she needed to be connected. Henry hadn't trusted technology and so they had limped into the twenty-first century without *Google* in their lives. A day after the funeral she had found a tiny computer shop in Northallerton run by a friendly young chap called Anthony. It transpired she'd taught him and as a result the two of them got on famously. He called at the cottage the next day and got everything running in only an hour. According to her ex-pupil, she was now a 'silver surfer'. Mary would have preferred 'blonde surfer', but was grateful to the lad nonetheless.

Today's excursion was far more important than a shiny new laptop. Forty minutes after setting off, she was walking through the swing doors to the *Dogs Trust* centre on the outskirts of Leeds. She'd already been there three times before, being assessed, then paired up with an appropriate dog, but she was there today to finally collect her new canine companion and take him home.

There had always been a dog in the house when she was growing up. Her father regularly found strays wandering around the docks at night, and would feed them a bit of his sandwich and on occasion would be so soft-hearted he would bring them home. He'd feed them, get to know their character, and try to find each dog a new home. Mary would regularly come home from school to find her father's latest project running around the enclosed back yard. She shared her childhood with dozens of dogs, some of whom would stay for a few days, others became permanent residents. She particularly loved to walk along the beach with her father and his latest group of strays. Henry had been allergic to many things, including virtually all animal hair, so allowing a dog to live in the house had been out of the question.

Charlie was a three-year-old short-haired Pointer, although Mary was sure there was a smidgen of something else mixed in there that meant his profile wasn't as sleek as a pure bred. He had soulful brown eyes and a large flat muzzle. A deep brown head gave way to countless small flecks of brown on white from his neck down. The overall effect produced a rather ungainly appearance. He also wobbled with an accentuated swagger when he walked, throwing his hips around like a ballroom dancer, which had made Mary giggle behind her hand at first. However, everything seemed to come together perfectly when he was running, as he loped along with a strangely balletic fluidity. His jaunty look only served to make him even more appealing. Charlie's chances of finding a new owner hadn't been enhanced by the loss of half his right ear. It had been bitten off, leaving a ragged edge. Upon spotting him on the re-homing website Mary had immediately been smitten; she loved an underdog.

Mary and Charlie hit it off within moments of meeting at the re-homing centre. Whilst playing fetch, Mary bent forward to pick up the ball. As she grasped it, Charlie stepped forward and a long, hot tongue softly wiped a path from the tip of her nose, up to her forehead, sending a shiver of delight through her. He then sat down, tilted his head and inspected her, as if to say, 'Well?'

'I'm not just saying this,' commented a member of staff overseeing the playtime, 'But I've never seen him act like that. He's always been a bit… well, boisterous and uninterested in most people to be honest.'

The moment she was passed his lead and took him through the reception swing doors for the last time, Charlie's tail was wagging so hard it seemed to be causing a ripple effect on his ribcage. His excitement upon leaving was palpable, bouncing around on his lead as they headed for the car park. When the boot of her Volvo opened he needed no encouragement to leap enthusiastically into the back of the car before settling on an old rug, dropping down to lie sphinx-like when Mary closed the boot.

Once the car started to move, he was straight up on his feet, staring out of the back window. He stayed rooted to the spot throughout the entire journey home until a motorcyclist stopped a few yards behind the Volvo at a junction. Mary looked back and watched as the hair on the Pointer's back rose to stand on end. Standing on his hind legs and scraping his paws against the back window, Charlie began a frustrated barking and snarling session that lasted until the rider turned off at the next junction.

Mary called a few soothing phrases to him and Charlie returned a mournful look, snorted in disappointment and settled to resume watching the traffic.

Five

During the course of the next week Mary and Charlie fell into a routine of sleep, food, walking and internet. The latter consisted of Mary researching various topics on her new laptop, sitting on one end of the sofa. Meanwhile, Charlie lay beside her, half asleep, taking up every other inch. He preferred it when he could rest his head against her hip, opening an eye when he guessed Mary might be leaving her seat. The two of them were getting on famously.

Having done her research, Mary made a phone call and the next Tuesday morning was up at six-thirty. She bundled a sleepy Charlie into the back of her Volvo and set off for the village of Middleham with both trepidation and excitement coursing through her. Of all the possible ways to spend a large windfall, she and her father had always fanaticised about owning their own racehorse. Mary had considered Malton as a potential training centre but had been drawn to Middleham in the Yorkshire Dales because of one name – Fitzpatrick.

Donald Fitzpatrick had been known in the sixties and seventies as the 'King of the Sellers' due to his mastery in enabling moderate horses to win races. He bought cheap, working man's priced horses and successfully dominated the smaller handicaps and selling races, especially in the North. He was one of the first trainers to advertise syndicates for his horses, and was extremely popular with punters and small owners, being a blunt, straight-talking Yorkshireman. Fitzpatrick loved to beat the expensive southern horses with his bargain buys at the horse sales, and was vocal when doing so. When he reached sixty winners in his third season of training, he got noticed, and was soon being sent quality horses with which he proceeded to win races at the higher grades, culminating in several Group One successes in the seventies. Mary's father had followed the yard from his first few runners in the late fifties, rating Donald as a shrewd operator and landing a few betting touches before bookmakers became savvy to his ability to lay out a horse for a specific race. He was the trainer her father would have chosen.

Donald had left the training ranks more than thirty years ago, handing the business over to his youngest son, Adrian Fitzpatrick. The yard hadn't enjoyed the same roaring success under Adrian, but nonetheless Mary felt drawn to him.

***

Later that afternoon, Mary reflected on her first experience of a racing yard as she walked Charlie around the edge of the Middleham Moor. The trainer's wife had recommended the walk as it was popular with local residents.

A steady flow of horses were using the gallops, and she watched in interest as they paired up and cantered or galloped across the plateau of land on top of the limestone hills. Keeping the lead on Charlie, she walked along the rough road around the edge of the gallops, keeping clear of the moor so as not to upset any of the trainers or their horses. Not that Mary minded, the track beside the cliff provided a jaw-dropping view of the Ure Valley, down to Wensley. A fresh autumn breeze was raising tears in her eyes, but she happily blinked them away to take in the impressive vista. Casting her mind to her stable visit, it had been a less than impressive experience. In fact, her encounter with the Fitzpatrick family and their stables had been underwhelming.

At the western end of Middleham Moor, Mary had found a garish multicoloured sign advertising the entrance and she'd pulled into the Adrian Fitzpatrick stables at eight-thirty. Walking into the yard had been an intimidating experience. The initial sprawling mass of concrete and windowless barns didn't reflect the photos of finely mowed grass-covered areas in front of immaculately white-washed stable walls advertised on the Fitzpatrick website. The barns were built in varying sizes and designs, seemingly placed against each other in a haphazard fashion as the yard had grown over the years. Everything was relatively neat and tidy, yet the place felt a little run down and in need of some attention.

Leaving Charlie to stand guard on the passenger seat of her Volvo, Mary had picked her way between the first few barns. After a minute of losing her bearings and walking in circles, she spotted a girl approaching carrying a saddle and tack. Barely out of her teens, she gave Mary a wary glance and with her head down, adjusted her path to walk past without speaking. Forcing a request for directions upon her, a stilted conversation gained Mary a route to Adrian's wife and an apology: Adrian Fitzpatrick had been called away and he wasn't at the yard.

Trying not to show her disappointment, Mary had been given a whistle-stop tour around the stabling blocks by Tracey, the trainer's wife. A round, red faced woman, she plainly knew every horse, bustling around the expansive yard with an enthusiastic zeal. It had been hard to get a word in edgeways, as the robust fifty-year-old whisked Mary through barn after barn, horse after horse, whilst passing dozens of staff seemingly engrossed in their work. For the most part, Tracey walked around and between the staff as if they weren't there, apart from stopping to chastise a young lad for not bolting a stable door properly when he dodged out of stable for a few seconds to retrieve a rake.

'Don't you *ever* leave a stable door unbolted, boy!' she'd lambasted the young lad, 'It only takes a second for a horse to bolt and then you, me or any of your workmates could end up in its way.'

It became apparent Tracey played a major role in running the stables. Eventually she stopped talking long enough to discover that Mary wanted to buy a young, unraced horse. She gave Mary a date for her to attend the Doncaster Yearling Sales, and promised her husband Adrian would be there to ensure she chose a decent individual for the next turf season.

Mary's attention snapped back to her dog walk when a string of five horses were suddenly upon her, coming up on both sides from behind. She'd been daydreaming, and before she could move out of the way, she was being closely passed with Charlie whipping around on his lead, clearly agitated as the huge animals trotted within a few feet of him.

'Walk your wretched dog somewhere else,' shouted a male rider, laughing. He had a sharp nose to match his tongue and carried on at a trot without stopping. Mary stood stock still, one hand to her chest, unable to vocalise a response. She watched as the last two riders shared a grin and instructed the group to slow to a walk once they were forty yards ahead of her.

Mary bobbed down to calm Charlie. As she did, a man's voice called, 'Everything okay?'

From growling softly after the horses, the unexpected query from afar silenced Charlie and he now copied his mistress in switching his focus to a figure on a grassy knoll about thirty yards away. The sun was behind him, but Mary could pick out the outline of a man who was looking down on her. With the sun in her eyes, the only discernable features were his long brimmed Breton cap that cast a shadow over his face, and a walking stick, or was it a cane, she couldn't tell.

He waved and repeated his question. Mary stood and shouted back, 'I'm fine, thank you.'

The figure responded by waggling his stick, turned, and was gone.

Six

After cracking open two windows of the Volvo and promising Charlie she would check back soon, Mary approached the Doncaster sales complex with trepidation. As she navigated her way through the grassed car park, she'd noticed it was stuffed full of expensive cars and understood now why the parking attendant had regarded her ancient Volvo with some amusement. She tried to ignore the butterflies in her stomach, telling herself she had just as much right to be here as anyone else, gathered herself for a moment, then strode purposefully through the gates.

She had planned to arrive thirty minutes early for her appointment with Adrian Fitzpatrick and almost an hour before the sale started, intending to get a feel for the place before meeting her trainer. Letting her curiosity determine where she went next, she spent most of her spare half hour walking around the multitude of stabling areas, feeling nervous at first, but quickly started to enjoy the experience. She plucked up the courage to approach a few of the vendors, who it turned out were more than happy to share their view of their yearlings with her.

Noticing that many people were holding inch thick, glossy catalogues, each with hundreds of paper thin pages, Mary found her way to the administration building and tried to buy one, only to be informed that they were free. Inside the catalogue she found a wealth of detail. She could now identify each horse via its lot number, read through their pedigree and locate where they were in the huge complex of stables. In the eighties she had been in touch with the breeding of racehorses, reading *The Sporting Life* cover to cover whenever her father bought it. Two decades later there were a whole new crop of sires to consider.

Her laptop had introduced her to the *Racing Post* website. She'd bought the paper when she went racing with Henry or her friends but discovered the digital version was an excellent source of form and easy to use. However she was pleased to find *The Sporting Life* still existed online, although any comparison to its former self had been lost in its transition to new ownership.

Eventually she returned to the pre-sales ring and from there, ventured into the virtually empty indoor sales ring before finding her way into the heart of the main building to locate the café.

She found Adrian Fitzpatrick not in the café, but instead, leaning against a small bar sharing a joke with a younger man. With only a photo she'd found on his website to go on, Mary needed to check twice before making a positive identification. From the evidence on the internet she had been expecting Fitzpatrick to be in his early forties. It transpired his website was woefully out of date. Fitzpatrick was probably only a shade younger than her. His countrywear wardrobe was similar, however his tanned, muscular appearance online had been replaced with a pasty face, a receding hairline and a spare tyre around his stomach. She decided not to be disappointed, bought herself a cup of tea, and went over to introduce herself.

Despite being careful to approach the men in Fitzpatrick's line of sight, so as to signal her arrival, the trainer was oblivious; being caught up in an apparently comic story the younger man was sharing. Mary waited patiently on the periphery of the two men, sipping at her tragically weak cup of tea. Once the anecdote had concluded and the braying laugher had subsided, she stepped forward.

'Ah, you must be our new owner, Mrs Romano,' Fitzpatrick cooed once Mary had introduced herself. He had a light voice and a smile that folded the skin under his chin. The other man was introduced as his head lad.

'I understand you want to buy a yearling.'

'Yes, I've already been looking…'

'Come into some money then, love?' Fitzpatrick asked with a wink as he finished off the dregs of his pint.

Mary tried to ignore the condescending tone in the trainer's voice, and wondered at the fact the trainer was drinking alcohol at quarter to ten in the morning, but tried to remain open-minded.

'Let's just say I can afford your training rates,' she responded tartly, her eyes never leaving Fitzpatrick's.

The head lad raised an eyebrow and grinned at his boss over his pint glass. All credit to Fitzpatrick, he'd read the signs coming from her and creased his features in apology.

'I'm sorry, Mrs Romano, please forgive me, I can be a little blunt. We get a lot of timewasters in this game. I'm sure you can afford the twenty or thirty thousand it will cost…?'

He left this assumption hanging, and his anticipatory expression melted into a frown when Mary didn't respond. She wasn't sure of Fitzpatrick, and certainly wasn't keen on volunteering her budget just yet. As she stood waiting for Fitzpatrick to realise she wasn't going to reveal the depth of her windfall, Mary was struck with how confident she felt. She'd enjoyed so few new experiences and opportunities for social interaction in the last three years, and was actually enjoying playing this man at his own game.

'So what sort of youngster are you looking for?' queried Fitzpatrick, once he couldn't stand the awkward silence any longer.

'I'd like a winner, please,' she fired back. The younger man laughed and Mary felt a jolt of recognition. She examined the head lad intently for a few seconds and his pinched features confirmed her initial thought; he'd been riding the horse that tried to scare her during her dog walk around Middleham Moor.

Fitzpatrick eyed her, trying to work her out. Mary turned her gaze on him and gave a tight smile.

'Well that's something we can agree on,' he exclaimed, breaking into a smile, 'Come on, I'll show you a few youngsters I like the look of.'

Mary followed the men around the stabling yards for the next half an hour, as they pulled out a number of yearlings from their boxes to evaluate them. She did eventually give them her budget of a maximum of £20,000 to buy a yearling, but soon decided she didn't want her horse trained by Fitzpatrick. However, Mary reasoned she could put this experience at the sales to good use, and from then on smiled, nodded, but added very little.

Mary and her dad had once caught up with Fitzpatrick Senior at the races in the early seventies and he'd come across as a modest and thoughtful man. He had a steely obstinacy and an obvious drive to succeed, but there was none of the pomposity his son was displaying. Upright, spick and span, Mary could remember Fitzpatrick's father had worn a white and blue spotted bow tie which he became famously associated with in his later years as he and his owners believed this adornment brought him luck. As she continued to follow Adrian Fitzpatrick around the sales barns she could understand why his yard was half empty.

With the sale now underway, the auctioneer's voice was being piped throughout the stabling area via a loudspeaker system, but also a number of television monitors. They were up to the eighth lot of the day when Fitzpatrick introduced Mary to his most likely candidate for her yearling.

The filly was indeed a nice looking sort, although to Mary's untrained eye, every single horse she'd seen that morning looked beautiful. The head lad had been educating her about the looks of some of the horses, for which she was grateful, but Mary was really no wiser. She was careful to make non-committal noises when Fitzpatrick asked if she liked the filly.

Clearly frustrated at Mary's apparent lack of interest, Fitzpatrick told her he would have a word with the breeder and see whether there was a reserve on the filly, as he felt she would be an early type for next season; just right for her. Mary was about to interject and explain that he was wasting his time, but he didn't wait for a reply and turned on his heel, leaving her with his head lad. Fitzpatrick took the breeder by his elbow, guiding him away in order to have a private conversation. Mary watched him intently as Fitzpatrick spoke. He glanced up and gave her an encouraging smile as he discussed the filly with the vendor.

Presently, he strode back grinning broadly, only to be met by Mary with a face like thunder.

'I think we can get her for a value price,' he ventured, still grinning but starting to grasp that something was wrong. However, he blundered on.

'He wants thirty thousand, but...'

'But you think we can get her for twenty?' Mary interrupted sternly.

Fitzpatrick's mouth dropped open.

'Yes, that's right,' he replied after a few, long seconds. He was holding the back of his neck and wore a troubled expression. 'Did you overhear our...?'

'You were planning to commit fraud, Mr Fitzpatrick.'

Mary almost spat the words, unable to contain her indignation any longer.

'My husband died of throat cancer,' she continued, her voice low and threatening, her eyes blazing, 'He had to have his vocal chords cut out for the last eighteen months of his life, so I learned to lip read.'

Fitzpatrick stared at the woman, struck dumb.

'I may be new to this, but even I know that pre-arranging a kickback from the vendor of a horse is illegal,' Mary hissed.

'I think you used the term 'run it up' which I'm pretty sure means artificially bidding a horse up so that I pay my top budget, and you share the difference with the vendor.'

Mary paused, trying to slot the conversation together in her head once more.

'You said you'd split the extra with him, five each. I'm guessing the filly is only really worth about ten thousand at best?'

The head lad was looking anywhere except at Mary or his boss. Fitzpatrick's eyes narrowed and he went to reply but Mary cut him off.

'Does it make you proud to be duping someone new to the sport, Mr Fitzpatrick?' She was aware this came across like she was scolding a naughty schoolboy, but Mary didn't waver. Now she put that twenty-three years of school teaching to good use and fell silent, waiting for her reply.

'Screw you,' Fitzpatrick eventually snarled under his breath. He scowled at Mary and stepped toward her, cocking his head aggressively. Mary stood her ground and tried desperately not to flinch, resolutely maintaining eye contact. He stopped an inch from her face. Beside her, the Head Lad twitched nervously and cast his gaze around the stables to see if anyone was witnessing the stand-off. A few stable lads and the odd catalogue-carrying buyer looked on, but the area was devoid of any sales officials.

'I don't know what you think you saw, but breathe one word of this and...'

Mary had been bullied before and Fitzpatrick's words only served to strengthen her resolve. She decided she'd had enough of Fitzpatrick's nose hair quivering in her face.

'I believe that is a CCTV camera up there,' she remarked in a crisp tone, nodding upwards to where a small white camera sat atop a thin pole, 'I suggest you walk away now and find yourself another owner to fleece.'

'Come on boss, leave it,' suggested the Head Lad, his hand on Fitzpatrick's shoulder. The trainer slowly licked his lips before a snort of derision sent a waft of stale beer toward Mary that filled her nose and throat.

'Not one word,' he repeated before peeling away and stumping off toward the sales ring with his employee in tow. The head lad looked back at Mary and was about to say something, but thought better of it and turned to chase after his red-faced boss.

Mary watched them disappear and found she was gasping in unison to her heart thumped against her chest. She took a few steps and steadied herself against the door to an empty stable until a regular heartbeat returned.

When she least expected it, she found a smile returning to her lips, and then a girlish giggle bubbled up. She'd gone searching for a racehorse in order to bring some excitement into her life. Well, her pulse was racing already... and that was *before* she'd found her racehorse.

Seven

Leaning against the plastic railings of the sales pre-parade ring, Danny Carter hummed quietly to himself without being aware he was making any sound. Holding the bridge of his nose in an attempt to alleviate the beginnings of a headache, he inspected his dog-eared sales catalogue to check on the breeding of one of the horses milling around in front of him. The loud, and annoyingly tinny, public address system had been his constant companion for the last two days, leaving him with the ringing of tinnitus, noticeable in the odd moments of silence. He was starting to fear he wouldn't snag the two yearlings he had planned to buy. His meagre budget of a few thousand pounds for each had so far been woefully insufficient. Ever hopeful, he followed lot four-hundred and seventy-nine as it made its way into the sales ring.

Doncaster's August Yearling Sales had already been running for two days and over four hundred juveniles had already passed through the ring. Now it was day three; the Silver Sale. Supposedly the day for the lesser lights, lower prices for horses possessing slightly less appealing pedigrees, or perhaps carrying minor conformation defects. Danny had assessed the pedigrees of every single one of the one-hundred and seventy horses in the Silver Sale catalogue and spent the last two days watching them walk, feeling their tendons, and most importantly for him, trying to determine their personality and attitude.

If you stayed in one place for long enough, a day at the sales could became a constant wall of horseflesh. Horse after horse called from their stabling area, walked around the pre-parade ring, pulled aside to be examined by potential buyers and finally taking their turn inside the indoor sales ring. During this process stable lads and lasses would pull their charge into viewing walkways where prospective buyers would run their hands up and down legs, looking for defects that might slow them on a racetrack. Then they would walk once more, every buyer's eye searching for fluidity and athleticism. Finally, the unbroken yearling would become the focus of an amphitheatre populated by owners, trainers, bloodstock agents, breeders and sales staff.

Danny shut his tired eyes tight and blinked them open a few seconds later in an attempt to maintain his concentration. A racehorse trainer needed horses to train, and with every youngster he lost out on, so his frustration grew. Danny's downward spiral of despondency was already well established, as once again he moved away from the sales ring having lost out to a higher bidder. The latest horse he had earmarked as a strong candidate was going to a new home with one of the large, well-established northern yards for twice the amount he could afford. He'd known it wasn't going to be easy, but the market was much stronger than he'd expected. He might have to settle for only one yearling in his first full year of training.

'Tough on your own, ain't it, son.'

Danny whipped round and found a man with short, silver streaked hair grinning at him.

He locked eyes with his ex-boss, George Lilley, who was wearing an expression of amused contempt.

'That one's coming home with me. I thought you liked her. Shame you've not got the cash,' he sneered, 'Should've thought about that before you jumped ship and took a member of my staff with you.'

'And you wonder why I left to set up on my own...' Danny replied flatly.

George smirked but didn't reply.

'She's shy,' Danny replied after a pause, still not breaking his intense gaze with the trainer, 'She'll take time, but she's an athlete. Make sure you give her the time.'

George shrugged, looking beyond the long-haired, fresh-faced twenty-five year old, a look of resignation on his face.

'You need to spend more time finding owners with folding cash and less time pampering your horses, Danny.'

'Don't give her to Jonnie to break,' Danny pleaded, 'He'll scare her witless. She'll need tender handling.'

George sucked his teeth, his tongue clicking as it disengaged. With a disappointed shake of his head, he pushed past Danny, heading to the stabling area.

Danny watched him go, wishing the words that were only now coalescing in his head had been there a few moments before. But even if he told George, yet again, how badly his son Jonnie treated the horses he was supposedly caring for, he doubted he would listen; George had selective hearing where his only son was concerned. George's recent divorce had only increased his reticence to see Jonnie for who he really was.

Danny started to hum a tune; the Imperial March from *Star Wars*. He often did this when he was thinking, even though the stable staff around him would become irritated by his incessant humming. Usually he was oblivious to the fact he was even doing it.

His two years at George Lilley's yard as an assistant trainer looking after his own group of thirty horses, hadn't ended amicably. Thanks to a bust up with Jonnie, the trainer's son, he'd had to leave. On reflection, perhaps it was the push he'd needed to take the plunge and risk his savings. A small yard in need of renovation had become available right next door to the Lilley's and he'd decided to strike out on his own. It had been so exciting at first, but with a quickly depleting savings account, only a handful of horses, and a single member of staff, three months down the line his dream of running a successful training business was already starting to lose its lustre. Today was a risky throw of the dice: with the last of his savings he'd come to Doncaster to buy a couple of nice, but cheap yearlings. The plan was to find owners for them, and with those new training fees he'd just about be breaking even each month, instead of watching his bank balance being slowly eroded.

What could possibly go wrong, he thought to himself gloomily, turning to lean on the pre-parade ring rails. George was right though, he did need to find more owners. Just a few horse lovers with deep pockets... and an unlimited amount of patience; that wasn't too much to ask for, was it? He almost laughed out loud at how ludicrous he sounded. Unearthing owners had proved challenging, they didn't just fall in your lap. Danny knew he could train winners, he'd already done that as an assistant for two other trainers, but what he hadn't counted on was also being required to fulfil the role of salesman, receptionist, builder, maintenance technician, and accountant.

That reminded him, he'd had a letter from the local authority. As he contemplated when he would have time to work through the fourteen page form, Danny's attention was easily distracted to the number now showing in green on the wall mounted screen. Lot four-hundred and eighty-nine was going through. He checked his catalogue and was relieved to find his next horse of interest was two lots away. He wanted to look this colt over one more time.

It was mid-afternoon now, and there were plenty of people milling around the open-air pre-sales ring. Making his way to the left-hand side of the ring, he had to push his way through the crowd and move up the rails to find a clear view of which horses were touring around. The colt he was looking for was on the other side of the pre-sales ring.

Danny recognised the bay colt immediately, as he'd already viewed it twice outside its stable earlier in the day. He'd also stuck around the area for a further twenty minutes, loitering against an unused box to simply watch the young horse as he was pulled out of his stable every few minutes by potential purchasers. The colt was a good size and correct. His pedigree was decent enough, however Danny had come to the conclusion this young horse wasn't just headstrong - he had a streak of devilment in him. It was the way the colt eyed his handler, how he would flick an ear at anyone who came close.

Danny was sure the colt wasn't a 'headcase', as some of the buyers viewing him had suggested as they walked away; far from it. His view was that the yearling was intelligent and easily bored. Misbehaving helped pass the time, although he also seemed to dislike anyone fiddling with his ears. The colt was doing the same thing in the pre-sales ring right now.

Every four steps the colt was snorting and planting himself, refusing to budge for a few seconds. No amount of tugging on his lead rein from his increasingly crimson-faced handler would see the colt move. Then, totally unbidden, the moderately sized, unremarkable liver chestnut would assent to saunter forward, before repeating his locked-legged stance a few steps later. The teenager handling him was starting to let his anger spill over, yanking on the rein. This only served to make matters worse. The colt was playing his handler, showing him who was the boss. And Danny *liked* that.

As the colt rounded the corner closest to the sales ring entrance he looked poised to rear, shifting his weight onto his back legs and gave a desultory whinny. The handler, sensing the impending swipe of metal hooves through the air in front of him, let out some rein and stepped back and braced. With a touch of arrogance spawned from this success, the colt stepped forward and gently head-butted his handler.

Danny almost laughed out loud. The more he saw of this fellow the more he liked him. He continued to watch closely as the chestnut treated his handler to further embarrassing antics as he made another circuit of the ring. The colt was toying with him, but there was no malice in his actions, he was simply having an enormous amount of fun with a stable lad who was wet behind the ears.

A check of the colt's pedigree reminded Danny that he was by a Group winning son of Invincible Spirit out of an unraced Showcasing mare who had a sister with a Listed win to her credit. As he traced his finger down the catalogue page the auctioneers hammer rang out like a gunshot over the public address system; lot four-hundred and eighty-nine had just been sold. A bellow went up from behind Danny and he swung round.

'Mind your backs!' screamed a man's voice. This was followed by a number of exclamations from the group of people at the corner of the ring. Danny caught sight of a horse rearing at the start to the viewing chute, the thin, straight railed walkway which ran parallel to the right-hand side of the pre-sales ring. It acted as a final opportunity for any interested buyers wishing to examine a horse up close, both stood and walking, prior to them entering the sales ring. The single railed lane was expressly for horses and their handlers only.

A line of people quickly backed away from the rails as a filly rose into the air, her front legs bicycling. She whipped the lead rein from her handlers grasp then crashed backwards into the plastic rail behind her. Danny's attention, however, was elsewhere. He was looking into the eyes of a small, blonde, well dressed middle-aged woman who inexplicably, was standing in front of him, only on the other side of the rails, in the middle of the viewing chute. More importantly, the woman was directly in the path of the filly, if the animal was to take flight.

Danny stole a glance to his left and saw the filly's front feet returning to the ground, her back legs braced against the bottom end of the chute. The woman inside the chute followed Danny's gaze, looking to the filly, and then quickly returned to lock eyes with Danny. Her expression altered from one of bemused innocence to wide-eyed terror as she comprehended the situation; the filly was setting herself to bolt down the thin walkway and she was trapped in its path.

Everything slowed down for Danny, and what he needed to achieve became crystal clear. Telegraphing his intentions to the lady with his eyes only, he dropped his sales catalogue, stepped a yard forward to the base of the four foot high rail, bent his knees, and leaning over into the walkway chute, thrust both arms out wide and shouted, 'Come here!'

The woman ripped her eyes away from the filly as it sprang forwards, closing the fifteen yards to her in what seemed no more than a heartbeat. Seeing two outstretched arms, the woman instinctively obeyed, launching herself into an embrace with Danny, the white, plastic encased railings between them. Once he had her, he released the strength in his legs, springing upwards and pulling the woman up and over the rails towards him. The two of them toppled backwards in a desperate embrace.

The filly thundered past and upon reaching the end of the chute encountered a dead end, whereupon she came to a shuddering halt and was immediately caught. Danny missed this, as he was lying on his back with a small middle-aged woman on top of him, a profusion of blonde hair in his mouth and the smell of perfume up his nose.

Witnesses to Danny's actions soon had the two of them onto their feet, checking them over and bombarding them with concerned inquiries. He placed a gentle hand onto the lady's upper arm, 'Are you okay?'

Clearly shaken, the woman nodded whilst trying to straighten her clothes. 'I must have taken a wrong turn,' she muttered, 'I wondered why I had to open a gate to find my way around this side of the parade ring.'

'Easily done,' Danny retorted with a smile.

He was about to introduce himself when the sound of the auctioneer's hammer cracked through the air once more. Danny froze, craning his neck to read the current lot number. The number four-hundred and ninety-one flashed onto the external lot number screen.

'Sorry, I have to go,' he told her, and dashed off through the crowd towards the sales ring.

Mary watched the tall, rather gawky young boy dance through the throng, his knees and elbows somehow out of time with the rest of his wiry frame, his long, straggly hair whipping around his head. She followed him until he vanished into the sales ring entrance. Above the entrance the lot number was being displayed.

'Well look at that,' she whispered, unaware it was loud enough for the small cluster of people around her to hear. There was a spark of incredulity in her voice.

'Lot four-hundred and ninety-one,' she noted, 'That's a prime number.'

Around her a number of eyebrows were raised and the queries about her 'feeling quite alright,' resumed.

Eight

Bidding for the colt was already at £7,500 when Danny reached the standing area in the entrance to the sales ring and the auctioneer was repeating the colt's pedigree in an attempt to conjure up another bid. Danny let out a relieved gasp as he stuck his hand in the air, delighted with the fact that the colt had once again planted itself, this time in the centre of the sales ring, where it was now noisily relieving itself whilst eyeing the mass of people sat in a tiered horseshoe around him.

'I have £8,000. New bidder,' the auctioneer called into his microphone upon taking Danny's bid. He switched his attention to the floor above and added 'Against you, Madam.'

With a budget of only £12,000 for the two horses he wanted to buy to bolster his fledgling training yard, the next minute seemed to drag on forever. The auctioneer got to the third request of any more bids before he nodded upstairs.

'I have £9,000, thank you, Madam,' and his gaze fell to Danny once more. 'Do I hear ten thousand?'

His heart thumping, Danny held up a hand with fingers splayed.

'I have a bid of nine five, which I'll accept,' came the response from the auctioneer's pulpit.

Again, there was a long wait, and two tours of the sales ring, but finally the words Danny was desperate not to hear rang out over the public address system. 'I have ten thousand upstairs.'

Danny nodded immediately, taking the bid to £11,000. Sweat broke out under his arms. That was as far as he dare go. With the bidding now going up in thousands, his next bid would have be £13,000, a price for one horse he simply couldn't afford. He waited, tensed, willing the auctioneer to close out the bidding. Again, there was a prolonged request for a final bid.

The auctioneer smiled benignly and waved his gavel upwards, 'I have £12,000 from the lady upstairs, do I hear £13,000?'

Danny's chin dropped and he felt himself deflate. The auctioneer now transferred an expectant look toward him. With a disconsolate shake of his head he regarded the colt, who was still giving his handler a hard time in the sales ring.

'Ah, come on, Sir, one more bid may do it,' teased the auctioneer, sensing the young man's disappointment. Once more Danny shook his head and turned to leave. It only took a few more seconds for the auction to finish.

'Not today I'm afraid,' the auctioneer declared without dropping his gavel.

Danny was already walking out of the bottom entrance of the sales ring into the warm summer air outside, ruminating on how unfair it was to be lacking in funds when you were trying to build up a racing yard. Six horses, that's all he had, and one of those was currently lame. He'd be bust by Christmas at this rate.

Clearly happy to be led out of the noisy, human filled auditorium, the colt Danny had been bidding on was now dragging his handler out into the fresh air. Still cursing his luck, Danny watched the headstrong young horse toss his head about before opening its front legs wide and planting itself in the gangway, his tail swishing. Without thinking, Danny went to the plastic rails and leaned over in front of the horse and started to whistle in a high register, modulating the frequency every few seconds. It sounded like a songbird. The colt flicked an ear backwards for a few seconds then both went forward, standing bolt upright and flaring his nostrils as he listened. Danny smiled and still whistling, held up a flat palm. A snort and a step forward and the colt relaxed, pushing his muzzle into Danny's palm.

'Where did you learn to do that?' queried a female voice behind him. A few tugs from his handler, and the colt soon trotted amiably across the oval of turf in the centre of the pre-sales ring. Danny swung round and found a small, shapely blonde haired woman standing with her hands on her hips. She wore a silk shirt, jeans, heeled boots and a pleasant smile.

Mary's smile deepened when recognition flickered across Danny's face, 'I'm Mary Romano,' she told him warmly and offered him her hand, 'You saved me from being knocked over by a horse and I never got a chance to say thank you.'

She watched with interest as the boy opened and closed his mouth, then he blushed. 'I'm so sorry… I was desperate to bid on a horse,' he replied, grasping her hand in both of his and pumping it up and down.

'Danny Carter,' he told her apologetically.

'Oh, gosh, don't be sorry!' Mary laughed, 'I just hope you got there in time… I assume that was the horse. Did you manage to buy him?'

Mary watched the lad's eyes dull for a moment and his cheeks hardened, 'No, I'm afraid he was just too expensive.'

He immediately wondered why he'd shared this nugget of information with her, but the lady's soft North Eastern accent and her concentration when he spoke showed she was genuinely interested. They exchanged small talk for another minute, Mary explaining she was a prospective owner and Danny that he was probably the newest trainer at the sale. On hearing this, Mary pursed her lips, appearing to have made a decision.

'Come on, can I buy you a cup of coffee and a piece of cake to say thank you?' Mary asked hopefully, 'It might make up for not buying that colt. I could see you connected with him just now. I'd love to know more about that whistle of yours.'

Apart from being relieved she hadn't been trampled by the filly and wanting to show her gratitude, Mary was starting to get a strong impression this lad was in need of someone to talk to.

With only a ten pound note in his back pocket, Danny considered the offer, worried he might be embarrassed at the café till. He paused, only for Mary to slip her arm into his and start to guide him away. What could be the harm he decided, as they toured around the sales building. Besides, he'd not eaten since seven o'clock this morning and the thought of cake had his stomach rumbling.

He need not have worrie. Mary insisted on paying for everything. The café bar was filled with the light buzz of conversation without being too busy and they found a small, two-person table against a wall. Screens strategically placed on each wall maintained the atmosphere of the sale, the lot numbers relentlessly ticking over when a lot was sold or jumping up by a couple if a horse had been withdrawn. Danny kept his eye on the numbers, as he still had one lot, a small May-born filly he wanted to check out in case she went cheaply.

Mary asked the questions and Danny talked. She discovered he was in his mid-twenties and had just taken a lease on his first racing yard, a twenty-box barn with a small house included, on the outskirts of Malton. He was so new to the training ranks he was yet to field a runner. That was about to change as he was hoping to race a three-year-old gelding in a small handicap at Pontefract in a few days time.

'So what does it take to get a training yard up and running?' asked Mary, quickly becoming engrossed in the business of being a racehorse trainer.

'I'd already done my trainer's courses and I managed to pull together the thirty-five thousand pounds I needed to get started, with savings and a little bit of luck with one of the horses I used to look after in my previous job,' Danny explained between mouthfuls of cake, 'I'd been thinking about having a go myself for a while and a lease came up at the same time things got a bit sticky with my previous employer, so I jumped at the chance.'

Mary watched Danny polish off his second slice of cake and wondered when he'd last had a square meal. When you looked closely there were rings around his eyes and his skin seemed to cling to his bones. She found herself quashing an almost overpowering urge to mother him.

'I've only got six horses, which is why I'm here,' he explained, 'I was hoping to buy a couple of cheap yearlings and find owners for them once I'd got them home.'

'Why did you need thirty-five thousand pounds?'

'Oh, it's just a figure you have to prove to the BHA you have available in cash before you can get your trainer's license. Ten thousand of that disappeared straight away on paying for three month's lease and sorting out the rates bill,' said Danny with a roll of his eyes.

Their conversation continued, the two of them settling into friendly chatter. Danny was more than happy to share his plans for his yard, especially with a listener who picked things up quickly and showed genuine interest. They had been sitting for twenty minutes before Danny realised he'd not found out anything about Mary.

'So why are you here today?'

Mary placed both of her elbows on the table and clasped her hands together. She was finding it difficult to contain herself, 'I wondered when you were going to ask that question,' she replied with a hint of excitement, 'I was here to…'

'Don't be sending this rogue a horse,' said an eerily whiney voice from over her shoulder, crushing her reply. Mary looked round and into the steely eyes of a short young man, who boasted perfectly sculpted black hair and a mouth that turned down at both sides.

'He's a liar and a thief,' the young man continued, 'You'd be mad to give him a horse to train.'

Danny was on his feet and towering over his accuser before Mary could reply. The young man backed off a few paces and he gave a crooked sneer, enjoying Danny's reaction.

'Leave us alone, Jonnie,' Danny warned. His voice was low and measured, but even so, conversations halted on a couple of nearby tables as the occupants assessed the two men facing off.

'Ooh! There's that short temper,' Jonnie baited, 'You going to attack me again? Go on, have a go…' He filled his last few words with contempt.

Jonnie's challenge was met with silence. Mary noticed Danny's teeth were clenched so hard his jaw muscles were rippling. She leaned out from her sitting position and took Danny's hand in hers. He flinched a little, before realising who had touched him and grasped her hand properly. It was soft and warm.

'Sit down, Danny,' Mary told him, calmly indicating his empty chair with her eyes. Danny relaxed and returned to the table. Switching her gaze to the young man she added, 'So, Danny, can you tell me about the horses you want to buy, I'd be very interested in you training for me,' in the same warm tone. However, she spoke slowly and loud enough for the rest of the now silent café to hear her and was careful to never let her gaze leave Jonnie's. The young man understood the significance of her words and squirmed uncomfortably under the woman's icy cold stare. He considered adding a parting rebuke but felt the attention of the room on him; the woman had spoilt his moment. Instead, he sniffed in disgust, turned on his heel and pushed his way out of the door of the café.

'That was Jonnie Lilley,' Danny explained once the room had settled back into a burble of conversation. 'He's the son of my ex-employer, the trainer George Lilley.'

Mary nodded and raised an eyebrow, prompting Danny to explain further.

'I gave him a black eye a few weeks ago,' he admitted quietly.

'And did he deserve it?'

Danny locked eyes with the petite, well-turned out lady across the table and considered his answer carefully.

'No. In truth, I over-reacted.'

'But..?' she prompted once more.

He became sheepish and eventually shrugged before continuing.

'I caught him smacking a horse over its back with a whip because it wouldn't stand still. So I grabbed the whip and hit him over his back to see how he liked it. Then it developed from there…'

Mary pursed her lips and nodded again, examining the man, almost thirty years her junior.

'I could have handled it better,' Danny added hurriedly when Mary remained silent, 'Like just now. My words don't come to me when I get angry. Thank you, by the way… for what you did.'

Mary inclined her head and stared at the floor for a few seconds. She sniffed, grabbed her handbag, stood and started toward the café exit. Danny watched her go, a mixture of surprise and disappointment written across his face. He must have read her wrong; he'd assumed she was still on his side.

Mary halted after three yards, her back to him. She looked back over her shoulder and gave him a coy, mildly suggestive glance. It seemed to Danny that Mary's eyes sparkled as she raised an eyebrow. Loud enough for the entire café to hear, Mary called back to him.

'Come on, Mr Carter,' she urged, feigning impatience, 'Let's buy us a racehorse.'

Nine

Mary was outside and walking round the sales building when Danny caught up with her. She was striding on with purpose and they soon reached the pre-sales ring. It was flooded with people and the crack of a gavel signalled another sale. He looked up to the nearest monitor; lot five-hundred and twenty had just been sold.

Mary found a space on the rails and waved Danny over to stand with her. She watched the yearlings walk around the ring for a minute, beaming excitedly at each one that passed.

'It's entirely your choice,' she told him, 'I trust you to get the right one for me and your budget is twenty-thousand pounds.'

She couldn't help giving a yelp of laughter when Danny's eyebrows disappeared upwards beneath his ruffled fringe. His eyes danced in their sockets as the sum registered.

'Really?'

He sounded like a little boy who couldn't quite believe what he'd just opened on Christmas morning. Mary drank in every second of his astonishment, delighted with his reaction. She produced an affirming expression and watched as Danny's eyes glazed over. A few seconds later he was rifling through his sales catalogue.

'There's so many nice horses I'd ruled out because I knew they would go for more than my budget,' he explained as he leafed excitedly through the wafer thin pages.

'What about that horse you bid on, I don't suppose we could buy that one? It's just that you seemed to… get on with him quite well. I see he was bought by someone called Vendor.'

Danny looked up from the catalogue and frowned.

'No, you can't have that right. A woman bought him. The vendor was a chap from Ireland, I know the stud.'

'It says Vendor on here,' Mary countered, turning her mobile phone round and pushing its glowing face toward him.

It only took Danny a minute to find the right area of the stables and track the colt down. A small, plump girl inadvisably dressed in jodhpurs that accentuated every ripple of skin, was leaning against the stable door when Danny and Mary approached. They both independently feared they were too late, as the stable was completely shut up.

The girl didn't look up and was bent over, engrossed in her mobile phone screen. She had a small leather case beside her and a head collar lay across it. She gave an irritated sniff when Danny asked if the colt was still in his box.

'We bought him back,' she reported, momentarily glimpsing up at the two of them before dropping to eyes to her device once more.

'But still for sale,' an Irish accented voice announced from behind them, 'Linda, let's open up and allow these good people to see the colt.'

The man shot out a hand and gave Mary a firm and vigorous handshake during which he wore a businesslike smile and assessed her intently with pale blue eyes. He was about the same age as Mary and introduced himself as Rory Dermott. He nodded a greeting to Danny in a way which Mary took to mean the two men were already acquainted.

Galvanised by Rory's request, Linda busied herself with the stable door latches and bolts. As the door was cracked open, a dark mass moved in the back of the box, almost as black as its surroundings. A thin layer of straw crackled as the colt shifted its weight from one foot to another and issued a nervous snort.

'This one has plenty of spirit. Don't be getting too close, and leave his ears alone,' Rory warned Mary, then to Danny he added, 'I thought you'd be bidding for him. You could see beyond his immature temperament.'

'He was a shade too expensive, I'm afraid,' Danny replied, followed by a sigh so dramatic it made Mary bite her lip in order to stop her giggling. Danny didn't notice, he was already with the colt in the back of the box, whispering to him.

Mary joined Danny and looked the colt over, careful to maintain her distance from the horse. The chestnut shifted forward a few feet and the light from the open stable door struck the colt's chest, transforming his previously dark hide to a vibrant, shining golden colour.

'What a strange marking,' Mary said, squinting at the colt's neck, 'It resembles the petals of a flower.'

'I think it suits him,' said Linda from the stable door, 'It's like he's wearing a rosette.'

Danny ran a hand over the circular, three-inch wide irregularity. It looked like an extra layer of folded skin which seemed to be bunched at the edges, covering a small, round indentation.

'That's a Prophet's Thumbprint,' Danny said, gently touching the area before sliding his forefinger under the fold of skin and rotating it a full three-hundred and sixty degrees, 'It's supposed to be lucky. A small number of horses have them like this. It's just a minor abnormality in the muscle tissue that makes a dip, and the skin around creates a sort of frilly edge.'

'Is it something to worry about?' asked Mary.

'No, not at all. It's like a birthmark; he won't even notice it's there.'

Danny resumed feeling the colt's legs, and then switched to running his palm down the horse's spine. The colt tossed his head upwards a couple of times, but didn't shift his position.

'Would eight thousand pounds in cash buy him?'

Danny swung round, his eyes wide in surprise at Mary's offer. She had retreated to the stable door, leaning against it with her arms crossed and adopting an expectant expression, patiently waiting for an answer from the breeder.

Rory rubbed a couple of fingers thoughtfully across his chin.

'Well now, I've had plenty of interest in this lad since he went through the ring…'

Before he could continue Mary produced an understanding nod and spoke again, careful to use a conciliatory tone.

'I noticed you had your keys in your hand when you joined us, Linda was packed, and if I'm not mistaken, there's a passport of some sort sticking out of your pocket. I think you were about to leave, Mr Dermott.'

Mary paused and became contemplative, 'I imagine the last thing you need is to take him all the way back to Ireland. In the circumstances, I think eight thousand pounds is a fair offer, so what do you say?'

The Irishman kneaded the back of his neck with a palm, looking Mary up and down. The colt had been difficult from the day he was born, and he winced inside at the thought of taking him back home. Trying to bid him up through Linda and trusting a young lad to lead up had been a mistake, and he'd had no further interest since the sale. Besides, they needed the room at home for the new foals.

With the colt's muzzle dipping under his arm in the back of the stable, Danny watched the breeder reach into the back pocket of his jeans and pull out a plastic coated equine passport.

'I do like a lady who knows her own mind,' Rory stated softly and handed Mary the passport. She went to accept it, but found the Irishman playfully refusing to let go. He was examining her closely, both eyebrows raised, demanding her attention.

'He's yours…' he said, locking eyes with Mary, 'For eight thousand five hundred pounds… and if I can take you for a coffee while your trainer does the paperwork.'

Mary felt her cheeks redden. She contemplated all sorts of excuses and reasons to let the man down but instead found herself curtly nodding her acceptance, only breaking eye contact with the Irishman to flash an excited girlish smile in Danny's direction. Danny beamed back, but soon transferred his attention back to his newly bought colt. He started humming a tune Mary only recognised as D:Ream's *Things Can Only Get Better* as she was walking away from the stable with Rory.

Ten

In the first week of September, a few days after her Doncaster Sales trip, Mary spent a raucous evening with her three best friends. It was the first time since Henry's funeral that all four of them had been able to synchronise calendars. Mary had been looking forward to catching up; it had been over five months since they'd all been together, although she had met each of them individually in the meantime. However, it was when they all got together that the real fun happened.

Like Mary, Audrey, Sarah, and Maisie were all in their fifties. The four of them had become firm friends whilst Mary was in her first few years teaching. Until Henry became ill, Mary had been the one who arranged their nights together, or afternoons at the races, usually to coincide with Henry working late or being away for a few days on business.

Mary thoroughly enjoyed her time with her friends, and indeed, their days out together. Despite the constant push and pull of their family lives, the three ladies didn't fill their chatter with stories about their children, work, and husbands. Instead, their evenings were dedicated to playing poker for money, and their days out together tended to be at the local racecourses.

Henry had once asked Mary whether she would describe the three ladies as close friends, the types she could rely upon to drop everything for her at a moment's notice. Mary had thought long and hard, finally answering, 'Yes.' Henry had immediately challenged her response. He had reasoned they couldn't be that close if she'd had to think that hard about it. A little hurt, she'd not argued further. However, when Henry became ill, Audrey, Sarah, and Maisie had all rallied round, proving Henry was wrong.

Maisie, married with two children, worked as a full-time Matron at the local hospital. Audrey was always the most vocal, ran the local swimming pool, chaired several charitable events in the town and was a larger than life character. Sarah was a housewife who had endeared herself to the group at the age of twenty-two by announcing she was a trophy wife for her husband, twenty years her senior. Money was never an issue for Sarah.

Tonight it was Sarah who had suggested they meet at her house for some supper and, almost certainly, a game of cards. With Sarah's husband banished to the other end of the house, Mary had enjoyed re-joining the group after her enforced absence. By the time she waved goodbye at the end of the evening, she prided herself at having left with plans for all four of them to go racing the following week, and with a small profit from their game of poker.

***

Mary turned into the short row of terraced houses to find someone waiting outside her cottage. Her headlights picked out the shiny new silver car parked at the bottom of the lane. Her heart missed a beat. Eddie Romano's name, never too far from her thoughts, now leapt to the fore.

A dark figure, with head leant back, was sitting in the driver's seat. As Mary drove slowly toward the parked car, the outline of a man's face was picked out through the driver's window by the dim lights of his dashboard. As she passed, the head rocked to the right in order to peer at her. For a moment she locked eyes with the man. He was sunk into the seat of his motor car, was about her age, perhaps a little older, but it was his eyes that gave him away. It took a few moments for Mary to place him, but as she switched the Volvo's engine off, it came to her. She knew who owned those bulbous pop-eyes. Mary glanced into her rear-view mirror and caught her own reflection as her look of concern turned into a scowl. It was Vinny.

Vincent Raggert slid out of his car and bounced on his toes to Mary's garden gate. He watched with arms crossed and a smirk on his lips as Mary opened her boot. Picking up on Mary's nervousness, Charlie immediately started to growl the moment the boot lid started to rise. At the first opportunity, he jumped down to the drive and looked primed to leap into action, the hair on his back standing on end. He pointed his nose at Vincent and showed a fang at the side of his mouth during a low, threatening growl. It made Mary proud, but she held firmly onto his lead all the same.

But what was she to do? She couldn't set her dog on him… could she? She rubbed the dog's leather collar between her fingers, allowing the thought of Charlie jumping on Vinny's chest and dribbling saliva all over him to fill her mind for a few seconds. Instead, she crossed to her garden path, stopping a few yards before the gate and adopted an expectant expression.

A shiny-looking grey suit, at least a size too big for him, clung to a pair of bony shoulders. An off-white shirt and a thin red tie did little to disguise a small, yet perfectly rounded pot-belly and a pair of battered black, faux leather shoes provided him with a passable version of a rent collector.

He's virtually the same as he was thirty years ago, as creepy as they come, just older, thought Mary. Vincent's protruding stomach was the primary alteration; he'd previously been rake-like. However, his jet black hair, now receding, was just the same as it always had been; combed into a quiff at the front, with the rest plastered to his skull.

Eddie and Vinny. Her two least favourite men. They had been inseparable in the eighties and apparently the two of them were still in each others' pockets. Although Mary and Eddie had their long-standing grudge, her husband had remained in touch with his brother. He'd never announce he was seeing Eddie, but Mary had always suspected they watched Newcastle United home games together. She hadn't minded; after all, it was Eddie who had the problem with her, not the other way around. Besides, it was Henry's way; he was a natural peacemaker. If the two of them argued, which was rare, it would be Henry who made the first move towards reconciliation. However, Henry's skill had never been enough to reconcile Mary and Eddie.

Despite his patience and understanding, Henry had no time for Vincent, believing him to be a bad influence on his brother. Mary hadn't known Vincent well, but during those couple of years in Newcastle she had reached the conclusion the man stuck to Eddie like glue, shadowing him and providing fuel for Eddie's temper. She'd had no time for him in the eighties and doubted she would muster much more than a couple of minutes for him this evening.

She strode up the path, trying to exude an air of confident impatience whilst battling internally with why Vincent, Eddie Romano's right-hand man, would be smiling at her.

With dread churning in her stomach she swallowed hard and forced herself to stare into the face of a man who she had been reliably informed, threw people out of their houses for a living.

'It's been a long time, Mary,' Vincent burbled through a false smile that faded quickly. He offered nothing more, standing arms crossed at the garden gate. Mary noticed the weak streetlight made his slicked hair glisten and wondered whether anyone would find that effect alluring; she certainly didn't.

She took another step closer, halting outside of fist-swinging distance from the gate, sniffed the night air and mimicked Vincent by crossing her own arms. He would be under orders from Eddie. She needed to discover what those orders were and get rid of him as quickly as possible. He wasn't here to hurt her, at least she doubted it. Even Vincent would have enough sense not to do his dirty work out in the open.

'What do you want, Vinny? It's late.'

Vincent sniffed his disapproval at the use of his old nickname.

'Vin...cent,' he said slowly.

'Such a shame,' Mary replied conversationally, 'I always thought you suited 'Vinny', you know, it's so...'

'We need to talk. Inside,' Vincent interrupted, losing patience. 'I've a...'

Mary watched Vincent trying to locate the right word. His bottom lip pushed in and out as he searched through his lexicon. It can't be an extensive search she decided. He'd always been a man of few words.

'…proposition,' he managed finally.

Mary rolled her eyes, but didn't move from her pitch half-way up the path. She considered her options.

'We're being watched,' Vincent noted, 'Your next door neighbour has been twitching his curtains ever since I got here.'

Mary's shoulders slumped. He'd have to come into the house. She couldn't conduct the entire conversation out here for Bert to hear.

A few minutes later she closed the door of the kitchen on a very disgruntled Charlie and joined Vincent in her lounge. She was empty-handed, having refused his request for a 'brew'. She found him sitting in her favourite armchair with his bony legs crossed, displaying a couple of inches of terry-towelling sock. She reasoned they had to be decades old, she couldn't believe shops still sold them.

'This is cozy,' he said without warmth, as she entered the room. Mary shivered, clasped her arms around herself and remained standing.

Vincent uncrossed his legs, leaving them wide open and looked the small woman up and down whilst swallowing. Mary watched as his hideously large adam's apple rose and fell, hiding her revulsion by gritting her teeth. Oblivious to the effect he was having on her, Vincent concluded Mary Romano still had that look about her, despite her age. The fine boned face, intelligent eyes and sculpted waist and… he stopped himself. He could see why Henry had fallen for her.

There was something a little different about her, but he couldn't quite put his finger on it.

Mary read the man's silence as an attempt to intimidate her and took a breath in order to steady herself.

'Come on, *Vinny*, tell me what Eddie wants to say then get out of my house,' she challenged.

With his wandering thoughts interrupted Vincent frowned up at her and began tapping the arm of his chair with a little finger.

'You always were too clever for your own good. And look where that's going to get you,' he said irritably, as the drumming of his finger becoming quicker, 'Eddie is gunning for you now Henry is gone.'

'Really? Well he certainly knows how to throw threats around, but I haven't seen any action from him.'

'Ha, no, you're a special case,' said Vincent, his wire thin smile returning, 'Eddie's going to sort you out himself.'

He watched Mary's reaction closely before adding, 'I wouldn't worry. I'm sure he'll make it quick… as you're family.'

'I'm no relation to him anymore. Oh, and he's not going to intimidate me,' Mary insisted, glaring at the seated man, 'All I've ever received from Eddie is hollow threats. He's all mouth and no trousers.'

Vincent's throat crackled with a forced laugh.

'What is it they say about revenge?' he asked rhetorically, his finger-tapping slowing as he felt his grip on the conversation begin to tighten.

'Surely you know, Mary, you being so *clever*?' He waited patiently but when a reply didn't arrive he continued.

'Well... however it's best served, Eddie's going to serve it that way.'

'That's enough *Vinny*, get out of my house,' Mary said irritably. Her patience with this horrid man was wearing thin and she pointed to the door, 'You've got nothing to tell me I haven't heard before, so just get lost. I'll wait for the organ-grinder to pitch up and see what he's got to say.'

'I was surprised he let you walk away from the funeral,' Vincent replied, unmoving in his armchair. He was comfortably in command now, and allowed another reference to his teenage nickname to pass unnoticed this time, 'I would have dealt with you straight after Henry passed if you'd killed *my* father.'

Mary swallowed hard. It had been a lifetime ago since she'd heard those words. Vincent grinned, displaying a rack of yellowy-grey teeth.

'It's your lucky day, Mary,' he said, delighting in the confusion it brought her, 'Eddie's given you a way to…' he paused, again scrabbling for the words, eventually settling for '...pay him back.'

Mary was now standing behind the empty sofa, her arms crossed tightly below her bosom and wearing a bemused expression. Vincent raised both his pencil thin eyebrows, as if what he was about to say was momentous.

'He wants something from you. It's rightfully his anyway, so when he gets it, he'll leave you alone.'

He said this in a much softer tone which caught Mary by surprise. She could almost believe Vincent was *pleased*. Pushing the thought away, she fought to remain poker-faced.

Vincent was a shade disappointed. He'd hoped for more of a reaction from her. Instead she'd continued to stare uncomprehendingly. Yes, Eddie was right, she *was* a slippery one. There was certainly more to her than you could imagine from following her around. He'd done plenty of that in the last three years.

'We know you must have it. You and Henry lived like church mice, then he dies and you're suddenly buying racehorses. Didn't you think we'd get to know?'

Mary's mind was racing. She was still glaring at Vincent, but wasn't seeing him. She needed time to think. She wandered around the sofa and down toward one end, the one furthest from Vincent.

'Trousers!' Vincent exclaimed unexpectedly as she passed him.

'What?' queried Mary, turning to stare intently at her uninvited guest.

'Trousers,' Vincent repeated, nodding at her bottom, his bug eyes sparkling, 'You've *hardly ever* worn trousers. All the times I've seen you, you've never…'

Mary's stare intensified as she allowed Vincent's words to filter through and settle on her. So it was true. She hadn't been imagining it, at least not *all* of those times. Those movements in the shadows, the snap of branches when no one was there and so, so many times… that strong sense someone was watching, in the street, through her back window, at work and with her friends. Was it the figure of a man she'd caught in the corner of her eye all those times, or just a trick of the light… had Vincent been there to cause a shiver of fear that made her pulse quicken?

His outburst had revealed a truth, but Mary now considered the lengths Eddie had gone to in order to monitor her. It was almost *thirty years* since his father had died. Mary felt a wave of nausea rush over her as she reached the conclusion that Eddie's threats may not be as hollow as she imagined.

Vincent hadn't noticed Mary's reaction, as a tinge of colour had flushed his own cheeks.

'… you've never worn jeans,' he finished tamely. His eyes were glued to the walls for a few seconds as the magnitude of his embarrassment registered. But he had been watching her for such a *long* time. He *knew* her. He knew all about her. He knew her secrets. All of them. And over the last three years she had become his guilty secret. He *enjoyed* watching her.

A short, awkward silence was broken by Mary. She prayed her face didn't reveal her new found fear. In fact it was masked – by her revulsion for Vincent. Simply by being in her home, he was now making her flesh creep. She consoled herself a little in the knowledge Vincent had proved he was capable of making mistakes.

'So, you've been watching me?' she asked, her brows diving into a demanding stare, 'For how long?

Of course she was right, Vincent thought. He had been watching her, and decided there was no harm in admitting it. Things were different now. The objective of the game had altered, at least in the short term. Eddie wouldn't be pleased if he discovered he *liked* following Mary around, and looked forward to seeing her… but there were plenty of secrets he kept from Eddie.

Vincent cleared his throat and resumed the spiteful persona he'd relied on for most of his adult life.

'We've known where you were living for years, but you had

Henry protecting you. We took closer interest three years ago, when Henry got sick. He couldn't give us the run around anymore. I've been checking up on you every week,' he told her with a sneer, 'I've seen you at school, at the swimming baths, out shopping… and most of all, in this house. The monotony of your life is truly tiresome.'

He grinned at his put-down, his confidence returning.

'Eddie gave me you as a project. He's never forgotten you, or what you did. Eddie's a strong believer in family, so as long as you were married to his brother, you were safe. I just kept tabs on how things were going. I didn't want to miss a quickie divorce and for you to skip the country!'

Vincent gripped the arms of his chair and paused to admire Mary's expression. She hadn't been able to disguise her initial indignation, but it had dissolved as he'd been speaking; instead, her face was limp, her mouth slightly open.

'Stunned are we?' he enquired with an inclination of his head, 'I know all your friends, your work colleagues at that school you used to teach at, and I've even sat in Suzie's front room, you know, the young lass you took on part-time to look after Henry for the odd evening, so you could meet up with your poker playing friends? I know how much you and Henry earned, what you've got in the bank... I even know that you couldn't have children…'

'Shut up!' snarled Mary, jumping up from her seat. From behind her Charlie produced an angry growl and began pawing at the kitchen door.

Vincent shuffled into the back of his seat, clasped his hands and rubbed them together. His dry skin made a quiet rasping noise.

'Get out!' Mary insisted, throwing out her left arm toward the front door, 'Get out now you, you…'

'Monster? Wicked, evil slime-ball? I've heard them all, Mary, ' Vincent interrupted with a bored sigh. He waved her back to the sofa with a few flicks of his wrist.

'I know you inside out, you're my mark. The longest I've ever had. If you get to know your mark well, the opportunity, method and timing used to extract what you need from them becomes obvious. You should know that; it's how you killed Eddie's father.'

Mary remained standing, glaring down at him. It was clear Vincent was going nowhere until he'd imparted whatever it was Eddie wanted her to know.

'Tell me what the hell Eddie wants and then get out.'

'Sit down,' Vincent demanded. Mary's eyes narrowed and was about to repeat her own demand at increased volume, but stopped herself. This weasel probably got a kick from seeing her out of control. She took a breath and returned to her seat on the sofa. Charlie's pawing at the door had stopped, replaced with a low, insistent whining. She wished she'd kept him with her, and imagined for a moment how she could have set him on Vincent.

'The only way you can afford to buy racehorses, even a cheap one like you bought the other day, is if you've come into some money,' Vincent pointed out when he was satisfied he had Mary's undivided attention.

'You're comfortable, but that's about it. You've enough to cover the rent on this place but thirty to forty grand a year per horse for training? Come on, Mary, that was a rookie mistake.'

Mary opened her mouth to fire back an answer and tell this lizard how wrong he was, but instead coolness descended onto her and she controlled the urge. He clearly didn't know *everything* about her. She almost flicked her eyes up to the mantle to check the Premium Bond letter wasn't still there, worried it was on show, but resisted.

'Eddie reckons there's only one way you could have come into that sort of money,' Vincent continued, 'And that's if you, or Henry, found Joe's Stone. Have you got it?'

Mary's mind was racing once more, the years peeling back to those few months in the eighties. She'd tried to forget them, but such stark, strong memories were hard to bury.

'Well?' Vincent prompted.

Mary rubbed her chin between her thumb and fore-finger, as if contemplating the question. In truth, she had no idea how to respond.

'So where did Joe hide the Stone? You or Henry must have worked it out, y'know that meeting with someone called 'Jam', or 'Jay' or something?'

Mary wrinkled her nose in search of a suitable response.

'So not satisfied with his parents' house and all the money, Eddie wants the Stone as well?' she ventured.

Vincent's eyes widened, 'So you *do* have it?'

'Not here,' Mary answered quickly. After a short pause she continued, 'It will take weeks, maybe months, to get it.'

'You've raised money against it, haven't you?'

Mary remained silent, choosing to react with a hard stare consisting, she hoped, of suppressed anger. It seemed to work, as Vincent broke out into his wiry smile. He slapped the arms of his chair with two flat palms and let out a single word; 'Aha!'

Vincent pulled himself to his feet, but Mary hardly noticed. She was staring into the unlit fireplace, into another world, another place.

Digging in the top pocket of his suit, Vincent tossed a plain white business card onto the other end of Mary's sofa. It displayed a mobile number and nothing else.

'Tell anyone about Eddie, me, or the Stone, and you'll regret it. Involve the police and you'll... regret it. Don't think for one second the authorities will stop Eddie, you will…'

'Yes I get it. I'll regret it!' Mary cut in, her anger fizzing within her once more, 'What does that even mean?'

Vincent grinned as he walked to the lounge door and opened it before turning back.

'It means your life will not be your own until Eddie gets what he wants. Whatever you've done with the Stone, get it and call me.'

He paused and Mary witnessed Vincent's stance softening. He remained serious, but the petulance was replaced with something else, something quite alien for him. It was as if he'd suddenly become bored with his act.

'Eddie says he'll leave you alone if he gets the Stone back,' Vinny said softly and with an element of pleading in his eyes, 'Give him the Stone, Mary. Do the *smart* thing and give it to him.'

Eleven

Once the familiar click of her front door being closed reached her Mary rushed to ensure it was locked and the dead-bolt was engaged. She opened the kitchen door and stood back as Charlie charged into the front room, dashed straight to the window and sprung up, his paws on the sill so he could bark at Vincent's car as it swung round and disappeared up the lane in a cloud of diesel smoke.

Thirty minutes later, the two of them were curled up together on the sofa in front of an open fire, Mary drinking soup from a mug. She'd decided to leave her armchair empty for tonight; it somehow felt tainted by Vincent. As she raised her mug to her lips, she caught the faint smell of paraffin. She hadn't washed her hands thoroughly enough after setting the fire, and a waft of firelighter block suddenly filled her. She'd been trying to distract herself, but it was no good, the paraffin smell awoke her memories, transporting her back to the mid-seventies.

She saw herself and her father, lighting the fire in the back room, holding newspaper to the grate to make it draw and then toasting bread on cold Sunday evenings. She paused there a few moments, enjoying the sense of calm it brought her. Then she sped forward to the eighties, the day she enrolled as a Mathematics undergraduate at Newcastle Polytechnic. She thought of the daily commute from Sunderland, reading the situations vacant ad in a copy of the *Evening Chronicle* someone had stuffed between two seats on the train the previous night. What better for a mathematics student than to become a croupier? She was eighteen, she was quick with numbers, she may not be tall, but she was presentable… Money was tight, despite her grant, so she had applied. And it was at the casino that she had met Henry.

She'd fought these memories for so long, thrusting them deep down, trying to obliterate them, knowing where they led. Tonight she would allow them to bubble up, take shape and become real once more.

The night she met Henry, he was with his brother. The two of them had glided up the stairs to the Grey's Casino gaming floor and after a pause, crossed the thick, crimson carpeted gambling room. It was a few minutes before midnight on a Friday in December and after perusing the available tables, Henry touched his brother's arm lightly and indicated Mary's blackjack table. Henry was a large, broad man. He stood well over six feet, towering over Mary and yet he moved with the grace of a dancer. He seemed to float over to Mary's table. Eddie was a couple of inches smaller and darker, with hair and eyebrows the colour of coal, but he possessed the same ease of movement. She knew they were brothers immediately; despite the difference in size and shape there was something about their jaw line that gave it away. Both were immaculately turned out

47

in three-piece lounge suits, something Mary had admired in those days.

Henry smiled as he sat down. It made his eyes shimmer, and it was his smile that always created a shiver which started at the top of Mary's neck and travelled like an eruption of hot lava down her spine. She hadn't worked well that night; she couldn't concentrate.

Their romance had taken hold of them quickly. They had lived around the bars, clubs and pubs in a city known for its nightlife. Before long she was meeting his family. They were Italian immigrants. Henry's father, Joe, ran a small, popular pasta restaurant situated down one of the many backstreets in the centre of Newcastle. It was a family affair; Joe's wife Nina, and both their boys, worked the tables while Joe cooked.

Mary got to know Eddie, Henry's younger brother by two years. He was good looking, arguably more so than Henry, and the women flocked to his side, but it was only the needy, damaged girls prepared to be victimized that stuck around for any length of time. Eddie had Latin looks and a quiet, smouldering charm, yet he lacked all the empathy and generosity of his brother. He lost interest in new women, clubs, and pubs quickly, always seeking the next new experience. And his temper was never too far from the surface. If his partners didn't run after a night or two, Eddie would cast them aside within a week at most. On more than one occasion Mary found herself giving his latest female companion private, subtle hints of what to expect, especially if they were naive.

Initially Mary forgave Eddie's treatment of women, agreeing with Henry that it was most likely a foolish, adolescent phase. That was until she witnessed Eddie punching a young girl in the face when she wouldn't let go of him, leaving her unconscious outside a night club. From that moment on, Mary distanced herself from Eddie. He was a driven young man, possibly destined to succeed in his chosen path, but he had no thought for the mental, and sometimes, physical distress he left behind.

But Eddie was a minor irritation, for Mary's love for Henry would have transcended anything his brother might do or say. For eighteen wonderful months, Mary had the time of her life with Henry. She entered the third year of her degree with plans to teach and expectations of finding a place with Henry to live together. Those plans fell apart in the space of three days in the summer of 1986.

Henry's father's birthday party was when her perfect world started to unravel, her first and only visit to the Romano family home. It was bigger, and much grander than she had anticipated, located in an old area of Newcastle called Summerhill Park, to the West of the city centre. Inside the spacious four storey town house every room had tall walls with intricate cornices and ornate ceiling roses from which spectacular lighting dazzled her. The house was decorated immaculately throughout. Mary had been awestruck when she had been given a guided tour of Joe's house.

It had to be ten times the size of dad's house in Sunderland. All the appliances were brand new, the carpets and curtains were thick and oozing quality, and two virtually new, top of the range cars were lined up at the back of the house behind radio controlled garage shutters.

When she had sheepishly asked how his family could afford all this, Henry had shrugged, his eyes darting away from her gaze.

'I suppose the restaurant has had a few good years,' he had replied, slightly embarrassed. She hadn't pursued the matter further. Oh, how she wished she had.

Joe had been on great form that evening; the centre of attention and the perfect host, until she was leaving. He manufactured a moment alone with her and asked which shifts she would be working in the coming weeks.

'I have perfected a little system on the blackjack. I want to make sure you'll be there to see it working,' he explained with a touch of mischief about him. She'd been polite and naively answered without considering what her prospective father-in-law could be planning.

A week later she'd taken Henry home to meet her father, and the two of them had clicked immediately, as she had known they would. Henry's staunch support of Newcastle United had become an immediate source of jibing and good-hearted mocking by her dad, himself a dedicated Sunderland fan. The two men could happily argue for hours over the relative merits of players, managers and enjoy berating the owners of the two football clubs.

Mary emerged from her reminiscing to find Charlie asleep beside her and the fire reduced to a few dots of stubborn red embers. She slid off the sofa, leaving Charlie to continue his slumber, closed the curtains and added a few choice pieces of coal to the fire. She sat back down and watched the thin wisps of smoke curl around the newly added fuel and found herself grimacing. She was delaying the inevitable. She didn't want to think about *that* night, but knew she had to.

The Royal Victoria Infirmary had been ablaze with light when they pulled into the hospital car park, even though it was three o'clock in the morning. She remembered there had been large cracks in the paving stones making progress perilous in her high-heeled croupier working shoes. She'd still been wearing her bow tie and jacket too, making her feel incongruous among the inhabitants of the accident and emergency room.

By the time she and Henry had finally arrived at his father's bedside, Joe was slipping in and out of consciousness. Nurses whisked in and out of the room, warning he was being prepared for surgery. Nina wasn't there, which immediately placed Henry on edge; where was she? Did his mother even know what had happened?

Joe's cheeky grin, usually a fixture on the sixty year-old's face had been replaced with an almost serene expression painted in a pallid grey. Mary remembered the pain in Henry's eyes when they traded a glance, felt sure that her own feeling of dread was being reflected back at him.

'You've no right to be here,' an agitated voice interjected from behind them. She recognised Eddie's throaty North Eastern accent and a shiver of fear stopped her from turning to face him.

'It's *your* fault he's in here, you bitch! That's right, don't you look at me!'

Tears had never come easily to Mary as a young woman, so when she did turn, it was with a dry eye and her make-up still perfectly in place.

'He was cheating. I warned him…'

Mary tried to remember how it happened, but Henry, much the bigger and stronger man, had fended his brother off. Eddie had flown across the small curtained space, his fists clenched. Henry stepped in front of her before Eddie's blow could reach its intended target. As the two young men struggled face to face, Henry pleading with his brother to calm down, Mary heard a groan behind her.

'Go to… the Ron… Rendez… Vous. Ask for…'

Joe tried to swallow in order to finish his sentence but a rasping cough contorted his face into a mask of pain.

The boys stopped arguing and rushed to the bedside, Eddie on the opposite side of Henry and Mary.

'What is it, Pa?' Eddie asked, grasping his father's pale white hand in his.

Joe turned his head to his youngest son and tried to speak, tears of frustration welling from the corner of his eyes as the waves of pain ripped the words from his vocal chords and replaced them with an unintelligible gurgling.

'He said to go to the rendezvous and ask for someone, he didn't say who,' Mary told the brothers.

Henry shook his head. 'Forget that, Pa, just hang on. You're going into theatre soon. Stay strong.'

A female nurse swept the curtains apart and ordered the three of them to step back. A male orderly appeared and started to click the mechanisms of Joe's trolley with practiced efficiency, repeating the nurse's request for room to work. Henry and Mary stepped back, but Eddie stayed, leaning close to the old man's face, maintaining his grip on his Father's hand.

'Where's the rendezvous, Pa? Who do we ask for?' Eddie whispered urgently.

Another nurse was now placing a hand on Eddie's shoulder and trying to prise his fingers from his father's hand.

When Eddie tried to shrug her off, she leaned over the trolley until she was almost nose to nose with him.

'We have to get this man into theatre. Please step back now, Sir!'

Joe's eyes rolled upwards and he coughed again. In defiance of the drugs now invading his bloodstream he raised his head off his pillow and his tongue darted over his lips.

'Ask… Jay,' their father croaked to Eddie before whatever medication he'd been given finally overcame his will to stay awake.

The trolley departed along with its entourage of medical staff, leaving Eddie, Mary, and Henry standing in an empty emergency bay. It took a few moments after the trolley banged its way through the swing doors before the sounds of other patients and hospital staff pushed in and reminded them they weren't alone. Their moments of anxiety with Joe had been shared with dozens of other people behind the thin plastic curtains.

Mary stole a glance at Eddie and immediately sought shelter by moving closer to Henry and grasping his hand. Eddie seemed to be experiencing a host of emotions all of which were overlaid with rage.

Even though Henry stood between her and Eddie, his eyes locked onto her with such intensity that when she recalled the scene they were always alone. Everyone else, including Henry, dissolved away.

Eddie's anger quickly drained from him as his eyes drilled into her. The rage was replaced by an almost placid, dull expression. He relaxed, dug his hands into his trouser pockets and cleared his throat.

'If Pa dies, you will suffer,' he said slowly and deliberately.

As Eddie spoke there was no menace in his words. Instead, his hard blue eyes seemed to penetrate Mary's skull and bury a bomb in her brain. It was a device filled with enough menace it immediately started to leak its promise of violent rage the moment it was planted there.

It only took twenty minutes for a tired, bespectacled young doctor to emerge and confirm that Joe had died on the operating table due to complications arising from the blows he took to his stomach.

'You won't be protected forever,' Eddie had told her in the same implacable tone, ignoring Henry's protests. He broke eye contact with Mary and turned to address Henry.

'She will pay, when you've done with her,' he told his brother. Henry said nothing, there was no point. He'd seen Eddie like this before.

'I will make you suffer,' Eddie repeated to Mary. He left the hospital and Mary never saw him again until the day of Henry's funeral.

***

Mary had been padding around the house for two hours. She was tired, but her mind was racing with thoughts of Eddie, Vincent, Henry and her father. So she wandered aimlessly, deep in thought.

She had found the Stone… Vincent's words tumbled around her. They were meaningless rubbish. She'd never heard of a 'Stone' in all the years she'd been married to Henry. Did it have something to do with Joe's last words in the hospital? It must have, as Vincent had said so… she had worked it out… apparently!

Thank goodness she hadn't revealed the true source of her windfall. At least this turn of events might buy her some more time before having to face Eddie again.

Mary finally got into bed at two o'clock and lay rigid, fretting for the first twenty minutes. The most sensible thing to do was to go to the police and tell them all about Eddie, Vincent, and their threats. But she'd done this before, several times after Joe died, and again about three years ago when she was sure someone was following her. Given what she'd learned tonight, it had to be Vincent who had been tracking her from school and around Northallerton.

The police had done nothing previously. Both times, sympathetic police officers had taken statements from her, but no concrete evidence had resulted from what little enquiries they conducted. She had no evidence either - no paper trail or email correspondence - just unrecorded verbal threats and a stalker caught in the corner of her eye on several occasions.

If she couldn't work out where this Stone… A thought struck her and out loud she asked, 'Stone?' Her voice bounced around her bedroom. It couldn't be an actual piece of stone could it? She considered Vincent's words again. Perhaps it was a gemstone? But what gemstone, and where? Henry had never mentioned a stone of any sort. Perhaps it was Henry's mother's? Yes, that made sense. Maybe Henry was given some jewellery of some sort by his mother before she died?

Following their father's death, Henry's reaction to his brother's accusations and threats had been to try and make Eddie see sense. When Eddie wouldn't back down, insisting he was going to exact revenge for Mary killing his father, Henry had lost patience. The two brothers' had argued bitterly, and when four months later their mother died of pneumonia Eddie piled further blame onto Mary, claiming Nina had given up after losing her husband, and died of a broken heart.

Inexplicably, the reading of Nina's will revealed she had altered it recently and left the house, the money, and the restaurant business to Eddie. Henry had been deeply hurt, and there was a suggestion Eddie may have had a hand in the alterations to Nina's will in the last two weeks of her life. Henry was left a little money and a few photos.

Cutting him from the will seemed to spur Henry on, and certainly helped harden his resolve. With Eddie constantly haranguing Mary at work and on occasion, in the street, Henry made plans to leave his beloved home city of Newcastle. He sought a new life that would put distance between his fiancé and his brother.

They were married soon after Mary completed her degree and the two newlyweds left Newcastle the same week, moving fifty miles south to Northallerton. Henry never spoke of his brother with Mary. She guessed they made up eventually, and Henry simply wanted to keep her and Eddie well apart. He did return to Newcastle on a regular basis, as he was offered a job by his oldest school friend and within a few months was working around the North of England, successfully selling training and building management services such as security, pest control, and general maintenance.

Mary's thoughts returned to the Stone. Tomorrow she would sift through all those old boxes she and Henry had shoved in the loft when they first moved in. Maybe she would strike lucky and find whatever it was Eddie wanted so badly. Henry's will made no mention of a Stone, and he'd never broached the subject of Joe or a Stone with her in thirty years of marriage. It was infuriating. She was playing with half a deck and bluffing like crazy. Perhaps she needed to pump Vincent for more information, but how to do that without raising suspicion that she didn't possess the Stone?

She tossed and turned for another few minutes before remembering her arrangement to visit Danny Carter's yard in the morning. She'd have to search for the Stone in the loft and indeed, the rest of the house, when she got back. Anticipating a visit to her new trainer and her racehorse led her mind down a calmer, more alluring path. She fell asleep within a few minutes and dreamt of racehorses, jockeys, winning betting slips and her dad.

Twelve

When Mary slowed her Volvo and wound her window down, she knew she had the wrong place. This couldn't be Danny's yard; it seemed far too big based on the description he'd given at Doncaster. She was almost at the bottom of the tree-lined single-track road and the Danny Carter yard was nowhere to be found.

It was around seven thirty in the morning, eight days after Doncaster sales and this was Mary's first visit to Malton. It was a perfect September morning. The sun was slowly climbing into the sky and the hint of a cool breeze provided the only indication autumn was on its way. She was just about to continue to the end of the road when she heard a warning shout which made her slam on her brakes. Eight horses, walking in pairs, filed out of a gap between the trees, passing close to the back of her car. In the back, Charlie was on his feet, nose to the back window, giving a soft whine as the horses passed him only inches away.

Mary was treated to mutterings from at least three of the riders and she responded with a wave and apology delivered through her open window. One of the primary complainers was easily recognisable. Even with his riding helmet obscuring from his eyebrows up, Mary was able to place the pinched features of Jonnie Lilley. She waited for the group to disappear down the lane, relieved they were walking away from her direction of travel.

Danny had warned her that there were three training yards right beside each other down this quiet backwater, reached by following a single track B-road located a mile outside Norton, on the south side of Malton. The road traversed the side of a hill, which she had determined must be a part of the Yorkshire Wolds. Originally built in the seventies as a single yard capable of housing one-hundred and fifty horses, it had subsequently been split in two, and then more recently into three, providing two fifty-horse yards, and a smaller twenty horse yard. Each set of stables were leased from a single landlord and Danny occupied the smallest yard.

Another thirty yards further down the lane, Mary came across a crudely hand-painted sign planted into the rough roadside earth declaring she had reached Danny Carter Training. The entrance to the yard was easy to miss, as a line of mature leylandii had been allowed to grow beyond a controllable height. Mary stopped the car and leaned forward to eye the trees through her windscreen. Each one had to be forty feet high. She eventually located the entrance between two of the towering trees and edged her car into the yard, slotting her Volvo in alongside a small, day-glo yellow coloured horsebox.

Mary had to swallow down a feeling of dread as she made an initial scan of the yard. She'd had her expectations managed to some extent by Danny at the end of their time together at the Doncaster sales, but the reality gave her a sinking feeling. The premises of Danny Carter Training looked in need of a substantial upgrade.

The back of what she presumed was a stabling building had grass, and even a butterfly bush growing out of its guttering and the once whitewashed walls were now a dull, dirty grey colour. There were two jagged holes in the wall, each about four feet square. To her left, a large oblong ménage was surrounded by a wooden fence with posts at angles and several broken or completely missing fence boards. A large round wooden structure sat next door. Beyond was rough ground populated with weeds and rubble and finally at the back of the plot stood a small two storey 1970's redbrick house that gave the impression it needed more than a lick of paint. Its four windows and a centrally placed door seemed to stare mournfully out onto a once proud, but now dilapidated, set of training facilities.

Road scalpings crunched underfoot as Mary made her way toward the house. There seemed to be islands of the bluey-grey stuff placed around the yard in haphazard fashion. On closer inspection, it appeared they were for filling the numerous potholes. She managed to brighten her mood slightly by reminding herself that Danny had only been in this yard a matter of weeks, and felt much better when the man himself loped into view around the corner of the stabling block.

'Welcome to Cordike Stables, Mary!' Danny announced as he approached her in his strange, jaunty walk, 'I thought I heard your car.'

His movement amused Mary. There was so much wrong with the way he swung his arms, and his knees and elbows seemed to bend outwards, yet it all came together somehow, propelling the young man forward as if he was on springs. His enthusiasm was immediately infectious and the two of them broke into easy conversation about their day at the sales.

'Come and have a look around,' the trainer said excitedly once Mary mentioned her horse, 'Your colt has settled in really well.'

In the end, Mary had stuck with the one yearling at the Silver Sale. However, as well as her colt from Ireland, Danny had bought a small filly for two thousand pounds later in the day. She had gone through the ring at a price that Danny had assured Mary was too good to miss, given her breeding. He seemed sure that he would find an owner for her.

Danny guided Mary around the corner of the barn and she was greeted by a sight that helped replenish her faith in the yard's ability to operate as a training base. It also explained why Danny had flecks of white concrete dust in his hair and a dusty smudge down one side of his face.

The barn she had parked behind formed the first side of a horseshoe shaped arrangement of horseboxes. They were large, much bigger than she'd seen in Middleham, and significantly bigger than the boxes at the Doncaster sales. Each box had a split wooden door, some of which appeared to be new, others looked original. All the stables had waist-high lightly stained wood panelling from which ornately twisted steel bars rose to the ceiling of each box. Having burnt through the early morning mist, the sun now illuminated the facing wooden walls and cast shadow beneath the covered walkway outside each box. Sculpted red tiles topped the roof and the stables created a natural courtyard. What looked like recently poured concrete produced a broad, flat walking surface once the horses exited their stables. A small area of grass had been left in the middle of the courtyard.

Mary drank long arc of stables. The boxes looked terrific, and with at least five horses poking their heads out into the courtyard and the smell of the residents on the breeze, a warm feeling of belonging suddenly filled her. As she spun around to take in the full effect, she noticed the house behind her had been built at an angle which meant its windows faced the horseshoe of boxes. Presumably you would be able to see right into each of the boxes, from your kitchen or bedroom window.

'I really like it,' she found herself saying quietly. She hadn't meant to vocalise the feeling, it had simply bubbled to the surface.

'Yeah, it'll be even better when I get it finished.'

She hadn't expected a reply and swung round to face the trainer who stood, one hand on hip, the other shading his eyes from the sun as he ran a critical eye over his yard. Danny wasn't a looker, Mary decided. His bent Roman nose, puppy fat cheeks that reddened too easily, and long, unruly mousey coloured hair that constantly flopped forward, put paid to him falling into the 'good looking' category. His appearance would no doubt have potential suitors passing him over. Yet he had a passion for his horses which surrounded him like an aura and there was undoubtedly a quiet charm about the boy.

'It's certainly got bags of potential,' noted Mary positively.

'It was the old stud,' Danny beamed, plainly pleased with Mary's reaction. He gestured for her to follow him to the first of the stables.

'When this place was a single yard, these boxes are where the broodmares would be stabled. That's why they're so spacious. It means my horses have plenty of room and there's less likelihood of them getting cast in their boxes.'

Danny received a querying look from Mary.

'Sometimes a horse can panic if they can't get up to their feet,' he explained matter-of-factly, 'And they end up hurting themselves because they thrash around trying to stand up. The bigger the box, the less chance there is of that happening.'

'So why are you cutting a big hole in the back of this box?' Mary asked as they walked into the vacant stable. There was rubble on the floor, a variety of tools scattered around and a sheet of Perspex leaning against the wall.

'Ah, that would be for Ivor.'

'I'm guessing Ivor is a horse?'

Danny grinned, 'Ivor is a horse with issues. I'm trying to modify his stable so he'll stop box-walking.'

'Box-walking?' Mary echoed.

'Round and round, all day long,' sighed Danny, 'Not good for him at all.'

'And a big hole in the wall will stop him going around in circles?' asked Mary, perplexed.

'It's going to be an open window, so he can watch everyone coming and going. It will hopefully distract him. And if that doesn't work, then I have this.'

Danny grabbed both sides of the Perspex sheet and flipped it around to face Mary, 'It's going on the opposite wall,' he added.

Mary saw her own image reflected in the sheet. The reverse had a mirrored surface. It wasn't glass, but provided a fairly decent version of a mirror, 'What's Ivor going to do with that... his hair?'

Danny smirked, 'Possibly, although I thought if I got him some make-up...'

He rolled his eyes, 'It will hopefully distract him. Between looking out at the coming and goings of visitors to the yard, and his reflection, he'll take the pressure off his knees created by the constant walking. He's a decent racehorse, but he's just a bit too active. I need him to chill a bit. Come on, he's next door, I'll introduce you.'

It turned out that 'Ivor' was a compact four-year-old bay gelding who had won twice before in sprints. He had a lovely wide face with a white blaze, which ran from his left ear to the right-hand side of his nose and it transpired he loved being petted. When Mary tentatively touched his nose, the gelding stepped forward and gently sank his head into her armpit, prompting her to scratch him between his ears.

'He loves the attention,' Danny pointed out, 'He'd follow me into the house and sleep at the bottom of my bed if I let him. The box-walking is just because he gets bored.'

'What's his racing name?' asked Mary.

Danny responded with a small chuckle, 'His owner is a Welshman with a sense of humour. This lad is called Ivor in the yard, but his racing name is 'The Engine'.'

Mary transferred her attention from the horse, looking up at Danny, who was standing with his arms crossed, one eyebrow raised.

'Ivor... The Engine,' she stated deliberately, 'I see...'

'Want a cup of something hot?' said a young female voice from the stable door.

A boyish girl of about eighteen swung from the doorframe by one hand. Devoid of make-up, she was the same height as Mary and looked fit and full of energy. She was wearing a riding helmet and a bulky looking body protector.

'I've just washed Harry down, and, like, put him on the walker, but I'm desperate for a coffee. Want one?' she asked amiably. When there wasn't an immediate response she added, 'Oh, sorry. I didn't know you, like, had company, Danny.'

'This is Mary Romano,' Danny offered brightly, 'Mary owns one of the horses I bought at the Silver Sale. Mary, this is Juliet Good.'

The young girl moved into the stable. Now standing self-consciously erect she removed her helmet, flattening her hair when a loose brown curl fell across her face. Her eyes met Mary's momentarily then awkwardly flicked away, uncertain whether she should offer to shake the older woman's hand.

Mary put the girl out of her misery by stepping forward and proffering her hand and a smile, 'Really pleased to meet you, Juliet.'

Juliet shook gingerly, her awkwardness reduced, 'So…' she asked in a timid voice, '…two coffees?'

Once Mary and Danny had agreed, Juliet's relief to be leaving on an errand was palpable, the concerned lines on her forehead flattening out as she hurried away in the direction of the farmhouse. There was something about the girl that reminded Mary of herself at that age. Perhaps the uncertainty, mingled with a touch of fear in her eyes. The age of eighteen seemed such a long time ago and yet the young girl's awkwardness had unearthed the memory of the sounds and sensations of her first few weeks in the casino. She could hear the roulette wheel spinning, chips riffling, the calls of croupiers and tinny music providing the background over which gamblers' chatter percolated.

Danny noticed Mary watching Juliet as she crossed the courtyard and gave his owner a few seconds before speaking.

'She's seventeen. She's happier around horses than she is with people, just like me.'

'You seem perfectly fine with people.'

'Oh, I don't know about that. Talking to you I'm fine, but I'm useless in front of more than one person.'

'Are the two of you…' Mary queried, purposely leaving her question hanging.

'No, nothing like that,' Danny replied positively and without embarrassment, 'I think she has a boyfriend in Malton. We don't tend to talk about that sort of stuff; we concentrate on the horses.'

'So it's just the two of you?'

'Yep, and eight horses. Juliet came with me from Lilley's next door,' explained Danny as he led Mary out of the stable, 'We get on. She's reliable, works hard, and is a great little rider. If things work out next summer, we might get her an amateur licence to ride under rules.'

As they walked to the far side of the crescent of boxes, Mary recognised the head of her own colt. It had appeared over the door of a stable at the end of the horseshoe of stables. A thrill of excitement ran through her once more. Oh, how she wished her dad could have been here to experience this feeling.

'Here's Jake,' Danny announced as he moved a hand up to scratch the colt's neck.

'Jake?' Mary gasped, shocked by the trainer's apparent ability to read her thoughts.

Perplexed with her reaction, Danny looked round and found Mary with her hand held to her mouth. Her eyes were glazed over and he was suddenly aware of Mary's petite stature. In that moment there was an air of vulnerability about her.

'That's right, isn't it?' he asked, concerned he'd upset her, 'That's what you called him at the sales. You said it a couple of times. I started calling him that without thinking. It's his stable name, but we can change…'

'I didn't…' she took a breath, '…realise I'd called him Jake.'

It was Danny's turn to show relief, as Juliet arrived a few moments later carrying two mugs. Mary had produced a hanky from her handbag and quickly dabbed a stray tear away from both eyes before accepting her coffee. Juliet gave Danny a look which dripped with, 'What have you done?' and he tensed once more.

Mary registered the concern on both young faces and gave a croaky laugh.

'Don't mind me, I'm just a sentimental old fool,' she remarked, recovering her composure and waving away any awkwardness, 'Jake is fine. In fact, it was my father's name. It was just a bit of a shock to hear it, I didn't realise I'd mentioned his name to you. But now I'm here, standing in front of 'Jake', I think it suits him perfectly.'

Danny found himself checking Mary's face closely for signs of discontent. However, she seemed to have recovered. The sudden show of emotion had passed and was soon forgotten once Mary produced a bag of carrots from her handbag and tried to feed one to her colt. Jake sniffed tentatively at the long orange object offered up over his stable door, cocking an ear. The colt toyed with the end of the carrot between its lips, but refused to take a bite.

'He won't have been offered a carrot before,' explained Danny in response to Mary's frown, 'We'll have to teach him. Grass, hay and horse nuts are probably the only food he's come into contact with so far.'

He dug deep in the front pocket of his jeans and teased open a small penknife, running its blade along the length of the carrot, producing a thin peeling.

'He needs to realise how good it tastes,' he said, giving Mary a knowing smile and pushing the stringy morsel between Jake's lips. The colt ran the sliver of carrot around his mouth, but eventually it fell out of the side. Danny patiently repeated the process but this time the shaving of carrot disappeared and after some mastication, didn't re-emerge. He sliced the carrot into a couple of thicker strips and gave one to Mary.

'Try now. Hold on though, so he has to bite into it.'

Mary followed his advice and this time Jake bit down on the slice of carrot with a jaw rattling crunch. Within a few minutes the sound of carrot being joyfully bitten and noisily chewed filled the courtyard.

The door to the farmhouse opened and a Dachshund puppy dashed out and came bounding over to Danny, followed by a harassed Juliet carrying her own mug of coffee. Mary watched with amusement as the little dog skittered over the concrete courtyard, almost losing its balance in its haste to reach its goal. Danny dropped to his haunches and the young black and tan bundle of awkwardness sprang into his waiting arms.

Danny stood up, trying to avoid the little dog's frenetic attempts to lick his face.

'Meet Milo,' he said, trying to calm the dog's writhing by clamping him against his chest, 'He's...'

'...a bit of a handful?' Mary suggested, trying to keep a straight face as the puppy's pencil thin tail whipped around manically.

'You could say that...'

Juliet looked apologetic when she reached them.

'Sorry, Danny, he shot out as soon as I opened the door.'

'No worries; he can follow us around for a bit,' Danny replied, holding Milo tightly and allowing Mary to stroke him.

'Anyway, where's your dog Mary, Charlie isn't it?' he asked.

Once Danny discovered Charlie was waiting patiently in the back of her car, she was despatched to collect him in order for Milo to meet a new friend. Mary hadn't been too sure how Charlie would respond to an energetic puppy, but after an initial dance around the older dog's legs and a couple of intimate sniffs, Milo accepted Charlie was the boss and then proceeded to follow him everywhere he went.

'How long have you had him, he looks so young?'

From behind her Juliet interjected, 'He's only three months old and Dan shouldn't have agreed to take him,' she said in a mock stern voice.

'To *take* him?'

Danny turned and aimed a dramatic roll of his eyes in Juliet's direction. It was plainly a story she enjoyed telling.

'Dan broke in two difficult yearlings last spring for a trainer based in Norton and, like, instead of paying him, he produced this bundle of fur four months later and told him he was worth a grand.'

Juliet's lifted her eyebrows expressively and Mary acknowledged her playacting by doing the same in return.

'Dan, being, like, a sucker for a nice cuddly animal took Milo instead of the cash,' she concluded, stepping forward to join Mary in stroking the puppy.

'Yes, definitely the wrong decision,' Danny stated sarcastically, as the two women fussed over Milo, 'Come on, I've a couple of other things to show you.'

Danny led Mary around the back of the crescent of stables to where a separate line of five boxes faced a set of paddocks that rolled gently down several hundred yards to the bottom of the hill. The paddocks were neatly edged by a line of tall conifers denoting the end of Danny's property. Two bay geldings turned to look their way from the nearest paddock and once again Mary buzzed with the *feel* of the place.

'The fillies are separate for now, just until we get the colts gelded,' Danny told her as he led Mary away from the stables, unaware she'd become entranced with the view down the paddocks. 'Don't want the young boys getting too excited,' he added, without any indication of humour.

Once Mary could tear herself away from the tranquil vista, Danny's tour continued. He guided Mary over to a circular, wooden building that turned out to be an equine walker, currently populated by a single mare who was snorting impatiently as she slunk around in circles. Danny explained she was the laziest on the yard, and needed the exercise. Behind the walker was another circular contraption, this time sunk deep into the ground and with a long entrance ramp to one side. Mary recognised the layout from the Fitzpatrick yard.

'My equine pool!' Danny stated proudly as they peered down into a huge concrete hole filled with dead leaves and at least a foot of black sludge.

'It's in need of some attention,' he admitted, 'But this could make all the difference to my results. Any horse who might find regular galloping too much will be able to get fit in the pool. Once this is full of water, and I've improved the ménage and lunging pen, we'll have everything we need to send out winners.'

Mary smiled generously, admiring the young man's enthusiasm, and hoping his optimism wouldn't be dashed when he realised the enormity of his task. In her experience, young people tended to underestimate how much time these sorts of projects could devour when you did everything yourself.

Danny turned and returned Mary's smile. However, he detected the faintest flicker of concern in the woman's eyes.

'I haven't made a mistake you know,' he said with feeling.

Mary was impressed. It wasn't only horses the boy could read correctly, even if he was riddled with self-doubt when it came to dealing with groups of people. This thought was quickly followed up by a wave of embarrassment at having been so judgmental. After all, what did she know about running a racehorse stable? What she did know about was taking on too much, getting weighed down and letting down everyone around you. She found herself wincing at the memory. She'd thought she could cope with Henry's illness alone, but boy, had she been wrong.

Danny cocked his head to one side.

'Your ears have gone red,' he pointed out, smiling again.

Mary's right hand automatically went to her ear, and the tips of her fingers felt the heat transfer into them.

'I'm sorry, Danny. I have every confidence in your ability to train the horses. But you have a big job in getting the yard to where you want it to be. There's only the two of you, and you have a business to run. You might be taking on more than you can chew…'

Danny held up both hands in a shushing motion. He was nodding his head in agreement. Mary placed her hands on her hips and gave him an expectant look.

'You said you used to be a mathematics teacher, didn't you?'

'Mmmm,' Mary murmured, trying not to give away her delight at the direction their conversation was taking.

'I wonder if I could ask a small favour…'

Thirteen

Mary stood on the farmhouse doormat and wondered whether she should remove her boots. She quickly realised there was no need once Danny leaned past her and flicked on the unshielded light bulb that hung from the hall ceiling. The stark light revealed a track of muddy footprints that led down the hall and into what appeared to be a sitting room beyond. The hallway felt damp and looking up the stairs, a line of cobwebs followed the right-angle where the roughly painted orange walls met the white stippled ceiling. The scalloped swirls appeared to be stained yellow and the smell of cigarettes confirmed its provenance. It was a symphony of seventies kitsch, abandonment, and tobacco.

'I did warn you,' Danny said apologetically from behind her, 'It's not been lived in or touched for… well, quite a while, and I've not had enough time to…'

Danny paused for a couple of seconds, then added, 'You know, you could be right about the size of the job I've got here. I was only thinking about…'

'…what the horses needed,' Mary finished for him. The two of them exchanged a look which immediately put Danny at his ease and filled Mary with another powerful need to mother him, which she resisted.

Danny pushed a door to their right open and invited Mary into his kitchen. Rather like the entrance, the décor was tired, but it was the taste of grease in the air and the thick layer of dust on the shelves that made Mary's nose uncontrollably wrinkle up. Danny offered her a seat at a small rectangular table with a plastic tablecloth.

In an attempt to distract attention from her severe reservations regarding the cleanliness of the kitchen, Mary took a seat on one of the rickety wooden chairs, fighting the impulse to clean the ripped vinyl cover before sitting down. She leant an elbow on the table as she waited for Danny and found the tablecloth rising with it when she tried to pull it away. Eventually the plastic sheet pinged away from her elbow and the cloth that had risen in the shape of the table edge, slowly returned to fit snugly into position. With a closer fingertip inspection, Mary found the table was covered in a layer of grime with the consistency of sticky tape.

'I wondered if you could you take a look at this please?' Danny asked, fishing out a manila envelope from behind the kettle and removing its contents.

'I'm pretty good with physical stuff, y'know, riding and looking after the horses, but I struggled at school with reading.' He paused, his face screwed up as if the merest thought of school was allowing painful memories to surface.

'To be honest, I was even worse at sums,' he admitted with a sigh,

'I failed both at GCSE and was working full-time in a racing yard a week later.'

He handed Mary some official looking sheets of paper that she quickly ascertained was a rateable value calculation for the stables, sent by the local authority.

Mary read the first two lines then looked up at Danny, eyeing him thoughtfully. She placed the first page onto the table in deliberate fashion.

'Read the first paragraph for me, would you.'

Fear filled Danny's features and he seemed to crumple. However, Mary was pleased when he took a breath, furrowed his brow and slowly started to read. Forty seconds later she placed a hand gently onto his shoulder and asked him to stop.

'Has anyone ever tested you for dyslexia?'

Her query was received with a narrowing of the eyes and a shake of his head.

'Did you realise you read the second line twice?'

Danny shook his head once again, but this time it was more of a twitch than a shake. He looked so glum. It was the sort of reaction she might have elicited from a scolded schoolboy. A wave of regret suddenly drained her of the schoolmistress's fervour she'd just experienced. She met Danny's eyes and gave him as bright a smile as she could manage.

'My apologies, Danny,' she said lightly after the awkward pause, 'That was my retired teacher persona. It's difficult to keep it under control sometimes. If I do it again just kick my ankles!'

She collected the pages of the letter together and was relieved to see Danny had brightened.

'Now then. Let's see what we can make of your rates bill.'

Danny took a seat opposite her and waited in silence as Mary dug in her handbag for a pair of reading glasses and settled down to consume the five page letter. After half a minute he started to speak but was halted by her raised palm, followed by a stern glance. After what seemed to Danny to be an awfully long time Mary finally refolded the letter and shot a look of concern across the table at him.

'In short, it's a rates bill.'

Danny leaned back in his chair, which immediately complained with a squeak married to the sound of screws biting into old wood. He scowled and asked 'I thought as much. How bad is it?'

Mary sucked air over her teeth 'A little over ten thousand pounds, payable in a fortnight.'

Danny gave a quiet groan.

'But…' Mary said, holding an index finger up, 'I think we might be able to… I tell you what, let me make a few calls and we'll see what can be done.'

'No,' Danny insisted, 'I will get it sorted. I didn't mean for you to do anything more than decipher the letter.'

'Nonsense,' Mary responded, 'Have you got an accountant Danny? A limited company set up? Have you got the ability to invoice your owners yet?'

Danny's cheeks turned bright red. Mary let them burn for a few seconds before pushing him for an answer.

'I'm sorry to have burdened you with this,' he blurted, 'I haven't got any of those… *things!* It's just so difficult. I spent three hours last night trying to read that bloody letter and couldn't…'

'Not surprising really, as it's pretty complex.'

Danny rubbed his forehead with the heel of his hand, turned his head to the window and stared out toward the stables.

'I'm not a businessman, but I thought I'd be able to wing it. Jules is okay with some of the paperwork and is pretty good on the computer, but like me, she has no idea how to run a business.'

He called her Jules, thought Mary. She momentarily allowed her mind to dwell on Juliet and how she and Danny had spoken and traded looks with each other. A warm feeling grew in Mary's stomach.

Danny returned his gaze to Mary and was surprised to find her relaxed and smiling expectantly. He self-consciously placed a hand on the back of his neck. How could she find his situation amusing? She had a pitying expression now, damn it. This latest flash of embarrassment sent a new rash of red rushing around the collar of his polo shirt.

'I shouldn't have asked you, it was…'

'You needed help and asked for it,' Mary interrupted, her tone forthright. Realising the boy was uncomfortable she waved his attempted apology away, 'Now, it's *my* decision whether to help you, or not.

'Mary, please, I…'

'I've decided,' she broke in, 'You are a brand new racehorse trainer with little time on his hands and with need for an accountant, invoicing clerk and…' she cast her eyes around the room, '… possibly a decorator. I am a retired lady, with experience in financial planning, I know my way around a set of accounts and what's more, I know a good decorator. Most importantly, for the next few months at least, I have time on my hands.'

She paused, still locking eyes with Danny over the table.

'It seems fate has delivered you someone with the ability, means and time to solve your current problems, Mr Carter.'

The first wrinkle of a grin started to form at the corner of Danny's mouth, before receding quickly.

'But we've only just met. You're my *owner*. I know I need help, but you know nothing about me, how can you trust me not to cock everything up?'

Mary burst out with a loud guffaw. The look of unbridled surprise on Danny's face only led her to laugh even harder. After a few seconds he returned a cock-eyed smile, the redness from his cheeks transferred to his ears.

'Goodness Danny, you saved me from being trampled by a charging horse! I think I owe you quite a debt,' Mary managed between crackles of laughter, 'I would *love* to help you get your business going.'

She thought for a second before adding, 'A bit like the horse I own, I can only commit to being around for the next few months, maybe up to a year. But that should be enough to get you started.'

Mary clasped her hands together and her eyes widened. 'So shall we give it a go?'

A glint had entered Danny's eye. Was it excitement or simply relief? Mary didn't know, but it really didn't matter, she already knew what his answer was going to be.

'Besides, I'm also extremely cheap,' she pointed out, 'I'll be happy to do it for nothing.'

Fourteen

The soles of Eddie Romano's footsteps rang out on the steel grilled staircase as he climbed two rungs at a time to his second floor office. Pausing halfway to retrieve his car keys from his suit pocket, he peered down into the small, cobblestoned courtyard below and clicked the lock button to ensure his newly acquired Aston Martin was indeed, locked. The shiny white car blinked its parking lights reassuringly at him. You could never be too careful, even in a private car park in the centre of Newcastle.

He stopped a few paces before a door with 'Romano Services Ltd' cut into the two-inch steel plate at its centre. Checking his Patec Phillipe watch to ensure he was fashionably later than he'd indicated to his staff, he ran a hand through carefully coiffed jet black hair. Satisfied he was suitably presented, Eddie rapped three times on the steel with his car keys before dropping them into his jacket's inside pocket; they would make his suit hang awkwardly in any other pocket. He crossed his arms and stared belligerently into a small camera positioned high on the wall to his right so it caught anyone climbing the stairs.

The door swung open to the sound of reinforced hinges squeaking and an over-enthusiastic hail of, 'Good Morning Mr Romano,' from Harrison, followed by an escaping blast of warm air.

'Is it?' Eddie countered, striding into the building, his new shoes making a pleasing clack as he crossed the polished wood floor. As he walked, he cast his eyes around, taking in each person.

Bella, his receptionist and secretary, didn't react when he walked in. Experienced enough to keep the boys in check, she ruled her domain with an iron fist. She was also sensible enough to keep her eyes and mouth shut when required. She was seated at her desk, as she had been for the last ten years, against a grilled window that would have looked out onto Grey Street if security wasn't the order of the day. Apart from Vincent, Bella was his oldest employee, and the only other person on his payroll he referred to by first name. She nodded an acknowledgement Eddie's way but did not smile.

Burke, a Debt Recovery Manager in his forties, groaned as he got up from one of the four armchairs that doubled as a waiting room and a place for the other eight managers to await instructions. The stylish leather chairs were placed loosely around a modern, glass-topped coffee table and an open fireplace that was roaring heat in to the Victorian room. Arguably overweight and with a nose flattened with eighteen years of service, Burke was still around because he did what he was told and added a certain amount of threatening gravitas when he knocked on a defaulter's door. He was unflappable, patient and consistent. In stark contrast, Harrison, in his late twenties, was fit, handy with his fists and keen to intimidate, which to

Eddie's mind, made them perfect working partners.

Harrison closed and locked the door behind Eddie. The hinges complained again.

'Get some bloody oil on that door, Harrison,' Eddie called back as he strode toward another door set into the far right-hand corner of the reception.

'You got no work today, Burke?'

'Out to Blyth soon for a car repo, boss,'

'Good, don't let me keep you,' Eddie replied flatly whilst concentrating on tapping a code into a panel on the wall. The lock buzzed and he entered another room half the size, where Kevin Forrester, his financial manager, was busy placing some paperwork in one of the long row of filing cabinets that filled the left-hand wall. It was an austere room. Rather like its single inhabitant, the room was plain, functional, and highly productive.

'Forrester! How are things adding up this month?'

Eddie smirked at his clerk's perfectly bald head. It always made him smile, it was so... shiny. When Forrester made his way back to his large, leather-inlaid desk, Eddie noticed that, as always, he was dressed neatly, but without style. But then Eddie didn't employ this man of few words because of his good looks or dress sense.

'Steady, Mr Romano,' came Forrester's reply, once he'd pushed his glasses up his button nose and was seated. He didn't look up, and Eddie noticed how childlike Forrester appeared behind his huge workstation monitor.

'Only steady, eh! We might need to drum up some business then.'

Forrester peered over his computer monitor, making eye contact with Eddie for the first time.

'No need. Five new jobs have come in.'

Forrester grinned open-mouthed and the tip of his tongue poked out beyond his bottom teeth, reminiscent of a panting terrier.

Eddie adjusted his tie, the image of Forrester as a child had vanished. The man resembled a ghoul when he attempted to smile. Regardless, Eddie maintained a straight face.

'Great, put the details on my desk.'

'Already there, Mr Romano.'

Eddie typed a code into another panel on the wall and entered the last room on the floor, his office. He liked this set-up; it was the main reason he had chosen these premises. Anyone who got through the armoured front door or securely barred windows in reception would have to make it through two further rooms protected by strengthened doors and pass-codes to get to him. Even if they did, he would be long gone through the small staircase at the back, across the roof, down the fire escape and into the busy city centre.

Eddie's office was akin to a Victorian sitting room. The first time he'd walked into this large, almost square room he'd known immediately how he would make it his own. This was where he brought his clients, seating them in beautifully refurbished armchairs and plying them with freshly ground coffee and stories of how he extracted payment from people who didn't pay.

Eddie quickly learned that eliciting debt recovery contracts from large companies with plenty of defaulting customers required nothing more than for him to play a role. It was a role he was born to play. You had to look the part, speak the language of finance directors and exude a detached professionalism which hinted at violence. In Eddie's experience most finance people neither had the stomach, nor the balls to get out from behind their desks and into the grill of people who owed them money. They just wanted the problem to go away. His company had quickly garnered a reputation for collecting debts by adopting a robust, single minded approach, often mistaken for intimidation.

There was a large desk with a laptop placed at its centre, but it was rarely opened. Eddie was a talker, not a typist. A brace of exquisite cut glass chandeliers gave the room balance and threw enough light to give a warm glow in the winter, aided by a sumptuous open fireplace with a period arched mirror above. At all other times, sunlight would fill the room in both summer and winter as three tall windows complete with seats, allowed those with time on their hands to gaze in the direction of Northumberland Street.

Vincent was standing at the central window, hands in trouser pockets, watching people scuttle up and down the frosty street below. He spun round on hearing the door buzz.

'Boss! Good morning!'

'Vincent,' replied Eddie with a slight inclination of his head, 'Good trip south?'

'I spoke with her. Was invited in...'

Eddie had been on his way to the corner of the room to where a set of chrome coffee making apparatus sparkled. He stopped abruptly and pierced Vincent with narrowing eyes before becoming thoughtful.

'Good work,' he replied, then raised his voice, 'Forrester! Get in here.'

Forrester buzzed himself into the room and the three men sat facing each other, Eddie lounging on the sofa, the other two in armchairs.

'She said she didn't have the Stone in the house,' Vincent reported, 'But, she reacted strangely when I asked for it. She admitted she's got the Stone, but it would take a few weeks or a month to get it.'

Eddie couldn't keep the excitement from his voice.

'Did Mary agree to give it to you?'

He was sitting on the edge of the sofa. Forrester looked on, maintaining a doleful expression, but was following the conversation intently.

'Pretty much,' smirked Vincent.

'That's great!' beamed Eddie, 'So where is it?'

Vincent gave a shy smile, 'She didn't say. Mary was, y'know, pretty upset by the time I got her to confess she had it. I couldn't push her further.'

'Al... right,' Forrester said, punctuating the syllables with a stab of his pen into his notepad, 'So Eddie has successfully tracked the Stone to Mary Romano, but you've not located it.'

Vincent cocked his head toward the financial controller and Forrester flinched a little. Vincent disliked him for one reason; he played Eddie in exactly the same way he did, with compliments, and by undermining the people around him.

'Yet, Forrester, I haven't located it *yet*,'

The brinkmanship between the two men went unnoticed by Eddie. He jumped up and started to pace the polished floor in front of the windows, turning smartly with a click of his heels each time he reached a wall. His stride was well practised, he liked to see the little people with their little lives scurry up and down Grey Street as he paced his empire.

'You think it's in her house?' he asked after two passes of the trio of windows.

'Unlikely,' Forrester piped up, 'Not secure enough.'

'We know she can't have sold it, otherwise we'd have heard something,' Eddie murmured, 'You can't sell a piece as valuable as that without the trade getting to know. Could she have found a private buyer?'

'No,' Vincent cut in before Forrester could offer an opinion. He'd done the hard work on this one and he was going to make sure he got the credit, and the reward.

'I suggested to her she had raised money against its value, and she went very quiet. Mary hasn't been anywhere near a jewellers or an antique valuation service in the last three months. However she has visited her solicitor and her bank on several occasions. Either of them could have arranged a loan on the basis of the Stone's value.'

The room fell silent, save for the tap of Eddie's shoes as he continued to pace backwards and forwards in front of the windows.

'How long do we give her?' Eddie wondered out loud.

'I'll keep monitoring her,' Vincent said quickly, 'If she has it on deposit with the bank, it could take a month or two to repay the loan and get the piece back.'

This received an unconvincing murmur of agreement from Eddie, but without an alternative suggestion, he moved on.

'How much time do you need to get the potential buyers ready to start bidding on the Stone?' he asked Forrester.

'Six to eight weeks to get the parties interested. We have to be careful; after all, it has a chequered history.'

'Yes, yes, so we need to be careful. How long to get it sold?' Eddie pressed.

'I estimate a week to ten days to conduct the negotiations and the transaction. But I must stress, they will need to *see* the Stone. It must be in our possession that final week so that the number of carats can be confirmed prior to a bidder completing the transaction.'

Eddie stopped pacing, 'Remind me, Forrester, how much is a Burmese Ruby currently worth per carat?'

For the first time during the meeting, Forrester managed something resembling a genuine smile, 'A million pounds sterling.'

Eddie beamed at his two colleagues, 'Pa always told us the ruby alone was eighteen carats. That's some payday, and all we have to do is pluck it from the thief who stole what is rightfully mine.'

'You want me to continue full-time surveillance on Mary until she's got the ruby in her hands?' Vincent queried. His heart missed a beat when he was given a definite nod from Eddie.

'Let her know you're around and if you get the slightest indication she has the ruby back in her hands, we go in and take it, understood?'

Vincent closed his bug-eyes and nodded sagely.

'And you can start drawing up the list of potential buyers now,' he told Forrester.

Eddie took a long look at himself in a cheval mirror almost as tall as his crimson painted wall. He rubbed a rogue crease out of the arm of his suit and admired his reflection for a few seconds before eyeing Forrester and Vincent in turn.

'I want this dealt with by spring. Let's take the bitch down and come out of this as millionaires.'

Fifteen

Mary rubbed the back of her hand across her forehead and leant back from the computer she had been working on for the last two hours. Daniel Carter Racing letterhead started to spew out of the printer on her desk in the back room of Danny's farmhouse. She picked up the first page to check the copy invoice was correct.

Satisfied, Mary walked into the kitchen, clicked the kettle on and slumped into one of the six newly acquired wooden chairs that surrounded the kitchen table. She placed her elbows onto a tablecloth she didn't have to worry about sticking to, and closed her eyes for a few seconds, enjoying the mellow darkness. Mary allowed herself to relax. The sounds of the yard outside soon invaded the house, stable chatter and hooves on concrete. Feeling the sun on her face she opened her eyes and blinked until she could focus on the view through the window.

Outside, a muscular bay gelding was being washed down, the fine sprays of water bouncing off its back creating small rainbows which flickered in and out of existence as the stable lass worked with her hose. Danny emerged from the feed room with a wheelbarrow loaded with two large feed bins and shouted a few instructions over to Juliet. Mary drank in the atmosphere, reflecting on how much her life had altered in the last two months.

It was the first week of February. The start of the flat season was only eight weeks away, and the big plus, she reflected wryly, was that she'd managed to keep Vincent at bay. She was sure he was out there watching her now, as he kept popping up every fortnight or so to remind her he was still waiting for her to produce the Stone.

In mid-November Mary had managed to enlist her friends from Northallerton on a cleaning mercy mission with the promise of a day out at York races in the summer. She and her three fellow card players, Sarah, Audrey, and Maisie had come over and spent an entire day cleaning Danny's farmhouse from top to bottom in order to make it presentable for potential owners and liveable for Danny.

Sarah, who tended to speak as she found, commented, 'It may not be pretty, but at least it's clean now!' There was also a promise from Maisie, the green fingered member in her little band of helpers, to return in April in order to add a dash of floral colour to the yard.

A couple of decorators cum handymen had followed, to give the place a lick of paint and generally tidy the house up. Danny had fixed the half dozen tiles that were broken or missing, the kitchen now sported new doors on the units and Mary had gone to the local auction house and managed to buy some cheap equine prints to hang on the walls and a few great value rugs which added a touch of warmth and colour to several rooms around the farmhouse.

December turned into January without any sign of Vinny, and Mary started to hope Eddie had lost interest. Did he really think her money was linked to some family heirloom she had magically discovered? It soon became clear he hadn't forgotten her, as Vincent had confronted her a few days into the New Year. His pop-eyes cornered her in Tesco during her weekly shop and while he had been willing to accept her excuses, he did ask why she hadn't sold her racehorse. She'd scolded him for his lack of patience and raised her voice enough to turn a few shoppers' heads, so he backed down and soon sloped off. She had redoubled her efforts to get to the bottom of the 'Joe's Stone' issue after that.

The search of her cottage had taken much longer than she expected. Three days to be precise. Although it didn't reveal a Stone of any description, Mary had made a few interesting finds. She managed to clamber into her loft space, up a rickety pair of wooden step ladders she'd found in the shed, and was baffled to find she and her next door neighbour shared one huge loft space. She got the shock of her life when her torch beamed into the darkness and found nothing more than a couple of chimney stacks. The entire floor had been boarded out. Bert had a neatly stacked group of identical boxes, and Mary's side of the loft had a large pile of bin bags, suitcases, fruit boxes and cardboard boxes of every size and shape, some of which looked like they'd been thrown up through the trap door.

It did strike her as odd, and a potential security risk, but then her terrace was over a hundred and fifty years old and frankly, if Bert wanted to wander over and pick through her loft junk, he was welcome to it. She imagined his wooden storage crates no doubt housed something far more valuable than her pile of forgotten bric-a-brac.

Inside one of Henry's old briefcases she found a small bundle of letters, presumably the family items left by his mother. Inside a dog-eared envelope, Mary discovered a stash of old Romano family photos, some from Italy, taken before Joe and Nina had migrated. Several pictures provided evidence that Joe had looked the spitting image of Eddie as a teenager, whilst Henry was definitely his mother's son.

One of the older photos made her stop and examine it in more detail. It was a shot of Henry's parents, Joe and Nina, and another couple at the docks, their arms linked around each other, the four of them barely into their twenties, happy and excited. They were standing in front of the prow of a ship and emerging from the background fog you could just make out a ghostly Tyne Bridge. Mary turned the thick card photo over and written in pencil in Nina's hand was; 'A new life in Newcastle: Gia and Elena Lombardi, 1959.'

Mary checked through the envelope for more photos of the Romano's friends, to no avail. She had no idea why, but that photo had nagged at her for the rest of the day. Later that evening she searched for Gia and Elena Lombardi online and after going through many pages of results Mary found a reference to a brand of ice-cream. It was a single line of a blog posted in 2008 by a lady lamenting the loss of some of her favourite things from her childhood, growing up and holidaying on the North East coast.

Mary read the paragraph out loud to Charlie: 'We used to visit the caravan site beside Saint Mary's Lighthouse in Whitley Bay where my brother and I would buy a Lombardi's Ice Cream from a proper Italian chap in an old Austin van hand painted yellow. It had images of Goofy and Cinderella on the side that somehow weren't quite right, but we loved it all the same. As the tide came in, we'd watch the waves start crashing over the causeway to the lighthouse as we ate, and would laugh at the tourists who got stuck on the island. The ice-cream was sublime.'

Despite another hour of searching, Mary couldn't locate the Lombardi's or their Ice Cream and decided it was a dead-end. She was considering climbing the stairs to bed when Joe's words came back to her: '…ask for Jay.' It sort of made sense he might give some pertinent information about his most valuable possession to a lifelong friend.

She returned to her laptop and searched for Gia and Elena, then got Italian translations for their names, but nothing matched Jay. Gia was a womans' name, as was Elena. In desperation she dug deeper and on a website dedicated to European forenames discovered that Giacomo was a version used for James in some areas of Italy, and of most interest, it was regularly shortened to Gia.

Mary spoke the name 'Ja…mes' a few times to Charlie. Each time she repeated the name Joe's 'Jay' sounded like a cut-off version of James.

'I think I'm busting the elastic on this one,' she lamented to Charlie, who gave a little snort, lay down and closed his eyes in response.

'A lot of help you are. Not only am I talking to myself, I'm boring you too!' The dog half opened his eyes, sighed, and promptly fell asleep.

Even if she was right about Gia being 'Jay' or 'James' she still needed to find out what Joe had meant by meeting him at some rendezvous. Which rendezvous, where? It felt like three steps forward and two back. Mary decided she would have to take a different tack. She'd try and find out more about Joe and his friends.

Mary had telephoned Henry's best friend, Adam, in late December on the pretence of wishing him a happy Christmas but really to discover whether he knew anything about a Stone connected to Henry's father. Apart from receiving an open invitation to visit Adam up in Newcastle, she'd learned nothing of any substance regarding a Stone. Adam had known Joe was a flamboyant character as a younger man, through stories Joe had spun to Henry and himself when they were just boys, but it transpired Henry hadn't spoken to him in any detail about his father's past.

Adam had surprised her by asking about Eddie. It caused her to wonder whether Henry had told Adam about the circumstances of Joe's death. It was likely, given the length of time they'd known each other.

'I noticed Henry's brother at the funeral. I hear he spoke with you alone,' Adam mentioned. He had a steady, concise way of speaking that encouraged you to engage with him. And he listened. It was probably why Henry got on with him so well. Henry never had time for irrelevant small talk.

'Yes, he thanked me for looking after Henry when he was ill.'

'He's a dangerous man, Mary. I've heard rumours around Newcastle, you know, given the services to the security community my company provides. Henry was constantly worried about him.'

He paused, perhaps hoping Mary would reply. When she didn't he added, 'Has he been in touch since?'

Mindful of Vincent's warning, Mary replied, 'No, I've not spoken to Eddie.'

This was arguably true. She liked Adam, and didn't want to lie to him, but what options did she have?

'Good,' Adam said, sounding relieved, 'Henry did tell me the two of you didn't get along. I wanted to make sure Eddie wasn't trying to get you involved in anything...'

'Hold on a second,' Mary interrupted, 'Henry was a salesman and trainer for you wasn't he?'

'Yes, that's right.'

'So why are you getting information about Eddie?'

The line went quiet for a few seconds before Adam answered, 'To be honest, it is hearsay. My company provides security management and training for our clients, so I have people who have been bouncers and personal security guards in the past. You know the sort. A few of them have worked for some pretty unsavoury types in their time, and they tell stories.'

'What do they say about Eddie?' Mary pressed.

'Oh, just not to cross him. He's got a reputation for being... uncompromising.'

'You mean he hurts people?'

The sound of Adam exhaling suddenly crackled down the line, followed by another pause.

'Listen Mary, all I'm saying is I know Henry wanted to keep Eddie well away from you. Henry was my friend and I miss him. I count you as a

75

good friend too and if you ever need my help, just pick up the phone.'

By the time Adam had disconnected, Mary was convinced she needed to do something more to protect herself. She spent Christmas considering whether to involve the police, but decided against it. It wasn't as if the police could provide her twenty four hour protection. No, she'd have to arrange some sort of security for herself.

The big change in Mary's life over the last few months had been her rapid integration into Danny's yard, and unexpectedly, his business. She was now, very happily, integral to the smooth running of the stables. Mary had originally intended to simply do a few spreadsheets and get a basic accounts system going for him, then leave him to it, but the success of two of Danny's older horses on the All-Weather tracks at Newcastle and Wolverhampton in December had prompted the arrival of another three new owners and five horses. The yard was now up to thirteen, with the hope that they might get sent another couple before the turf season got underway. Danny's business was now breaking even, thanks in no small way to Mary.

By his own admission, Danny was useless when it came to anything more than simple maths. When he had shown Mary his 'accounts' they consisted of some scrawled figures in the back of an A4 pad. Initially with Juliet's assistance, Mary got his invoicing up to date, creating systems and processes for dealing with owners and suppliers and soon learned how to make entries and declarations, order transport, deal with vets, the blacksmith, work riders and jockeys' agents and a chap called 'the back man' who worked wonders with some of the older horses.

An early success came with the local authority over the rates demand. Mary not only managed to agree a phased payment schedule, she succeeded in getting it lowered by applying for new business relief. This reduced the bill by sixty percent and cemented her as an invaluable resource in Danny's eyes. His cash flow had been dangerously low soon after she grabbed the reins of his financial situation, but with some negotiation with suppliers and chasing of owners, Mary was able to get things on an even keel. By mid November she had settled into a three-day week and felt as much at home at Cordike Stables as she was in her cottage outside Northallerton. What's more, Charlie was in his element, running around the place all day long and alerting everyone if a visitor arrived with a few woofs.

They also had a new member of staff. Danny had known Graham for some time and he now came into the yard two or three days a week. In his sixties, he didn't ride out, but when it came to handling a horse Graham was in his element. Forty years in the business meant he could drive the horsebox, lead up at the races, long rein horses and knew about Danny's feeding regime and countless other tasks around the yard. He was a safe pair of hands when Danny couldn't be in two places at once.

Mary had found the process of training racehorses fascinating. Being at the yard on a regular basis, she'd been able to watch her youngster being lunged, taught to turn, to walk and trot and obey the basic commands. She had watched as Danny had put a saddle on Jake's back and finally a few days later lain across his back while Juliet held the colt tight. A week later Danny straddled Jake for the first time in the ménage and he walked in a circle a few times for him, turning on command. The colt wasn't as naughty now, and had grown another two inches.

She'd even seen him being gelded. That was an experience that had stayed with her for some time. The way the vet had sedated Jake then made one simple cut, then squeezed… She shuddered and concentrated on the sunny scene out of the farmhouse window. There were some things you didn't need to experience more than once.

The farmhouse phone saved her from further images of gelding. On answering, a soft Irish accented man caught her out a little by asking for her by name.

'Yes, its Mary Romano speaking.'

'Ah, I'm glad I managed to catch you Mary, it's Rory. Remember me?'

'Oh yes Mr McDermott,' Mary replied lightly, 'The last time we met it cost me eight and a half thousand pounds and two coffees.'

They traded pleasantries and Rory asked about the colt and wasn't too surprised to discover he was now a gelding.

'Will do him the world of good,' he assured her.

She'd not really thought too much about Rory after the day at the sales. She'd enjoyed their conversation over a cup of coffee, but had got the impression Rory was simply good at customer relations. It hadn't occurred to her his motives for taking her for coffee might actually be more than good business.

Ten minutes later, Mary replaced the handset having agreed to accompany Rory to the races at Newcastle for the Eider, a race in which a horse he bred, and still part-owned with a few friends, was due to compete in a couple of weeks time. Rory had sounded pleased when Mary revealed she knew all about the race, having attended the meeting several times with her dad.

'Waggoner's Walk won for us in 1981,' she told him, 'We had fish and chips on the bus to celebrate on the way home. I'd have been about fourteen.'

'Really?' marvelled Rory, 'I hope my lad can do the same! He's called Misty Creek. I've got a couple of owners' badges, so it might be a slightly different experience for you this time. I'll even spring for some fish and chips afterwards.'

Mary stood in silence for a minute afterwards, enjoying the little buzz of expectation the conversation had brought her. She was rocked out of her halcyon moment by the sound of shouting, the movement of horses and a lot of expletives being screamed.

Her butterflies of anticipation drained from her. It sounded like Danny was arguing with Jonnie Lilley again. It was a regular occurrence, usually initiated by Jonnie who took every opportunity to deride every aspect of Danny's training style and abilities. It didn't help that the two yards were only separated by a small brick wall and both the Lilleys' and Danny's lunging pens backed up to each other.

She ran outside to find Danny screaming at Jonnie Lilley over the small brick wall between the two yards.

Jonnie Lilley was outside his lunging pen, ignoring Danny's protests, holding onto the head collar of a frightened, edgy young horse with one hand, and in the other, brandishing a short riding whip over his head.

'You stay out of this, Carter, you soft social boy. This filly is a bloody screwball and needs to be taught who's boss.' Jonnie shouted back, becoming red in the face.

'She's frightened, you fool,' Danny screamed from the other side of the low wall, 'Put her back in the pen and let her calm down!'

Jonnie ignored the advice and went to lead the filly away but she planted her front feet on the concrete. He glanced disdainfully over his shoulder at Danny and released another volley of swear words at him as Danny was repeating his advice. The filly steadfastly refused to move and after yanking on the lead rein again without success, Jonnie brought his whip down on the shoulder of the horse with a sickening crack. The filly responded by rearing up, losing her balance, and crashing backwards onto the concrete walkway beside the lunging pen. Jonnie let go of the filly's lead rein and watched her fall, raising his whip over his shoulder and stepping forward to inflict another blow. Mary cringed at the noise the filly made as over half a ton of horse toppled backwards onto the concrete. She held her face in her hands, dreading what the boy was about to inflict next on the frightened animal.

She need not have worried. Danny vaulted over the wall and onto Jonnie's back within seconds, tearing at the boy's whip hand. Jonnie, smaller and stronger than his foe, struggled free and turned his attention away from the filly and concentrated on braying a cowering Danny with his whip.

Stable lads and lasses were suddenly running toward the two men from every direction on the Lilley side of the wall. Juliet appeared from nowhere, leapt over the wall and cannoned into Jonnie on his blind side, cutting short his whipping onslaught. Jonnie, Juliet, and Danny were all on the floor now. Between them all, the filly managed to struggle ungainly to its feet and stood stock still. Blood ran down her front legs and a number of welts started to stand out on her back, neck and shoulders; evidence of Jonnie's handiwork with his whip. As if only now becoming aware she was free, the filly took two steps forward, broke into a trot and jumped the brick wall between the yards and trotted to the bottom of Danny's yard.

Juliet was up first, helping Danny to his feet. Angry red marks were coalescing on his forehead and cheeks. Blood dripped from his right ear, sending dark red rivulets down his neck. A couple of the Lilley lads were around Jonnie now. He was holding his stomach where Juliet had rammed into him, and was still shouting obscenities when his father loomed up behind him.

'Shut up, Jonnie,' George Lilley cut in harshly, 'Control yourself.'

Jonnie's tirade of swearing ceased abruptly and the lads stood back to allow the trainer to pull his son to his feet.

Mary approached the wall and waited, her heart pounding, ready to enter the argument and defend Danny's actions. George said something quietly to his stable lads and they started to wheel Jonnie away, both gripping an arm each.

'The snotty nosed bugger was trespassing, he got…'

'I said shut up, Jonnie' George growled, 'I saw the whole thing from that stable over there.'

He nodded to the lads and they pulled Jonnie away.

Danny watched them disappear before he spoke. Still filled with anger and shock, he addressed George shakily.

'I could hear him in your lunging pen; he was losing his temper… I mean to say, who the *hell* takes a riding whip into a lunging pen in order to teach a young horse…'

Danny stopped talking. He'd caught the look on his ex-bosses face. He'd expected defiance; but George wasn't shaking with rage. He had glassy eyes and his shoulders were sagging forwards.

Mary took this lull in the conversation to straddle the wall with care and join Juliet and Danny. She placed a hand on Danny's shoulder when she reached them.

'So what now?' Mary enquired firmly of George, 'I'm sure the BHA, the press, police or RSPCA would be interested.'

Danny peered at her incredulously and she returned him a stern stare and hint of a dart of her eyes toward the filly now standing stock still in his yard, forty yards behind them.

George shook his head. He was sullenly looking Danny up and down.

'I'll talk to him. Jonnie I mean,' he said after a short pause, 'It won't happen again. Can I get someone to go catch the filly?'

'No,' Mary answered immediately, 'Isn't that the filly you tried to buy at Doncaster?' she asked Danny.

When he indicated it was, Mary eyed George again.

'It's not working with you, is it? Who owns her?'

'I do,' George replied, narrowing his eyes.

'Given what's gone on, it seems to me she wants to be on our side of the fence…'

'Forget it, Mary,' Danny cut in, 'She's too expensive.'

Mary was now watching George's reaction as she spoke.

'Oh, I wasn't expecting to pay *full price* for her. I was expecting Mr Lilley would accept *half* what he paid for her. After all, it would probably be best all round. If Jonnie was reported to the police, the BHA, or even the RSPCA, I hate to think where he could end up. It would certainly put an end to his race riding career…'

As Mary's voice trailed off, George's eyes hardened once more and he screwed his mouth up toward his nose.

'Take her for four grand,' he said through gritted teeth, 'She's a wobbler, and probably untrainable now anyway. But no authorities, okay?'

'Three thousand pounds, plus, you guarantee us your son will leave Danny alone from now on. In return this incident will be forgotten. Do we have a deal?'

George examined Mary. Holding her in his stony gaze for several seconds, his eyes finally dropped to the floor and without speaking he offered Mary his hand. She shook it without any flicker of emotion. George turned on his heel and stumped off.

'Juliet will be round with a cheque and to collect the filly's passport in a few minutes,' Mary called after him. George waved a hand in acknowledgement, but didn't look back.

***

The filly took no time to catch. Danny managed to loop a head collar over her and then spent fifteen minutes simply calming her down and building a rapport with her. He looked the filly over and treated her cuts and bruises with iodine. The worst were where Jonnie had laid into her with his whip down her back and a scrape down her right flank where she'd fallen.

'She's sound at the moment, but we'll know more tomorrow. If there's any lasting physical issue it will show itself soon enough. She'll be pretty sore for the next few days,' Danny reported to Mary and Juliet.

'Will she be okay to still race?' asked Mary.

'Physically, she should be fine. Mentally, she's probably going to struggle. I knew she was tender when I saw her at the sales, but with what

Jonnie's put her through, there's a chance she might not recover her confidence enough to race.'

The filly was installed in a stable in the quietest part of the yard, the very last box overlooking the paddocks.

With Mary back in the farmhouse, Danny looked over the filly's stable door while Juliet dabbed at his split ear with a bloodied cotton ball. She was tutting each time the bleeding re-started.

'Yeowch!'

'You are such a baby,' Juliet sniggered, 'It's a tiny cut. Man up!'

Danny theatrically sucked air through his teeth. His ear and face were hurting like hell, but there was compensation; he was enjoying the attention.

Their conversation stalled and Juliet continued to dab at Danny's head and neck. It was three-thirty and with only another hour of sunlight available at best, they still had plenty of stable work to finish. However, it was an unseasonably warm day and the winter sun still had a little heat in it, so neither of them felt guilty for lingering at the stable door to watch over the filly. She was wrapped in several layers and stared dolefully at them from the back of the stable. She'd not moved for ten minutes. All of a sudden she appeared to make a decision. Blinking rapidly a few times, the filly folded her back legs, flopped onto her thick wood chip bed and dropped her head carefully to the floor. Danny gave a satisfied grimace; the filly was finally settling. He turned his back on the stable door and viewed the scene down the paddocks and then upwards to the blood red sun that was starting to dip behind the Wolds in the far distance.

'Mary's been a bit of a godsend,' Juliet stated matter-of-factly, 'And she's so good at managing, like… well, everything really…'

'I sense a but coming,' Danny said, lifting an eyebrow.

'Yeah, but isn't it a bit odd like, that she insists she can only be around for one season?'

Danny thought for a few seconds before answering.

'I don't know why,' he admitted with a shrug, 'What I do know is that Mary has made a big difference. I don't think I'd have been able to sort out the business stuff without her.'

'I can't believe she bought the filly like that.'

Danny grinned, 'Yep, that was worth a few cuts and bruises!'

'I think you should ask her,' Juliet suggested, prodding Danny gently in the side of his ribs.

'Ask her what?'

'Why she's only going to be with us for a season!' Juliet responded, becoming a little exasperated.

Danny shrugged again, 'That's for her to tell us. Remember, she's an owner who is helping us out. I can't start quizzing her about her private life!'

'But I'm worried, Dan. What if she's ill?'

Danny mulled this for a few seconds, then shook his head, 'No, that can't be it. I think she's keeping her options open, you know, wanting to see how things work out before committing to any longer.'

Juliet allowed a silence to develop before she suggested, 'Still, it would be, like, nice to know.'

Danny didn't reply. The seed of doubt successfully planted by Juliet, was germinating in his mind. However, his thoughts were interrupted by Mary herself who had just wheeled around the corner of the short line of stables carrying three coffee mugs.

'Here you are you two, get this down you,' she said brightly, 'It will do you the world of good. So how's the filly?'

Mary gave Danny an expectant look, but found his attention was elsewhere. He was staring down the paddocks with lines of concern furrowed into his forehead.

'What?' Mary asked, 'Something wrong with a horse?'

'No, nothing like that,' Danny said softly, 'I think someone is watching us.'

Juliet and Mary followed Danny's gaze to the bottom of the paddocks and the line of mature fir trees that marked the end of his property.

'There!' Danny exclaimed, pointing down the paddocks, 'Can you see it? The third tree along, there's someone in the lower branches. You can see them moving. There! Did you see them?'

Mary had seen a figure. It must have been over five-hundred yards away, but there was definitely someone there. The tree branch was quivering. Whoever it was had reacted to Danny's raised arm and from the way the branch bowed then sprang back, they had jumped from their vantage point to the ground a moment ago. A sickly feeling started rising from her stomach and an image of Vincent flashed across her mind, stayed there for a few seconds, to be replaced by another possibility.

'Hold this,' Danny said quickly, shoving his mug carelessly in Juliet's direction, 'I'll go have a look.'

'No, there's surely no need,' Mary advised, 'It looked like a bird to me, maybe a large hawk or a pheasant. Besides, even if it was someone, it'll probably be the trainer's kids from the yard at the top of the hill messing around. I'm more interested in how my new filly is settling in.'

She put a hand on Danny's arm and gently turned him toward the filly's stable. He shot Mary a questioning look, which she returned with an easy air of expectancy. Danny checked the trees again. It all looked quiet.

'Okay, I guess it could have been Mike Kirby's kids,' he agreed grudgingly, only partially placated. The possibility of someone being so close to the geldings in the bottom paddock warranted investigation. But he had to remember that Mary was an owner, and currently she was an owner who had just added another horse to his yard and in so many other ways was critical to his business. He pushed the incident to the back of his mind and joined Mary at the filly's door.

As Danny was explaining that the filly needed some time alone, he caught the strangest expression on Juliet's face. She was watching Mary, carefully and closely, as if she was trying to weigh her up, but not quite able to reach a conclusion. It occurred to Danny there were a number of things that didn't add up where Mary was concerned.

Sixteen

As a child Mary had always been daunted by the entrance to Newcastle racecourse. It reminded her of a grand old mansion, the sort she'd only ever seen on television. Its austere stone block exterior was only slightly diminished by the addition of modern buildings being glued to its sides in later years. Of course, she and her father had never actually entered the course through the mansion's front door in the seventies; that was reserved for owners, trainers, jockeys and Tattersalls customers. Mary and Jake had used the ugly concrete turnstiles that gave entrance into the lesser enclosure. The Silver Ring was much cheaper and lacked the grandeur of Tattersalls, but it did mean you could still get up close to the horses as they paraded.

Not that Mary, aged five, had been too bothered, as the Silver Ring had also boasted a well equipped children's playground that helped maintain her enthusiasm for racing in the days before she became hooked on race form and betting.

Entering the racecourse through the mansion's front doors for the first time on Eider day with Rory proved to be something of a letdown. There were oblique references to the buildings' distinguished past, such as the columned entrance hall and grand central staircase ascending to the upper levels, but there was little real grandeur in evidence. However, Mary noted it was pleasingly warm compared to the near-freezing late February conditions outside. Rather like when taking tea with him at the sales, Mary had felt a little awkward at first, but Rory proved to be the consummate host, and she was soon enjoying herself.

After climbing the stairs to the first floor, they decided to take advantage of the free lunch in the Owners and Trainers room, an airy space that could have been a ballroom in the dim and distant past. Lunch consisted of a two course self service meal and a place at one of the dozen round tables that each seated up to ten people. She and Henry had eaten at racecourses around Yorkshire when their finances had allowed, and the Silver Service treatment had always impressed, even at the small courses like Catterick or Beverley.

The owners dining experience had so far left Mary unimpressed. It was as she was poking a thin, over-cooked slice of pork around her plate that she spotted a face she recognised. Deciding she wouldn't risk another forkful of the watery mixed vegetables, she caught his eye.

'Mary, it's wonderful to see you,' said a smooth North Eastern accented male voice, 'I thought I saw you earlier, and had to come and find you.'

Adam East had such a deep vocal register he immediately demanded attention, especially from women. Several people, mostly women, looked around to discover the owner of the baritone voice. Mary had first been introduced to Adam only a week after she had met Henry. The two men had remained friends for the rest of Henry's life. Adam had also been the last person to see her husband alive.

'Adam, this is lovely, it's so good to see you,' Mary said as she stood to kiss Adam's cheek.

She allowed him to run through the standard, 'How have you been?' and 'You're looking well...' small talk before noticing Rory had put his fork down and was waiting for an introduction.

'This is Rory,' she cut in quickly, moving aside to indicate her companion, 'He's kindly invited me to watch his runner in the Eider.'

Adept at social manoeuvring, Adam was soon engaging Rory in a conversation discussing breeding in a thinly veiled attempt to sound her partner out. Mary stood between the two men, easily a foot smaller, watching with some amusement as the two men sized each other up.

Once their conversation descended into a discussion of how many horses Rory had bred in the last year, set against how many people Adam employed, Mary steered the conversation away from their male supremacy contest.

'Why are you here, Adam?' she asked with wide, expectant eyes that flashed a warning at him.

'Oh, yes. You must both join us upstairs. We're the sponsor of the Handicap Hurdle at the end of the card,' then in a conspiratorial whisper, he added, 'And the food is *so* much better up there.'

Rory looked back to the table where his half-finished tomato soup was slowly congealing. Within five minutes he and Mary were enjoying smoked salmon in Adam's palatial private box on the top floor of the main stand.

As was Adam's way, he had ushered the two of them into his corporate entertaining room and introduced them to the entire body of twenty people as, 'Mary, a very old friend, and Rory, who owns a runner in the feature race of the day.'

'Are you okay with us being here,' Mary whispered to Rory as the first race of the day went off. They had moved onto the balcony of the box, along with a dozen other guests who Mary assumed were clients or suppliers.

Rory took a quick look around before answering 'Yes, sort of,' he replied uncertainly, 'Have you noticed the lack of women in this box? I've only counted three. When we walked in about a dozen of the men's eyes popped out of their heads when they saw you.'

'Really? I...'

Mary spent a few seconds inspecting the guests around her. Even though the race was in full flow, two men made eye contact with her, one of them smiled back in a manner that made her feel slightly uncomfortable.

Just as Mary was about to speak with Rory again, Adam appeared at her side and bent his head as if he were about to speak. On the track, the two novice hurdlers at the head of the betting kicked a few lengths clear into the home straight and the crowd's reaction meant he had to remain silent.

'I hear you bought a two-year-old at the sales,' Adam inquired once the two horses had crossed the finishing line locked together and the cries of encouragement from the crowd had subsided.

'Yes, I was lucky enough to come into a little money and decided to treat myself. I found a rather good young trainer as well,' Mary replied as the guests began to filter back into the warmth of the room.

Eventually, only the three of them were left outside in the cold, Adam peppering Mary with questions about her new-found interest in racehorse ownership. Rory remained close, but silent as Mary became quite animated about Danny Carter's yard and his training abilities.

'I have someone I'd love you to meet, Mary. I also happen to know he's looking for a trainer for three of his flat horses,' Adam revealed, once Mary had completed her sales pitch for Danny's yard, 'It sounds like this trainer of yours is an exciting young chap.'

Adam disappeared inside and Rory leaned against the balcony rail, perusing the winners enclosure and parade ring which was now devoid of equine athletes.

'Do you know Adam very well?' he asked quietly in his soft Irish drawl.

Mary joined him, linking his arm in hers. She was still buzzing a little from her conversation and the prospect of finding Danny a new owner.

'Yes, of course. Henry worked for him for almost thirty years.'

'But do you really *know* him?'

Mary paused to consider this for a few seconds, 'Not in the biblical sense, if that's what you're trying to get at!' she replied in a slightly less jovial manner than intended.

'Of course not,' Rory countered, 'I mean, is he above board, or a bit of a chancer?'

Mary was unable to reply. Adam was sliding the doors to the balcony open and came through with an immaculately turned out Asian gentleman of about forty following behind.

'This is Yousef,' Adam declared, his arm around the man, 'He is a longstanding client and I believe he'd be very interested in hearing about Danny Carter.'

'Yousef Amari,' the man stated graciously. He flashed an easy smile at Mary and ignored Rory.

'I'm pleased to make your acquaintance Miss Romano. It seems Adam is quite keen for us to meet.'

Adam produced a rumbling laugh, 'I must apologise to you both if I seem a little enthusiastic, but when I see a match which will benefit both parties, I can't help myself.'

'Please Adam, networking is the grease that keeps business flowing, there's no need to apologise,' declared Yousef.

This received a round of polite agreement, although Mary was aware Rory didn't join in. Adam must have realised too, as he proceeded to ask him a direct question.

'Rory, perhaps you'd like a drink and we can leave these two to discuss their horses and trainers?'

After querying the suggestion with Mary via a lingering glance, Rory accepted the offer and followed Adam back inside. However, he didn't cross to the well-stocked free bar in the corner of the room. Instead, he visited the cloakrooms, then returned and opted to select a seat close to the sliding glass door. Sitting alone, Rory pretended to be engrossed in his racecard, whilst keeping a close eye on Mary's conversation.

**

As the off-time for the second race drew closer, Mary and Rory made their excuses to Adam, thanking him for his hospitality and found their way downstairs and out into the crisp winter air, having decided to watch the race from trackside.

They reached the parade ring, joining the bustle of people watching the ten runners circling prior to the second race on the card. Rory had been uncharacteristically quiet for the last ten minutes and Mary linked arms with him once again and squeezed his arm through his heavy coat as he checked the runners number cloths against his racecard.

'Forty minutes to Misty Creek's race, are you nervous?' she asked quietly. Rory regarded her through wisps of her condensing breath and emerged from his thoughts with a weak smile.

'Yes, I guess so.'

He paused, as if contemplating how to phrase what he was about to impart. Mary dropped her hand from Rory's arm, sensing whatever he was about to say wasn't going to be positive. She watched as her companion avoided her questioning eyes and instead focused his gaze at a point on the top of the stands. He took a breath.

'You really are a complete bitch, aren't you?' an angry voice protested behind Mary's shoulder.

Rory's eyes grew wide and he instinctively drew Mary toward

him and stepped forward, placing himself between her and Adrian Fitzpatrick. The trainer had created a space in the crowd as racegoers backed away from the agitated man who was now gesticulating with a pudgy finger toward the middle-aged couple.

'You couldn't leave well alone could you?' Fitzpatrick accused loudly, apparently oblivious to the attention he was attracting.

Mary moved from behind Rory, who was holding both hands out as part of a protective stance.

'I have no idea what you mean,' Mary said, forcefully enough to ensure her voice carried to the ring of racegoers enjoying the spat.

'Yousef Amari ring any bells?' Fitzpatrick hissed, stepping forward into Rory's outstretched hands, so they were pushing on his puffed out chest, 'You've stolen three horses from me.'

Rory tried issuing a few threats to get Fitzpatrick to back off. This only made the trainer lean in on the Irishman, keeping his own hands at his side. Realising Fitzpatrick was attempting to elicit a physical response, Rory dropped both arms to his side and stood his ground. He tensed, expecting the man, who was slightly taller, to fall into him, instead, the two men ended up nose to nose, bumping chest to chest. Rory could smell beer on Fitzpatrick's breath.

'Walk away. Now,' Rory stated into his aggressors face. Fitzpatrick didn't move, his features contorting into a snarl.

'I'm going to make it my business to hurt her.'

No-one around the two men heard Fitzpatrick's words as they were faint and almost inaudible. They were only intended for Rory, and Rory heard them. The trainer's steely eyes didn't flinch, waiting for a reaction.

Having staged the spat on the edge of the parade ring, the disruption to the viewing public hadn't gone unnoticed. A burly paddock attendant was pushing through the crowd. Fitzpatrick saw the crowd parting and stood back. Before the attendant reached them Rory backed further away from Fitzpatrick, took Mary's hand and pulled her into the forest of people. Fitzpatrick watched them disappear with a frustrated sneer before making off in the opposite direction before the attendant had chance to buttonhole him.

With his temper still raging at the loss of three horses, one of which was his only hope of landing a heritage handicap that season, Fitzpatrick fought his way to the entrance to the parade ring. He had a runner in the next race, and had left his owners standing alone in the ring when he'd spotted Mary Romano in the crowd.

A thin faced man leaning up against the white plastic rails caught his arm as he passed and Fitzpatrick was forced to halt, anger still surging through him.

'What do you want, I'm busy?' Fitzpatrick blurted angrily.

The man looked thoughtful, sizing Fitzpatrick up. He waved his index finger from side to side as if scolding the trainer before beckoned Fitzpatrick closer simply by changing the direction of his digit. The two men had a short, quiet conversation and Fitzpatrick moved into the parade ring to rejoin his owners with a newly acquired spring in his step and a gleam in his eye.

Seventeen

Mary decided Misty Creek looked like a bull of a horse. Compared to her two two-year-olds back at Malton, being faced with a strapping ten-year-old chaser made her realise her young horses were still very much babies.

She'd tried to tell Rory as much as she could about Fitzpatrick and thanked him at length for standing up to his bullying, although since the confrontation her Irish partner for the day seemed preoccupied and distant. As they stood waiting for Misty Creek to appear from the racecourse stables, she asked Rory what it was he'd wanted to say to her prior to Fitzpatrick's arrival.

Rory considered telling her about the man who had cornered him in the cloakroom, slyly offering money in return for information about Mary. He debated whether to potentially ruin their day by sharing the man's agitation with Rory's refusal, and his subsequent attempt to intimidate him with the threat of violence. It hadn't worked. Rory had pushed the man aside and walked out.

Rory liked this woman. He liked her a lot, and was desperate for this day to go well. Following the face-off with Fitzpatrick, he decided adding further complication to Mary's day would only turn everything sour. So he made an excuse. His news could wait.

Instead of pushing for attention, Mary contented herself with a background role when she met with Misty Creek's Irish connections. Rory slipped into his breeder persona with the other owners, the same Rory she'd experienced at Doncaster Sales before they'd had coffee together.

The gelding was walking around the pre-parade ring at the back of the racecourse, watched by Rory, the other two shareholders in the horse and their six guests, all of whom were being entertained by their Irish trainer. Mary was fascinated to learn the horse had travelled from Ireland by sea the day before and spent the night with his stable lad in the racecourse stables. The trainer, a grizzled old man of seventy, possessed a truly impressive beard and spoke with such speed and depth of Irish accent, Mary was unable to tune into what he was saying before it was time to set off to the parade ring.

As they approached the small chute leading to the entrance to the parade ring, Rory pulled her to the side. He was troubled by something and Mary knew it was more than just nerves ahead of the Eider.

'I'm sorry, Mary, I didn't realise there was going to be so many of us. I'm afraid I have to leave you here. The course will only allow eight owners to enter the parade ring. My fellow shareholders brought more people than I was expecting.'

Mary looked down the parade ring steps two yards below them.

'But it's huge. We could have a game of football in there and not bother anyone.'

Rory shrugged, 'I'm sorry, they're the only racecourse I know of that has this draconian rule.'

Mary examined Rory's face. There was something around the eyes that told her he was troubled by more than just gaining access to the parade ring.

'Listen, I'm sorry about Adam taking over your day... and Fitzpatrick...'

'It's not that, they're both... well, Fitzpatrick is an arse, but I knew that before I met you,' he said, closing his eyes and shaking his head, 'It's something else... Listen, I've got to go. Wait here and I'll be back in a few minutes.'

Suddenly feeling hollow, Mary watched Rory dash down the parade ring steps to join his trainer and seven other friends on the bright green artificial turf inside the centre of the parade ring. Fifteen minutes later Misty Creek crossed the finishing line in second position after a superb round of jumping, beaten four lengths and belying his odds of 20/1.

Mary had been thinking hard during the race. As the gelding crossed the line, she reached her conclusion. She couldn't drag Rory into her messy life any further and it hadn't been fair to come here today. Rory was a nice chap, and didn't deserve to be treated this way. He had probably reached the same conclusion and was having difficulty letting her down. She'd make it easy on him.

Inside the winners' enclosure the members of the Misty Creek partnership gave the gelding congratulatory slaps on his neck, listened intently to the jockey's feedback, and complimented the trainer on the performance. Rory stood apart from the happy throng, reading, then re-reading a text message from Mary on his mobile phone, unable to enjoy the moment.

***

From his position up in the stands, Vincent trained his binoculars onto Mary and followed her as she headed for the racecourse exit. Once she had disappeared toward the taxi rank, he returned to watching the parade ring.

He passed over the breeder who had been Mary's partner for the day; he wasn't of interest. It only took a few seconds of searching the crowds before he caught Adam East in his crosshairs and found Yousef Amari in animated conversation with him. He tracked them for a while, eventually deciding he'd seen enough and wasn't going to learn any more.

91

Vincent knew he had a problem. Mary's conversations with East and Amari up in their private box had been enough to depress him. He hadn't been able to hear them, but the fact those two men were together, and had approached Mary, meant his job had just become far more complicated. The argument with the trainer had been interesting, the same trainer she'd argued with at the horse sales. He could be bought, which was more than could be said for the Irishman with Mary.

Whichever way you cut it, the outlook for acquiring the Stone had been complicated by what he'd witnessed today. Eddie would not be pleased.

He called his boss's number and spoke for a minute, then listened for two, and hung up without uttering another word.

You're in for a rough ride, Mary Romano, he said to himself.

Eighteen

'Danny, is that you?'

'Yes Mary, I was asleep. What time is it?'

'Five-thirty, I waited until I knew you'd be getting up.'

Mary heard a faint groan and the muffled sounds of movement.

A few seconds later a comic voice told her, 'You're going to have to stop phoning me like this, Mary. People will talk.'

'Let them!' she countered, 'Listen Danny, I need to ask a favour...'

Five minutes later Mary ended the call, tossed her phone onto the sofa and taking both sides of Charlie's head in her hands, gave the fur behind both his ears a simultaneous scratch which sent the Pointer into leg tapping ecstasy.

'He said yes!' she told the dog.

The breakthrough had happened when she was watching late night television. Mary had been half watching a re-run of an old detective television series when the Whitley Bay coastline popped up with St Mary's Lighthouse in the background. As ever, the detective and his sidekick were on the trail of a suspect, and after showing the two actors walking down the Whitley Bay promenade with the lighthouse in the background, the camera angle changed to follow them into an old-fashioned cafe on the seafront.

As the camera panned, the name of the cafe was on-screen for only a split second, but that was enough. Mary had walked down that promenade with Henry many times before, and she kicked herself for not making the mental leap required to see its significance.

The filmmakers hadn't bothered changing the name of the establishment, they'd used its real name. The Rendezvous Cafe.

Mary had felt a tingle of recognition, followed by a wave of euphoria as she considered the breakthrough she'd made.

'Meet James at the Rendevous,' she told Charlie excitedly, 'That's what Joe was trying to say!'

His parents would often head to the coast, according to Henry. They would walk on the sands in a morning, come back to Newcastle, and open the restaurant in the late afternoon. It all made sense now. She'd visited the cafe with Henry, sipping superb hot chocolate drinks in the middle of the winter at the fifties style tables, unable to see the beach because of the condensation on the windows. In summer they bought ice-cream cones...

Her heart jumped. Of course, ice cream! Lombardi's Ice Cream. That's where she had seen it before. There was even a little sliding window they still used to serve cornets to passers-by in summer. The cafe was kept practically the same as it had been sixty years ago. Had Gia and his wife run the Rendezvous Cafe in the sixties, when it was primarily an ice-cream parlour? Thinking hard, Mary was sure she could remember a faded out old painted sign on the other side of the cafe which said 'Lombardi's Ices'. The more she thought about the cafe and Joe's words, the more sense it made.

The final pieces of the puzzle were falling into place, but to take it further she had to find James, thirty years after Joe had told Henry, Eddie, and possibly inadvertently, herself, to speak with him. It was one-o'clock in the morning by the time she decided what to do. She would go there, but not alone, and she'd have to take precautions; Vincent might be watching. She corrected herself; Vincent would almost certainly be watching.

***

Two days later, Mary drove down the slip-road onto the A19 and pointed the nose of her Volvo toward Newcastle. Danny occupied the passenger seat and dozed whilst Charlie watched the traffic out of the rear window. It had already taken an hour, as Mary had been determined to ensure they weren't being followed, touring around small, minor roads, then doubling back to catch out anyone tailing them. They'd never seen anyone, or caught anyone out.

There had been plenty of talking in the first half hour of their journey north, but little conversation, as Danny had immediately launched into an excited monologue of how his yard was faring. Mary found his enthusiasm both amusing and enthralling, and allowed the young man to rattle through his horses, their plans for the turf season and the couple he still had racing through the winter months on the All-Weather. Danny had an air of enthusiasm which was contagious.

'Another new horse in the yard!' Mary exclaimed in delight when Danny told her of a Mr Bruce, an owner who had phoned, and then delivered his five-year-old filly only two days later.

'He's a breeder,' Danny added knowingly, 'Has a specific task in mind for his mare.'

After a short silence, Mary checked her rear view mirror and looked over at her passenger.

'You're going to have to explain, Danny. You have to remember I'm new to this.'

'Ah, yes. Sorry. He's a breeder and this mare is well bred and is set to go to the paddocks. She's already been covered by a decent sire, but she's never won a race.'

'You mean she's pregnant?'

'Yeah, I think she's gone to a sire called Mayson.'

Mary put on a glazed expression as she ran this through her mind.

'Surely she can't run when she's carrying a foal?'

'Oh, she'll be fine to race up to about July time. Sometimes mares actually see their form improve once they are in foal. But you haven't heard the best bit, she came from your favourite trainer's yard...'

Mary shot her passenger a tight-lipped grimace.

'Fitzpatrick?'

'Yeah, the owner fell out with him. Didn't say why, but he wanted to get his horse out of there quickly.'

'Don't blame him,' Mary concurred.

'You'll have to get them to sign the yard agreement...'

'Already done!' Danny announced happily, 'You've got me well trained, Mary. And I got a set of silks off him as well.'

'Hey! I'm impressed. You'll be doing the accounts and all the paperwork as well by the end of the season!'

Danny went peculiarly quiet following this compliment. Mary stole a look at him and got the impression he was uncomfortable, or possibly nervous. He was scratching the seam of his jeans close to his knee with his nails and staring straight ahead.

'Danny? What is it?'

His concentration broken, he swivelled in his seat in order to face Mary.

'Juliet... Well, Juliet and me. We were just wondering why it was you keep saying you'll only be with us for a short time?'

He paused, trying to read the older lady's reaction. He stumbled awkwardly on but was interrupted by Mary.

'That's a very fair question and it deserves a proper answer. To do that, I need to tell you a story and I guess an hour-long car journey is just as good a place as any.

She sighed, 'Sit back. It's not a nice one, and it might mean you don't want me to continue being involved with the yard.'

'Oh, I'm sure...'

'Wait until I've finished,' Mary insisted, flashing him a serious look.

For the next half hour, Mary took Danny through her experiences with Henry, and then Eddie. She told him how she'd met Henry in Grey's Casino, the night at the hospital, Joe's dying words and eventually Henry's death. She went on to describe how she'd won the money that allowed her to buy a racehorse, and her father's love of racing that he'd passed on to her. Finally, she revealed Vincent's involvement with her, and the story surrounding the Stone, and the reason for todays trip to the North East, or, more accurately, Whitley Bay.

'I didn't want to do it on my own, and I only have a couple of people I can trust, and most of them are too old to go on such a wild goose chase!' Mary admitted as she cruised on the inside lane of the dual carriageway, going as fast as the Volvo could manage without complaint.

Danny had sat quietly throughout the story of her life. Now he looked fit to burst. She nodded for him to speak.

He grinned, 'You're a dark horse aren't you?'

It took until they had passed through Billingham to answer all of Danny's queries. He saved the most difficult question until last.

'But there's one thing I don't understand about Eddie,' he said whilst scratching the seam of his jeans with even more gusto, 'Why does he think *you* killed his father?'

Mary paused, took a sharp intake of breath and tried to stem the emotion already massing in her throat.

So what happened? Danny asked quietly.

Mary didn't reply. She'd tried to forget that night in August 1987, but it was all there, every single minute, playing constantly in her head, as if it had been digitally captured and was available for replay at the touch of a button. But it had always played internally, never out loud. Until now.

'It w-was my fault,' she stammered, 'If it wasn't for my actions, Joe would never have died.'

With those words spoken a weight lifted from Mary and the story started to trickle, then pour from her.

'I knew he was cheating...' she stopped after glancing over to the passenger seat and reading the confusion written across Danny's face.

'You know, I said I was a croupier?'

Danny nodded.

'I've always been good with numbers, and I tried a few times to count cards on a four deck shoe. It's difficult, but if you adopt the right combination of Hi-Lo counts and betting correlation...' Mary glanced over and saw Danny's forehead was either creased in concentration or confusion, 'Never mind that now, I need to tell you about Joe, my husband's father.'

Relieved, Danny relaxed. Nonetheless, he concentrated on Mary as she drove and spoke, becoming absorbed with her story.

'Joe started coming into the casino the odd night after his restaurant closed. Always alone, he'd never bring a friend, his wife or his sons. Joe was a solitary, conservative gambler, only risking a couple of pounds a hand. He won a little and lost a little, and he always chose my table to play.'

Mary continued, holding the wide, thin steering wheel with both hands, staring at the road just above the top arc, 'I sensed there was something wrong that first night...'

As she told her story Mary imagined Joe, sitting in front of her on a tall stool, unsmiling, concentrating on his game. A thin, muscular man with a pointed chin, Joe's skeletal cheekbones gave him a sharp, undernourished appearance. He was starting to show his age, with an abundance of wrinkles and a large, slightly bent Roman nose that twitched as he made his betting decisions. A fruit machine spitting coins into its steel payout tray cut through the ambiance created by the smattering of clients and the constant chatter of croupiers.

'He started to increase his stakes, to the point where he was up to two-hundred pounds per hand. It was classic card counting', Mary reflected, 'He would play small stakes, and then increase them hugely when the odds fell in his favour.'

'So he knew what cards were left in the pack?'

'If you count accurately you'll know when the table is in your favour,' Mary corrected, 'By matching the size of his bets to the probability of receiving a winning hand, he was able to beat the house. The problem was, he was far too obvious. I noticed the first night, but I said nothing. On the second night I warned him to ease off and lose a little, otherwise I'd have to report him to the casino management.'

'So is this card counting illegal?' Danny broke in.

'No,' Mary replied, shaking her head, 'But casinos keep a keen eye on that sort of thing. They don't mind an occasional winner, but like bookmakers, if you consistently win they'll tend to put a stop to it, one way or another...'

Mary's voice trailed off. She realised she was gripping the steering wheel so hard her nails were biting her palms. She eased them off, flexed her shoulders and made an effort to relax before continuing.

'I told Joe to stop, or at least be less conspicuous, but he wouldn't. He was an arrogant man, just like Eddie. He thought he was being so clever. I *told* him I would have to report him to my boss, it was my job.'

'How do you mean?' asked Danny, who was now caught up in Mary's story, locked on her face and hanging on every word.

'No casino likes to lose money,' she sighed, 'They have spotters or pit bosses that scan for people card counting. As a croupier they expect you to report anyone you suspect, but it was so obvious with Joe, I had to report him. How could I not? They knew I was dating Henry, his son. For all I knew the casino may have believed I was working with Joe to defraud them.'

'So what happened to Joe? I assume he was warned off?'

Mary winced, 'Not warned off, they told me he would be 'sorted out'. Casino owners aren't the sort of people who take losing money on the chin, and this was thirty years ago. The world was a different place.'

She paused and her cheeks inflated as she exhaled. The car wobbled a little in its lane and Danny realised Mary's hands and arms were shaking. He was about to say something, but then she started to speak. Quick, sharp and crisp words came forth and she didn't stop until her story was told.

'I was worried about Joe that night,' Mary said with feeling, 'He was carrying a huge amount of cash and I feared what the casino people would do to him. They employed some very powerful, rough men who weren't too fussed about who they used their fists on, and how hard they hit. I got Joe to stay in the casino until my shift finished at three o-clock in the morning and told him to wait for me so I could walk him to his car. I imagined they wouldn't do anything bad if I was with him.'

Mary closed her eyes for a second. Danny stayed silent, but readied himself to grab the wheel if she started to waver out of her lane.

'He must have got impatient. I was only two minutes getting my handbag from my locker and when I got to the casino entrance he wasn't there. I waited for about a minute and then heard shouting across the road in High Bridge Alley. I found him being beaten...'

Mary blinked a tear from her eye, but didn't wipe it away, allowing it to draw a moist line down her cheek.

'Two men ran off once I appeared and started shouting. Joe was lying on his back on the cobbles,' she finished, glancing over to a wide-eyed Danny, 'He was trembling, his arms held tight to his chest, with cuts and bruises all over his face. It was only later I realised he had been having a heart attack.'

'Eddie had been at a nightclub and was passing the alley on his way to a taxi rank and ran to help. He called an ambulance and we waited together. I can't remember exactly what I said to him, I was in shock. But I told him about the card counting and that I shouldn't have told the casino and he suddenly went crazy, screaming I was to blame for his father taking a beating. Thank goodness the paramedics arrived when they did, otherwise I think Eddie would have taken his anger out on me.'

Mary shuddered and took a deep breath.

'So that's the story. We followed the ambulance to the hospital where Henry joined us. If I hadn't been dealing blackjack at the tables that night, Joe would still be alive and Eddie wouldn't be dogging my every step with his threats.'

Danny cocked his head to one side, deep in thought, his eyes on the road ahead.

'I assume the police didn't charge anyone then?' he asked eventually.

'No-one saw what happened in the alley and Joe only spoke a few words at the hospital. The police interviewed the casino bosses and bouncers, but they all had alibis. That said, they claimed they were all together at the casino. It was reported as a mugging in the press and I lost my job because I'd spoken to the police about the card counting.'

'Yeah, I can imagine a story about a winning punter getting mugged outside your casino might damage business a little,' observed Danny, straightening himself in his seat and looking over at Mary, 'For a woman who is terribly straightforward, to the point of being blunt with people, you've got yourself mixed up in one hell of a complicated bundle of trouble.'

Danny's statement rattled around Mary's mind for a few seconds before the relief at having shared her story grew and she found herself smiling widely, then stemming a laugh. The young man smiled back uncertainly, not quite sure why she'd found his statement so humourous, but content Mary's reaction seemed to be positive.

'I tell you what,' Danny offered, glancing at the road ahead.

'What?' Mary managed as her amusement subsided.

'You can keep giggling if you pull over and allow me to drive. You're all over the place!'

Mary started to laugh and another, wholly different type of tear, eventually washed down her cheek.

Nineteen

During winter, Whitley Bay promenade is bleak at the best of times. A testament to what could be created with concrete blocks, a grey sea slapped against its twenty foot sea walls throughout the winter, only scaling it once or twice when a storm whipped the breakers into a scum-ridden froth. Yet Mary had always felt the winter was the time to visit the promenade. It possessed a stark beauty once the day-trippers and the heat of summer evaporated in autumn. She'd enjoyed her weekend winter walks with Henry along its broad, mile long gentle arc, often fighting a bitingly cold wind. On some days you would taste the salt on your lips within moments. Whatever the weather, their stroll would culminate in a visit to the old-fashioned cafe built into the promenade where they would sip freshly created whole milk hot chocolates' together.

Mary and Danny arrived at the Whitley Bay seafront car park mid-morning, accompanied by a persistent drizzle.

'Popular little place,' Danny noted as he toured the Volvo around the empty car park.

'The cafe will be open. It always is.'

'You willing to put money on that?'

'No,' Mary replied following a contemplative pause.

It was with a good degree of relief that Mary spotted the lights on inside the cafe when the two of them, plus Charlie, emerged from the small red-brick tunnel that led to the promenade. She was pleased to find neither the promenade nor the cafe had changed since she had previously visited the seafront over twenty-five years ago.

Danny rattled the double doors and a hard-faced middle aged woman eventually appeared behind the cafe counter. She was carrying a tray of assorted cups and mugs and her stained white apron only just clung to her ample waist.

'Fifteen minutes,' she shouted over, 'We open at eleven, pet.'

'Come on,' Mary said, pulling at Danny's arm, 'Time for us to introduce Charlie to sand!'

Half an hour later, they returned to the Rendezvous Cafe, the two of them cold and very wet and with a dog covered in sand and sea water. There were already two other tables occupied. To Mary's relief, Charlie was allowed to come in with them and he and Danny chose a spot close to a radiator, while she bought two hot chocolates and quizzed the rotund lady behind the cafe counter.

Charlie lay down with his back almost touching the small radiator set into the ancient parquet floor. Danny noticed wisps of steam were rising from his fur. From a table a few yards away, a man with skin resembling a walnut was watching Charlie too. He acknowledged the pensioner with a kindly shrug and received a knowing smile back.

'She's never heard of a James or Gia Lombardi,' Mary whispered as she set the whipped cream topped mugs onto the small round table, 'New owners took over two years ago, and before that the people weren't Italian.'

'So where do we go from here?'

'I was thinking the local records office or library. Maybe we can look at the...'

'That lad would make a decent gun dog,' said the man two tables away, 'What's his name, pet?' he added in a thick Northumbian accent.

Mary was used to this. She hadn't bargained for the attention Charlie would attract and had found the intrusions from dog lovers bewildering at first. However, this dog owning etiquette, which seemed to allow anyone to engage her in conversation regarding the breed, age and wellbeing of Charlie, had soon became a normal, regular occurrence.

'He's a two-year-old pointer called Charlie,' she responded automatically.

The old man stroked the silvery two-day old growth on his chin, his gaze set on Charlie's steaming underbelly.

'Does he like ice-cream?'

Mary blinked a few times, somewhat thrown. Meanwhile, Danny suppressed a chortle.

'My pointer loved ice cream,' continued the wizened old man, shuffling in his seat. His eyes left Charlie and came to rest on Mary. They were misted over in remembrance.

'She particularly liked their raspberry ripple.'

'I'll have to try Charlie with that flavour,' offered Mary amiably.

'Oh you won't get that here anymore,' he explained with a shake of his head, 'It's all that whipped up crap that keeps forever now. Not even ice cream if you ask me. Wouldn't feed that stuff to a dog, it's full of chemicals.'

Danny examined the man in detail for the first time, the kernel of an idea forming.

'You remember when this place sold proper ice cream then?' he asked hopefully.

'Oh aye,' replied the pensioner, 'I've been coming here every week for the last fifty years.'

***

A fret was busy rolling off the sea by the time Mary and Danny reached Cullercoats. The Volvo's lights hardly seemed worthwhile, making no difference at all to the impenetrable wall of freezing fog. They crawled along in silence, searching for road signs which popped into existence only yards in front of them.

'Saint Oswald's Avenue,' Danny muttered.

'Oswins,' Mary corrected, 'He said the middle of St Oswins' Avenue.'

A right-hand turn loomed up out of the gloom of the coast road and Danny indicated, edging the car slowly across the junction.

'Here!' Mary said excitedly, 'Turn right here.'

St Oswin's Avenue was as the old man had described: a wide Victorian terrace with small, well kept gardens and lines of cars parked on both sides of the road. The first two hundred yards contained two rows of large three-storey houses boasting prominent bay windows.

'This is it,' Danny said, parking the car as soon as he found a kerb space big enough to accommodate the Volvo.

'He said it was a black door with railings outside.'

'I can see five black doors from here,' Danny moaned.

Mick, the pensioner in the cafe, had been very helpful. He had told them about his time working at the now-defunct Spanish City funfair, at the end of the promenade. As a young man he'd worked in several arcades, on fairground rides and for a period in the seventies and early eighties became the caretaker for the Empress Ballroom. In those days, Lombardi ice cream had been sold all over the sea front and he'd got to know its creator and owner. And as a result of Mick trawling his memory, here they were, on the street where Gia and the Lombardi family had made their home thirty years ago.

It took a knock at three black front doors on the avenue before a kindly octogenarian lady directed Mary to the far end of the street and a mid-terrace with a well-maintained garden and a freshly painted ornamental lintel. It was a few minutes after noon when the door opened and a harassed looking woman wearing a plastic apron, and with a very young child clamped to her midriff, pierced Danny and Mary with a hard stare.

'This better be good, I've had to walk down two flights of stairs to answer this door.'

'I'm sorry. I see you've been bathing him,' Mary said warmly, having noticed the woman's child had wet hair and was naked apart from being wrapped in a towel, 'I believe the Lombardi's once lived here?'

Mary gave the woman a hopeful smile. In return the woman frowned whilst making an attempt to hitch the wriggling baby up her hip.

'Er, yeah. I think they did, but a while back.'

'I don't suppose you know where they live now?'

'No, they moved out about twenty years ago. We've been here three now, the umm... Fletchers were in before us...'

The woman stopped speaking abruptly as a shrill scream of 'Mummy' rang out behind her. The woman's face drained of colour as she glanced behind her. A very young girl with a cheeky face ran up, repeating her scream until she saw Mary and Danny. Her silence only lasted a couple of seconds. She sized the visitors up, found them of little interest and grabbing her mother's leg, started to pull at her and demand more biscuits.

'I really must get on, sorry I can't be of any help,' said the woman, starting to close the front door.

'We were supposed to pick up something from them, the Lombardi's, Gia Lombardi,' Mary said in desperation as the door started to swing closed.

The door halted and opened again.

'Are you a relative of Gia...'

'Gia Lombardi, yes! I'm Mary Romano.'

The woman opened the door wider, looking Danny and Mary up and down once more.

'You best come in then.'

Twenty

'I still can't believe you found it!' said Danny as they sat in the Volvo half an hour later with a tray of fish and chips each on their laps and plastic forks in their hands.

'And you were great with that little girl,' Mary responded, nodding whilst swallowing a vinegary chip.

'Had plenty of practice.'

'Really, when?'

'I was brought up by a string of foster parents. There were always a ton of kids younger than me that needed looking after.'

Mary was reminded of something Jonnie Lilley had screamed at Danny the day of the fight over the filly; 'Social Boy'. That's what he must have been alluding to, as an insult; Danny's upbringing. On reflection it had been a poor, cheap shot and Mary didn't want to sour the moment by mentioning it.

'You had that little girl eating out of the palm of your hand. Her mother was amazed,' added Mary.

Danny chuckled, 'All kids love magic. I think they should teach every parent the basics before they have kids.'

Mary eyed the letter that was propped up on the dashboard and was reminded of what lay within.

'You're right,' she agreed, spearing another chip with her tiny plastic triton, 'We were lucky.'

'You over the shock?'

Mary glanced over to Danny and produced a sad smile to assure him she was.

'I wasn't expecting Henry to be involved. It threw me for a minute,'

In fact, Mary had needed to grab Danny in order for her knees not to buckle when she'd first read what was written on the letter's envelope.

The mother of the two children had introduced herself as Jilly and escorted Mary and Danny through the house and into a warm, modern kitchen with plenty of windows at the rear of the house. She had dressed her baby and placed him into a square pen that Mary thought resembled a padded cell, and then found a handful of custard creams for the little girl, using the few minutes of respite from the youngster's protestations to relate to her guests the tale of the 'letter in the tin'.

'It's become a bit of a family favourite,' Jilly told them excitedly, 'I never thought anyone would actually knock on the door asking for the letter in the tin.'

'You have a tin for Mary?' Danny checked, slightly bemused.

'Oh, yes. On the day we got the keys to this house, we walked in and there was an old sweet tin on the counter top,' Jilly replied, indicating the kitchen units behind her.

'There was a post-it note from the Fletchers; that's the previous owners. It said the tin belonged with the house and that the people they'd bought the house from had insisted the tin remained here, as at some point in the future it would be collected by its owner. So when we moved in, the tin was passed onto us for safe-keeping.'

Mary had explained in broad terms how she had followed the trail to find Gia Lombardi, but that it had taken thirty years to decipher the instructions. Skirting around the circumstance behind Joe's death and with no reference to the threats from Eddie and Vincent, she realised her journey to Jilly's door sounded rather like a benign treasure hunt. She tried to keep it that way.

From being a tired, washed-out housewife on the doorstep, Jilly's whole demeanour had become charged with bright interest as Mary's story unfolded.

'Nothing like this has ever happened to me,' she told them with wide eyes once Mary's tale had reached its conclusion, 'Of course, we've all tried to work out the clues in the letter, but now you're here, we're going to find out!'

Apparently thrilled and full of suppressed anticipation, Jilly had disappeared upstairs, leaving Mary bewildered and Danny attempting to amuse Jill's rather dumpy daughter with some magic tricks using a coin, rather than dose her with sugary treats.

'Here you are,' Jilly announced with some reverence, returning to place a battered tin with an art-deco picture of pear drops on the kitchen table. Scratched roughly onto the lid were three letters; 'GIA'.

Mary had considered simply leaving without opening the tin but thought better of it, given Jilly was watching her with bated breath. After years of waiting, it only seemed right to allow her to enjoy watching the finder's reaction to its contents.

'You've read the letter then?' she asked.

'Oh yes,' replied Jilly without any sign of embarrassment, 'Plenty of times. It was open when we got it. There didn't seem any harm in trying to work it out.'

The tin popped open easily enough, revealing a grubby white envelope with the words, 'Hello Eddie', handwritten in ink. Mary recognised the writing immediately. It was unmistakeably Henry's hand.

Mary's sharp intake of breath found Danny at her side, holding her tenderly under her elbow.

'What is it?'

'It's... Henry,' Mary managed, 'My husband.'

While Danny and Mary shared a concerned look, Jilly had clapped her hands together in enraptured glee.

'This is sooo... dramatic,' she bubbled, 'Can I take a photo? No, actually, a video would be great!'

She started to dip into her trouser pocket in search of her mobile phone.

'This is rather private,' Danny pointed out sternly, holding Jilly's enthusiastic gaze until it transformed into something rather hopeful instead of expectant.

'So, just the photo then...' Jilly ventured.

'No!' Danny and Mary answered in unison.

Realising how crestfallen their host was, Mary managed to placate her with a promise of a few photos once they had read the letter.

The letter inside the envelope was similarly tarnished with many years worth of handling by interested parties. A faded brown coffee ring was the most obvious addition to the original document.

'Yeah, sorry about that,' Jilly said upon seeing Mary trace the outline of the stain with a forefinger, 'Uncle Colin was a bit tipsy at Christmas and plonked his cuppa down on it.'

Danny guided Mary to the kitchen table where she read the couple of paragraphs seated, with Danny waiting patiently and Jilly picking at her fingernails with her teeth between shushing her little girl.

Once she had read the letter through twice to herself, Mary leaned back in her seat and closed her eyes, silently passing it over to Danny.

The first thing he noticed was the date: September 14th 1986. He guessed it meant Henry had retrieved the Stone and written his letter only a few weeks after his father died. Apart from the handwritten envelope, it was typed throughout and Danny noted a few horizontal smudges of ink and realised Henry must have used an old-fashioned typewriter.

Dear M or E,

I could have taken the Stone Of Shiazzano (M: it's a gold brooch with a ruby) and left nothing behind. However, you know how I love a treasure hunt and this was too good an opportunity to miss! Eddie: I'm impressed you got this far but don't waste your time, I will always be one step ahead of you. Mary: If you ever need the Stone I'm sure you'll be able to work my little conundrum out.

H. xxx

Etfa. Chfeq yct uxscagu vrbg sjha ayn. Dywtgg phftaos oo. B

hugnujd bh owlh vy ifblxqv ihi sjha vrx drgizg S gsrv mc fotz jamv. Dem krde rqxx tbj pctubbt gnh yrth Cs fscxm. Huw lhqxx wf zbrfog wa s izcmx gcwvwcv mc ogmv qp ng. V utb'v dkifl uopul oav xbvbnggagu kd mc sjbspnl kbmer rem huwf wp ntbtwk. Uq dh chj yoxynfvlx pgxvv. Gg mvg vxtg al o vbxs jamv vgh hemgyu. Vhcx xhf vrx pnlmstow fvfz ch cbziwk. Onv fm ygos. Jogfl.

'What's all the stuff at the bottom?' Danny asked once he'd read the message through.

'I... don't know,' Mary responded distractedly.

From the other side of the kitchen, Jilly gave a despondent sigh, 'We thought it was a code you would be able to read.'

'Maybe. I guess I might be able to work on it,' Mary said, getting up from the kitchen table and tucking the letter into her handbag, 'But it's clear that this 'Stone Of Shiazzano' that was in the tin has gone now. It looks like my husband, as he loved to do, is playing games.'

She stood up, catching Danny's eye in the process. One knowing look, and another two minutes of thanking Jilly and sorting a couple of photos for her, and the two of them were back inside the car.

'What is it? What's up, Mary?' Danny queried once they were moving.

'It isn't a code, it's a cipher. There's a difference.'

Danny rolled his eyes as he drove the car but realised his reaction was wasted on his passenger. Mary was staring dreamily at the gloomy sky through the windscreen.

'So?' he prompted, allowing a hint of irritation to show through, 'Come on, help me out here, Mary. I failed most of my GCSE's. What's a cipher?'

***

As he ate a chip Danny watched a bead of condensation as it gained mass at the top of the Volvo's windscreen and started travelling downwards. A combination of the food, chat, and body heat from the two of them had misted up the windows inside the car. The Grand Parade coast road was empty, as was the car park beside the aquarium where they'd pulled in to eat their fish and chips lunch. Danny had parked facing a few grassy dunes and the sea, although it was barely visible through the sea fret. Up until a few minutes ago it had been gloomy, but the scene had transformed when the sun unexpectedly started cutting through the mist, lighting it up.

But Danny wasn't delighting in the light as it reflected sparkles from cresting waves. He was concentrating on the man currently standing menacingly on the Volvo's hood, brandishing a baseball bat.

The thump of his feet, the swaying of the ancient car, and the staccato metallic slap as he smashed his aluminium club into the car roof, was enough to ensure all three occupants of the car hunkered down in their seats. Charlie was the first to react after the initial shock, standing on his hind legs and snarling through the estate car's back window.

'Lock your door,' Danny shouted, allowing his lunch to tumble to the floor. He fumbled on the steering rack, searching for the keys, his fingers greasy from the chips.

'Throw out your bag,' commanded a growling male voice through the passenger side window.

'Crap, there's two of them,' Danny's internal monologue informed him. He found the keys and turned them; the wrong way.

A large gold signet ring rapped sharply on Mary's window three times and she flinched away from a set of fat knuckles.

'Down *now* or I smash it,' screamed the man, 'Start the car and you're both dead.'

This time a pair of hard blue eyes encased in a ski mask appeared at Mary's window, forcing a squeal from her as she pushed herself away from the door and onto the car's automatic gearbox.

Placing his arms protectively around her, Danny took in the seriousness of the situation for the first time.

'Give him your bag.'

'What... No, I can't do that,' Mary countered, pulling away from Danny's arms momentarily.

'Mary,' insisted Danny gruffly, 'Your bag. *Give it to him!*'

On the hood of the car the batter swung again, this time slamming into the top of the windscreen, denting the roof and sending a series of cracks racing down the glass.

'Oh, bugger it,' Mary complained, much to Danny's surprise. She was holding her hands to her face in case another blow shattered the windscreen. They locked eyes for a second. Danny was struck by what he saw in her. It wasn't fear. Far from it, instead, Mary looked *seriously* pissed off!

'Alright, alright you thug,' Mary shouted in a tone dripping with condescension, 'Here it is.'

She was holding her handbag up and shaking it at the second man whose masked face was now pressed to the passenger side window. Mary reached over and wound the window down by hand just low enough to squeeze her bag through the crack, but then stopped short of poking it through, instead placing it on her lap and opening it.

'Here,' she said, dipping into the bag and fishing out Henry's letter, 'That's what you want, isn't it?'

Danny watched as a flash of indecision registered in the masked man's eyes. There was enough in that split second for Danny to realise what Mary had done, and moreover, what they had learned. This wasn't a random mugging. The thief's goal wasn't money. His hesitation had signalled as much, but now it was confirmed as he eyed the letter hungrily before realising his mistake.

'Too late!' Mary told him in a spritely voice that oozed victory, 'Here, take it.' She posted the letter through the open window and the man's head disappeared below as he scrabbled on the tarmac to retrieve his prize.

A high-pitched crack sounded from further off down the car park. Mary and Danny reacted by sinking into their seats and sharing a worried glance.

'What the hell... was that a gunshot?' Danny panted.

The car pitched as the batter leapt to the ground and within a few seconds both men had disappeared. Charlie snarled and barked as the figures receded behind the car into the wall of white mist. A few seconds later a high-powered motorbike screamed past them. Mary peeked over the sill of her window and watched the bike, complete with its pillion passenger, vanish into the thinning sea fret.

Half a minute of tense silence ticked by during which the two of them inched themselves back up to an almost upright position. Mary turned to Danny and shrugged, 'Easy come, easy go. They've gone now, whatever that noise was, it scared them off.'

'I can't believe how cool you are!'

'Huh!' Mary replied with a roll of her eyes, 'It's easier when you know who sent them and what they're after. They were Eddie's thugs.'

'How do you know?'

'Who else would be following me around... which reminds me...'

To Danny's further surprise, Mary took her mobile phone out of a small pocket in her bag and agitatedly tapped a few icons.

'Where are you, Mr Bennett?'

There was a pause, during which Danny could hear a man's voice squeaking from the phone.

'So, you've managed to miss the mugging I hired you to prevent because you were buying your lunch,' Mary continued, anger rising in her voice with every word.

There was a frenetic few seconds of speech from the phone before Mary shook her head in disbelief.

'No, Mr Bennett, that's enough. You're fired,' she barked, ending the call with a frustrated poke of the phone's screen. Mary leaned back into her seat and issued a disgruntled sigh. Cocking her head toward Danny once more, her anger evaporated and she adopted a look of concern.

'If you're wondering, that was the person who fell out of the tree at the bottom of your yard a few weeks ago. I must apologise, it's my fault. I should never have hired a private bodyguard on the basis of his website alone.'

Danny's confusion was now complete. He sat in the drivers' seat, lumps of battered fish and greasy chips scattered around him, his mouth opening and closing, unable to conjure up a reply.

Twenty-One

Danny hadn't said too much since leaving Cullercoats. Mary was driving once more and he was sitting arms crossed, staring out of the passenger window, trying to make sense of the last few hours.

Every minute or so Mary would glance over at him, look like she was about to say something, think better of it, and return her attention to the road. She maintained a steady fifty-five miles an hour up the coast road, heading for the Tyne Tunnel turn-off.

Once the immediate shock of the mugging had worn off and the dents to the car had been examined, Danny had assumed they would call the police, however, Mary had persuaded him not to.

'Remind me again, why we didn't call the police?' he asked as a means to break the silence.

'Eddie has what he wanted, which means he will leave me alone. Going to the police would only complicate matters. I've a dented roof and a windscreen that is roadworthy but needs replacing. Otherwise we've not lost anything.'

'Not *lost* anything? They got the letter!'

'True,' Mary replied smoothly, 'But it won't do Eddie any good. He'll still have to crack the cipher and recover the Stone, wherever it is.'

Danny was about to continue pursuing this line of questioning, but at that moment Mary leaned over and placed a hand on his knee and patted it.

'I was never interested in keeping that Stone,' she told him gently, 'Now that Eddie has the letter, he will know Henry got there first. Once I tell him I bought the horses with money I won on the premium bonds, he'll leave me alone.'

She leaned back into her seat and took both hands off the steering wheel for a moment, waving them madly in the air.

'He can go off hunting for the damned Stone himself now.'

'So you never wanted the Stone of Sh... whatever it's called... for yourself?'

'No, not really. The hunt was fun, but Eddie can keep his family heirloom. Until a few weeks ago I didn't know it existed. To be honest, I'm still a bit sore Henry decided to keep it a secret from me.'

'And I was brought along...'

'For protection. And because I like and trust you.'

'Well thanks... but what about this Mr Bennett. Wasn't that his job?'

Mary winced a little and curled her mouth into an odd shape.

'He was my attempt at an extra level of protection for both of us.'

'But was as much use as a chocolate fireguard,' agreed Danny gloomily, 'I never even saw him.'

'Oh he was about. I saw him parked up outside Jilly's house, but I get the impression he's used to watching out for philandering husbands, rather than taking a bullet for a fifty-three-year-old woman and a racehorse trainer trying to track down a gemstone.'

'Does this mean you're keeping the horse in training, and staying involved in the yard, or do you need to sell up and get out?'

Mary noticed Danny was nervously scratching the side of his jeans again, so she thumped her palm on the steering wheel. She hoped it would signal her commitment.

'You don't get rid of me that easily! I've still got eighty-thousand pounds, less the cost of a windscreen, to get through from my win, and I'm going to spend it on something I care about. I promised my dad. And I'd like to keep helping out with the yard, if you'll still have me. You know all about me and my family history, there's no more secrets to tell. And you now know about my lack of long-term funds.'

'I'm glad. This morning has been one of the weirdest I've ever had,' Danny said in a relieved voice, 'You have to be one of the... strangest ladies I've ever met. I'm not bothered about your family secrets. I had five foster families and all of them had secret stuff that would make your toes curl. I'd love you to stay around as long as you can.'

There was a pause during which both of them stared straight ahead at the dual carriageway, Mary contemplating whether she was strange, and Danny wondering whether he'd said too much. Eventually, Mary gave a dry sniff.

'You're right, we've had a hell of a day so far. Let me make it up to you,' she said brightly, 'Will you allow me to treat you?'

Danny gave Mary a quizzical look.

'I've also got an idea which might help fill the rest of the boxes in the yard before the season starts.'

That evening Danny returned to the yard with a host of new clothes including two new lounge suits, complete with shoes, shirts and ties. On the drive home, Mary had shared her 'idea' with him which turned out, with a few modifications, to be a startlingly decent one. It seemed Mary the teacher and accountant, was also adept at marketing.

Danny examined his face in the bathroom mirror that night, running his fingers through his fringe. Mary had also talked him into trying a new hairstyle. His shoulder length locks had been left in Newcastle. The newest young trainer in Malton now sported a short, neat cut. It was the best, and definitely the most expensive haircut he'd ever had. And he loved it.

'I've got the look, and I've got the horses,' he told his shaving mirror, 'All I need now are the results on the track.'

Twenty-Two

Mary would never have imagined that standing in a windswept field in March, up to her ankles in mud, could be so exhilarating. Yet here she was at the top of the Wolds at seven forty-five in the morning, waiting for her young racehorse to complete a piece of work which would determine whether he was ready to go racing in a few weeks time. With the bulk of his two-year old's prep work completed, Danny had invited her to join him and see how Jake, and her filly went during their first full racing pace workout over five furlongs.

Naming her two youngsters had been both interesting and frustrating. Many of her preferred names had been rejected because they'd already been the names of racehorses in the past. However, Jake had been given the racing name 'Lucky Jake' and the nervous filly acquired from the Lilleys' would compete with the name 'Gentle Jill'. According to Danny, it had required painstaking work to get her backed and ridden away, and as he'd expected, the young filly had proved to be extremely skittish, although George Lilley's assertion she was a 'wobbler' had proved incorrect, due to a growth spurt that had seen her put on bone and significant muscle.

The filly's mistrust meant she would turn away and stand at the back of her stable if a stranger approached, but made good progress once she'd been to the gallops a few times and realised what her real job entailed. Juliet rode her gallop work and Danny was always on hand when they were teaching her anything new, such as stalls work. Mary wasn't surprised to hear from Juliet that he was able to cast a blanket of calm over the filly when he dealt with her.

It transpired the stable staff's hard slog to bring the youngsters up to speed had proven worthwhile. In the first week of March Danny announced Gentle Jill had impressed him on the grass gallop, and Lucky Jake had covered three furlongs on the uphill stretch of the All-Weather gallop in thirty-six seconds. When Mary questioned the significance of this timing, Danny excitedly informed her it meant the gelding had a decent engine and should be more than capable of winning races if he continued on his upward curve.

Charlie sat on the long grass at Mary's heel, shivering every now and again when the late March wind whipped up and increased the chill factor. He looked up at Mary when she stamped her feet, hopeful they were heading back to the car. He looked away again when it became obvious she was concentrating on the four dark blurs at the bottom of the All-Weather gallop.

Beside Mary, Danny was holding his mobile phone out in front of him, concentrating on the small screen, keen to catch the four horses on video over their last two furlongs, for review back at the stables.

'Who are my horses working with?' asked Mary.

'Ivor is up front; he's there as a yardstick against the youngsters and also to lead them up. He's a solid seventy horse. Don't worry if he beats your two out of sight. You'd expect that at this time of the year. Lucky Jake will work with him and Gentle Jill is working with the cheap filly I bought when we were at Doncaster. She's stayed on the small side, but I've found an owner for half of her.'

The four horses were no more than dots at the bottom of the dog-leg gallop and disappeared out of sight behind bushes for a few seconds. When they emerged from a tight corner, the front two had kicked off into a strong gallop. They were followed by the second duo fifty yards behind. A furlong later, the front two entered a sweeping left-hand turn and straightened up for the straight four furlongs up the hill, climbing about thirty feet in the process.

'Ivor is leading, with Lucky Jake on his outside, and the two fillies are stride for stride in behind,' Danny called through the wind.

Mary narrowed her eyes against the stiff breeze, determined not to miss a single stride made by any of the horses. Seconds later, both sets of horses had stormed past her. The dull thumps made as their hooves hit the sand of the All-Weather surface faded away as they reached the top of the gallop.

'How did they go?' she asked, slightly frustrated that trying to follow the progress of both her youngsters had proved to be impossible, 'I know Ivor pulled a little clear.'

'Yes, but he was working hard,' Danny explained as they turned their backs to the wind and started to walk towards the four horses that were returning down the dirt track towards them.

'Jake was caught out when Ivor quickened, but when they hit the rising ground he stuck his head down and was able to go with him. I'm delighted with that.'

'What about the other two?'

'The small filly is still pretty backward. She's going to need more time. When you see the video back you'll see she couldn't get into a rhythm at pace. Gentle Jill was surprisingly good though. I liked the way she picked up. You wanted a run for your money, and for three grand, that's what you're going to get. She's not got a turn of pace like Jake yet, but she tries hard and is growing in confidence. She just needs to muscle up a bit more.'

'So, I've a good one, and a moderate one,' Mary stated matter-of-factly.

Danny chuckled, 'It's still very early days. These three are just babies. With the budget you and I had, finding a horse capable of winning *any* race, even a lowly seller, would be an achievement, and I think you've already got that in Jake.'

Mary nodded in agreement, 'And we were lucky to get him in the end.'

'Yes, I suppose in a weird way we have Adrian Fitzpatrick and Jonnie Lilley to thank for my best two-year-olds this season! Your breeder chap, Rory, will be pleased when he sees how well Jake runs in his first few maidens. It'll add value to his mare.'

'He's not my chap,' Mary said absentmindedly.

Danny glossed over her comment, aware Mary had been very quiet about her trip to the Eider.

'George is going to be spitting feathers when he realises he's gifted us a nice horse,' he noted.

Jonnie Lilley had not put in an appearance recently, partially due to a new seven foot fence his father had erected against the short wall dividing the two yards, but also because Jonnie hadn't been seen on the yard or at the gallops for a few weeks. The talk among the stable lads was that he had gone to live with his mother after arguing with George, following the whipping incident.

'If I'd met you a little earlier, I'm sure we would have bought Gentle Jill anyway, so I think it's fair enough we ended up with her. After all, I understand George Lilley only bought her to spite you for leaving and taking Juliet with you.'

'Who told you that?'

'Rory overheard George trying to bully you at the sales.'

Danny's stride shortened, his head bowed. Eventually both of them were standing still. Mary waited expectantly.

'I feel responsible for Jonnie going off the rails. I've known him for five years and I knew he was never in love with racing. I reckon he only stayed around the yard for his dad. He was frustrated, I think. George is a decent enough chap, but he is blinkered when it comes to Jonnie, and when his wife left...'

'Now, you wait just a minute,' Mary cut in sternly, 'Don't go blaming yourself for the Lilley's problems. That lad has a mean streak and was brutal with that filly.'

Danny didn't answer immediately. It only came out rarely, but Mary's teacher voice was sharp, and unerringly correct. He cast his eyes toward Charlie, who was watching the two of them with his head cocked to one side as if contemplating the situation.

'One of the Lilley's lads told me Jonnie's giving up racing. I might go round and see if I can have a word with George, to smooth things over. What do you think?'

'A good working relationship with your next door neighbour

would be much better than a bad one, but I'm not too sure he'll listen. He strikes me as a rather narrow-minded man.'

The four horses were fast approaching and Mary and Danny resumed walking towards them.

'But that shouldn't stop you trying,' Mary added, after becoming aware she had come across as unnecessarily negative.

Danny discussed the horses' work with each of the riders, picking up on the nuances of each concerning their galloping style, pointers towards their ideal racing distance and level of fitness. A few minutes later the foursome turned to complete their walk down the hill and the fifteen minute trek over rolling hills back to the yard. Danny and Mary jumped into a small twelve-year-old Renault, recently bought for a few hundred pounds expressly for ferrying owners to and from the gallops.

The Renault turned into the downhill lane a few minutes later with Danny running through possible races for Jake and Jill in the next four to six weeks. Caught up in their discussion, Danny turned into the yard and almost ran into the back of the police car that had been left parked sideways a few feet into the yard entrance.

'What the...?' Danny exclaimed, and was immediately out of the car and striding purposefully into his yard. He found Graham waiting beside a uniformed police officer, both of whom were displaying concern. Relief spread through Graham's features once he caught sight of Danny.

'Sorry Guv, we couldn't get hold of you on the gallops...'

'That's okay, Graham, what's going on?' asked Danny as he scanned the stables for any signs of a problem.

'It ain't the horses, Guv. It's the farmhouse. I think you've been burgled.'

***

It was early afternoon by the time Mary thanked the last police representative and watched them pull out of the yard. She met Danny back in the farmhouse and together they started to clean up the mess.

'That plain clothes chap knew they were searching for something, that's why he was spending so much time questioning you,' Mary pointed out.

'I didn't say anything about your... treasure hunt,' Danny replied, stooping to recover a crumpled copy of *Owner Breeder* magazine from the floor of his sitting room.

'You could have told them.'

'It would have complicated everything. Anyway, I think the police were more worried about the two men in the lane outside arguing and one of them pulling out a knife. I've sent Graham home, by the way; he was a

116

bit shaken up. More by all the questions the police were firing at him than the experience of seeing two blokes arguing.'

'He said one of them drove off and left the other behind?'

'That's right, in a silver car. He didn't get a good look at either of them. The one with the knife was tall, and the other short, but that's not much for the police to go on. Graham looked through the trees to see what all the shouting was about and once he saw the knife come out he backed off and called the police. Both men were gone by the time they arrived.'

'I assume he didn't see who entered the house?'

'No. The door was open as usual and anyone could have slipped in while Graham was mucking out. He was the only person on the yard because we'd all gone up the gallops. Whoever it was must have been watching for when we left and waited for Graham to do the stables facing the paddocks. You can't see the farmhouse from there.'

Mary surveyed the room once more, 'You're absolutely sure there's nothing missing?'

'Yeah, I'm sure. I suppose it's a good job I've got nothing worth nicking!'

Danny and Mary worked through the house. It didn't take long to put things right; Danny didn't own a great deal. It was mainly rugs, carpets and the odd poster or picture that needed attention. Upstairs in his bedroom, Danny looked across the room to where a loose floorboard lay, exposing a matrix of dusty cobwebs.

'I can't for the life of me understand why they would think I was hiding anything under the floor,' he muttered, placing the board back into place.

'That board is shorter than the rest, and has a cut in it,' Mary stated from over his shoulder, 'My guess is they were searching anywhere that looked like it might hide a small tin.'

Mary had thought of little else during the time the police were at the yard. The lack of obvious items going missing like Danny's television, iPod or the office computer ruled out any standard thief. This was a search for something specific. That's why the police had spent so much time questioning Danny.

'I reckon the police thought I was hiding drugs or money,' he told Mary over a coffee in the kitchen once the clean-up was complete, 'As if *I've* got a stash of money!'

'I know exactly how much money you have,' Mary replied lightly, 'And as you suspect, you've nothing spare.'

'I think it means your brother-in-law hasn't found that Stone,' Danny said with a heavy sigh following a moment of silent reflection by both of them. Mary was impressed; she hadn't imagined Danny would be thinking along the same lines as herself.

'Yes, it does look a rather desperate effort though. It's not really Eddie's style. I thought he was far more professional.'

Danny took a sip of his coffee and a grin started to grow across his face.

'What?' Mary enquired.

'Are we going to search for the Stone ourselves?'

'Whoah! Holster your guns there, partner. For one thing, I've not seen Vinny since our day in the North East and for another, we don't have a copy of the letter, and more importantly, the cipher. For all we know this could just be a bungled burglary and two thieves arguing when they didn't find anything worth stealing.'

'I've been thinking about that cipher,' Danny said in a low voice over the brim of his coffee, 'What if we *did* have a copy of the letter?'

Danny watched Mary's eyes narrow and a frown develop, 'You remember the woman in Cullercoats... What was her name, Jane?'

'Jilly,' Mary corrected.

'Yes, Jilly. She wanted a photo of you and her together. I took a bunch of shots on my phone and sent them to her by email. Well, look at this...'

Danny turned his mobile phone toward Mary and she peered at a photo of a beaming Jilly and a rather less excited image of herself, standing together in the young mother's kitchen.

She shot Danny a blank look, 'Sorry, I think I'm missing something.'

Danny groaned, took the phone back and swiped the screen a few times, using two fingers to enlarge the image.

'There!' he said triumphantly, holding the phone up to Mary again, 'Jilly was holding the letter up for the camera in a couple of the photos, and look, my phone is so clever you can actually read it when you zoom in!'

Mary squinted at the small screen and sure enough, the lines of text, and most importantly, the lines of the cipher could just be made out.

Twenty-Three

By the time Mary returned to her cottage, it was early evening. She and Danny had spent another two hours discussing the pros and cons of pursuing the Stone and had even had a crack at trying to break the cipher, but found it difficult to make any real progress. The question uppermost in Mary's mind was whether it was sensible to even embark on another Stone hunt.

She had stayed around the farmhouse into the late afternoon, doing a bit of work on the business accounts while Danny went next door to try and smooth things over with George Lilley. He'd come back a much happier man. It had taken a few minutes for George to thaw, but he had accepted the olive branch and grudgingly admitted Jonnie had been out of order.

'He mentioned you,' Danny told her when recounting his visit, 'George reckons you're a force to be reckoned with and I'm lucky to have you on my side!'

Mary wasn't so sure, but accepted Danny's report as a positive step forward. Jonnie had unexpectedly shown his face, although Danny hadn't spoken with him. Appearing at the kitchen door, Jonnie recoiled when he saw who his father was speaking with, immediately turning on his heel.

'He looked... scared,' Danny said when reflecting on this brief glimpse of Jonnie. Regardless, Danny had left the Lilley's yard in good spirits and returned with a spring in his step. George also accepted an invitation to their Fire Engine Day, the marketing idea Mary had discussed with Danny on the way back from their Newcastle trip.

With her head full of the burglary, her horses, Eddie Romano, and the Fire Engine Day, Mary absent-mindedly pulled into her drive, switched the Volvo's engine off and sat still for a few seconds, thinking about her day. The only sound was from Charlie in the back, providing a soft whine that signalled he was keen to get out and be served his supper.

The cottage was dark and Mary suppressed a strong urge to reverse out of the drive and go back to Malton, or even to one of her friends' houses in Northallerton. Without any solid reason for doing so, she rose up in her seat a few inches and peered down the row of small front gardens. Everything was normal, right down to the twitch of Bert's curtains as he checked her out. It actually helped; that touch of normality.

Mary approached her front door with only one thing other than her keys in her hand; Charlie's lead. The Pointer sniffed around the front door and sat, licking his lips in anticipation of receiving his supper. Mary peeked in through the bay window and found her front room untouched, just as it was when she'd left early that morning. Everything seemed normal. There was no sign of a break in.

Standing still with her key in the door, there was only silence from inside the house, which was in marked contrast to her own heart, which was pounding so loudly Mary imagined Bert would be able to hear it from next door. She shook her head, and told herself to stop being so jittery. It had been a long day and the burglary had put her on edge. It was as simple as that. She'd soon have Charlie fed, some food prepared, and she might even run herself a bath later.

Pulling in a deep, silent breath she turned the key and she and Charlie entered the cottage, immediately flicking the hall light on. Again, everything looked perfectly normal.

With a sigh of both relief and a small chuckle at her over-active imagination, she let Charlie off his lead and hung her coat up on the end of the stairs. The dog headed straight for the kitchen door and Mary's pulse quickened as Charlie's fur stood on end as he sniffed up and down the closed kitchen door. He soon began to paw at the door, growling in a low, menacing tone. He stared up at Mary, standing statue-like, imploring her to let him into the kitchen.

'Alright,' she told Charlie, 'Wait.'

She backed away from the kitchen and grabbed one of Henry's old walking sticks still leaning up in the corner beside the front door, returned to Charlie and placed a hand on the kitchen door knob.

With a single twist Mary flung the door open and Charlie bolted through. He growled and let off a subdued bark. Mary followed him through, brandishing the walking stick above her head and in a loud voice issued a largely unintelligible threat. Her hand went straight to the light switch on the wall and she readied her stick for a slash at anything that moved.

The strip light slowly flickered into life, providing a few bursts of retina burning flashes before slowly becoming a dull yellow glow. It finally stuttered into life with a ping, revealing nothing exceptional. She followed Charlie, as he traversed every corner of kitchen with his nose clamped to the floor and realising she was holding her breath, Mary closed her eyes, and breathed out.

'Are you ready for me?' a scathing voice whispered above Mary's right shoulder. The man was so close she had heard a soft click as his jaw opened in readiness to speak. Jumping forward in fright, Mary spun around, wildly flailing with the walking stick, sending it singing through cool, empty air.

Eddie Romano was leaning languidly against the door frame, one hand in his trouser pocket, the other holding the jacket he'd slung over his shoulder. He lazily watched Mary as she took up a side-on stance, the end of her walking stick pointing at him as if they were about to duel with swords. He languidly examined the tin tip hovering a few inches from his chest.

'You said you'd always be ready for me,' he challenged.

Charlie had been eying Mary for the past few seconds and belatedly announced his dislike of Eddie by placing himself between the two of them, tensing, and growling in a low register.

Eddie grinned humourlessly down at the dog, baring his own teeth in response to Charlie's quivering upper lip. He feinted to the left and aimed a kick at the dog but Charlie was too quick, deftly moved out of range and clacked his jaws together as he attempted to take a bite at the swinging foot.

Mary steadied herself, her focus entirely on her unwelcome guest. She considered screaming; Bert next door would be sure to hear her. Or should she run? It was her curiosity that won the day.

'What do you want?' Mary demanded, finally finding her voice.

Eddie laughed, feigning a couple of quick movements for no other purpose than to bate Charlie. He took a step forward and received a prod from the end of Mary's stick.

'What the...' he remonstrated, 'I've come here to *speak to you*. I know you've lost the instructions for recovering the Stone.'

Mary renewed her grip on the walking stick whilst furiously attempting to analyse Eddie's response.

'Vinny was watching us at the coast?' she murmured, wondering how many people must have been following Danny and herself around Whitley Bay and Cullercoats.

'Of course! It's what we do. You're out of your depth, Mary, so you better listen to what I've got to say.'

Mary tried to level her breathing. She had to get this right. Whatever forces had brought Eddie to her, she had to play her hand to its maximum potential. She took a moment to assess the watchful man in front of her. He was surprisingly well toned for a man of fifty. It seemed Eddie had taken care of himself over the years, and enjoyed holidays in the sun if the tan on his face and hands was anything to go by.

'Are you willing to listen?' Eddie enquired petulantly.

'Why should I? You're of no interest to me. All you ever do is threaten me. Your threats meant Henry and I had to leave the North East. You threatened me at my husband's funeral, and Vinny threatens me every time he pops up!'

Eddie didn't answer immediately, thinking through his next response. When he spoke, it was with a careful touch of resigned regret.

'Threats and intimidation become part of who you are in my line of work. Vincent is the same. It's difficult to switch them off when you're a debt collector.'

He paused, pleased with the confused expression his little remark had caused. Taking a sideways step, he placed his jacket onto the kitchen units, and to the sound of Charlie's insistent growl, leaned his backside against them and crossed his arms, as if settling himself for a longer conversation. He stared at the dog, imagining for a second what it would feel like to give it a good, hard kick, and tried hard not to smirk.

Mary appraised Eddie carefully, seeking meaning from this change of tack. Despite her initial shock having subsided, she was still pointing the end of her walking stick his way. Eddie's relaxed attitude was unnerving, and the stick was a helpful reminder that she was alone with a potentially dangerous man. She told herself that should things go the wrong, one loud scream would have her neighbours running.

Eddie ran the opening lines of his pre-prepared speech through his mind and adopted what he hoped was a slightly conciliatory tone.

'I'm not going to waste time pretending I can forgive you for Pa's death,' Eddie started, waiting a few seconds for Mary to process his opening statement.

'Put your little stick down and *listen*, Mary,' Eddie continued insistently. He waited, holding her gaze until she capitulated with an irritated sigh.

'I need you to save a little girl's life.'

Twenty-Four

Mary hadn't believed Eddie at first, then as the rabbit hole deepened, was filled with uncertainty, and finally, became determined to learn more. Everything he had explained fitted neatly and gave a very real, positive reason for him to wish to uncover the Stone. But, this was Eddie Romano, and rather like Charlie's way of handling the man, Mary was careful not to be drawn in too close for fear of being caught out.

Eddie's story had started with a surprise, leading to further astonishment; 'Pa was a thief,' was what he opened with, and the rest came tumbling behind.

'He was a petty thief over in Italy after the war,' Eddie told her, 'Ma knew all about it, she actually helped him and even got involved in jobs on some occasions. It was nothing big though, he was simply good at picking locks and squeezing through windows.'

The twenty-five year old Joe Romano had been doing very well for himself, executing a string of successful burglaries until he unintentionally stole the Stone Of Shiazzano. He broke into a mansion in the south of the country and thought he'd hit the jackpot when stumbling small, intricate gold brooch with a large ruby at its centre. In fact, this piece of jewellery would be responsible for ensuring the Romano's left Italy and headed for England.

'It turned out the mansion was owned by an associate of the Mafia. When Pa tried to move the Stone on, things got ugly and he and Ma had to pack and get out fast,' Eddie reported, 'In a way, the Stone is the reason you met Henry. Otherwise, Pa would never have left Italy.'

'He chose Newcastle at random from a list of ports in England and they jumped on a ship. When he got here he used the Stone as security against a loan on a house and the restaurant business. That's what Henry and his business partner, Adam, used it for. Pa didn't trust banks and he didn't want to have the Stone in the house with us kids around, so he got his best friend to hold it for him. Henry realised what Pa was saying in hospital... I didn't make the connection.'

Mary detected a hint of sadness and possibly regret in Eddie's rendition of this chapter in his family history. Eddie was either a devoted family man, or a hell of a good liar. She was pretty sure the latter was more likely.

Mary's eyes widened as Eddie started to peel the layers from her husband's working life. He told her Henry worked for Adam, but according to Eddie, Henry had used the Stone to set up the finance for Adam's company.

'After Pa died, Henry recovered the Stone. There was no way to sell it, as would have led straight back to him and probably a prison term for handling stolen goods. Besides, it was worth far too much, the legitimate jewellery trade would never have touched it.'

'How much is it worth?' Mary queried.

Eddie twitched his nose and shuffled his shoulders, ending the motion by massaging the back of his neck. Mary had picked up that this was one of Eddie's stalling techniques, so stared intently until he answered.

'As kids, Pa would get the Stone out every now and again. The ruby is about an inch across and is Burmese, so it's among the purest in the world. In the seventies Pa said it was worth half a million pounds.'

'And now?' Mary prompted.

'I don't know, I'd be guessing,' Eddie said levelly, 'But you can see that the Stone is valuable enough for someone who knows about it to befriend you in the hope you'll lead them to it.'

'Including yourself,' Mary stated pointedly.

Eddie grimaced, 'I have no wish to be your friend. I'll come on to why I need the Stone.'

'So if it isn't you following me around, banging my car with baseball bats and breaking into my trainer's farmhouse, who is?'

'I don't know anything about break-ins or baseball bats. Sure, I admit Vincent has been keeping tabs on you, but Adam East is involved in this somehow,' said Eddie positively, 'He knows about the Stone and its value.'

Mary mulled this over and decided it made a modicum of sense. If the Stone had been used to keep Adam's company afloat as Eddie propounded, he had to know of the Stone's existence and its potential value. Yet Adam had told her he didn't know anything about the Stone when she'd spoken with him at Christmas.

'I've met Adam recently. He didn't seem to have any money worries, in fact, quite the reverse.'

'The man struts around like a peacock. Everything is always wonderful according to Adam East,' Eddie said sourly. He'd allowed some of his spite to rise to the surface and Mary watched in fascination as Eddie shivered, regrouped, and continued in a mellower vein.

'When the recession hit, East's business suffered more than most. From what I hear, that Stone's power to raise cash saved him from going under. Perhaps he's still paying his debt off, or maybe he can't afford to be without it...' Eddie left his suggestion hanging for a few seconds before continuing, '...however, I have a very personal reason to be pursuing the Stone, and it concerns someone who is dear to me.'

'Really?' asked Mary, reacting with a little too much sarcasm in her tone.

Eddie eyed her balefully, 'It may come as a shock, but my life continued once you disappeared and Henry disowned me,' he said in rebuke.

'I have a family,' he added defiantly.

Mary didn't react, remaining stoic in response.

Eddie sniffed, pushing his head back against a cupboard.

'I still live in the family house,' he announced deliberately endowing his words with as much gravitas as he could muster, 'I never married... I had no compunction to share my life with a woman. Vincent needed somewhere to live, so he moved into the top floor. It's a big house, and he is a generous house guest. We've never had a cross word in thirty years.'

Probably because he's a little weasel who sucks up to you all the time, Mary thought.

'However, eight years ago our little arrangement changed...' Eddie continued, switching his gaze to Mary's legs and slowly sliding them up until he settled on her face.

'... Vincent had a baby girl, and she lives with us.'

This news did elicit a response from Mary. Eddie was pleased to see her mouth fall a little open and a hand rise to rub her chin thoughtfully.

'To my complete surprise, I found myself utterly enthralled by this addition to our household. Emily is now eight years old and she has transformed my view of the world,' Eddie stated with a mixture of pleasure and triumph.

Mary frowned, 'This is all very illuminating. However, you'll have to forgive me for not going all gooey inside. I can't see how Vinny's little girl has anything to do with you breaking into my house.'

'Read this,' he said, producing an envelope from his trouser pocket and holding it out. I received it two weeks ago. That's why I'm here, *that's* what I came to discuss with you.'

Mary stepped forward and snatched the envelope and withdrew three thin pieces of paper.

'I'll save you the bother of reading them, it's a threat against Emily's wellbeing, and in return for her safety, the blackmailer requires me, and therefore *you*, to solve Henry's riddle.'

'I don't suppose you'll consider making me a cup of tea?' he added hopefully.

Mary was through reading the first page and shook her head before continuing onto the second. The letter was stark, and the demand was exactly as Eddie had outlined; either the location of the Stone was provided or the girl would be targeted. The letter didn't say how or when.

Eddie groaned and set off talking again, but Mary wasn't listening. Concentrating on the letter, there was one phrase that had leapt from the page, and she kept returning to it: '...or an injury will befall your child.' Mary said the word 'befall' several times in her head. Where had she heard that word before, perhaps recently? It was so old-fashioned; who did she know that would use such a word?

'... and of course it's obvious from Henry's letter that only you can solve the riddle,' Eddie finished off, peering down at her. 'Mary? Are you listening to me?'

'How do I know you aren't just making all this up?' she queried after a pause. She was inspecting the third page, which was a copy of Henry's cipher letter. She placed the papers back in the envelope, and levelled her eyes expectantly back onto her unwanted house guest.

Eddie rotated his neck around in circles. Mary heard it crack on the second revolution and shuddered. Another delaying tactic, she thought.

'I'm getting my mobile out,' he said eventually.

'Why?'

' I'm going to introduce you to Emily.'

Twenty-Five

An image of Vincent standing in front of a wooden door surrounded by purple coloured wallpaper coalesced on Eddie's mobile phone. He greeted Mary with a rapturous smile. She acknowledged his pixelated face with a slight inclination of her head.

Eddie was holding the device out at arm's length as Mary had refused to take the phone for fear she couldn't keep an eye on him. Charlie sat attentively at Mary's ankle.

Vincent grinned at her and Mary got the strangest feeling there was a nervousness lurking behind his over-the-top welcome.

Following Eddie's insistence, he'd placed a call to Vincent, who in turn would introduce Mary to his daughter, Emily. Eddie was watching Mary carefully, smiling indulgently as he listened to Vincent's welcome.

'So where is she?' Mary asked.

She maintained a stern, businesslike expression and reminded herself that these two debt collectors *needed her* to find the Stone for them, so she *should* be safe... and tried to ignore how risky that sounded.

Vincent's grin widened and the picture bounced around as climbed a turning staircase to the first floor where he entered a large square room with high ceilings and ornate plasterwork. It certainly looked like the Victorian family house she had visited with Henry. For a few seconds the phone's camera was pointed downwards onto a thick beige carpet. Vincent's boots brushed through it as if he was walking through grass. He approached a ring of furniture facing an open fire and a huge, wall mounted television screen.

'Emily?' Vincent called.

A shrill shout of 'Here!' was returned and a petite, lean girl wearing be-jewelled jeans and a t-shirt emblazoned with a teddy bear, jumped up from one of the sofa's and came running right up to Vincent's camera.

'I've got someone here who wants to speak with you,' Vincent told his daughter from behind his phone.

The girl placed a thumbnail in her mouth and gripped it in her front teeth, shyly proffering a wave to Mary.

'Emily?' Vincent scolded gently. She looked away from the camera with wide eyes.

'Hello, I'm Emily,' she said sweetly whilst rolling her eyes at her father, 'I know how to say hello!'

Suitably chastened by his plucky young charge, Vincent ploughed on, maintaining his light tone.

'Mary wants to speak with you. That's why you've been allowed to stay up late,' Eddie informed Emily, 'I want you to tell her what happened on the road outside the house the other day for me. Is that okay?'

Emily nodded theatrically, still looking off camera, 'The silly man?'

'Yes, that's right, I want you to tell Mary about the silly man,' Eddie replied like an echo.

Emily fell silent and scrunched her eyes up.

'He wanted to take me in his car, but I wouldn't let him,' the girl announced proudly.

'That's right, you did exactly the right thing. Can you tell Mary...'

'Will I get a treat now?' Emily broke in, her smile evaporating to be replaced with a frown.

'Emily... Yes, of course. But tell Mary, what did this silly man look like and how did he make you feel?' Vincent prompted.

The image on Eddie's phone jiggled around for a moment. When the correct resolution returned, Emily's face was set in concentration and hugging herself, she unconsciously scratched her arm.

'I didn't like him. He didn't smile and he shouted at me when I wouldn't go with him, so I ran back to my house.'

The girl paused, concentrating, 'He had really big feet and shiny shoes... I can show you.'

With that, she launched herself backwards and started to waddle up and down, feet at ninety degree angles, her socks leaving long streaks in the thick carpet.

'So he was like a clown?' Mary suggested.

Emily stopped waddling and thought again.

'Mmm... A bit. His face was fat and he dressed like Uncle Eddie.'

'He was wearing a suit,' Eddie explained quietly. He couldn't see what was playing out up in his lounge in Newcastle, but the call had served its purpose. The eight-year-old had done her job perfectly if Mary's face was anything to go by.

The little girl continued to play act, the video jerkily following her as she crossed the large room. Mary watched for a few seconds, transferred her attention to Eddie when she sensed he was watching her too attentively.

'Thanks for that Vincent, and of course you Emily,' Eddie called out once their eyes met, 'I think it's time for Emily to go to bed.'

From the phone the sound of a young girl's disappointment rang out across Mary's kitchen.

***

'So will you find the Stone for me so I can protect Emily?'

It was the third time Eddie had asked this question. Again, she ignored him. She was still piecing together his story and trying to come to terms with the possibility that a young girl's life could now be at stake. His claims might possibly explain why Vincent, as Emily's father, was so interested in tracking the Stone's whereabouts down. But could she really believe Eddie was so attached to Emily he would forfeit a valuable family heirloom? Eddie's disregard for all people, unless they were fawning over him as Vincent did, made it extremely difficult for her to accept. It struck Mary that at the age of eight, perhaps the girl was like her father, and also believed Eddie was wonderful...

'Are you going to answer me?' Eddie challenged with a frustrated growl.

'Let me make sure I have this right,' Mary said, her head low and thoughtful, 'There are people out there who know about this Stone, and they are willing to threaten a little girl in order to secure it. They attacked me, and my trainer to acquire the instructions for finding the Stone.'

Eddie made to interject, but Mary held up a hand to indicate she wasn't finished.

'After a fortnight of trying to break Henry's code, they decide to send the instructions to you. Why not cut out the middle man and come straight to me?'

Eddie's chin dropped to his chest and he started to chew on the inside of his cheek, 'I don't know. I have my suspicions, but I'm in the dark on their reasoning.'

'Or you didn't realise the flaw in the concocted story you decided to spin to me today?'

Eddie had been leaning against the kitchen units for fifteen minutes now, but this comment pushed him to a standing position.

'We think word has got around organised crime in Newcastle,' he said quickly.

'What does that mean?'

'The letter, Henry's letter. Whoever took the letter has sold it to the highest bidders among the various groups that run crime around the North East. I'm guessing one of them couldn't interpret Henry's instructions and thought I could,' Eddie stated forlornly, 'But of course I can't... but you can.'

Mary glanced at the letter laid on her counter top, 'What makes you think that?'

'Henry says so!' Eddie exclaimed, 'It's there in black and white. He says you will be able to crack the code. My blackmailer is getting me to do his dirty work. I get you to tell me where the Stone is, I find the Stone, give it to them, and in return they'll leave Emily alone.'

'But I've seen the instructions, they were gibberish. Besides, if

Henry wanted me to have the Stone, why didn't he simply leave it to me in his will?'

'He was protecting you! ' Eddie replied indignantly, 'It's a *stolen* jewel. He used it more than once to raise capital to fund Adam East's business and he couldn't just waltz into a high street bank, slap it on the counter and ask for a loan.'

Eddie took a calming breath before continuing. Mary had backed off and Charlie's hair had risen on his back once more.

'That jewel is well known around the Newcastle criminal fraternity and Henry knew there would be a number of people who would start trying to get their hands on it, even before he had died. None of them knew about you until you pitched up at his funeral. And once you started spending wads of money on a racehorse they all leapt to the same conclusion I did – that you'd found the Stone.'

Mary slanted Eddie a look she hoped would signal she was unconvinced.

'So you're suggesting I have unknown criminals in Newcastle gunning for me, just because of this jewel, and I'm the only person who can work out where it's hidden?'

'Not all of them are unknown,' Eddie murmured, 'I'm pretty sure we know who is responsible for the threats against Emily.'

Eddie met Mary's gaze wearing a serious expression that demanded her attention.

'I wouldn't have involved you if it wasn't for Emily. She's far more important than a bit of stolen jewellery. I hoped by explaining everything, you'd realise Vincent and I don't want the Stone for ourselves. I'm sure Henry would have gladly given it over in return for her safety. We're asking for your help to find the Stone and protect a little girl's life.'

Mary eyed Eddie critically, searching for any indication he was lying.

'Who are these threats from then?'

Eddie licked his lips, 'Are you going to help?'

'Tell me who wants this Stone badly enough to hurt a little girl and I'll answer you,' Mary countered stiffly.

Eddie paused, glancing around the kitchen before returning to warily inspect Mary. She suddenly sensed an air of uncertainty about him. Eddie nervously rubbed his cheek on his shoulder before answering her question.

'He's called Yousef Amari.'

Twenty-Six

It was a little before ten o'clock when Mary was left standing on the ancient brick pavement outside her cottage with Bert at her side. She hadn't needed to scream at the top of her voice in order to elicit his help; he was already out of his front door and up her front path once she'd emerged from the cottage.

'Thank you for helping me, Bert. Sorry it's so late, it won't happen again.'

'Wasn't a problem,' he beamed, 'Your evening didn't work out with your new fella then?' he ventured, nodding in the direction Eddie had left.

'No, I'm afraid not,' she agreed, 'It didn't work out and I needed to get rid of him. Thanks for coming out.'

Mary had purposefully raised her voice once she and Charlie had stepped past Eddie and dashed out the front door, insisting he should leave by shouting the command back into the cottage from the front garden. She had relied on Bert listening out for her unwanted visitor to depart, and sure enough, he had immediately popped out of his house to see what all the commotion was about. A couple of the other doors on the terrace had also opened.

Eddie had emerged from the cottage and scowled at Mary. Ignoring Bert, he'd strolled to the top of the lane, and disappeared. Mary assumed he'd parked some distance away to ensure his surprise appearance wasn't spoiled.

It had dropped cold and Mary realised she was shivering. She wasn't sure whether she could bring herself to help Eddie and had told him so. His reaction had prompted Mary to force his exit. However, she was sure she was no longer safe on her own.

'I've decided to have a few days away, so the cottage will be empty,' she told Bert, 'Can you possibly keep an eye on the house for me whilst I'm away?'

Leaving Bert brimming with enthusiasm for his new role, Mary collected some essentials from the cottage and set off for Malton. Bert waved her off at half-past ten, promising to report any visitors, wanted or unwanted, whilst she was away.

Upon reaching the Cordike Stables she was relieved to find a light on in the farmhouse. The door opened before she had crossed the yard, spilling a warm, homely light onto her. For the first time in hours, Mary felt safe. Blinking back tears of relief she dropped Charlie's lead and he bounded over to Danny and then reacquainted himself with Milo.

Danny looked concerned, but didn't say anything as he took her bag and followed her into the sitting room.

'I'm so grateful,' Mary said quietly, 'I would have understood if you had said no.'

Danny looked at her as if she was crazy.

'I think you must be *really* tired,' he said warmly, 'You're making no sense at all. You'll always be welcome here. I've made up a bed for you in the spare room. Go on, get to bed, you look dog tired.'

Mary thanked him again and climbed the stairs, allowing Charlie to follow her. There wasn't a part of her body free from aches or pains and her forehead was thumping with every insistent heartbeat. She removed the photograph of her dad from her bag and propped him up on her bedside table, peeled off her clothes and got into bed. Charlie sprang up, twisted in circles, pawing at the bedclothes and finally flopped down and curled up. The last thing Mary remembered of that day was Danny humming a song, badly, under his breath as he climbed the stairs to bed.

**

Eddie's car purred up the A19. He'd driven in silence for the entire journey so far, delighting in his evenings work, replaying it in his head, and grinning at his success. The arrival of the blackmailing letter had been the catalyst for his plan; it couldn't have turned up at a better time. He wasn't bothered by some idiotic demand; he got them all the time in his line of work. Vincent may have taken it seriously, but he *knew* it was his enemies screwing with him, nothing more. Getting Emily to recount a fictitious meeting with a kidnapper in the street outside the house had been a nice touch on Vincent's part and arranging the burglary at her trainers stable earlier in the day had set the tone beautifully. He'd watched Mary arrive and enter her cottage. She'd been frightened even before he crept in behind her.

Eddie reflected on his performance at the cottage, and how he'd finally sold his predicament to the woman. When after numerous attempts she wouldn't commit to finding the Stone for him, his promise to conduct cruel retribution upon her friends had really shaken her up. Naming Barbara, Maisie, Sarah, Danny, and Juliet – whoever they were - one by one had been a master stroke. That was thanks to Vincent's detective work. It had been a delightful moment, knowing he had her cornered. The horror etched on her face had thrilled him.

Eddie drove on, happy in the knowledge he had Mary, the woman who had ruined his life, right where he wanted her; not only was she frightened, she had the fate of a young girl in her hands. He had never expected to gain her trust, which was why a combination of blackmail and threats had always been the plan.

The way the woman had got rid of him was evidence enough he

had terrified her. Involving her neighbours like that... he'd been ready to leave anyway. He could cope with that minor embarrassment, because the woman now had no other option; she had to lead him to the Stone after this encounter.

There was some serious competition in the race to acquire the Stone, but as of tonight, Eddie was convinced he was now strides ahead of them all.

Twenty-Seven

Mary woke to the sound of the front door of the farmhouse clicking shut at six-thirty. Twenty minutes later she was in the kitchen preparing breakfast and by the time Danny had done his morning walk round the yard and Juliet and Graham had arrived to start their day, the smell of grilling bacon, fried eggs, and freshly brewed coffee was wafting into the yard.

It felt good to cook for someone else. She'd found preparing a meal for one person an unfulfilling and sometimes depressive task in the last few months, opting for quick, simple meals eaten in front of the television instead of sitting at the table. Right up until a few weeks before Henry died, they continued to make the effort to sit down and eat together. Mary was even grateful for the mundane task of setting the kitchen table as it allowed her to focus on something other than the Stone of Shiazzano and how the wellbeing of a little girl may be dependent on her ability to crack a cipher.

'That smells good,' Graham commented as he led Danny and Juliet into the kitchen. Rarely a man of many words, Graham signalled most of his emotions via his hang-dog expression. Mary was pleased to see he was wearing an ear to ear grin.

'Where did this little lot come from?' asked Danny as Mary produced a serving plate full of bacon, sausages, black pudding, eggs, mushrooms and tomato for them to dip into.

'I brought a few things with me.'

'I hope you're staying for a while then!' Juliet exclaimed, spearing a sausage.

'On top of us having an unwelcome visitor in here yesterday, Mary went home to find someone inside her house...' Danny started.

There was gasp from Juliet, which he had anticipated, allowing a short pause.

'... although it turned out to be someone she knew. But while her locks are getting changed and her security is upgraded, she'll be spending a few days with us,' Danny explained.

This was accepted without question around the table. Mary had been wondering how to explain her sudden arrival at the yard and silently caught Danny's eye to express her thanks.

'Your Fire Engine day is this Sunday, so I, like, guess it'll mean you'll have more time to organise everything if you're here.'

Juliet's comment had the effect of making Mary's mind freeze for a few seconds as she ran through the long list of jobs the Fire Engine Day would require to make it a success. Amid the stress and revelations of the last twenty-four hours she'd forgotten there were only four days before the yard would host the local Fire Brigade and, hopefully, around eighty people. On the other hand, it could be a welcome distraction.

Danny was the last to leave the table after breakfast, hanging back to speak with Mary. She was clearly tired and he had noticed she had the same distracted air about her from the night before.

'You know you don't have to do the open day on Sunday,' he told her as they cleared the table together.

'Don't be silly,' she replied lightly, 'Besides, it's practically all sorted anyway, there's only a few things to organise.'

'Come on,' he told her, folding himself back into a kitchen chair and crossing his arms, 'Tell me what happened last night.'

Mary placed a couple of plates on the draining board and considered whether to share her situation with Danny. As she had listened to Eddie forcefully making his case after the video call she'd realised she had no wish to be on her own. She had phoned Danny immediately after ejecting Eddie from her cottage, having given him a shortened version of events. His offer to stay at the yard had been immediate.

She did have her friends in Northallerton. The strength of those relationships hadn't weakened during her three years looking after Henry, but even so, she doubted any of her three racing pals could help her in this situation. Sarah and Audrey had big families that were unlikely to cope with hardened criminals landing on the bonnets of their cars, and Maisie had a few health issues. Mary wasn't sure she could bring herself to plunge any of her friends and their families into the firing line. Despite only knowing him for a matter of months, Danny had been the first person she seriously considered asking for help.

'Okay, but I don't want you being involved any more than you already are,' she said, joining Danny at the table.

'Sod that! If it wasn't for you I'd have gone bust months ago. Whatever it is, we'll sort it.'

It took fifteen minutes for Mary to run through her story in more detail. Danny remained silent throughout. When she'd finished, closing with the news that Yousef Amari, the owner she had introduced into the yard, was in all probability a blackmailer, Mary leaned back in her chair and waited.

A minute of silence ticked away, during which Danny stared intently out of the window and hardly moved. It was dull outside, and the kitchen was filled with the quiet patter of a spring shower hitting the window pane and the roof.

Finally, Danny stirred.

'It sounds to me there could be any number of people after the Stone.'

Mary indicated she agreed, 'And I can't trust Eddie.'

'I'm glad you think so too. I wonder if we could check up on him, you know, see whether this Emily is actually Vinny's daughter.'

'It would help if we could find out if that blackmail letter was real as well,' Mary added, 'But I can't see how we can check either really.'

Danny watched Mary take another sip of her coffee.

'Isn't there a register that would at least tell us whether Vinny has ever had a daughter?'

Danny found himself staring blankly at her. He wanted to do far more; Mary had become still, as if a blanket of sadness had wrapped itself around her.

'I'm not sure it matters whether Emily is Vinny's or not. I don't know whether I can take the chance that she isn't in danger. I can't imagine how I'd feel if something happened to her...'

'Bloody hell,' Danny complained, slapping a palm on the kitchen table in exasperation, 'This... this *villain* has got you right where he wants you, hasn't he? You do nothing, you feel guilty. You give him the Stone, and you'll always wonder whether it was all a big con.'

Mary gave Danny a weak smile and got up to wash her empty coffee cup at the kitchen sink, 'I thought I'd go along with it and might get all these bloody men out of my hair. I suppose I did manage to get a decent copy of the letter and I'm in no immediate danger because Eddie now knows I have to be on his side.'

'Eddie may not be a danger to you at the moment, but I'm not so sure about everyone else who fancies having a shot at nicking the Stone for themselves,' Danny pointed out.

Mary scoured her mug and rinsed it vigorously, as if by doing so it would help wash away her worries.

'That blackmail letter looked horribly real and I doubt Eddie faked it. It certainly wasn't written by him. Emily came across as an intelligent little girl and she seemed genuinely scared when she told her story about the man who tried to kidnap her. I have a feeling she is being used as a pawn in a desperate race by a number of people to reach the Stone first.'

'If you go back to your cottage, is there anyone there to stay with you?' asked Danny.

Mary shook her head.

'That's settled then. You should stay here until we can find the Stone, or at least until you decide how you're going to deal with these people.'

Mary's immediate reaction was to intimate she couldn't possibly stay more than a day or two, but Danny quickly brushed her protests aside.

'It sounds like you have one or possibly two stalkers watching your every move.'

'They are probably watching us now,' he added, bowing his head toward the window.

Mary shivered. Danny was right, Vincent could be out there now. For a moment she imagined him hiding in the undergrowth on the other side of the paddocks with his binoculars trained on her. Another shiver of fear mixed with disgust trembled through her.

'If Eddie is to be believed, and you're the only person who can work out where the Stone is, you're going to be hounded until it's found, handed over, or destroyed,'

'I could do with that moment being as public as possible, so there's no doubt I don't have it anymore,' Mary admitted wearily.

Danny pushed his bottom lip up and out and began quietly humming something unintelligible.

'So... you need to find that Stone of... What was it again?'

'Shiazzano'

'Yes, that. I'll get some better locks on all the doors and windows and you can stay here until we can sort this out, one way or another.'

'I can't possibly...'

'You got anywhere better to go?'

Mary tried to conjure up an answer for a few seconds, knowing she would come up empty. She shrugged sadly at Danny.

'Then we're sorted,' Danny declared, standing up, 'You get on with finding the Stone. Meanwhile, I've a first lot to organise and ride out. Jake is due to have some stalls training and fast work today.'

With that, he strode out of the house. A moment later the front door opened again and Danny's grinning face appeared around the kitchen door.

'Excellent breakfast by the way. You made the farmhouse feel like... a home.'

Twenty-Eight

The Fire Brigade Day saw Danny Carter Training a hive of activity from five-thirty in the morning. Mary woke with a knot in her stomach that didn't disappear until noon, when she was relieved to find the Malton Fire Engine manoeuvring into place in the bottom paddock.

The idea had been a simple one, but grown to become complicated. It was brought about with Danny underestimating how long it would take to fill his equine pool. He'd roped an apprentice jockey from the Lilley's into helping him. A young, strip of a lad called Ewan had started riding work a few mornings for Danny and had jumped at the chance to earn some extra money labouring in the afternoons. It took the two of them the best part of a week to clean and patch up the outdoor pool so they could finally start adding water.

The filling of this mammoth hole near the paddock, supposedly the final and easiest of the tasks, had ended up being, frustratingly, the most challenging. Two weeks after completion, a hosepipe with limited pressure running night and day had only managed to fill the pool to twenty-percent capacity and Danny had glumly accepted that the notion of swimming his horses this season was a non-starter. Mary's solution had been to visit the Malton Fire Station.

The head of the two-vehicle outfit was close to retirement and had luckily taken a shine to Mary, although she soon realised she may have had an unfair advantage. The all-male staff seemed to be fans of rather buxom ladies, evidenced by the trio of topless calendars hung on the station walls, the Me Too movement not having reached this corner of Yorkshire just yet. Mary had to admit this was one physical asset she possessed in ample supply and her request for Terry to pop along and fill their pool had been accepted with his gaze firmly on her chest rather than her eyes.

'Of course we'll have to charge,' Terry had told her in as broad an East Yorkshire accent she'd ever heard, 'But I'm sure we can come to some arrangement,' he'd added with a comically suggestive but non-threatening wink. The arrangement they'd agreed upon consisted of Danny Carter Racing hosting a charity open day for Fire Engine funds. The highlights of the event would be tours of the yard, free hot dogs, the Fire Fighters' dumping gallons of water into Danny's pool from their biggest engine, and any excess water being sprayed onto a fifty metre long, ten metre wide slip and slide allowing the kids to slide down the paddock hill.

Mary need not have worried about a lack of people attending. A combination of good weather and last minute visits on Friday afternoon to the local schools with leaflets, meant that by two o-clock on Sunday, the yard was bursting at the seams with families enjoying the horses and kids crawling all over the fire truck. It turned out that Terry and his crew were decent entertainers, well drilled at keeping young children occupied with trying on their helmets and sitting at the wheel of the engine.

Sarah and Audrey, directed by Maisie, had given the yard a complete floral make-over. The yard's newly acquired hanging baskets and pots added a much-needed splash of colour. Danny complimented the ladies, telling them they'd done a 'bang-up job', and admitted the flowers lifted the stables.

It was two o-clock and almost time for Fireman Terry to fill the pool when Mary picked her way through about two hundred people in the main horseshoe of the stables. Danny was telling a group of about fifty people all about Jake, and Juliet was stood with Ivor, allowing people to pat and take photos with the horse. Ivor was in his element, loving every second of the adoration, standing motionless as the stroking hands rained down from every side. There was no need for box-walking today.

She'd half expected to see him, as all Danny's owners had been invited, but she still took a sharp intake of breath when Yousef Amari popped up in front of her.

'Mary! How lovely to see you. This is terrific,' he declared, passing a flat hand through the air so his gesture encompassed the whole yard.

'Good to see you as well Mr Amari, I'm so pleased you came to support us.'

'Oh, please call me Yousef. My horses are my pastime, my release from running my business, so first name terms today please. I am impressed with your little yard, but even more so with my new trainer. He is wowing his crowd and is a wonderful horseman. I am delighted with your recommendation.'

He's trying to be charming, Mary thought. It occurred to her that the man couldn't possibly generate a grin any wider. His neat black and silver beard bristled from the strain his facial muscles were under. Mary contemplated challenging him with a set of questions aimed to discover whether he was seeking the Stone Of Shiazzano, but quickly decided a confrontation here, among hundreds of onlookers was inadvisable.

'I'm so pleased you like the yard, Yousef,' she said sweetly, 'I understand one of your handicappers is set to race next week at Redcar.'

'Indeed,' Yousef replied, holding his arms close to his body, his hands resting on his ample stomach. Mary noticed his fingertips of each hand touched gently together as he spoke.

'It will be interesting to see whether the change of scenery and training regime has a positive impact,' Yousef added.

Mary tried to detect signs of insincerity but there was nothing to glean from his face or posture. Frustration started to build. Their conversation at Newcastle had been almost exclusively confined to her views on Danny and his training techniques and facilities. She knew little about Amari's business and private life beyond the fact he'd mentioned Henry had worked on his account, although quite what he'd done for Amari wasn't discussed. She'd intended to place her personal issues to one side today, but Mary found herself bursting to ask Amari pertinent questions whilst he was busy describing the chances of his runner in a few days time.

'Have you heard of the Stone Of Shiazzano?'

Amari abruptly stopped speaking mid-sentence and examined Mary curiously.

'Yes, of course,' he replied after a pause, 'In fact, my family provided your husband with a loan against it many years ago. Why do you ask?'

Amari fingertips had ceased drumming against each other over his stomach and were now locked together. It provided him with an air of a holy man and Mary found herself drawn to them as she considered his question.

'I'm having a problem locating it.'

Disguised behind a beatific smile, Amari's shrewd eyes drilled into Mary. She could feel them probing, assessing her with their dark brown irises.

'I didn't know anything about you until Adam introduced us,' Amari said carefully, 'Henry did a good job keeping you quiet, and well away from Eddie. '

Amari believed this to be a benign statement, but upon witnessing Mary's reaction he quickly moved to repair the damage.

'It's probably sensible if we discuss this later. Shall we convene in a less public place once the activities have concluded?'

Mary could feel her ears glowing and her mouth went dry. She'd heard Amari's suggestion, but for the moment was lost in the implications of his earlier statement. He knew Eddie. What's more, he had implied Henry wanted to keep her away from him.

'Mary, are you alright?' Amari pressed, taking hold of her elbow and cradling it in a warm hand.

'Yes. Yes, I'm fine, thank you,' she managed, springing back to the here and now, 'I think that's a good idea. Perhaps we could meet at the farmhouse. How about five o'clock?'

After accepting her suggestion, Yousef melted into the crowd listening to Danny.

The rest of the afternoon was a blur. Over the next few hours more than two and fifty hundred people came through the yard and almost all of them stayed to watch Terry and his men pump gallon after gallon of water into the equine pool and then send hundreds of children and dozens of adults down their phenomenally popular water slide. Maisie and Audrey served hot dogs and onions, whilst Graham, Juliet and Ewan helped Danny to take Ivor swimming in order to christen the pool.

The Fire Brigade's collection bucket rattled regularly and the yard took on the feel of a village fete. By four o'clock the crowd began to thin and by a quarter to five, Danny was rounding up the last of the visitors in order to start his evening feed. Before they left, Terry and his crew pulled up outside the farmhouse and announced they'd had a bumper round of donations and would be delighted to repeat the day again next year.

'And you can pop into the Station anytime,' Terry had crackled to Mary comically through his open window as they departed, ignoring the catcalls received from his colleagues.

The Cordike staff, plus Mary's friends looked out onto an eerily silent yard at a few minutes before five o'clock. Danny started to thank people. Mary watched him move around the group shaking hands and inviting them into the farmhouse for a coffee. He looked tired, yet still full of enthusiasm and it occurred to her that she had witnessed him and his staff growing today; they'd handled the crowds, spoken to hundreds of people and done it with confidence and authority. She allowed herself to swell with a little pride.

Danny was complimenting Audrey and Maisie on their ability to serve over two hundred hot dogs in less than half an hour, when Graham made a shushing sound from the edge of the group.

'I heard something,' he said, cocking his head to one side, 'It sounded like...'

A moan and the sound of a slap on wood travelled across the yard.

'It's coming from the round wooden thing,' said Audrey, pointing to the corner of the yard.

Danny and Graham ran over to the lunging pen, an enclosed circular, wood built enclosure with eight foot walls used to teach the younger horses basic commands on long reins. Danny wrenched open the inset door and dodged in, quickly followed by Graham.

A few seconds later the two men emerged with Yousef Amari between them. He was able to walk, supported around their shoulders, but was dazed and his knees kept turning to jelly as they walked him to the farmhouse. Mary winced at the significant smudge of blood across his cheek. Yousef's once perfectly sculpted silver flecked hair was matted with the waxy sand from the lunging pen floor and most notably, his white silk shirt had been ripped open revealing a red surgeon's incision mark down the centre of his chest.

'He's been beaten pretty badly and it looks like he has a heart problem,' Graham called over as they approached.

'I can speak for myself,' Yousef protested, 'I'll be fine, there's no need for any fuss, I'll...'

Yousef stumbled and had to be lifted up by Danny as his right knee gave way. The three men ground to a halt.

'A chair if you would, and I'll be fine. No fuss, please,' he insisted.

Danny nodded at Graham and they man-handled the protesting businessman into the farmhouse and deposited him gently onto the sofa in the back room. Mary made him comfortable, collected the medical kit, wipes, and hot water from the kitchen and returned to treat Yousef's wounds, shooing all the onlookers, apart from Danny, out of the room.

Kneeling beside him, Mary's initial investigation of Yousef's injuries concluded he'd only suffered cuts and bruises. He was breathing heavily but that was probably as a result of being overweight and almost certainly unfit. He was shivering and a bruise above his eye had started to swell, contorting the forty year-old's face.

'Get him one of your jumpers, will you,' Mary asked Danny. He set off upstairs, a jumble of knees and elbows.

'I'm okay,' Yousef croaked, leaning back in the sofa with his eyes closed. His stomach bulged with each breath and Mary caught sight of the surgery scar again as his shirt fell open. Angry red marks around his ribs were punctuated by a line of three deeper marks in several places. Someone had been using Yousef as a punch bag. She pulled his shirt closed, and got on with treating his cuts.

'Heart operation?'

'Double bypass two years ago,' he grimaced.

'Then you need to go to hospital to get checked out.'

She dabbed at the two major cuts on his face and he winced, pulling away from her.

'Who...' Mary started.

Yousef's eyes sprang open and he tensed, which in turn caused him to emit a pain stricken groan.

'It's complicated. It could be any of them,' he rasped in protest.

Mary drew back from treating him and frowned. He was a husk of the man he'd been earlier in the day. Someone had achieved their goal; Yousef was scared. Yet Mary detected a streak of proud defiance in the man.

'Just tell me what you can.'

Yousef avoided her gaze and eyed the door.

'If you want to leave I won't stop you,' said Mary getting to her feet, 'But, you'd be helping me and yourself if you could tell me who did this to you, and why.'

'I must leave.'

'Then leave,' Mary said, allowing a touch of anger to inject an edge into her tone.

'My family ran most of the organised crime around Newcastle in the eighties and nineties,' Yousef said dejectedly, 'Even after twenty years of slowly going legit my family history still dumps it's crap on me.'

Danny entered holding a bundle of jumpers but came to a halt when he felt the tension in the room.

Yousef struggled to his feet, refusing help from either of them and limped to the door, baring his teeth as the spasms of pain shot through his battered muscles. He opened the door, but stopped, staring down at the doorknob.

'Dangerous people are waiting for you to find Henry's ruby. Once you have it, they will stop at nothing to take it from you. They know who you are, thanks to you attending your husband's funeral and being involved in this...' he rolled his eyes around the room, '...and that you're the only one who can lead them to the Stone. Believe me, they won't think twice about hurting you, or your friends, in order to get to it.'

Yousef leaned on the doorknob and took two short breaths as a ripple of pain flowed down his right-hand side where the knuckleduster had pounded into his ribs. He paused, and it occurred to him how lucky he'd been. The man with the walking stick and strange military hat had intervened just in time... Henry really had created a mess of complicated problems for his wife.

'My advice is...' he paused to swing the door open, '...Don't find it, Mary. Leave the Stone where it is. If you do recover it, someone will end up getting hurt.'

Yousef lurched through the door, past the set of bewildered people in the kitchen and out of the farmhouse. Mary and Danny joined the group at the kitchen window to watch their owner stumble across the yard and struggle to pull his car keys from his trouser pocket. He made it into his driver's seat with such a high-pitched yelp of pain they could hear it from within the farmhouse.

Maisie was the first to break the silence once Yousef's executive car had departed in a cloud of dust.

'So what happened? Did he slip and fall? I'm a bit confused,'

'No, you daft bat,' Audrey piped up, 'He's part of a criminal gang and he got beaten up by another mobster to warn him off trying to find a precious gem that Mary's husband has hidden.'

The room fell silent.

'What?' Audrey questioned defensively, looking from one shocked face to the next, 'We all heard it! The walls in this place are wafer thin!'

She caught Maisie's baffled reaction and added, 'Well, some of us heard it.'

'Not all of us were standing with our ear to the door, Audrey,' Sarah commented, whilst peering thoughtfully out of the kitchen window.

Mary sighed and plonked herself down on one of the kitchen chairs. She put an elbow onto the table top and grumpily rested her cheek into her palm.

'It looks like I have some explaining to do.'

Twenty-Nine

'I've been poring over the blummin' cipher for four days now, and I'm no nearer to solving it,' Mary complained when she'd concluded her briefing. She'd purposely left out certain elements, such as Eddie blaming her for his father's death. She didn't know why. Pride came to mind, but it was an unsavoury piece of self-analysis, so she pushed the thought away.

Her friends were scattered around the farmhouse's small kitchen and instead of concentrating on the tablecloth, as she'd done throughout her story, Mary lifted her eyes and scanned the room. Maisie and Sarah wore worried expressions, as did Juliet. In contrast, Audrey's eyes were ablaze with excitement. Graham was rubbing his chin thoughtfully and Danny seemed to be experiencing a strange mixture of pride and relief. They had all remained in rapt silence throughout and that continued for a few seconds longer until Audrey couldn't contain herself any longer.

'Where's the cipher? Can I see it?'

'Sure, I don't see why not,' Mary replied, 'Although according to Yousef we should leave it well alone.'

Mary went to her desk in the back room and returned with a sheet of A4 that got passed from person to person.

With her enthusiasm dampened by being unable to immediately crack the code herself, Audrey settled down to quiz Mary.

'Do you think Eddie could be telling the truth?'

'Not a chance.'

Audrey frowned, 'Really? But the way you explained what happened at your cottage a few nights ago...'

'I'm sure he's a liar,' Mary cut in sternly, 'I'm not even convinced the little girl was Vinny's.'

A number of concerned looks were shared among those standing in the kitchen, but no one challenged Mary.

Danny hadn't seen Mary so frustrated. Keen to move the conversation on, he asked, 'Eddie is definitely after the Stone. He's admitted that, whether it's for him, or to give it to someone else, but who else could be involved?'

'What about Adam East?'

Danny and Mary swivelled round to where Ewan was standing, leaning against the wall. He was almost obscured behind one of the kitchen units, tapping his mobile phone with his thumb and engrossed in its small screen. He held Henry's letter in his other hand.

'Have you been there all the time?' asked Danny.

The seventeen-year-old looked up, becoming self-conscious when he realised all eyes were on him. He stood up straight.

'I followed everyone in when you brought Mr Amari inside,' he answered defensively.

'He's been here all along; you and Mary must have missed him,' suggested Sarah.

'That's okay, Ewan,' Mary said reassuringly, 'Why do you think Adam is involved in all this?'

'I just think Adam East is a likely suspect, given he runs a company that has been dependent on loans guaranteed by Henry's Stone of Shiazzano,' he remarked, before returning his attention to Henry's letter.

'I spoke with Adam on the phone yesterday,' Mary revealed, 'He was a bit cagey at first, but eventually admitted he knew about the Stone. Apparently Henry made Adam promise to never mention the Stone to anyone. Henry had dealt with the loans when the business needed them. Adam didn't have any contact with the people the money came from, he just made sure they were paid back with interest.'

'Did you ask him about Henry and Eddie?' asked Audrey.

'Yep, he was vague about their relationship and he claims he didn't know anything about Henry knowing any criminals. He was just a Training Manager.'

Sarah dropped into a chair beside Mary and put an arm around her.

'You look tired. Perhaps you shouldn't try to work the cipher out. That Amari chap could be right.'

'It's a Vigenere Cipher,' Ewan said into his mobile phone, 'I've Googled the first line of the code.'

'Ewan?' Danny said in a bemused tone, 'I know you're a bright lad, but how do you know it's a... whatever you said?'

'I'm doing A-Level maths at college. My lecturer told us to read around the subject and I was interested in secret codes. I'm pretty certain we can crack it, but I will need the key.'

The room fell silent in a way that tends to indicate the people around you are either confused, or not following. Ewan raised his head and realised he had some explaining to do.

'The cipher can be decoded if you have the key. It's usually a word when it's this sort of cipher. The person creating the cipher will share the keyword with the person they want to be able to decode the message.'

Ewan looked expectantly at Mary, which prompted the rest of the group to do the same.

'I already know all this,' Mary admitted, 'Henry and I used to write notes to each other in code just for fun. When I first saw it, I thought it would be easy to decrypt, but nothing I've used has worked. I've tried a few, but it takes hours to test each one because it uses interwoven Caesar ciphers.

Audrey opened her mouth and only managed to get a 'Wha...' out before Mary answered.

'Please don't ask. You don't want to know. It's about movable alphabets.'

Audrey deflated and gave Mary an accepting nod.

'It must have taken him ages to create in the early eighties,' said Ewan, checking the date on the letter, 'He wouldn't have had the internet then.'

'What do you mean?' Mary asked, getting up from her chair and crossing the room to peer over the boy's shoulder. A couple of the others joined her.

'You can decipher any Vigenere Cipher online. I've already found a page which will do the decryption. If you don't have the key, you can try and guess as many times as you want. It only takes a few seconds to type them in. Here, take a look.'

Ewan handed his phone over to Mary who took it and gingerly pushed her finger up and down its screen.

'I've typed in the first line of the cipher, you enter the key in that box there,' Ewan said, pointing. 'Just tap on the box, enter the key, then click the decipher button. If it starts to make sense, we can enter the rest of the coded message.'

'You're suddenly making me feel very old and out of touch,' she told him, 'I should have realised there was something like this out there.'

Ewan didn't react. He was re-reading the letter.

'So your husband didn't give you a key?' he asked without looking up from the page.

Mary thought for a few seconds, 'No. Not that I am aware of.'

'And you didn't have any pet names, passwords or joke sayings the two of you would share. The key will probably be a single word or phrase run together without spaces.'

Mary's ears started to tingle and she fought the urge to touch them, fearful they would already be glowing red and she'd only bring attention to them. Audrey caught her eye and Mary realised her friend had already noticed. She was smiling mischievously.

'I suppose there's a few I might try,' Mary said quickly in an unsuccessful attempt to kill the conversation.

Audrey giggled, 'Can I watch you type them in, Mary? I'd love to know what Henry's pet name for you was!'

Maisie broke into a laugh that was so infectious she soon had the rest of the room joining her. Mary didn't reply, shaking her head, but wearing a wry smile.

Keen on ensuring such a rich vein of potential comedy should continue, Audrey started to suggest possible keys.

'How about cheekychops or rumblebum,' she offered.

'Dumpling! My Stan calls me that,' exclaimed Sarah to more laughter, especially from Maisie, which spawned even more jollity.

'Ooh, I know,' Audrey said, 'Big B...'

'Be very careful,' Mary interrupted, eying Audrey intently in the forlorn hope she wouldn't continue. This had the effect of drawing another round of giggles, especially from the ladies present.

'I was going to say Boy,' Audrey replied innocently, 'Big Boy. Your Henry was a big, broad chap. What on earth did you think I was going to say?'

Mary's eyes narrowed, 'Mmm, I don't know how helpful you're being, but thank you for lifting our spirits.'

'You're welcome,' Audrey said warmly, a twinkle in her eye.

Ewan had been watching the interchange with interest, although slightly bemused by what a group of fifty-year-olds rated as funny. Now that Audrey had settled somewhat, he spoke again.

'When there isn't a known key, there's usually a clue within the code, or in this case, the letter. It will be something only the person the code is intended for will recognise. Have you had a good look through the letter, Mary.'

Mary stopped typing. She had just tried 'twentynineblack', Henry's favourite number on a roulette table, but the code had remained stubbornly unreadable.

'I've scoured every word in that letter a hundred times. I couldn't see anything,' Mary opined, 'I'll just have to sit down with my laptop and try every code word I can think of until I find the right key.'

Mary tried typing 'Northallerton' and once again received a negative response from the decoder.

'Could I, like, see the letter?' Juliet asked. Up until now she'd been peering over Ewan's shoulder, but he could see she was screwing her face up to try and look more closely.

She blinked at the letter and took it over to the kitchen window and tipped it from side to side. She called Ewan over and began a small satellite discussion.

Sarah put her hand onto Mary's shoulder, the two of them watching the younger members of the group apparently finding something of interest in the letter, 'Are you really sure you *want* to find this Stone?'

Mary gently rubbed her temples; it had already been a long day.

'Even if we manage to solve the cipher, I don't suppose I need to go and find it,' she said with a shrug. Sarah didn't look so sure.

'Remember, I play poker with you. There's no way you could stop yourself if you discovered where this Stone was hidden. You're the sort of girl who goes 'all-in' on a pair of tens for heaven sakes. It would eat away at you...'

Ewan and Juliet's discussion was becoming animated and their voices started to carry across the room. Mary heard the words 'font' and 'embedded' scrambled into their quick-fire conversation. A moment later they spun around.

'Have you got a highlighter pen?' Ewan asked expectantly.

Mary produced a yellow highlighter from her desk drawer and Juliet and Ewan sat down side by side at the kitchen table and started to mark-up the letter. The rest of the group traded blank expressions.

'Your husband was a devious man,' stated Ewan as he pored over the letter, dabbing his pen at a word as he spoke.

Mary looked to Sarah, who raised an eyebrow.

'If Juliet is right, the key is in the letter,' Ewan continued, 'It looks like he had some individual letters typed in a different font, or perhaps even on a separate typewriter, given it was the 1980's. It isn't so clear on this copy, but the original letter would probably allow the letters to stand out.'

As Ewan traced his finger along the lines of words, Juliet wrote 'C', 'E' and 'O'. By the time they had reached the end of Henry's letter she had added 'A', 'E', 'U', 'C', 'R', 'S' and 'R'.

A humming was coming from within the little group watching the two youngsters work. Mary and Graham turned their attention to Danny.

'Sorry,' he whispered, 'I don't...'

'...know you're doing it?' Mary and Graham enquired in unison.

Juliet started to re-arrange the letters, but from over her shoulder, Sarah, a word puzzle fan, was already there.

'Racecourse!'

'Bloody hell!' Danny blurted.

His outburst received a crackle of laughter. There was a buzz of excitement in the room and all attention now transferred to Mary, still holding Ewan's phone. She started to tap the device's screen.

After half a minute she handed the phone back to Ewan in frustration.

'I keep making mistakes, you do it.'

Within seconds Ewan was also frowning at the screen.

'Racecourse isn't the key, it doesn't decode the message,' he announced, looking up at the expectant faces and watching as the excitement faded.

'Perhaps it's a specific racecourse?' suggested Audrey, 'Try York.' This received murmurs of approval.

Ewan tapped, coming up blank once more.

'Well there are fifty-odd racecourses in the UK. Try them all, start with Aintree,' instructed Danny.

Twenty minutes later, a completely deflated group of people were starting to make their excuses and file out of the farmhouse, having exhausted the name of every single racecourse in Europe. Mary was thanking everyone and reminding them to keep quiet about her story and Yousef being beaten.

'Perhaps its best that we can't solve Henry's code,' Sarah suggested as she gave Mary a consoling hug in the hall of the farmhouse on her way out, 'It could bring you bigger problems. I was on the fringes of that world when I was growing up. It's inhabited by desperate people.'

Mary released her friend from their hug and gave her a weak smile.

'I know. It's just... I need to know about my Henry, who he was when he wasn't with me. I want to know the truth. Giving Eddie what he wants might...'

Sarah shook her head, 'From what you told us about him, I doubt that.'

Mary was unable to provide an answer. Confusion and exhaustion were clouding her thoughts.

Sarah raised both her eyebrows and whispered, 'If you do decide to go 'all in', just be sure you've got the cards to beat him.'

A crestfallen Ewan was the last to leave the farmhouse. He had a copy of the letter in his hand. Danny thanked the lad and made off to do his evening feed leaving Mary alone with the apprentice. He awkwardly extended a hand for Mary to shake, but instead Mary pulled him toward her and gave him a quick hug.

'You were great,' she assured him, pleased when he seemed to brighten a little.

'I'll keep working on it. I must have missed something,' he said, still looking down at the letter as he started to cross the yard.

Mary closed the farmhouse door and dropped her shoulders. She was properly exhausted, both mentally and physically. Her sole thought now was whether to go for a shower or a bath. She started to climb the stairs.

As she reached the top step the front door burst open, causing Mary to twist around in fright. She grabbed the banister and sat down to steady herself. Standing at the foot of the stairs was Ewan, brandishing the letter triumphantly.

'I missed the kiss,' he said breathlessly.

Thirty

'Racecourse X?' Mary questioned, having descended the stairs and inspected the letter once more. When she examined the line of x's, one of Henry's kisses at the bottom of the letter was indeed slightly different to the others.

'Not x. Ex!' Ewan told her excitedly, 'I think it means an ex-racecourse, one that doesn't exist because it closed.'

He watched as Mary mulled this new possibility around her mind. As inspiration hit, she raised her head upwards and closed her eyes.

'God, you are clever,' she said.

Ewan got a feeling Mary wasn't talking to him, so waited patiently.

'Henry and I used to go to Teesside Races. It was quite close to us and we loved it there, but they closed it down in the early eighties. It has to be the ex-racecourse. We went to their last ever race meeting together.'

Ewan was already tapping his mobile phone.

'No,' he reported, 'Both Teesside and Teesside Races are no good. I also tried it with one 's' instead of two. None of them work.'

'Try Teesside Park.'

Ewan tapped it in, growling in frustration as the mixture of intelligible characters from Henry's code remained stubbornly unaltered.

Mary lowered herself onto the second step at the bottom of the stairs, leant her elbows on her knees and planted her cheeks in her hands. The constant highs and lows were starting to take their toll. Ewan, standing in front of her, continued to tap at his device.

'According to *Wikipedia* Teesside Park is also known as Stockton Racetrack,' he mumbled to himself.

More tapping followed, followed by a sigh. Ewan turned his phone toward Mary and told her, 'Read.'

She blinked, trying to focus on the dancing line of text on the small screen. It took a few seconds before she could make out what Ewan had highlighted.

'marysorryforkeepingthisfromyou'

'Stockton is the key,' Ewan said through a huge grin.

'You did it?' Mary tried to confirm with a croaky voice. Her mouth had gone dry and she swallowed a few times, trying to wrap her mind around Ewan's breakthrough.

'Yep. I just need to type in the rest of the code.'

Without answering Mary jumped up and shot out of the farmhouse. Five minutes later, the entire group of eight had reconvened in the kitchen. Danny and Graham had scouted around outside to make sure there wasn't anyone listening, whilst Maisie and Audrey were making teas and coffees. A boggled looking Mary was sipping a neat whisky.

Ewan finally kicked back from the kitchen table and the room fell silent.

'Well, here you go, Mary,' he said, offering her a piece of paper upon which several handwritten lines of block capitals were printed.

'No. Can you read it please, so everyone can hear. I trust everyone in this room,' instructed Mary.

Ewan cleared his throat and started to read, conscious there were seven people about to be hanging on every word he spoke.

'*Mary. Sorry for keeping this from you. Please forgive me. I thought it best to protect you from the people I need to deal with. But well done for working out what Pa meant. The Stone is hidden in a place special to both of us. I can't trust banks and entrusting it to friends would put them in danger. Go to our favourite bench. To the left is a tree with two trunks. Look for the battered ring of silver. All my love. Henry.*'

'Short, and sweetly ambiguous,' Audrey pointed out.

All eyes went to Mary, who was tapping her chin with two fingers, pondering.

Presently a smile of understanding creased her face, 'Leazes Park,' she said, 'He means Leazes Park.'

A number of confused looks were shared between her audience.

'Leazes Park! Behind the Newcastle United football ground. It's where Henry and I used to meet before we were married. After I'd finished my lectures at the Poly we'd walk around the gardens and sit together... on a bench beside the lake.'

'So when do we go and find the Stone?' Audrey asked eagerly.

'Whoa... cool your jets, Aud,' said Sarah, waving her hands in a calming motion.

'Here it comes,' Audrey muttered dejectedly, 'Sarah the pragmatist is about to tell us why we shouldn't go find a jewel that could be worth millions of pounds...'

'... that has been stolen!' Sarah warned, 'So Mary could never sell it, and just possessing the Stone could pitch all of us against a whole heap of trouble from people who are happy to attack cars with bats and beat up people at our open day!'

Mary squeezed her eyes shut, 'Put like that..' her voice tailed off as she inhaled a breath to steady herself, 'I've put all of you in danger.'

Throughout this exchange Maisie had been scratching her head, not paying attention to the discussion around her. In the lull created by the group contemplating Mary's statement, she spoke up.

'I had a strange thing happen in the supermarket yesterday.'

Audrey snorted, 'Come on Maise, keep up. This is serious. We don't need to know about your shopping trip just at the minute.'

'A man came up to me when I was choosing fresh fish...'

Audrey sighed dramatically and rolled her eyes.

'He said it was shocking how much they were charging for cod these days,' Maisie continued, 'But if I could give him the right sort of information I wouldn't have to worry about the price of fish.'

Maisie had been staring into the middle distance, however she snapped back, looked around the mixture of amused and confused faces for a moment, then started to dig in her handbag.

'There!' she announced triumphantly, 'He gave me this and said to call him, and he would make it worth my while.'

She placed a small white business card on the kitchen table, 'I had absolutely no idea what on earth he meant. Is that what you're talking about, Mary?'

Mary didn't need to pick up the card, she knew whose it was. It held nothing apart from a mobile phone number printed in the middle; Vincent's number. She locked eyes with the totally innocent, and unsuspecting Maisie and couldn't speak. A feeling of dread surged through her.

'I got given one of those,' Juliet piped up, distracting Mary from her downwards spiral, 'I told him, like, get lost. He stopped me outside the Saddlery shop on Langton Road the other day. I thought he was after racing tips. He was, like, creepy.'

Mary swallowed hard. 'Yes, he is a bit,' she said quietly, 'Anyone else been offered money by Eddie's right-hand man, Vinny?'

This was greeted with a round of blank looks, until Mary reached Danny. She knew something was wrong when he started a low humming.

'Danny?'

He rubbed the back of his neck sheepishly, unable to disguise an inner turmoil, 'It's George and Jonnie Lilley.'

'Come on Danny,' Mary prompted. Her demand came out sounding a little strident and she immediately corrected herself, 'I'm sorry. It's just that it could be important.'

He nodded, 'I promised I'd keep it to myself. They came to see me together yesterday. It's simple really. It was Jonnie who broke in here a few days ago.'

Graham whistled and there were a few gasps. Maisie and Audrey had a muffled conversation behind their hands to catch up with who Jonnie was, and Mary encouraged Danny to continue.

'Jonnie was... well, I've never seen him like that. He was scared, a completely different lad. You could see George was pretty worried too.'

Danny squirmed a little before he started speaking. Mary assumed he was trying to square the breaking of a promise to himself.

'Some chap caught up with Jonnie at the races a few days after he and I had... argued,' Danny said in a low voice, 'He offered him five hundred pounds to go into our farmhouse and make a mess and make it look like he was searching for something. I guess Jonnie was still pretty angry with me and said he'd think about it. The chap caught up with him the next morning in the lane outside here and convinced him to break in when we were out riding. After he'd run through the farmhouse turning things over Jonnie went back to get paid and the chap pulled a knife on him and threatened to hurt his dad's horses if he told anyone. It scared the hell out of Jonnie.'

'So George made him come round here and confess,' said Mary in an assumptive tone. Danny caught her eye and confirmed this with a sad nod.

'Someone wanted to scare us,' Mary added.

Sarah's voice cut through the hushed kitchen, 'If I'm not mistaken, either the man with the knife didn't know about Henry's letter and the code... or he purposely made it *look like* the intruder didn't know.'

'Why would they do that?' asked Danny.

'To ensure continued pressure was applied on us to find the Stone,' Mary replied, 'If Sarah is right, it also makes it appear there are more people out there hell bent on getting their hands on it.

A heavy silence descended on the group, eventually broken by Danny who felt he hadn't completed his admission regarding the Lilley's.

'Jonnie was still scared after he'd told me, but a little calmer, and George was really cut up. Just disappointed I guess. I told them I'd say nothing, after all, there wasn't anything taken or broken, but I warned them if I heard of Jonnie doing anything similar in the future, I'd go to the police. I think George was grateful. He shook my hand harder than he's ever done before and said he owed me one.'

'This is awful,' moaned Audrey, 'By the sound of it there are people ready to pop up everywhere and buy information, or worse. All of them are waiting for you to find this blessed Stone, Mary.'

'So what are you going to do?' asked Maisie.

Nobody moved. Even Milo and Charlie were standing stock still, their eyes wide, watching pensively. Mary scanned the faces in the kitchen, finally locking eyes with Sarah.

'Knowing me, I'll be going all in.'

Thirty-One

Danny didn't have a runner for the first few days of the new flat season. Ivor, or 'The Engine' as he appeared in the racecard, was the first horse to be sent out on turf at Redcar in the first week of April. He returned to the yard a hero, having got up in the final stride to nose ahead at odds of 9/1. Mary even got a phone call from the local school, as it seemed many of the parents who had attended the Fire Engine day had backed him, and wanted to thank Danny.

'Ivor has become quite popular with the children,' the deputy head had admitted over the phone, 'Perhaps we could bring a class to see him before the summer holidays?'

The yard was now up to nineteen horses. Surprisingly, and also a shade worryingly, Yousef Amari's horses had remained with Danny. He was paying his bills on time, but hadn't revisited the yard in person. If anything, the beating he'd taken had somehow convinced Yousef to become a staunch supporter of the yard. He'd sent Danny another two horses only a week later, both were expensive unraced two-year-olds that had come straight from a breaking yard.

'Bred to need a mile as a minimum,' Danny told Mary when the youngsters arrived, 'They won't see a racecourse until August at the earliest.'

'Do you get the feeling Yousef may be trying to ingratiate himself?' Mary asked.

Danny had replied with a shrug and said as long as Mary was okay with it, and the man paid his training bills on time, he didn't have an issue with Yousef remaining an owner.

Mary was still living at the farmhouse. Danny insisted she remained, at least until, 'We know you'll be safe sleeping alone in a cottage in the middle of nowhere.' Mary had reluctantly agreed. Danny had made it quite clear that she was doing him a favour by being there, and after thirty years of having Henry around, she found she was appreciating the company, especially in the evenings. She'd been back to Northallerton a few times to pick up odds and ends, but always felt vulnerable and ill at ease, despite Bert fussing over her.

Danny had been amazed at Mary's apparent acceptance of evenings entirely composed of racing highlights. However, he'd suffered a bout of guilt after a few days and ensured Mary squeezed *Coronation Street* into their viewing schedule. The soap was one of Mary's guilty pleasures, another throwback to growing up with her dad; together they had never missed an episode. After a week of The Street, Danny had become hooked too.

Vincent kept arriving at the yard, although he tried to time his arrival to when Danny and most of his growing team of stable staff and work riders were on the gallops. Mary preferred it that way; it meant he couldn't stay more than about twenty minutes before the yard was awash with returning people and horses. It was clear Vincent preferred her Northallerton home as he kept asking when she would be returning. Mary assumed it had made her an easier target for him to keep an eye on.

His visits came every seven to ten days now, and were increasingly filled with ever darkening overtones. As well as the emotional blackmail concerning Emily, Vincent had begun to intimate some of her friends and colleagues at the yard could be targeted by a number of unknown interested parties if the Stone wasn't recovered before the start of summer. When Mary had confronted him with the fact that he had already attempted to bribe some of her friends, he had casually replied, 'What did you expect? My little girl's wellbeing is at stake.'

With every visit from Vincent, Mary's patience was being stretched. She'd always disliked him, but had come to loathe the man. During one visit he produced a metal object from his jacket pocket which he toyed with, turning it over in his hands as his veiled threats were issued. After he had left, Mary hadn't been able to get the chrome plated device out of her thoughts. With a shudder, she remembered Vincent had at one point tensed his fist and three arcs of the metal device had risen above his knuckles. She had realised with growing dread that the loops of sparkling chrome matched the angry red marks she'd seen on Yousef Amari's abdomen.

Mary continued to supply Vincent with excuses throughout April, and if he was being particularly insistent, suggested a little progress had been made. Mary knew it was only delaying the inevitable. She could only see two possible outcomes. Either she reported to Eddie the Stone was lost and faced the consequences, or follow Henry's instructions, retrieve the Stone (if it was still there!), pass it to Eddie, and hope that whoever else was pursuing it would accept they had lost the race to the ruby. Either way, she would then be forced to sit back and pray that Eddie, and his thugs, or any other unknown entity, didn't take umbrage and decide to inflict retribution on her, or her friends.

It hadn't failed to register with Mary that both options meant either handling stolen goods, or at the very least, withholding information regarding a criminal act. Mary had never been involved with the police, beyond the odd parking ticket. It was a strange feeling though, weirdly liberating, that Mary Romano, the perfect citizen, was on the wrong side of the law.

Since the Fire Brigade day Mary had applied her mind to unearthing a solution where she could rid herself of the Stone and guarantee the safety of everyone around her. It wasn't until she and Danny shared a conversation on the gallops ahead of Lucky Jake's racecourse debut, that the seed of a plan was planted.

Lucky Jake was being aimed at a five furlong maiden at Wetherby in the second week of April.

'He's better than selling class,' Danny had shared as the gelding came up the grass gallop alongside an older horse on his final workout.

'He's working with one of Amari's four-year-olds and is staying with him. That horse is rated seventy five. Considering he was a cheap horse, you're going to get a run for your money.'

'You think he can win a seller?' checked Mary.

'At the very least. I think he can win a Maiden if we find the right race for him. A small race at a Northern track which doesn't attract too many horses from the powerful southern-based yards would do us. But he will need the experience from his first outing, as he's still a big baby. His stalls work is perfect but he tends to run too keen behind other horses.'

'But if all else fails, he could win a selling race?'

Danny had curled his brow downwards, 'Where's this interest in selling races coming from? He's far better than a selling-plater. You might lose him if he wins well.'

Mary went straight back to the farmhouse, switched on her computer and logged onto the Weatherby's website. Her search for two-year-old selling races in the entries and declarations section confirmed what she had expected; the top selling race for youngsters was The Rous Stakes at York in mid-June, over six furlongs.

From that moment Mary became engrossed in her scheme. She found herself still at her desk at seven in the evening with copious notes strewn across every available inch of space around her. She pushed her chair back, surveying the mess, and memories of her dad came flooding back. He would often sit at their kitchen table well into the evening, working on his latest pools permutation, with notes and calculations littering its entire surface.

'Having fun?' Danny asked rhetorically from the door to the back room, taking a slurp from his mug of cup-a-soup.

'I got my own tea. You seemed a bit busy,' he added before Mary could answer, 'You want some soup?'

Mary rubbed her eyes and yawned.

'I might have found a way to sort this mess out,' she said in a tired voice.

'A bin would probably do it,' Danny joked, moving into the room and casting his eyes over the mountain of paper. He lifted more paper off the seat of a chair and settled in.

'Come on then, Mary, let's hear the plan.'

Thirty-Two

Mary knew she was biased, but Ewan really did look wonderful in her racing colours. It helped that the sun was out on this fine late spring day at Wetherby, but even Danny, not one for caring too much about presentation, had approved of her red and white striped silks and red cap.

She and Sarah watched Graham leading the young lad and Lucky Jake out of the parade ring and behind the assorted outbuildings on the way to the track.

'He looks so small on Jake's back,' Sarah commented as the apprentice disappeared down the chute at the side of the stands.

'How much do you think he weighs?' quizzed Mary.

'No idea, about nine stones?

'Seven stones ten pounds,' she answered, 'Jake's carrying almost a stone of lead in his saddle bags today.'

The two women walked from the parade ring through the gap between two stands and, ignoring the lines of bookmakers, climbed the steps so they could watch Lucky Jake canter past on the way to the five furlong start. The gelding exited the chute, took a few steps onto the track and flicked his ears forward. Graham removed his lead rein in anticipation of the horse jumping off down the track but instead Jake planted himself.

Ewan tried a couple of pushes with his hands to no effect, followed by an encouraging dig with his heels to get him to move, and when he did, it was to take half a dozen steps backwards. Mary's heart was in her mouth. Danny had emphasized how important it was that Jake had a good experience first time out, and they had discussed whether to put a professional jockey on him. She had insisted Ewan got the ride, as he did most of the home work on Jake.

Another three runners emerged from the chute before Ewan called over to the next jockey out, who walked his mount over to Lucky Jake and turned in front of him to face the five furlong straight. As if by magic, Jake kicked off with the other horse, sticking about a length behind.

'He just needed a lead,' Mary told Sarah as Lucky Jake cantered down the straight. She noticed the gelding's ears were flicking around as he passed, taking in the people on both sides of the track.

'Danny did say he would be as green as grass today. Speaking of which, where is Danny?'

'He always watches the race alone. He can't stand with owners, he gets far too... animated,' Mary explained.

Down at the start, Ewan walked around the stalls and parked the gelding's head over the rails at the end of the track in an attempt to get him to relax. The gelding had been fighting him all the way and was behaving extremely green, so much so, Ewan was worried he could have issues with entering the starting stalls. Behind him, the starter was calling the stalls positions and Ewan was reminded he would be one of the first to go in; not exactly in his favour.

At most racecourses the start to a five furlong race would be a quiet place, well away from people and other equine distractions. This wasn't the case at Wetherby. Ewan cursed as the sound of several large vehicles thundering past on the A1(M) motorway came over the embankment. The noise managed to spook Lucky Jake enough for him to shy away from the rail, whip around and snort angrily. Ewan clung to the gelding, gripping his neck with his knees, losing his foothold in his irons but remaining on top. Now, both horse and jockey had their blood racing around their bodies.

A stalls handler peeled off and approached Ewan and, to his relief, managed to attach a lead rope to Lucky Jake's bit. It took forty-five seconds, and the addition of two more handlers to man-handle the gelding into stall three. Ewan sat, praying for the stalls to open as the gelding began to jig-jog, then paw at the ground.

Slowly, far too slowly, the eleven other stalls began to load. Ewan moved off Lucky Jake's back, standing on the stanchion at the edges of the stall and started to stroke the gelding's neck through his glove, careful not to touch his ears.

'Two to go,' called the starter.

Ewan got back on Lucky Jake and dug the toe of his boots into his irons. It seemed the gelding had finally calmed down and stood still, his nose touching the gates.

Two stalls down from Ewan, a horse rose on its back legs, whinnying, and its rider screamed, 'No, Sir.'

Lucky Jake turned his head at a right-angle, trying to see what was going on at the same time the rearing horse returned to the ground.

'Jockeys!' shouted the starter.

Before Ewan could alert the starter to his lack of preparedness, the stalls flew open. As the gates clanged and eleven other runners jumped forward Lucky Jake, still with his head held to one side, backed into his stall. He stayed there, poised for half a second, saw his exit was now clear and sprang awkwardly up and out of the stall, scraping his head against the steel strut dividing the gates. In one thrust of power, Ewan's leg was sandwiched by Lucky Jake's ribs and the side of the stall, ripping his toe from his stirrup.

In the stands, Mary searched in vain for her red cap and groaned as she realised her colours weren't with the field. By the time the racecourse commentator had confirmed his late stalls exit, the gelding was ten lengths off the back of the field with Ewan fighting to find his right-hand iron.

Two furlongs into the race Ewan finally managed to dip his toe into his flapping stirrup and he and Lucky Jake began to travel like a racehorse and jockey, albeit fifteen lengths behind the leaders and with any chance of getting competitive having evaporated. Ewan kept hold of the two-year-old's head, whilst allowing him to bowl along at his own pace behind the main body of the field. Over two furlongs out he started to push, and was disappointed with the response. Lucky Jake kept up the gallop, but the turn of pace he had on occasion shown Ewan at home was nowhere to be found. Nevertheless, under instructions from Danny, Ewan continued to push. He would ride the horse out to the line regardless of where he was going to finish, in order to educate him.

The magic happened when he managed to pick up one of his competitors at the rear of the main pack. As they swept past the furlong pole, Ewan felt a surge under him as Lucky Jake got onto the weakening horse's flanks. Through the last two-hundred yards, Lucky Jake powered past three other rivals.

'It's a shame Aud and Maisie couldn't make it today,' said Sarah as she and Mary left the stands, 'His final finishing position won't tell the whole story.'

The two women hurried past the parade ring, which also doubled as the winner's enclosure, and up to the back of the racecourse where the unplaced horses would unsaddle. Danny was already there, waiting for his horse.

'He lost the race before the stalls opened,' Danny said in greeting, 'We need to work on getting him relaxed, maybe some headgear to make him concentrate. But on the plus side, he loves passing horses and on that showing will get six.'

Ewan arrived, slid off the gelding's back and after apologising, told his story of how the stalls had been released with Lucky Jake checking out other horses.

'He'll be better next time,' Ewan promised, 'He was really green. It was like his first day at school.'

Ewan concluded by thanking Mary for the ride and headed off to weigh in but stopped after a couple of paces and turned back.

'Cheekpieces,' he said, 'Might just keep his mind on the job.'

Danny thanked him and glanced Mary's way once Ewan was out of earshot, 'For a young lad, he's not so daft.'

'Can solve ciphers and knows his horses,' Sarah noted, 'He could be your son, Mary!'

'That's what you get when you employ idiots.'

Mary's smile fell away as soon as she looked up and recognised Adrian Fitzpatrick. He stepped closer. Danny instructed Graham to take Jake back to the stables and placed himself between the advancing trainer and his owners.

Mary thought Fitzpatrick looked unwell. He'd appeared chubby at Newcastle, but the extra weight was starting to show in his red face; his cheeks looked like slabs of raw meat.

'No Irishman here to protect you today then, huh?'

Danny remained silent, not breaking eye contact with Fitzpatrick. He'd come to a halt a couple of feet from him; enough to be invading Danny's personal space, enough to intimidate, but not touching.

'I'm not interested in anything you have to say, Mr Fitzpatrick,' said Mary sourly.

'Really?' he replied sarcastically, 'I beg to differ. I have a message for you.'

Mary didn't miss a beat, 'So you're a messenger boy now. Well, I suppose it's better than being an untrustworthy trainer.'

Fitzpatrick scowled over Danny's shoulder at the small blonde woman. He couldn't wait to deliver his message and wipe that smug smile off her face.

'It's about the Stone,' he said, baiting his hook.

Mary blinked and tried to remain stoic, at the same time furiously trying to understand how Fitzpatrick knew about the Stone. Danny's bravado in the face of Fitzpatrick's intimidation wilted for a few seconds, but he recovered to square his chin and stare into the trainer's eyes.

A sneer worked its way onto Fitzpatrick's lips, his opening broadside had worked; she was unable to hold his gaze. Now he was going to sink her...

'They know you have the letter and if you don't give them the Stone...' he stopped and produced a false, hollow laugh. Once it had died away he lowered his voice and slowly and carefully told her, 'They are going to kill your horse.'

Danny had heard enough, his blood was boiling and Fitzpatrick was only two feet away. He took a small step backwards and with the slightest of back-swings, thumped his riding boot into Fitzpatrick's crotch. Danny watched in fascination as the subject of his ire went down heavily, his hands clutching between his legs. He started to gurgle, and with eyes bulging, cheeks flushed a beetroot colour, he finally ended up on all fours, panting like a dog.

'Time for us to go,' Sarah suggested urgently, pulling at Danny's sleeve. He was in shock. The last time he'd lost his temper was... he shook the childhood memory from his mind and followed Mary and Sarah toward the pre-parade ring, and the exit to the racecourse stables.

He glanced back only once, to check how many onlookers had caught his provoked attack. He was relieved to find Fitzpatrick was still kneeling, and not a single soul had come to his aid. There was a smattering of people around, but they would have missed the spat because Fitzpatrick had chosen to confront them behind the first aid building, shielding himself from onlookers.

At least the monster hasn't got too far to crawl for help, Danny thought to himself as he and his two owners left the racecourse and hurried down the hill to the stables.

'We're going to have to do something about that temper of yours, Danny,' warned Mary as they distanced themselves from the racecourse, 'But in this instance, I think your actions were completely justified.'

Thirty-Three

The BHA inspector arrived at the yard unannounced. According to Danny, these visits were always a tense experience, as inspectors would rarely leave without having found some sort of minor infringement. This was Mary's first experience of a snap inspection and had not expected all her own paperwork to be examined. She wasn't too enamoured with the inspector taking up residence at her desk either.

'A cup of coffee, Mr Fotherstone-Smyth?' Mary enquired though gritted teeth.

She'd been though OFSTED inspections when she was teaching, but you usually knew when they were coming. This ratty little man had just pitched up at eight in the morning and started to demand one thing after another, which wouldn't have been so bad if it wasn't for his brusque, officious manner. It made her bristle.

'That won't be necessary, Mrs Romano,' Fotherstone-Smyth rumbled, 'I have my own.'

He dialled a four digit number on his leather-look briefcase and it clicked open. Removing a plastic bottle and a small square packet he carefully placed them on his upturned case. Inspecting the items further revealed them to be a bottle of chocolate milk and a sachet containing two oat biscuits.

Mary rolled her eyes behind the man's back and wandered back into the kitchen. Just as she was about to sit down, he called through to her... again. It had been like this for two hours, up and down, answering a plethora of basic questions and producing evidence of invoicing, owner's agreements, bank statements, and payroll. She'd managed to entertain him with a fixed smile up to now, but her patience was wearing thin.

'Your yard prizemoney payments?' he said without looking up.

'In front of you. In the blue folder marked Yard Prizemoney Payments,' she replied from the backroom door, returning to the kitchen without checking he had chosen the correct file.

An hour later, Fotherstone-Smyth clicked his briefcase shut and without saying anything, made his way through the kitchen, past Mary and into the hall where he retrieved his raincoat and folded it over his arm. He had his hand on the doorknob when Mary caught up with him.

'Is that it then? You're finished?'

'Yes,' he replied as he opened the door.

'So did you find what you were looking for?'

Fotherstone-Smyth turned to regard Mary with a world weary gaze.

'Contrary to what you may think, I have simply been ensuring that, as a new trainer, Mr Carter is conducting his business correctly and

163

not bringing racing into disrepute.'

'And is he bringing racing into disrepute?' Mary persisted, crossing her arms.

Fotherstone-Smyth licked his lips, 'No. Your bookkeeping is, if anything, above standard. My findings will be in my report to Mr Carter, but in answer to your query, I didn't find anything, Mrs Romano.'

'That's because we have nothing to hide Mr Fotherstone-Smyth,' Mary responded tartly.

'Everyone has *something* to hide, Mrs Romano.'

Mary was about to fire a rebuke at the irksome little man, but the words caught in her mouth. Fotherstone-Smyth gave her a weak smile.

'In my experience, Mrs Romano, the best place to hide something is out in the open. But few people are clever enough to do that.'

With that, he turned on his heel and left. Mary watched him cross the yard, the wheels in her mind turning. He was right. Hiding something in open view could catch people out, if you were clever enough. Eddie and Vincent did keep reminding her she was far too clever for her own good.

A few minutes later Danny and Juliet came into the farmhouse kitchen, both in high spirits, talking about the latest lot they had just exercised.

'The BHA dude has left then?' Danny called through to Mary as he washed his hands.

'Yes.'

'All good?'

'It was illuminating and strangely satisfying,' she replied, apparently engrossed in her computer monitor.

'Jake has just done a great bit of work, he'll go to Beverley next week for another maiden,' Danny said, walking through to stand behind Mary, still drying his hands on a tea towel. He could see Mary was browsing a saddlery website.

'What are you working on?'

Mary pushed on her chair and swivelled round, 'I think it's time to see whether the Stone is still where Henry left it.'

'Wow, really? I thought you were going to leave it. You know, too dangerous, friends lives at risk, that sort of thing?'

'I doubt my life will be any less complicated if I leave it where it is... or at least where I think it is.'

Danny flicked the moist tea towel over his shoulder and put his hands on his hips, 'You've lost me.'

'Never mind, there's something I need to...'

'The last time you started saying *there's something I need*, we ended up being beaten with baseball bats, and I got a new hairstyle.'

Mary gave a little chuckle, 'I want to ask Adam East a few questions. In person. I wondered if you'd like to escort me to Durham?'

Thirty-Four

Mary had never been to Henry's workplace. In truth, he'd never offered her the opportunity, but she'd not shown any degree of interest either. He had always tended to play down his role as a security trainer for Adam, labelling it as pretty boring, and 'a way to pay the rent.'

When Mary and Danny rolled up to the offices of Adam East Business Services, she was slightly surprised to find a security man operating a swing gate at the entrance to the car park. They pulled up, and asked for Adam. Their names were taken and a short conversation via a walkie-talkie resulted in the gate being lifted.

First impressions of Henry's workplace were as he had indicated. AEBS was on a small business park outside Durham and consisted of a white steel box of a building, peppered with huge tinted windows. There were mature trees scattered among the corporate landscaping, and a grid of parking spaces outside was inhabited by a smattering of vehicles adorned with the AEBS logo.

When Mary's Volvo pulled into a parking spot with 'Visitor' painted on it, a glass door opened outwards from within the white box and a young, thickset security guard approached the car. It transpired a frown was his default expression. After confirming who they were, he asked them to follow him. He reminded Mary of *Marvin*, the paranoid android from *The Hitchhikers Guide to the Galaxy*. She found herself wondering if the cause of his grumpiness was a constant pain in diodes down his left hand side.

Danny was humming something as they followed the guard toward the entrance. Mary queried the song and Danny, snapping out of his daydream had to think before telling her he thought it had been *'Welcome To The Jungle.'*

The inside of the steel box was far more impressive than the outside. A waft of air-conditioned ambiance greeted them as they stepped into an impressive corporate foyer, complete with a row of palm trees in huge pots. There was a ridiculously large check-in desk occupied by a smiling receptionist who was plastered in make-up. To complete the welcome, Adam East was standing waiting for them, immaculately turned out, as always, with his arms wide and a huge grin on his face.

'Mary Romano! I'm so pleased you decided to take me up on my offer to visit,' he cooed, dipping down to plant a kiss on Mary's cheek.

'And this must be Mr Carter,' he continued, offering a hand to Danny, 'Mary was singing your praises at Newcastle races. It's great to meet you. Come on, I'll show you around.'

'Actually, we just wanted to have a word with you in private, Adam,' Mary asked politely.

His expression of delight didn't waver, 'Of course, Mary. Come on, follow me. We can use my office.'

Adam's office was nothing short of palatial. Placed at the top corner of the building, it enjoyed views over fields running to rolling hills to one side and the business park on the other. An imposing desk with a cluster of four computer monitors dominated the centre of the room, but Adam directed Mary and Danny to a black leather suite beside a small kitchen that acted as a lounge area.

Danny sank into an armchair far softer than his bed back at the farmhouse, and drank in the view from the top of the building, aware of a faint smell of citrus fruit.

'It appears business is good, Adam,' Mary commented whilst their host was making freshly ground coffee.

'Thirty years of hard work, Mary. But then you'll know all about that, as Henry was here right at the start,' Adam responded, placing a brace of perfectly sculpted lattes in front of his guests. He returned with his own double espresso and took a seat opposite his guests, still wearing the same warm smile that greeted them ten minutes earlier.

'So, Mr Carter, how are your horses running at the moment?'

Danny was under strict instructions to let Mary lead the conversation, so he produced a non-committal shrug. Mary gave Danny an assuring smile, took a sip of her coffee and placed it carefully back on its coaster. She lifted her head and locked eyes with Adam.

'How many times did Henry raise money against the Stone of Shiazzano for you, Adam.'

Adam's plastic smile faded and was replaced with a tight-lipped stare. He broke eye contact with Mary to adjust his tie, undo the top button of his shirt and switch his gaze out over the fields.

Mary tried to wait patiently for Adam to answer but started to feel a buzz of anger in her chest. She was about to bark, 'Well?' at him when he dropped his chin and trained a pair of sad eyes on her.

'I'd hoped we'd be having this conversation in six months time, on the anniversary of Henry's death,' he admitted meekly, 'You weren't supposed to attend the funeral. It would have all been *fine* if you hadn't attended the funeral and bought a racehorse.'

Mary started to bristle and felt a spike of indignant rage travel down her.

Adam read her reaction and waved a flat palm at her, 'I know, I know. It *sounds* crazy, but that's how Henry managed his working life. Nothing was straight-forward or normal.'

'You were Henry's friend. You knew him better than most and saw him regularly for the last three years of his life. Henry trusted you.'

Mary held her breath for a couple of seconds before starting to speak, 'A few weeks ago I rang and asked you whether you knew anything about Henry and a Stone. You told me you knew nothing. I now know you were lying.'

She leaned forward, bringing her closer to Adam, 'I need to know the story behind the Stone... because we've found it.'

Adam's eyes produced a flicker of interest before slamming shut. He dropped his chin to his chest once again.

'I told Henry,' Adam murmured with a disgruntled shake of his head, 'I warned him they wouldn't leave you alone. He thought a quiet year would do it, but...'

'Who the hell are you talking about?'

Adam screwed his face up as if battling with some inner turmoil, 'Some of the most dangerous people in the North East. Organised crime; the people Henry used to train.'

He jumped to his feet and started to pace his office with his head down, speaking as he went.

'Henry's father was due to lend us the start-up money for the business, but he died before we received it. A month or two later, Henry was left with nothing when his mother died. Eddie took everything; the family house, the restaurant business and his job with it. Henry retrieved the Stone of Shiazzano from an old friend of his father's and that's all he had. Because it was stolen and so recognisable, he couldn't sell it, so he did the same thing his father did; he used it to get a loan from the only people with pockets deep enough and crooked enough not to care it was originally stolen from the Mafia.'

Adam stopped pacing and opened his palms, 'That loan created this place. It all began with a thirty grand loan we secured from the Amari brothers. I owe Henry a lot; I built this business from the ground up and now it's thriving.'

'Henry secured a loan for you? Yet he was just a training co-ordinator, hardly making enough for us to go on holiday each year,' Mary complained.

Adam aimed an apologetic glance at both his guests, 'Henry wanted to keep a low profile. He loved doing the training, but didn't want to run a business. To him, the Stone was just something he got out every now and again to help the business, and to help me, when I needed it.'

Danny placed an inquiring hand onto Mary's, as she seemed to have frozen with her mouth open, gazing dreamily into space. Relieved when his touch brought her back into the room, he turned to Adam.

'Perhaps you should come and sit down and explain to Mary exactly why she has a bunch of Geordies following her around, trying to intimidate her into giving them this... this Stone!'

A downcast Adam returned to his armchair and told a story of how, using the Stone of Shiazzano as collateral, Henry received a loan from the Amari brothers, one of the major criminal families in Newcastle in the nineties.

'At that time, Henry and his brother were ready to tear each other apart. I never got to know the details, I imagine he was pretty sore over Eddie forcing his mother to sign over everything to him in her will, but Henry feared for your wellbeing if you had stayed around Newcastle. That's why he moved you down to Northallerton.'

'So their relationship must have improved over time?' Mary stated.

Adam frowned and pushed his bottom lip upwards as he considered this possibility.

'As far as I was aware, he loathed his brother. He went to extraordinary lengths to make sure Eddie was firstly unable to find you, and then prevented him from approaching you.'

'What sort of lengths do you mean?' Danny asked.

'Well, in the early days, a completely different house for starters,' Adam said with a flamboyant wave of his arms, 'At first he rented a house in Wallsend and would spend three nights a week there in the late eighties. He tried to convince his brother that Mary had left him and gone abroad. After a few months, he rented an apartment down the road here in Durham. It took him some time to find a suitable place, as he needed to be able to leave without anyone seeing him. He'd go back to his ground floor flat in the evening, and slip out through a maintenance door into a cellar and go back home to Northallerton. He had everything on timers to fool anyone watching into believing he was in the house alone. Eventually when Eddie worked out what was going on, Henry had to warn him off.'

Adam saw Mary cringe and quickly continued.

'I don't mean he threatened Eddie with violence, he wasn't like that. Henry was well thought of around Newcastle; you saw how many people turned up at his funeral. He had friends who could have made Eddie's life extremely difficult.'

'So Henry never went to watch Newcastle with Eddie? They weren't friends?' Mary asked.

'Good God, no. I think he entertained colleagues and clients at St James's Park, but they'd have killed each other if he and his brother were confined together in a small space.'

Frustration began to build in Mary, but she willed it to retreat; she needed to sift through the stories, the lies and the hearsay, and not become too emotional. Henry had kept secrets, that much was clear, but so many secrets, and so well hidden... she was close to being overwhelmed, and angry... so angry he didn't share this part of his life with her. And with each revelation Henry was becoming ever more distant. As each secret was revealed, Henry, *her* Henry, was drifting further away. Question marks hung over so much of Henry's life. And who was she to believe? Most of what Eddie and Vincent claimed to be true had to be taken with a pinch of salt. But what about Adam... could he be trusted? Mary steeled herself.

'You didn't answer my original question,' she said stiffly, 'How many loans did Henry get using the Stone?'

Adam paused, assessing his unexpected callers. The young lad was out of his depth, but had the sparkle of determination in his eye, while Mary was a shrewd, likeable force of nature, in many ways similar to her husband, albeit a pocket-sized version.

Henry had been the driving force behind Adam's company's growth into security, and personal protection training. After starting the business, Adam had managed to pull in a few small security contracts, but it was Henry who had seen a gap in the market. Through his dealings with the Amari brothers, and possibly his brother, Henry had realised security staff needed to be taught more than how to use their fists in order to be competent.

Henry had scoured the country, attending every security training course their competitors ran at the time. With that knowledge, he and Henry had developed several programs of training for security staff in areas their competitors never even touched upon. Their training courses on Close Protection, Conflict Management, and Behavioural Screening had all proved popular and profitable. On Henry's insistence they produced a Celebrity Protection training course which seemed to chime with the age. It quickly became their most popular course. Once they'd secured backing from the newly created Security Industry Authority, making their courses approved, the business took off. In particular, courses run by Henry himself were highly valued and could be run at a premium rate. The business grew through recommendation and some of the trainees would keep in contact with Henry for years afterwards, seeking his advice as a mentor.

Adam reflected on the fact that training was still the most lucrative service of the company's portfolio, and yet at the time, he'd had to be convinced. Henry had spoken to someone in the industry at length and wouldn't be shaken from the view that security guard training had been neglected and represented a business opportunity they could exploit.

'People and property will always need to be protected', Henry would say, 'And the people doing the protecting need to be equipped to deal with *every* eventuality.'

AEBS had probably trained half the bodyguards, bouncers, and security men and women in England. Of course, some of the trainees ended up working for organised crime...

'Three times,' Adam answered, 'Each loan came from a source

within organised crime, but that's not the question you should be asking, Mary.'

Mary's eyes narrowed, 'What do you mean?'

'You were a largely unknown, well protected school teacher until three years ago. Eddie and Vincent may have worked out where you were years ago, but couldn't get close to you. But when he became too ill to work, Henry couldn't keep you protected any longer. Then you attended the funeral, and that announced your existence to every criminal in Newcastle. They were all there... each gang knew Henry; hell, they respected him. He was one of them, even though he wasn't a criminal. Half the decent bodyguards out there were trained by Henry and knew him well. Henry knew Eddie and the rest of these unsavoury people would be at his funeral, which is why he wanted you to stay away, but you're so... single-minded.'

Adam leaned forward in his chair and held the bridge of his nose for a few seconds, as if trying to assuage the onset of a headache.

'The icing on the cake was when you bought a racehorse. You may as well have taken an advert out in the *Evening Chronicle*. Anyone in the North East who knew about Henry's Stone may have respected your husband, but you're fair game. In fact, I suppose you're a bit of a soft target when you consider the Stone could be worth several million pounds.'

'Okay, so I shouldn't have gone to my husband's funeral,' said Mary ruefully, 'Eddie has been pretty vocal, not to mention downright underhand, in trying to locate the Stone, so I know about him. Who else is watching me?'

Adam scratched his chin, 'Eddie has probably scared off some of the small fry with ideas above their station, but I would guess there are at least two others thinking they can snag the Stone of Shiazzano for themselves...'

'Are you saying Eddie is involved in crime?' Danny interrupted.

Adam returned a surprised look, 'He's clever enough not to be involved in stuff like drugs and people trafficking, but that business he runs is basically a protection racket. He is a very dangerous man. Eddie might look debonair, but you don't want one of his boys knocking on your door, there's no telling what could befall you. It's why Henry found him so detestable.'

Danny swallowed hard and took Mary's hand in his, as much for himself, rather than as reassurance for Mary.

'You weren't supposed to get to know any of this until the anniversary of Henry's death,' Adam continued, becoming quite animated, 'He thought a year of you lying low would mean everyone would forget about the Stone Of Shiazzano and Eddie would assume it was lost forever.

Instead, you've now got some seriously bad people buzzing around you and they know you're the only one who can recover the Stone.'

'I want their names, Adam. I need the contact details of anyone who might be following me. Also, the people you got loans from. Can you do that?' asked Mary.

Adam's mouth dropped open, 'You have to be kidding!'

'No. I'm perfectly serious.'

'Why, what could you possibly gain?'

'I'm keeping my friends close and my enemies closer,' Mary said quietly, 'I have the right to know who they are.'

After outlining a number of reasons why she shouldn't contact these people, and being met with stony silence, Adam capitulated. He went to his desk and after consulting a notebook and his computer, handing Mary a note containing a list of four names and addresses. Each possessed a North East postcode.

'Only four?' she queried.

'That's all I know, and more than enough,' Adam assured her, 'Yousef is okay, but you really don't want to go anywhere near the others.'

Ignoring his protest, Mary asked, 'Who gave you the loans?'

Adam told her the Amari's had facilitated loans twice, and the second name of the list, a woman called Weatherstone, had been the final source of finance against the Stone in 1993. Adam concluded by making it clear he thought she was playing with fire.

'You're crazy to think you can reason with any of these people,' he warned with a resigned shrug, 'And don't try to meet any of them either. You have to believe me, you won't be safe, Mary.'

Mary acknowledged Adam's advice with a perfunctory nod, tucked the note into her handbag, and thanked him. Signalling to Danny it was time to leave, they walked to the exit and Mary pulled the thick glass door open.

'Oh, just one more thing, Adam, if I may,' Mary asked, releasing the door and spinning back to face him.

'How did you know I was the only person who can retrieve the Stone?'

Danny watched the blood drain from Adam's face. The businessman was looking anywhere except at Mary. After an awkward silence he began to speak, but had to start again. He was clearly rattled, his brain working faster than his mouth.

'Yousef Amari, is an acquaintance of mine,' Adam managed to get out, 'He's been out of crime for many years, but a stigma like that doesn't go away...'

'And?' Mary demanded, her expression hinting at a white hot anger just below the surface.

'Yousef was a good friend of Henry's. I introduced him to you because he wanted to make sure you were looked after. He put a few horses with Danny to get close to you.'

The words were coming freely from Adam and Mary simply stared, making the man's tongue loosen further.

'Don't ask me how, but it became common knowledge that Henry's Stone was still hidden and only you could find it,' Adam added.

'Do *you* know where it is?'

'No,' Adam replied immediately, 'I never wanted anything to do with it. Henry always dealt with the blasted thing.'

'But you were happy to take the dirty cash loans against it when you needed them,' Mary pointed out sternly.

Adam fell silent. He looked flustered and frustrated.

'I wish Henry was still here,' he eventually uttered desolately, 'He would have known what to do.'

Mary opened the door once again and gestured for Danny to go through. She followed him, but not before she had spun round and pointed her nose up at the businessman, fire in her eyes.

'Well, Henry isn't here, so I guess it's down to me.'

Just before the door clicked closed she called over her shoulder, 'Don't worry, Adam, we'll see ourselves out. After all, I wouldn't want anything nasty to *befall* you.'

It took a minute for Adam to place Mary's odd parting comment. When he did, his heart quickened and he had to fight the urge to race after his visitors.

Feeling slightly queasy, he located his phone, pushed a few icons and waited impatiently for an answer. Standing at the window he watched Mary and Danny exit the building and walk hurriedly toward their car.

His call was answered as they backed out of their parking space and he kept his message brief.

'She knows about the letter.'

Adam listened to a short reply. He rang off as Mary's car passed through the security barriers and continued to follow its slow progress until it disappeared out of sight.

Thirty-Five

'I don't know why you needed me in there with you,' said Danny.

He was in a buoyant mood as he drove Mary's Volvo out of the AEBS car park, 'You were brilliant. You had him by the...'

Mary was upset. Danny glanced over at her again to make sure. He pulled the car over once they were out of sight of Adam's building.

Danny sat quietly and concentrated on the pavement on the far side of the road, not sure whether to say anything.

'I'm okay. You can drive,' Mary said, blowing her nose.

The keys in the ignition were left untouched.

'Are you sure? Wouldn't you rather tell me what's going through your mind?'

Mary dropped her hands to reveal tear scalded cheeks, yet it transformed immediately when her face cracked into a weary smile.

'You don't want to hear an old woman bleating on.'

'Old?' Danny retorted with a snort, 'You're certainly not old. You're as sharp as a tack. You ran rings around Adam.'

Mary settled her eyes on the road ahead, 'I'm certainly feeling old. All that time we were together... my husband wasn't the man I thought he was.'

Danny thought hard, aware his next few words could sound glib if he got them wrong. After a short silence, he tried, picking tentatively through the emotional minefield.

'I got the impression he, Henry that is, was trying... to protect you. He... obviously loved... well, you know. And he had these two, sort of separate lives... to keep you safe from Eddie. He did have a plan... as Adam said, something was due to happen in a few months time, it's just that other things happened and it all got a bit... cocked up.'

Mary had turned to watch Danny halfway through his speech and now wore an endearing grin. She made a fist and playfully punched him on the top of his arm.

'Hey! What's that for?'

'That's a thank you.'

Danny allowed his bottom lip to bend over and he ruefully rubbed his arm. He was pleased when his play-acting prompted a proper smile from Mary.

'God help me if you ever get *really* pleased with me.'

'Drive!' Mary told him through a throaty chuckle, pointing to the road ahead, 'Come on... we've got a Stone to recover and a bunch of greedy men to pacify.'

'Sounds good to me!' Danny cried, starting the car's engine, 'Where are we going, Newcastle?'

Mary didn't answer. Her thoughts had strayed back to their conversation with Adam. She'd realised the little girl, Emily, wasn't in any serious danger. If Adam had written the blackmailing letter to Eddie, there was no way he was going to hurt a child... he didn't have it in him. Which meant...'

'Mary? Where are we going?' Danny repeated.

They will be watching us, she decided. They have all been watching her. Eddie had been watching her for three years and perhaps more. Watching her... she considered the words carefully, allowing them to reverberate around her mind.

'We can't go and find the Stone,' Mary stated in a faraway voice.

'Eh? Why not?'

'No. I mean *you and I* can't go gallivanting around looking for the Stone. Someone else will have to do it for us. If we're being watched by several groups of nasty people, we may as well tell them all where it's hidden and let them fight it out.'

'Sounds good to me,' Danny said with a shrug.

'No. There has to be a way...'

'Ha! I didn't think for a minute you'd let someone else find it,' Danny cried, slapping the Volvo's thin steering wheel, 'But if *we* can't go searching, who will you send to find the Stone?'

Mary gazed through the car windscreen, thinking hard. After a pause, a crafty grin spread across her face.

'We need to distract and confuse anyone aiming to follow us.'

'How are you going to do that?' Danny queried.

'We'll send our least likely treasure hunters.'

Thirty-Six

Beverley was one of Mary's favourite country racecourses. If Henry wasn't able to make it to their Saturday meetings through summer, she would ask her friends, and on occasion make the hour and a quarter journey by car on her own if they weren't available. Beverley race meetings were always well attended, boasted decent racegoer facilities and possessed a quintessential East Yorkshire feel to them.

Mary had backed plenty of winners at the track over the years. Her memories of good wins were all linked to Henry and her friends though, as she and her father never ventured this far down from Sunderland.

Her fondness for Beverley had been cemented when she managed to land a sizeable Placepot bet one evening in high summer, thanks in the main to there being three five furlong races on the card. The track is idiosyncratic over many of the race distances, but none more so than five furlongs. It amused Mary that their sprint races were advertised as being run over a straight five furlongs when the track was anything but straight, and the actual distance was almost five and a half furlongs. What's more, there was a stiff uphill finish. A low draw near the inside rail was essential in order to save lengths on your rivals, especially in a competitive handicap with more than a dozen runners, as was a smart jump from the gates. Mary would often seek out a horse drawn well and needing six furlongs on form, in order for her selection to see out the trip properly. So it was with some trepidation that Mary climbed the large concrete steps into Beverley's grandstand in late May, knowing Lucky Jake's stall position was the worst of the sixteen runners.

Audrey and Sarah were beside her, leaning against the grandstand railings on the first tier, watching Maisie struggle up the steps.

'Thank goodness Jake went to the start early,' Audrey noted, inclining her head toward the slowly moving friend still climbing the steps, 'Maisie would never have got up here in time to watch the race!'

The three ladies watched as Maisie took a breather half way up.

'I did offer to help her, but she's a stubborn old boot. She still won't accept her hips need looking at,' lamented Sarah.

'Have I beaten Danny to the start?' Maisie puffed when she arrived beside her friends a minute later.

'Just,' reported Mary. 'He's about a hundred yards from the stalls.'

Danny insisted on applying for dispensation from the Stewards to lead Lucky Jake to the start, in an attempt to ensure the gelding went into the stalls in a relaxed state. An image of Danny leading Ewan and Lucky Jake at a jog popped up on the large public screen in the centre of the racecourse and the commentator mentioned them before he started to call the other runners as they were led, then released onto the track from the parade ring.

'What I'd give to be that fit all over again,' Maisie sighed enviously, eyes glued to the big screen and the jogging Danny.

'What wouldn't we all give,' echoed Sarah.

Audrey rolled her eyes at Mary, who shrugged and waited for the admonishment that was surely on its way. Audrey wasn't the sort to put up with people she categorised as 'Moaning Minnies'.

'For crying out loud, have you heard yourselves? Anyone would think you're on your last legs. Can you shut up about your aches and pains.'

Sarah and Maisie shared a wide-eyed look. A wry smile worked its way onto Sarah's face.

'Audrey, have you had a big bet on Lucky Jake?'

Audrey didn't reply.

'Because you always get a bit agitated when you've had a large bet...'

'Am I really that easy to read?' said Audrey grumpily.

'Yes!' her friends said in unison.

Audrey raised her eyes skyward, 'Remind me never to play cards with you lot ever again, no wonder I always lose.'

'So come on, he's trading at 9/1 at the moment,' Maisie said encouragingly, 'How much have you had on him?'

'Danny's view of the draw put me off if I'm honest. I was going to splurge, but in the end I've just had fifty each-way,' Audrey admitted.

'Blimey, Aud. I've had thirty to win and thought that was a splurge!'

'That's enough,' warned Mary, nervously tapping the rail in front of her, 'They're loading the stalls.'

The four women immediately switched their attention back to the big screen which was showing a static view of the front of the starting stalls from about a hundred yards away.

'I wish they'd get a camera behind the stalls, you can't see anything from here,' complained Audrey.

'Look for the red cap on the outside,' Mary instructed, 'But don't expect to see much of him in the first few furlongs. Danny has told Ewan to drop Jake in and ride him for luck.'

Behind the stalls, Danny stood still, patiently holding Lucky Jake's lead rein. The gelding was alert, flicking his ears, taking in every call, push, and shove the stalls staff made. With only two other horses to go in, a stalls handler approached and Danny handed Jake over. As he backed off, he glanced up at Ewan who had hardly said a word for the last few minutes.

'Don't touch his ears and don't stop riding him, right to the line. He'll keep finding for you.'

Ewan responded with a grin. He'd heard the same instructions three times from Danny during their jog to the start. 'Will do, Guv,' he confirmed, pulling his goggles down as Lucky Jake was led to his outside stall.

Danny backed away to the outside rails and waited. In the end, he'd not put cheekpieces onto the horse, preferring to save them for another day, but now wondered if he'd made the right decision. He was relieved when Ewan and Jake walked straight into stall sixteen without any hesitation and the gates closed behind them. Further down the line another runner slipped into its stall with a helpful shove, which left one to go. The remaining filly had already backed away twice, but with four stalls handlers now braced against her protests, she slowly edged forward into her empty slot in stall ten.

Danny saw the danger before it happened. A colt in the stall beside the filly started to get anxious. He rose on his hind legs and Danny saw its bay head bob up for a second, the rider leaning forward to maintain his balance. Danny took a step toward and leapt onto the frame beside Lucky Jake's stall. Two stalls down, the colt was up again, this time with its front legs pawing wildly at the front of the stall, his rider clambering onto the frame so as not to get crushed if the three-quarters of a ton youngster toppled over backwards.

Lucky Jake tried to turn his head toward the sound of the shouts. The distressed colt snorted as it caught one of its front legs over the side of its stall. Immediately there were two handlers up beside him. At the same time, Danny was up beside Ewan, talking into Lucky Jake's ear, holding his head. The gelding was anxiously bumping the sides of his stall, but Danny's words had a soporific effect and within seconds he was standing quietly once again.

Along the line of runners, the colt's leg was rescued from its neighbouring stall. Once he was standing with all four feet on the turf, the colt was reunited with his rider. Having lost patience with the headstrong filly who had planted herself once again, the starter shouted for the handlers to clear; they would go without her. Danny let go of Lucky Jake, dropped to the ground and a moment later the stalls flew open. Ewan simultaneously squeezed with his heels and the gelding jumped out with the field.

He allowed Lucky Jake to get to speed for a few strides, then pulled back on his reins until he was clear of the horse on his right. Then Ewan steering the gelding over toward the inside rails during their journey to the four furlong marker.

Mary squinted down the course, in a vain attempt to spot her colours but the race was still too far away. Returning to the big screen, she scanned the head-on view but was still no wiser, unconsciously crumpling her racecard in her fist in frustration.

'There he is, right on the inside,' remarked Audrey.

Her three friends scoured the picture and sure enough, a red cap and the smallest smudge of vertical red stripes could be picked out at the back of the field, right on the inside rails.

'He's going to find it difficult to win from there,' moaned Sarah.

Ewan had the same thought running through his mind. He was looking up at a wall of horses in front of him. The field had bunched in the last half a furlong and after tacking smoothly to the rail he had been shuffled back by some scrimmaging in mid-pack. There were at least five lengths between him and the leading duo, but with the cut-away coming up, he crouched a little lower in his saddle.

Over three and a half furlongs out, Ewan angled Lucky Jake to the right in anticipation of when the sprint spur would meet the circular track. This would offer him an opportunity, albeit within a very small window.

On his inside, the white rails came to an abrupt end and Ewan asked Lucky Jake to go forward. The response was immediate. The gelding's stride lengthened and he went up the inside of two horses and alongside another, making up five places in four strides. However, as the three furlong pole flashed past to his right, Ewan realised he would have to sit and suffer the consequences of opting for his inside route as two rows of three horses were now lined up in front of him, and he was boxed in on his left.

Mary cursed as the television pictures, now closer to the field and displaying the true condition of the race, showed Lucky Jake surrounded by other runners and still three lengths off the pace.

'He moved up well there,' said Sarah hopefully.

'Yes, but he's going to need the luck of the devil to find a way through,' Mary grumbled in response. More than thirty years of watching five furlong races at Beverley told her Ewan and Jake's chance had already evaporated.

In front of Ewan, the second rank of horses edged left and an enticing gap suddenly appeared one off the rail, but before he could react and move Jake over, it became obvious why the gap had opened; one of the pace setters had come under early pressure and was weakening back through the field and in doing so, causing the pack to splinter and spread. Anyone caught behind the spent runner would be forced to take a pull. Quickly glancing to his left, Ewan found two rivals matching strides with him. The closest jockey had recognised his predicament and began screaming for room as a set of hind plates flashed in front of his mount's nose. A second later he was gone, dropped out to avoid a collision, followed by the weakening horse only moments later.

Ewan waited, fighting the impulse to cross immediately into the vacant space. The race was changing shape as more jockeys adopted animated riding styles and he sensed he still had plenty of horse under him. He continued to hug the rail, Lucky Jake breathing in regular, forceful snorts.

He was still sitting motionless as the two furlong pole was left behind. Lucky Jake was now almost on top of the trio of horses in front of him, and another two rivals were a length ahead of them, contesting the lead. Ewan didn't waver from his course. The horse ahead of him had begun to shift away from the rail.

'He's got to switch him out,' insisted Audrey, shouting against the wall of sound coming from the stands.

Mary had stopped watching the big screen and was standing on tip-toe following Ewan's progress toward the furlong pole. Her heart was thumping despite having lost hope of securing a win. He's got to sit and suffer, she thought. It's too late to find a new path through.

Two strides before the final furlong pole loomed, Ewan started to push. The gap was there, and Lucky Jake was only too happy to oblige, squeezing between the rails and his rival who was jinking to his left. Lucky Jake quickly accelerated away, Ewan giving the gelding the faintest of encouraging slaps down his neck with his whip.

Audrey bellowed her encouragement as Lucky Jake appeared to breeze past the second rank of rivals, moving from sixth into third in a matter of strides. Sarah joined Audrey with a huge whoop as the gelding broke free of his incarceration.

There are moments in horseracing, split seconds where the impossible can become possible, and where the possible can suddenly become reality. The moment Lucky Jake pointed his toe and started to drag the front two horses toward him, Mary felt the flutter of possibility shoot down her spine and supercharge her heart. When Ewan thrust his mount between his final two rivals, only two strides from the finishing line, Mary had already been hollering at the top of her lungs and believed. When the three horses broke the line as one, she was sure she had witnessed her first ever winner. His momentum had surely carried him to the shortest of victories.

Caught in an ecstatic embrace, Sarah and Audrey were jumping up and down in each other's arms.

'He got there didn't he?' Maisie checked with Mary.

She didn't reply.

'Mary?' Maisie asked, her concern mounting. Tears of joy were streaming down Mary's cheeks and she was making no attempt to stop the flow or wipe them away. Staring at Beverley's finishing post and exhibiting a dreamlike expression, Mary remained silently rooted to her spot in the stands, allowing a flood of emotion to wash over her. An image of her father had swept into her mind and in that moment all thoughts, stresses, and strains of a stolen Stone, the secrets of a lost husband, and the threat from entities known, and unknown, were forgotten.

'That's for you, dad,' Mary told herself, slowly raising her eyes skyward and allowing the sunshine to warm her face, 'I hope you were watching.'

'Mary. Mary!'

Snapping back, Mary became aware she was surrounded by a trio of concerned faces and the offer of a tissue, which she gladly accepted.

'After assuring her friends they were indeed, tears of joy, she was hustled down the stands steps and toward the parade ring, which doubled as the winners' enclosure.

As her feet reached the immaculate turf of the parade ring, the public address system boomed into life.

'Here's the result, Mary,' Maisie said breathlessly. The four women halted in the middle of the ring, hanging on the photograph decision.

Ewan had pulled hard at Lucky Jake's reins soon after crossing the line and the gelding had flicked his ears forward in response, slowing before the track turned sharply to the right. He'd finished with a flourish, but not without sustaining a bump as he'd threaded the eye of the needle between his two rivals. One of those rivals called over to Ewan.

'What do you think?'

He shrugged, 'If my lad has got there, he'll have dug me out of a hole with his owners over the way I rode him!'

Ewan didn't discover whether his reception would be joyous or combative for another three minutes. He was sliding off Lucky Jake's back in the parade ring when the result came over the public address system.

'...Here is the result of the photograph for first place; First number nine, Lucky Jake, and a dead heat for second place...'

Danny heard the announcement as he was making his way across the track. He allowed himself a small punch of his fist to celebrate his first two-year-old winner as a trainer.

Lucky Jake's connections met up in front of the winners' podium, sharing congratulations, and in Ewan's case, their profound thanks for sticking rigidly to Danny's riding instructions. A few seconds later the public address system burst into life once again. This time the announcer's words were preceded by a trio of chimes that echoed around the racecourse, denoting a Steward's Enquiry.

Thirty-Seven

For the third time in the last twenty minutes, Audrey scowled at Maisie and told her she couldn't drive for toffee.

'I mean to say, left means *left*!'

Maisie screwed her face up, 'The left-hand lane will take me the wrong way!'

Audrey made a frustrated gurgling noise and riffled the paper map she had on her knee.

'For heaven's sake, will you stop crinkling that blessed map! It's not my fault my car doesn't have a... one of those...'

'A Sat Nav,' Audrey sighed.

Maisie's ten-year-old Rover edged forward to the junction, and St James' Park loomed up on the hill to their left.

'I *told* you!' Audrey complained, 'You're in the wrong lane.'

Maisie waited for a gap in the traffic, followed the lane which did indeed filter to the left, and eased over, following the road round and up past the Newcastle United football ground. She gave a little, 'Ahem,' and looked over her driving glasses at her friend.

Audrey stared straight ahead, avoiding Maisie's gaze.

'Bloody map,' she muttered.

A minute later Maisie had found her way onto Richardson Road and pulled over into a parking spot. On their right was a large hospital but it was the view on the other side that interested them. The two ladies peered over the road and through black iron railings to the trees, paths and parkland beyond. An expanse of water shimmered invitingly through the trees thanks to the springtime sun. It was fine and clear, hardly the day for lurking unseen in undergrowth.

'That has to be it,' said Maisie. She checked her rear view mirror, although uncertain what she was supposed to be looking for. She felt a tingling sensation; she hadn't been this excited for years. Even being dealt a pair of aces in poker, or watching a 33/1 shot win for you at the races didn't deliver this sort of excitement. She realised it must be the element of fear that was ramping up her blood pressure.

Their day had started in Danny Carter's car park at 9-30am, with Mary and Danny heading off in the horsebox to do a racecourse gallop at Wetherby, Graham and Juliet setting off for Whitby for a day out, and Ewan and Sarah travelling to Pontefract races where Ewan had two rides. They all left at the same time, with a lot of noise, and in a carefully co-ordinated convoy through Malton, so that when they eventually went their separate ways, anyone following would have to split into four to follow them all.

'Do you think we've been followed?'

Audrey gave her friend a tortured grimace, 'I think we would have noticed, you were driving so slow even the mopeds were passing us. There's no way anyone tailing us could have gone unnoticed.'

'I know you're only joking, but sometimes it can come across as rather rude, Aud.'

'I wasn't joking Maise,' Audrey replied deadpan, folding into a grin when she couldn't hold it any longer.

'Come on then, let's get going.'

'No. Give it a few minutes, just in case.'

They sat for another two minutes, nervously checking mirrors, watching the pedestrians pass by and cars swish past. None of them struck either woman as potential dangers.

'I have no idea what a criminal is supposed to look like these days,' Maisie commented after an old man with a wispy silver beard and a walking stick hobbled past her window.

'What did they used to look like?' Audrey enquired sarcastically.

'Oh, come on then, let's go. My leg's going to sleep sitting in here.'

They got out of the car, put their handbags back inside, got them out again, and had a whispered argument for two minutes about what they needed to take with them.

'We have to look normal!' Maisie insisted.

'So I guess we're leaving the spade in the boot,' Audrey ventured, 'Because it might look a little bit strange, two women in their late fifties carrying a spade into a public park...'

'We don't know whether we need it yet!' Maisie hissed back.

Finding the bench and the tree with two trunks hadn't taken long. Mary had given them detailed instructions. They sat down on the bench opposite the manmade lake and waited until a jogger went by and a young woman with half a dozen dogs on a variety of leads struggled past.

'My heart is pounding,' Maisie whispered.

'Never mind your heart, I'm having a hot flush. You'll have to give me a minute.'

The two ladies remained seated for another five minutes, smiling at anyone who came along and spreading themselves across the bench to ensure no one else could sit down. A scruffy young man entirely dressed in denim and a pair of Doc Marten's turned onto the path and made Maisie stiffen; however, he ambled past without giving them a second look.

'Weed,' Audrey noted with a knowing nod at her friend once she thought the denim clad lad was out of earshot.

'What?'

'Marijuana, Maise. He stank of it.'

'How do you make that out?'

Audrey raised a mischievous eyebrow, which prompted Maisie to catch on and comically shake her head.

A few moments later, Audrey tapped her friends hand.

'Come on, there's no one around. Let's have a look. Remember, we're looking for a battered ring of silver.'

Stepping over twigs, leaf litter and discarded crisp packets the two women pushed their way into the undergrowth and shortly arrived behind a mature silver birch with two trunks, each soaring forty or fifty yards into a clear blue sky.

'Keep watch,' Audrey demanded.

'You're kidding,' Maisie whispered, 'No one can see us in here. Besides, it's pretty obvious the Stone is going to be in that.'

Audrey followed Maisie's pointing finger and her heart sank when she caught sight of a bird box nailed to the left-hand trunk. It was old, its wood blackened and slightly warped. It was also a good twenty feet above them.

The two women traded a silent, knowing look that screamed, 'Don't for one minute think I'm shinning up there!'

'But it doesn't really fit with Henry's instructions; where's the battered ring?' reasoned Maisie.

Audrey had to agree. She scanned the two trunks of the tree again. Its bark was silver with streaks of black, and fresh green leaves shaped like hearts were fluttering in the light breeze. She followed the trunks down to their bases, where they disappeared into dry, bare earth. She repeated the process again, poring over every knot, every shave of bark peeling from the tree, right to the ground and then walking around the whole tree and scanning the earth. There was the odd sweet wrapper, cigarette butt and a crushed can of Pepsi; nothing seemed out of the ordinary.

Audrey returned to Maisie's side. She was inspecting the bird box, her eyes two slits against the glare of the sun.

'I don't think that box is for birds,' she commented, still squinting, 'There's no hole for a bird to get in. I think it's a bat box.'

She returned her gaze to the floor, blinking to remove the sun spots now dancing on her retinas and locked eyes with her friend, realisation lighting up her face, 'It's a *bat* box and it's on a *silver* birch.'

Maisie screwed her mouth to one side, unconvinced.

'Where's the ring of silver?'

'It's a *silver* birch and it's got a circular trunk. But more to the point, we're going to need a ladder,' Audrey breathed unhappily.

'I'm still not sure it's going to be up there,' said Maisie, peering up through the branches, 'If that's our battered ring of silver, then Henry was busting the elastic on his metaphor.'

'Yes, but Mary did say he liked word games and cryptic crosswords.'

Audrey crossed her arms and put her back up against one of the tree's trunks and muttered to herself about climbing ladders and where they would find one. She rolled a little against the trunk, as if she were scratching her back. Maisie dropped her eyes to the ground and the patch of bare earth where Audrey's heels were digging in as she rolled against the tree. Among the dirt was a ring-pull from a drinks can, in fact there were several, and Audrey's heel was disturbing them.

'Aud... How long ago was it that cans of pop stopped using the sort of ring pulls that used to come off in your fingers?'

Audrey, still rocking against the tree, perhaps in some vain hope that she could knock the bat box off its perch, shook her head.

'I dunno, I guess it could be five or six years.'

'I think it's a lot longer than that. Could you step over here?'

With Audrey removed from her spot against the tree, Maisie bent down to inspect a small area of earth between the major roots of the tree. There were two tarnished old-fashioned ring pulls that Audrey's heels had disturbed and were now lying on the surface of the soil. With a grunt of back pain, Maisie knelt down and picked them out of the dust and other leafy debris.

'A silver ring,' she said to Audrey, offering her the small aluminium ring. It still had the now defunct pull tab affixed.

Audrey looked unimpressed with her find.

'What's this got to do with the Stone? There must have been some kids drinking cans of Coke around here and...'

'What? Twenty years ago, and specifically under this tree?'

' You used to find them all over the place when I was a kid', Audrey ruminated, 'We would snap them and flick the rings at each other.'

Maisie wasn't listening; she was busy scraping the top layer of the soil away and had already found another two ring pulls. Her hand brushed over something sharp; the top of a bent ring pull was embedded tab end up in the soil. She tried to tug at it, but it was well planted, so using one of the other tabs, she scraped away the hardened earth around it until she could get a decent part of her thumb and forefinger gripped in the fat end of the folded over tab.

'Oh, good lord!' she exclaimed as the ring pull came away, pulling up with it the first four inches of a length of wire.

Audrey bobbed down beside Maisie and together they inspected the battered aluminium ring. Some sort of nylon, probably fishing line, had been tied to the ring. The first few inches had come up immediately, but whatever was at the end of the line was well buried.

'Don't pull too hard on it,' Audrey warned. Her voice was quavering and the two women shared an excited glance, 'It could lead anywhere, we don't want to snap it.'

'Good job I brought this then,' said Maisie, lifting a small hand trowel from her handbag.

It still took a full five minutes scraping away at the earth with the trowel, following the route of the fishing twine as it wound deep between the roots of the tree, but presently Maisie's fingers pulled away some more soil and her next dig with her trowel connected with something metallic. With her heart rate soaring, she traced the end of the nylon line to a metal clasp attached to a tin of some sort. Clearing more soil and wiggling it allowed Maisie to pull out a three inch square, flat tin box with tobacco advertising on its lid, almost obscured by bubbling rust.

'Go on then,' Audrey said eagerly. She bobbed down beside Maisie and the two women traded excited looks filled with schoolgirl glee.

The tin opened with a soft pop. It was immediately obvious they had the right box. Despite being wrapped in several layers of transparent plastic, an intricate golden brooch with a large red stone at its centre filled the tin.

Audrey giggled and was quickly admonished by Maisie, although both of them then descended into a fit of barely silent, uncontrollable excitement.

Maisie suddenly slapped the lid back on the tin, and tucked it into her handbag. Holding the bag to her chest, she peered furtively through the bushes beyond the tree and out toward the lake.

'Did you hear someone?' she silently mouthed.

Audrey placed her finger to her lips and the two of them telegraphed the same message with their eyes; don't move and try not to breathe. Audrey had heard it too now, a definite swish of bushes and snap of dry twigs underfoot. Both women were close together at the base of the tree, Maisie was on her knees, however Audrey was on her haunches, and after another thirty seconds the muscles and tendons in her legs started to complain.

Maisie grabbed Audrey's hand when she could see the pain register in her friend's face. Another twenty seconds of silence ticked by and Audrey considered getting to her feet, but this was quashed when there was another sound of movement, this time even closer to them. Maisie watched as a bead of sweat broke on Audrey's forehead and travelled down her eyebrow; she would have to stand or fall over soon. Maisie made her decision; she slowly leant the few inches toward Audrey and wrapped her arms around her.

'Come to me,' she said softly into her ear. Audrey didn't need to be told twice, her knees, hips and back were screaming in white hot pain. She toppled forward onto Maisie and the two of them went backwards, landing with a soft thump on the ground they had been digging until a few minutes before. They lay together, frightened to move, gripping their handbags, Maisie listening for movement, Audrey trying desperately to stay silent, both of them frozen in each others arms.

Maisie heard heavy breathing behind her, and screwed her head round. Come to think of it, it sounded more like...

A large golden retriever loomed over the women and regarded the two of them uncertainly. A half inch line of slobber was dripping from both sides of its panting jaw.

From behind the dog came the sound of snapping branches and a tall, middle-aged man wearing a garish hooped jumper and corduroy trousers crashed through a wall of whippy saplings and brambles to stand a yard behind them.

'There you are!'

Audrey and Maisie hadn't moved, and were still hugging each other. Together they looked up from the ground and in a surreal moment, both of the women realised the man hadn't been addressing them.

'Paddy, what have you... Oh dear God!'

The man's mouth fell open as he took in the sight of two mature women in an intimate embrace, staring up at him from the bare earth. Furthermore, they were hot, bothered, and appeared to have a fear of discovery in their eyes.

'I do apologise... er, ladies,' he said quickly, grabbing the dog by its collar. He whipped around and stumbled back through the thicket, dragging his dog behind him.

Audrey lifted her ample frame to a seated position quickly enough to watch the man disappear behind a clump of trees and, satisfied he was gone, looked over at Maisie. Her back was covered in dead leaves and dirt. Despite the remnants of pain in her legs, Audrey started to laugh.

Maisie, also on her backside, tried to silence her partner in crime, but soon succumbed to laughter too. A few minutes later, two slightly bedraggled ladies emerged from the bushes close to the lake.

They looked furtively up and down the lakeside path. There was only an old man with a stick and a Breton hat slowly walking away with his back to them, so they started back to their car.

'You know something,' Audrey whispered conspiratorially to Maisie as she brushed the dirt from her jumper and yanked her skirt back to her hips, 'I'm not so bothered that dog and his owner found us in each other's arms, I'm just relieved I didn't have to climb that blummin' tree.'

Thirty-Eight

'But you will definitely lose him!'

'I know.'

'It's an insane idea, he's far better than a selling-plater.'

'I know!'

'So isn't there any other plan you can come up with?' Danny was standing in the doorway to the farmhouse's back room, hands on hips and radiating indignation. Mary had expected this reaction, but that knowledge hadn't made telling him any easier.

'It needs to be in a public place and there has to be a definitive hand over so that you, me, and all our friends won't continually be hounded. You heard Adam, there are bad people out there who know I'm the only hope of them getting hold of the Stone. They are all waiting for an opportunity to jump in and steal it once it's obvious I have it.'

Danny screwed his face up, dug his hands into the front pockets of his jeans and began shaking his head slowly from side to side.

'It's the perfect opportunity and most importantly, the safest way I can come up with to bring this thing to an end,' Mary insisted.

'This hasn't got anything to do with Lucky Jake losing his race in the Stewards room, has it?

Mary scrutinised Danny with such an intense stare, he immediately crumbled.

'I didn't think so,' he said weakly, dropping his eyes to the floor.

'We didn't deserve to lose that race and to be demoted to third. Ewan hardly touched that runner up. And if you think for one minute I blame...'

'Yeah, I know you don't,' Danny interrupted irritably, 'I'm just sore we're going to be losing him. I'm sorry, It's just... well, it's not the horse's fault and I think sacrificing him is plain wrong.'

Mary got up from her desk, crossed over to Danny and tenderly took his hands in hers. She caught his eye and held it until she was sure she had his undivided attention.

'On June 13th, Lucky Jake will run in the Rous Selling Stakes and my life will return to normal. Everyone else who has been drawn into this mess will then be safe. And I'll be able to return to Northallerton and let you get on with your life.'

Danny nodded his begrudging acceptance. He had to admit, it was a clever way of disposing of the Stone. However the potential loss of Lucky Jake in a seller wasn't the only downside to Mary's plan. He would be losing her too.

***

Vincent burst into Eddie's office and found his boss standing in front of his mirror, evaluating whether a newly acquired cashmere coat squared his shoulders and made his backside look big.

'She's found the Stone. Mary has been on the phone...'

Perturbed by his sudden entrance, and being caught admiring his backside, Eddie's initial reaction was to stare maliciously at Vincent, but this quickly evaporated when the enormity of his news struck home.

'She definitely said she had Pa's Stone?' he checked.

'Yes, she's deciphered the letter,' Vincent replied gleefully.

Eddie removed his coat, hung it on a hanger and spent a few moments running the back of his hand slowly down its chic lines to remove any creases. Vincent remained silent, knowing Eddie was thinking. He noticed a movement out of the corner of his eye and realised Forrester was standing at the open door.

'What do you want?'

'I overheard your news,' he replied lazily, moving into the room.

'We'll let you know when we need you involved,' Vincent said, gesturing for the financial controller to leave. The edge to his voice was noted by Forrester, but he made no effort to retrace his steps.

'I've been keeping our buyers on the hook for far too long, Eddie. When can I tell them you'll have possession of the Stone?'

'I *told you*,' Vincent repeated forcefully, 'Eddie will inform you when he's good and...'

'Vincent,' Eddie interrupted in a soothing manner, 'He can stay. After all, Forrester is right. He needs to know when we can expect to conduct the sale.'

Vincent reacted kindly to Eddie, but gave Forrester an undisguised glare of distain. The greasy little man had been ingratiating himself with Eddie ever since his brother's death. He'd started to turn up at Eddie's house more often, sometimes on the flimsiest of grounds, and it had recently dawned on Vincent that the financial controller was trying to usurp his position as Eddie's trusted deputy.

Eddie took a seat, clapped his hands together and rubbed them in anticipation.

'Come on then, Vincent, when will she hand it over?'

This is why I didn't want Forrester in the room, Vincent thought. This news needed to be reported carefully, and that wasn't going to happen if Forrester started to fire questions intended to undermine him.

'I really think Forrester should...'

'Get on with it, man,' Eddie demanded, his open-eyed enthusiasm turning into irritation.

Defeated, Vincent replied, 'York, in ten days time.'

Eddie leaned back in his executive chair, 'Why so long? Can't we take it before then?'

'She's cracked the code, but she's not going to collect the Stone until the day before. We've been following her twenty-four hours a day for the last two months and there's no way she's picked it up yet. She's spent virtually all her time at Carter's stables apart from a couple of trips to the races and back to Northallerton to check on her cottage.'

'She's clever,' Forrester chipped in, 'She must know we'll take the Stone once she's collected it.'

Eddie curled his lip. The idea that Mary could be deemed 'clever' turned his stomach. Vincent noticed Eddie's reaction and smiled inwardly.

'So we pick it up from her in York,' he summarised, 'At least the bitch has seen sense.'

Vincent shivered uncomfortably. Maintaining his gaze on the leg of Eddie's desk, he delivered the rest of Mary's instructions.

'It's at York racecourse. On a raceday. She's going to send an owner's badge to you, Eddie, and you're to meet her in the parade ring twenty-five minutes before the third race at 3-00pm. Only you can enter the parade ring, as you'll be the only one of us with an owner's badge.'

Eddie stared incredulously across his desk and for once, Vincent was pleased it was ridiculously large. Behind him he heard Forrester cursing under his breath, just loud enough to ensure his words would carry to Eddie.

'What the...' Eddie started, 'She wants to hand it over in front of a crowd?'

'And television cameras,' Forrester added.

Eddie's fist thumped the desk and he shot bolt upright, sending his chair skidding backwards. He stood stock still, apart from his hands which he'd bunched into fists and was flexing, turning his knuckles white.

Still ensuring he was concentrating on the desk leg and ignoring the urge to chance a glance upwards, Vincent continued, 'Mary won't have the Stone; someone else will be holding it until just before the race. If she sees anyone else enter the parade ring with you, the Stone won't be brought in.'

'Is that it?' Eddie asked angrily.

'She's sending the owners badge and a copy of the instructions by post,' Vincent murmured.

After a short pause, Forrester spoke.

'At least you're going to get the Stone. The transfer will happen with other people in the parade ring and it should happen quickly.'

'In front of an audience of thousands, all watching as Eddie is handed stolen goods!' Vincent blurted contemptuously, trying to make his statement sound as derogatory as possible.

Silence descended. From outside the window, a pigeon cooed incongruously. Eddie remained standing, his face a mask of anger and frustration.

'Get out,' Eddie growled in a low whisper, 'Both of you. Get out.'

Forrester and Vincent stayed in the room next door without exchanging a word or a glance. After five minutes of the noise from Eddie's office, Vincent had made a phone call. Ten minutes later Eddie appeared at his office door red-faced and sweating. His car was already waiting outside to whisk him to wherever he wanted to go, and a small team of trusted cleaners were ready to reconstruct his trashed office.

Thirty-Nine

Mary paused a few yards in front of the York Racecourse owners and trainers entrance and checked her watch. Her hand was shaking so much, she could hardly make out the Roman numerals. Closing her eyes for a moment, she steadied herself. A confirming inspection of her wrist watch told her it was half past one; twenty-five minutes before the first race and an hour and a half until Lucky Jake would run in the Rous Selling Stakes.

It had been a nervy morning. Danny had been pensive at breakfast, which in turn had put Juliet and Graham on edge. Mary had done her best to be bright and breezy, with limited results. Their planning meeting with Ewan, Sarah, Audrey and Maisie the evening before went better. Any gathering with Audrey present could be relied upon to be upbeat.

It had been another new experience. A video call, with her three ladies in Northallerton at Sarah's house, and the stable staff huddled around Mary's computer in the farmhouse. Mary hadn't met with any of her Northallerton friends since they had all set off in different directions from the yard a week ago. She'd judged it was best not to draw any attention to her friends, especially since Maisie and Audrey had returned victorious from Newcastle.

The video call had been a humbling experience, not at the time, but afterwards. She had lain in bed, running the plans for the day ahead through her mind, trying to find any glaring errors and had slowly realised they were everywhere. Each scenario placed her friends and colleagues in very real danger.

There, in that moment she had reached an epiphany. Her friends, new and old, were willing to help her. They didn't have to, they wanted to, and at significant risk to their wellbeing. For thirty years it had been Mary and Henry. He'd said it often enough: 'We don't need anyone else, Mary, because we've got each other.' But she had a different life now, a family of people she cared about, and she was about to put them all at risk.

She'd eventually padded downstairs to the kitchen for a drink of water, only to find Danny already there in his dressing gown, softly humming some inane tune. They had talked. Only a few words of mutual support and determination, but that short interaction had strengthened her resolve. She'd thanked him. His humming had resumed by the time she'd reached the top of the stairs.

Mary was sure she'd been followed across the racecourse car park. Twice she whipped round and found what she believed to be a suspicious man or women behind her. She was sure a man in a Breton cap was there too, she'd caught a glimpse of him, watching her from behind a line of parked cars. She'd immediately changed direction and quickened her step to mingle with other racegoers.

Mary collected her thoughts and focused on the small queue just ahead of her at the owners and trainers entrance. She'd opted for a conservative outfit and now checked it for the umpteenth time before stepping forward to tack onto the end of the line. She had dreamt of this moment; entering York as an owner, with a runner that harboured a realistic chance of winning at an 'A' grade racecourse. Such a shame it was likely to be marred by a bunch of greedy thugs.

York had also been her dad's favourite racecourse. Mary treasured vivid memories of travelling down from Sunderland, via Newcastle, by train, and the half a mile walk from the station past the ancient city walls and tree-lined streets populated with huge, expensive hotels. Back in the early eighties the two of them never entered Tattersalls, but instead, it was two pounds fifty for her dad to get into the 'Course' enclosure opposite the stands, and as a child under sixteen, Mary would enter for free. The last time she'd gone with her dad had been just before he died, Mary had been eighteen, but due to her lack of height, had been waved through the children's entrance without a second look from the aged attendant.

York's June meeting had always been one of Mary and Henry's favourites. It might lack the top quality racing the Ebor or their May meetings boasted, but it also lacked the huge crowds, making the racing experience far more pleasurable. Mary had always looked forward to this two day's racing in the middle of June as it signalled the school year was soon coming to an end and summer holidays were on their way.

Reaching the head of the queue, her owner's badge was allocated by two efficient ladies who provided Mary with a thick card ticket, which she attached to her shoulder bag. She had considered taking no bag at all, for fear it would be ripped from her by a thug who thought she'd carry the Stone into the racecourse with her; that was someone else's job. In order to advertise the fact she didn't have the Stone on her person her outfit was made of thin material, had no pockets, and she wasn't wearing a hat. Mary had opted for a very small, thin bag, no more than a purse on a strap really, she wouldn't have felt dressed without it.

As the lady behind the desk passed her a complimentary racecard, Mary forced a bright smile and asked the question she'd been rehearsing in her head for the last few minutes in the queue.

'I see you make a record of each badge being allocated. I'm meeting up with some guests of mine with Lucky Jake in the third race. You should have their names, as I booked them in advance. Could you possibly tell me whether they've arrived yet?'

The woman shot a look at the expanding line of owners behind Mary, gave a little sigh and replied, 'No problem, Madam, give me a second.'

'Mr Romano and Mr Amari have arrived,' the woman recited from a clipboard, 'Your other guests haven't picked up their badges yet.'

Mary thanked the lady warmly and received a genuinely pleased smile in return. She entered the racecourse and walked slowly towards the grandstand down a wide path bordered with ornately potted plants and tall advertising banners that Mary imagined would normally be fluttering in the breeze, but today hung motionless.

Passing several lawns strewn with tables of champagne quaffing racegoers to her left and nondescript buildings to her right, the path opened up onto a view over the parade ring and beside it, to the right, the pre-parade ring. There were plenty of people moving around, and most of the seats around the parade ring were already occupied. It was a scene Mary found quintessentially English, as the runners for the opening race began to filter from one ring into the other.

She quelled her impulse to join the crowd around the ring, choosing to remain in the open; it was her job to be on show until Lucky Jake's race. If the attention was on her, then it meant it wasn't on her friends... hopefully.

'I thought I'd find you here. Alone are you?' said a soft, heavily accented voice in her ear.

***

Sarah was first out of the car when it came to a halt in the racecourse car park. The parking attendant jumped with surprise when a frustrated scream of, 'Will you stop complaining!' was accompanied by the slamming of the driver's door. He peered into the car to see another angry woman dressed in similar attire, and in the back seat a large woman with her hand over her mouth who appeared to be finding the situation hilariously funny. Satisfied they weren't going to come to blows, the attendant moved off to park his next car.

Maisie was next out, slamming the car door, which made another satisfying thump. She grumpily folded her arms and eyed Sarah with unconcealed contempt.

'How was I supposed to know you were going to wear the exact same outfit?' Sarah countered before Maisie could start to berate her once more.

Audrey hauled herself out of the back seat and rounded the front of the car, leant on the bonnet for support and touched away tears of mirth from her eyes with her forefinger. She'd been laughing since they picked Maisie up, and her ribs were beginning to ache.

'I told you this would happen!' Maisie continued, wagging a finger at Sarah, 'It's the last time I go clothes shopping with you!'

Sarah struck a pose, her hand on her chin, looking Maisie up and down, appraising her outfit. Careful to adopt a conciliatory tone, she offered her opinion.

'Look, I'm sorry we didn't have time to go back so you could change, but honestly Maise, you look better than me in it. Besides, the whole idea today is that we stay separate, so we're hardly going to clash.'

Maisie sucked her teeth and considered this before uncrossing her arms and hitching her bag over her shoulder.

'I suppose so,' she conceded with a pout that would have made a teenager proud.

Seizing her opportunity to kill the current topic of conversation, Sarah took command, 'I'll set off first, then Aud can come after and then you can saunter over in about five minutes, so we all enter the racecourse separately. Best of luck everyone, let's do this for Mary.'

With that, Sarah gave Maisie a quick hug and set off over the Knavesmire grass toward the racecourse enclosures.

'What were the chances we'd wear the same outfit?' Maisie asked, watching her friend disappear into the sea of cars, 'I've only got five decent ones, but Sarah has hundreds and rarely wears the same one twice.'

'Forget about it. It's just a daft coincidence,' Audrey said softly.

Maisie bit her lip, 'It's going to be a bit weird being on my own at a racecourse all afternoon, I've always been with at least one or two of you.'

'It's only going to be for an hour, Maise,' Audrey pointed out, 'Lucky Jake is running at 3-05pm'. She put an arm around her friend and gave her a squeeze.

'Do you think Mary's plan will work out okay?' Maisie asked, her voice filled with doubt.

'When has Mary ever let us down?' Audrey said brightly, 'Besides, we're only the supporting cast. Mary and Danny, and, I suppose Lucky Jake, will be the ones in the spotlight. By the way, I assume the Stone arrived okay?'

'Yes, Mary called this morning. I couldn't believe she wanted me to send something that valuable through the normal post, but she insisted it was safe. Apparently it's been done before with gemstones...' Maisie had been consulting her watch and now nodded at Audrey.

'Ten to two. Isn't it time, Aud? You'd better go...'

Audrey gave her friend another squeeze, reminded her she looked great in her outfit, and headed off.

Maisie waited until Audrey was out of sight, took a deep breath and set off, her mind full of the rules of selling races and baby blue chiffon dresses with princess cut bodices.

***

'Really, I promise you Mary, I'll be fine,' said Rory. He was sitting at a table on the Champagne Bar lawn, nursing a bruised cheek, dabbing it tentatively with a napkin filled with ice. Mary sat beside him, feeling wretched.

'I probably deserved it anyway, sneaking up on you like that,' he offered amicably, along with a painful smile.

'I elbowed you in the face,' Mary said flatly, 'You really didn't deserve that.'

'Well, maybe it was for leaving you alone at the Eider meeting. I reckon I do deserve some retribution for that.'

Rory stopped touching his swollen cheek to concentrate on Mary's response, but was disappointed to find she wasn't listening. Instead, she was alternating between staring apprehensively over his shoulder and cringing behind him, apparently hiding from someone.

'Er... please don't look round or move too much will you, Rory?'

He had no reason to acquiesce to her request, but found himself automatically doing so. It had been the same unfathomable urge he'd felt when he'd seen Mary's horse was running today. He'd been down at the Newmarket Sales when he noticed Lucky Jake's declaration and felt compelled to leave his staff and charge halfway up England on the off-chance he would bump into her again. It was maddening.

'Can I ask who you are hiding from?'

She weaved from side to side, peeping over his shoulders before glancing quickly at him.

'No.'

Rory allowed his eyelids to half close in an attempt to produce such a sardonic expression Mary would be forced to open up. It had the effect of making her recoil.

'Are you sure you're okay, Rory? For a moment I thought you were having a stroke.'

He ignored her and decided to jump in with both feet.

'Why didn't you return my calls after the Eider?'

He watched Mary's eyes twitch slightly, then slide away slowly to gaze over his right shoulder. The tension in her shoulders fell away and the anxiety washed from her face. She got up to leave.

'I'm sorry Rory, there's a lot going on today. Can we have a chat in a couple of days?'

'No,' he replied firmly, 'I've travelled three hundred miles to find out why you're ignoring me.'

She scrutinized him with a curious, preoccupied air.

'What is it?' he insisted, 'What's wrong?'

'I'll see you after Lucky Jake's race, outside the parade ring,' she called over her shoulder as she slipped through the tables on the lawn. He lost her when she disappeared into the snake of people heading to the stands for the first race.

Rory reapplied the icepack to his cheekbone, wincing as the cloth stung his skin. 'Fine, I'll see you later,' he muttered miserably to himself.

***

Lucky Jake poked his head over his box door in the racecourse stables and snorted. From her small stool situated below the gelding's chin, Juliet provided him with a few kind words and returned her attention to her phone. It was a welcome distraction, as she was nervous.

It had already been a long day and she allowed her eyes to close for a few seconds. Starting at five o'clock that morning, she and Graham had done morning stables together and she and Ewan worked two lots on the gallops before preparing Lucky Jake and themselves for racing.

'If you need forty winks, you can crash in the horsebox if you want,' said a booming voice.

Juliet snapped to wide-eyed attention to find Graham and Danny approaching her, returned from their lunch. It slowly dawned that it had been Danny speaking unusually loud.

He stuck out a hand and pulled her up to her feet, announcing in a similarly strident tone, 'Don't worry. Go have a nap in the horsebox.'

'Graham and I can look after Jake,' he added, catching Juliet's eye.

'She did a grand job this morning,' Graham confirmed in a low voice as Juliet departed.

'I know, I'm sorry you three of you had to do everything on your own.'

'That's okay. I assume you managed to complete what you were working on after the package arrived?'

Danny gave Graham, a full forty years his senior, a knowing look and tipped the brim of a dark blue flat cap he'd taken to wearing for the last week.

'Good. We don't want our part of the job goin' wrong.'

Danny consulted his phone. He'd become aware of a little more activity around this end of the racecourse stables, with the traffic of lads, lasses and horses starting to increase.

'Two o'clock. We need to set off in fifteen minutes,' he stated, casting his eyes over a line of nearby bushes to the racecourse grandstands over half a mile away in the distance. It was such a still day he was sure he could hear the sound of the crowd massing for the first race on the card, due off in a few minutes.

'Aye, it's a long walk over the Knavesmire,' Graham confirmed, 'I've done it enough times.'

Danny turned back to Graham and whispered, 'I'm going to look Jake over. Check out those bushes on the left. I thought I saw someone in there watching us.'

Presently, Graham joined his boss in Lucky Jake's box.

'Definitely a chap hanging around behind those bushes,' he reported quietly.

Danny scowled, 'Only to be expected, I suppose.'

Graham shuffled closer to Danny until he was standing at his shoulder, 'You're a young lad with lots of horses and racing ahead of you. I've worked for good and bad trainers, but I've seen the way you train, and you've plenty of winners to look forward to. Don't be trying to be no hero. You heard Mary, these people are villains. If they threaten you, give it to them.'

Danny removed his flat cap and turned it over. The two men bowed their heads and peered inside. Danny grinned as he carefully replaced the cap, making sure to make adjustments so it was firmly clamped to his head.

'I know you've had four decades in the business, Graham, but get ready for what could be the most exciting bit of leading up you've ever done.'

Forty

Eddie Romano didn't tend to mix. He spent most of his days on holiday, at home, or at the city centre office. When it was essential, late evenings and night-time were his preferred hours to be pressing reticent payers for his pound of flesh. However, in the right circumstances he would venture out on his own during the day. Being out in public places was always risky, and carrying an entourage of bodyguards wasn't his style, although there were times when it was necessary. This was one of those times.

'I can't believe all the private boxes were taken,' he complained to Vincent, aware there were three men on his payroll surrounding him as they stood in the stands, waiting for the first race to get underway.

'Everything was booked up, the only thing left was a table on the top floor of the stand in a shared lounge, and I know how you hate being in busy restaurants.'

Eddie grunted his discontent, rocked on his feet and scanned the crowd. He'd never held an interest in horse racing; his father and brother had dragged him to the races a few times but he couldn't see the point. He was passé when it came to gambling and disliked the animals themselves; huge, flighty things with bad teeth. He'd discovered there were easier ways to make money and the only animals he bothered with were the ones he could shoot at in the Highlands.

'I suppose I've only got half an hour to wait,' Eddie stated, checking his Patek Phillipe.

Vincent didn't reply, willing the race to go off so that Eddie would be forced to halt his constant complaining. The huge screen on the inside of the track showed a handful of horses had yet to load.

'Heard anything from our people following the stable staff or the woman?'

'No,' Vincent replied, checking his phone just in case he'd received a message in the four minutes since Eddie had last asked. He reflected on the fact that Eddie had taken to calling Mary, 'The Woman', since he'd returned from his meeting with her. It worried him a little. Eddie tended to start referencing people as homogenous entities when he wanted them dealt with harshly.

'And she definitely didn't have the Stone on her when she arrived?'

Vincent shook his head, 'We checked her over close-up. There was nowhere for her to hide it.'

'She won't have it,' Eddie agreed, 'It'll be with those friends of hers, you need...'

The commentator's announcement of, 'Three horses to load,'

suddenly echoed around the racecourse, drowning Eddie's words. A few moments later the race was off.

Eddie didn't watch the race; he watched the crowd, scanning the backs of heads and faces, at a loss to understand why so many people would want to part with money to stand cheek by jowl watching animals with small, brightly coloured men and women on their backs run down a strip of turf.

As the race reached its final stages, Eddie lifted his eyes above the track and the crowd, over the manmade hill and clock tower at the centre of the course enclosure, and focused beyond. He concentrated on the tree-line on the other side of the racecourse, to where he'd been informed the racecourse stables were located. A steady flow of horses were being led across this huge expanse of grass, each with one or two handlers. The huge beasts were being led down a thin, snaking track of white railings.

Vincent had told him it was called the Knavesmire, an area once known for hosting public hangings. Eddie grinned at this thought, oblivious to the race reaching its climax.

Once the roar of the crowd had died down, Eddie inclined his head toward Vincent, 'Tell them to pull Carter and that woman's wretched horse apart before it gets to the track. I want the Stone in my hand before the next race goes off.'

Forty-One

Danny checked Lucky Jake over one last time and pulled him out of his box. The liver chestnut's coat sparkled in the afternoon sun and Danny found himself contemplating his chances. He shook himself from his reverie. Today was no time to be dreaming of winners at York.

Danny checked his watch one last time, 'Are we ready?'

Graham took the lead rein and swallowed hard, 'Aye, we're ready.' Lucky Jake scraped a front hoof on the tarmac, keen to be on his way.

With Danny walking on the horse's right-hand side, Graham led the gelding to their first checkpoint; the exit to the stables. A few yards before passing out of the stables Danny feigning a check of the gelding's feet as he waited for some company. To his relief, a young lass leading up a filly came up behind them. They let her pass, then fell straight in behind. The lady at the gate checked their details and within seconds they were across the small entry road and into the grassed chute that led to the Knavesmire. They would cross the racetrack twice, before they reached the pre-race stabling area next to the parade ring.

Neither men spoke. Mary had been specific; If they were going to be intercepted she believed it would be on this first fifty yard walk to the second checkpoint; the back straight racetrack crossing. Danny and Graham surveyed each side of the walkway. There were bushes and trees to the left and buildings with recesses to the right, perfect for someone to hide and suddenly jump out on them.

It was easy to detect their nervousness. Danny was checking every corner of each building, seeing gangsters in the shadows on his side of the gelding and at one point Graham growled a challenge into a large bush, making Danny jump. It was with immense relief that they reached the attendant on the back straight gate without anything untoward happening.

***

In the back of the horsebox, Juliet's mobile chirruped an alarm. Napping hadn't been an option. She had changed clothes, tied her hair up, found the lead for Lucky Jake's canine travelling partner, and waited for her three minute alarm to sound after Danny and Graham had set off. The Pointer sat unperturbed in the dark horsebox as Juliet clicked a retractable lead onto Charlie's collar.

With her pulse racing, Juliet opened the side-door to the horsebox and she and the dog jumped down onto the tarmac. Her working clothes were gone, replaced with distance running garb. She was a vision in Lycra, as Graham often described her on the occasions she decided to run to work.

After being cooped up in the horsebox for an hour, Charlie was bouncing around, keen to get on with his walk which to his delight, immediately turned into a run. Juliet set the timer on her mobile, secured it in a pouch tied around her waist and with Charlie cantering beside her they were soon leaving the racecourse stables and turning a sharp right past the Holiday Inn hotel and down a tree-lined road only wide enough for single cars.

As they settled into a steady rhythm and the shaded road began to take them away from stables, Juliet stole a long look over her shoulder. She didn't see anyone suspicious and a rush of relief filled her. She slowed a little and Charlie started to gambol; she had plenty of time. The lane was deserted and soon the Knavesmire opened up in front of her. She was pleased to note the grassland was dotted with other dog walkers.

***

It was stiflingly hot in the Land Rover, but you couldn't put the windows down. That was the job. When the call came he was the first to open the door and take a welcome lung full of the fresh air. They'd been waiting for an hour and a half, and one of his colleagues definitely had a body odour issue.

He was given his instructions. Their man at the stables had been tracking the mark. It was a simple intimidation and search job, and they could be heavy on the intimidation according to the boss.

There was a mass of cars to walk through, and no one around. Some of them looked nice, better than he could afford. He slowed to steal a quick peek inside a Porsche with red leather seats and his two colleagues walked on. He bent to the driver's window.

'Lovely, isn't it?' said a voice.

He turned to reply and instead of words flowing from his mouth, an intense pain in the base of his throat meant he produced a constricted cough and his eyes filled with moisture. By the time he registered he'd been struck in the throat, his moment of opportunity had passed and the pain transferred itself to his shoulder blade as he was forced to the floor, his nose pushed into the grass by a vice-like grip around his arm. A foot pressed into his back and pulled his left arm higher, grinding the bones. He responded with a grunt. There was a sound of sharp, metallic clicking and the pressure suddenly left his shoulder.

Rolling on his side, he found something was nipping at his wrist. He chanced a turn of his head to view his attacker, and found he was alone. However, his left hand wrist was still raised and it was being held aloft by a silver manacle and chain which... Realisation dawned and a shiver of fear ripped through him. He had been handcuffed to the door handle of the Porsche and pulling at it only brought him pain. An attempt to call his colleagues resulted in a pitiful squawk.

He shuffled to a sitting position and leant up against the car door, trawling his mind for a solution, but was drawn to a far more pressing question. How was Eddie Romano going to punish him?

***

As soon as Danny and Graham walked Lucky Jake into the railed chute leading across the Knavesmire, two men emerged from the lines of cars parked and made a beeline for them. They were walking alongside the rails, on an interception course with Lucky Jake. Set on their course toward Danny and Graham, the two men sporadically called over their shoulders to some, unseen person.

'It's got to be a welcoming party for us,' warned Danny, 'Look at what they're wearing. They have to be Eddie's boys.'

Graham agreed; the two men were dressed like nightclub bouncers from the nineties, with matching shiny zip up jackets, black trousers and army boots. They didn't walk with any grace over the undulating ground. Both men were carrying excess weight around their midriffs and their perambulation couldn't be described as athletic. It seemed they were built for standing still.

'They don't look that scary,' Graham noted, 'They're washed-up boxers with noses that have been broken too many times.'

'That tells me they'll have plenty of experience of punching people and being punched. Just remember that you are sixty-seven and you're not made of steel. Stick to what we have been practising,' Danny replied, eyeing up the speed of the approaching men and the twenty yards to the stable lass and her filly in front of them.

By the time the two bouncers came into range there was still three-quarters of the Knavesmire chute to walk with Lucky Jake. Danny estimated it was six hundred yards. The horse in front was now thirty yards ahead of them, due to their slowing pace, and as expected, one of the men dipped under the rails and started to wave his hands at them in a slowing motion once the filly had passed him. His colleague also was calling for them to stop.

'Okay, time to go,' said Danny, switching to the left-hand side of Lucky Jake. Graham reversed the lead rein, allowed the gelding to take a step past him and was legged up by Danny onto the gelding's bare back. Lucky Jake didn't bat an eyelid, as Graham had done the same thing every day on the gallops for the past week. Graham grabbed Jake's mane and shouted an encouraging 'Ya!' and horse and rider immediately shot forward.

The bouncer in the chute stopped mid-wave and his self-satisfied expression immediately transformed into one of utter terror, as Lucky Jake put his head down and thundered towards him. The bouncer backed to the nearest rail and froze. Jake did what all horses prefer to do when faced with a human in their way, he shot straight past, giving the petrified man as wide a berth as possible. After a further five strides, Graham eased back, telling the horse to calm, and Jake trotted quietly past the filly and reached the holding area for entry into the saddling stables thirty seconds later.

Danny watched the two men trade a look of disbelief as Graham and Jake whipped past. Powerless to catch the gelding, they were momentarily confused. Deciding it was now or never, Danny seized his opportunity. He put his head down and ran.

The chap on the other side of the rails never had a chance; Danny left him for dead. After ten yards, he dodged under the rails to his right and tried to get his arms and legs in sync in order to pick up speed. His suit jacket tails were flying and pinpricks of sweat immediately bubbled up under the brim of his flat cap. To his horror, the second bouncer had recovered from the shock of almost being bowled over by a charging horse, was dipping under rails and making a decent fist of trying to intercept him. Danny tried to pick up his pace, immediately realising the Knavesmire's undulations were undermining his efforts.

The man loomed large in front of Danny. It was going to be a close run thing as to whether he would be able to avoid a close encounter. Mid stride, he whipped his cap off his head and when he got within a few yards, threw it at the man.

'Take the Stone, it's yours,' Danny yelled, spinning the cap like a Frisbee. It reached its target, flying with solidity uncommon in most flat caps.

The red-faced bouncer juggled with the unexpected headgear for a split second as it bounced off his chest, enough for Danny to fend him off, shoving a hand in his face, twirling away, maintaining his forward momentum and coming away with a waft of body odour from the encounter. He sprinted another hundred yards before looking over his shoulder. There was no one following. The two men were together, hunched over, making no effort to catch him.

Danny slowed, imagining them inspecting the cap, feeling something round and heavy sewn into the lining, ripping it open and finding a ring of steel horseshoes attached to a metal plate he'd had his farrier knock up to emulate a large brooch with a ruby at its centre. In this case, the ruby was a pebble he'd super-glued to the centre.

Graham had slipped off Lucky Jake's back and was presently processing the horse through the final stage of entry into the saddling area.

Danny jogged up to join him.

'Over there,' Graham indicated with a pointed finger as the attendant at the gate ticked Lucky Jake off his list of runners.

Panting, and with hands on his knees, Danny took in the sight of a man, dressed similarly to the two bouncer types he'd just evaded, sitting with his back against a car door. There were significant differences though. He was younger, maybe early twenties, and probably fitter than his colleagues as he didn't have the spare tyre around his waist. One of his hands was in the air and it appeared he was handcuffed to the car's door handle.

'Looks like we've got someone helping us,' Graham said quietly as they entered the protection of the saddling area. Danny didn't reply. He was wondering whether the result of his skirmish with Eddie's men would have led to a different outcome had this third man been involved.

***

No one had given Juliet and Charlie a second look so far. Charlie bounded along beside her, still full of beans. The two of them were sticking to the access road for race pursuit vehicles that ran beside the track. Reaching the three furlong pole, Juliet eased to a walk and reduced the length of Charlie's lead. His tongue was lolling out of his mouth and he looked questioningly up at her as she fished her mobile phone out of her bum bag and inspected it earnestly.

'We've got another five minutes,' she told the dog.

With Charlie padding close to her heel, she continued to walk alongside the racetrack. The noise of the raceday crowd reached them and the runners for the second race were being announced over the public address system. She checked her watch again; twenty-five past two. Reaching the east entrance to the Clocktower enclosure, they walked past the ticket booth, now bereft of queuing customers. Juliet had almost reached her goal.

She eyed the eight foot high steel reinforced mesh fence protecting the enclosure and prayed her tests in the bottom paddocks and in her parent's back garden at home would pay off.

***

Sarah checked her watch and injected a bit more pace into her stride. Transferring from Tattersalls into the Clocktower enclosure hadn't been as smooth as she had imagined, losing a few minutes waiting for the attendant to deal with the chap in front of her. It meant crossing the racecourse, and health and safety being what it was, there were only certain times this public transfer opened between races.

Timing was critical. Sarah visualised Mary hammering this point home to them on the video chat. It's why she'd chosen her for this job; Maisie and Audrey were always late for everything.

She headed for the centrepiece of the enclosure, the Clocktower, by picking her way around picnicking families sat on collapsible chairs or lounging on rugs. A listed building, the Clocktower sat proudly at the top of the manmade hill, raised above the ground on columns that disguised the fact that there were steps underneath that led downwards to the rear of the enclosure.

Vindicated with her decision to wear flats, Sarah scampered down the Clocktower steps, passing ice cream trucks and fast food vans and wandered onto the large area of grass at the back of the enclosure. Several games of football were being played between children and a smattering of adults, most with jumpers for goalposts. She plotted a route between the players and caught sight of Juliet and Charlie, walking nonchalantly on the other side of the steel mesh fence. Juliet's face lit up when she caught sight of Sarah.

Turning her back to the fence, Sarah surveyed the scene. There were scores of people, but none of them seemed particularly interested in her, or the dog walker on the other side of the fence. They were playing games, queuing for food and drink or had their heads buried in newspapers or racecards. She spun around and checked whether there was anyone on Juliet's side of the fence. A lone dog walker had just rounded the corner of the enclosure, but Sarah decided she was far enough away and nodded expressively at Juliet.

'Dear God, I hope I get this right,' Juliet confided to Charlie under her breath as she undid her bum bag. He sat on the grass and watched her with his head on one side, beguiled by this new game. She checked the bag was securely zipped, stepped forward onto the grass verge and started to twirl the bum bag by its strap. It felt heavier than the contents she'd been practising with. Out of the corner of her eye she noticed Charlie's eyes following the revolving bag as if he was judging her style.

The moment she let go she knew it was all wrong. She'd screwed up. The bag shot straight up in the air at an angle that ensured it wasn't going to cover enough ground to cross over the fence. Looking up, Juliet lost the bag in the glare of the sun and with arms over her head for protection, waited for her missile to return to earth.

The second attempt was just as bad. She released too early and fired the bag into the fence.

'Can you throw it over or shove it underneath?' Sarah asked urgently as Juliet retrieved the bag from the foot of the fence. They both inspected the bottom of the fence. It was new and solidly built, a quick check revealed they would need to dig down under the fence to make the gap anything like large enough.

'And I can't throw for toffee,' Juliet whimpered, starting to get upset.

'Try spinning it again. Just breathe out before you throw and only spin it once or twice before you let go,' Sarah whispered through the mesh, worried their antics was drawing the attention of people on her side of the fence. She looked around and found a small boy standing a few feet away watching both women with wide eyes. He smiled and his eyes lit up when she held her forefinger to her lips.

Juliet stepped back, a mixture of concentration and frustration on her face. The dog walker was almost upon her now but she tried to put the woman and her Pug out of her mind, focussing instead on the weight of the bag and the revolutions. This time the bag soared into the air at a perfect forty-five degrees, clearing the fence easily and coming to rest near the young boy, who started to clap.

'Brilliant!' Sarah called.

Juliet didn't reply, she was too busy doing a victory dance, Charlie leaping around with her.

The small boy ran over and picked the bag up and held it out. Sarah fished about in her dress pocket and produced a five pounds note. The boy's eyes were like saucers by the time he made the exchange.

Hurrying back to the enclosure transfer point, Sarah reached the crest of the Clocktower hill and could see the horses in the second race being led around the parade ring. As she set off down the hill the public address system crackled into life.

'Jockeys for the second race, would you please mount. Jockeys, please mount.'

Stumbling over racegoers lying on the grass and passing between groups of seated retirees, Sarah crashed on through the forest of people. She had a minute to get back over the track before the transfer gate was closed until after the next race.

Forty-Two

'I'm working with bloody amateurs,' opined Eddie, spittle flying from his lips as he spat the words into Vincent's face. He closed his eyes and waited for Vincent to start explaining, cutting in as soon as he began to create the shape of his first word.

'Four men we had out there, and they couldn't stop a bony kid and an old man with a bloody donkey. Why the hell are we employing these idiots?'

Vincent waited, he wasn't going to be caught out with the same trick twice. Besides, the occupants of the next table on the champagne lawn were nudging each other and swapping jokes; Eddie's voice was too loud. At this rate it would be a miracle if he could get him to the parade ring for the third race without him taking a swing at one of his staff or a racegoer. He really wasn't great at social settings.

Eddie's eyes narrowed as Vincent's refusal to reply extended the silence. 'Well?' he demanded loudly, banging his fist on the glass topped table.

'Because they earned you a quarter of a million pounds in profit last year,' Vincent pointed out in a low hiss, 'They collect debts. They're not trained for this... sort of work.'

The two young couples at the next table enjoyed another round of giggles aimed at the two stiff men. One of the lads pretended to copy Eddie's fist bang and received a rapturous peel of drunken laughter from the girls.

For the first time, Eddie became aware of the interest from the next table, and directed a disgruntled stare over at the group.

'Leave it, Eddie,' warned Vincent, 'We're only minutes away from getting the Stone from Mary. Come on, the next race is about to start, we'll watch it from the parade ring so you will be ready to meet with her straight afterwards.'

'Where is she now?'

'Same place as she's been since she got here. Staying outside in the open and hasn't spoken with anyone apart from the Irishman she met at Newcastle races a couple of months ago. Even so, it was only for a few minutes.'

Vincent got up to leave, and was left standing waiting for his ill-tempered boss to join him. Eddie remained rooted to his chair, petulantly draining his flute of champagne. He rose, and struck a pose in his Saville Row suit, tugging at the cuffs to his cream shirt in order to allow his diamond cufflinks to sparkle. He picked up their half-finished bottle of champagne and followed Vincent a few steps, but halted at the table that had been mocking him.

'Cheap rubbish,' he exclaimed in a voice loud enough to turn heads. The girls giggled and one of the young men got to his feet.

'You got a problem?'

Ah, thought Eddie, the universal opening statement of the yob. Behind him, Vincent kept an eye on the standing male, ready to move in if necessary.

'Absolutely not,' Eddie replied with the faintest smirk, 'It's these ladies who are in dire need of being treated properly. The champagne you have bought them is the cheapest rubbish they sell here.'

Before the young man could react, Eddie placed his half drunk bottle of Bollinger onto their table, 'Here ladies, try a glass of this each... you may find it more to your taste.'

The young man glowered at Eddie but was uncertain how to react. His female friends were now thanking this smooth interloper and besides, up close both men radiated an air of controlled aggression.

'Sit down, chum,' Eddie advised, 'Take this opportunity to pour your lady friends a proper glass of champagne.'

Eddie didn't wait for a reaction. He slowly turned his back on the table and walked away. Vincent allowed his boss to pass him. The young man, along with the rest of his table, watched Eddie walk away. Vincent crossed his arms, piercing the lad with an intense stare for a few seconds before leaving.

This was familiar territory for Vincent and he smiled to himself as he dropped down the steps of the lawn behind his boss. Sure, Eddie was difficult to manage, but he had a way of reading situations and bending them his way. He'd watched him do it countless times and the greater the reward, the better he became. If Mary was true to her word and handed the Stone over as promised, albeit in front of an audience, perhaps Eddie could be convinced to...

A tall, shapely lady in a blue dress passed Vincent and he lost his train of thought. He watched her walk away from him toward the weighing room and pre-parade ring and trawled his mind. He knew that face, but from where?

Leaving Eddie to kill time watching the runners for the second race filing out of the parade ring, Vincent went in pursuit of the lady. There was a fuzzy recollection gnawing at him, a connection he couldn't quite place. She was hurrying, skipping sideways between the crocodile of racegoers flowing against her, as she headed for the weighing room. He did the same, trying to keep her in his sights as she bobbed and weaved.

Upon reaching the corner of the parade ring, she left the path, dropped down the steps to the lowest level of the sunken parade ring and cut across under the trees towards the pre-parade ring. From his elevated position on the path, Vincent was able to snatch a view of the lady from head to foot for the first time, and it came to him. She had served hot dogs at Danny Carter's open day, she must be a friend of Mary's. He also noticed she was carrying something; a nylon bag of some sort, big enough to hold...

Vincent shot forward and downwards, dodging between the few racegoers still standing on the turf terraces around the parade ring and strode purposefully after the lady, not allowing her to leave his field of vision. She was moving quickly through the crowds, scuttling up a few steps and was about to disappear behind the wall of the weighing room. He was fifteen yards behind, but was sure he could catch her; it was a dead end at the bottom of the public area of the pre-parade ring. Dodging a man staring down at his racecard, Vincent cursed as he was forced up another two steps by a threesome engaged in discussion. It was as he was leaping back downwards that he felt a pair of meaty hands give him a firm push on his buttocks. His immediate reaction was to turn his head to discover what had caused him to lose his footing, however, the sudden, unexpected feeling of weightlessness forced Vincent to look down, just in time to thrust his hands out to break his fall. He plunged between two rows of pedestal seats and crashed head first into the neat white steel mesh below the parade ring railings.

'Oh my word! That *poor* man!' Maisie shrieked in mock incredulity, the tips of her fingers in her mouth. Her exclamation had the desired effect, as a battery of concerned racegoers rushed to aid the fallen man. Meanwhile, Maisie strolled nonchalantly to the corner of the pre-parade ring. She peered around the corner and down to the bottom of the public viewing area in time to witness Sarah passing Juliet's bum bag over the pre-parade ring rails to Danny.

She looked back and watched nervously as Vincent was helped to his feet. Disorientated, he staggered a little and was guided, under protest, onto one of the seats. Maisie didn't wait to find out how quickly he would recover. She looked around her, then hurried down the side of the pre-parade ring, wishing she hadn't worn heels.

Vincent pushed his well-wishers away, firmly insisting he was recovered, and tried to stand. A few moments of giddiness had him back in the arms of his helpers and onto his pedestal seat. As they fussed over him he screwed his head round towards the pre-parade ring. Horses for the next race had started to move around behind the rails, but there was no lady in a blue dress.

Behind him, Maisie and Sarah walked across the centre of the parade ring, their heads bowed closely toward each other as they conducted a clandestine conversation. They tagged onto another group of owners and were soon lost in the huddle of people slowly siphoning through the parade ring exit.

Forty-Three

From the racecourse side of the parade ring, Mary was still enjoying a combination of relief and levity from having been witness to Maisie bumping Vincent down the parade ring steps. Not only had he failed to catch up with Sarah, the Stone reached Danny safely and she'd been able to witness the two ladies in matching dresses sneaking across the parade ring behind Vincent and thus evading any payback for their actions.

Once Vincent was reunited with Eddie on the other side of the parade ring, her good mood ebbed away. Vincent made a call and seconds later another four individuals, all wearing dark lounge suits, slowly converged on the two men from differing directions. She recognised a couple; they had been close to her all afternoon, watching her every move. Danny had been right. Keeping herself separated from the Stone and the others had served as a necessary distraction. However, it was the Rous Selling Stakes next and that meant it was Mary's time to shine.

The commentary for the second race had started but it was just a background noise to Mary, as she wasn't following the spectacle behind her. Facing the parade ring, she watched Eddie berate and wag his finger at the newly formed arc of men around him. Presently, one of the men was allowed to speak a few words, after which he turned and pointed across the parade ring and six sets of eyes were trained onto Mary. There were plenty of people around her, but they were all following the race on the big screen; her pale face stood out from the mass of racegoers, as she was the only person facing Eddie and his entourage.

Eddie contorted his features into a tooth-filled grin as his gaze settled on Mary. He's still the same as he was aged eighteen, Mary thought; completely lacking in warmth. She found herself feeling repulsed, despite the thirty yards of grass, rails and walkways between them. It reminded Mary of the pre-fight weigh-ins professional boxers were so fond of; the nose to nose staring contest prior to trying to knock each other senseless.

Behind her, the second race reached its climax and the crowd's volume swelled as the closely packed field passed the winning post. Their shouts of encouragement quickly lost resonance as the commentary ceased. Mary could hear hooves slapping against the turf as the horse's pulled up behind her, but she remained still, stoically facing Eddie's group.

Once the winner and placed horses had returned to the parade ring, connections had been presented with their prize, and the horses had been led away, Mary tapped a short text message on her phone and made her way to the corner of the parade ring. She showed her owners badge to the attendant and at the age of fifty-three Mary walked out onto the finely mown grass inside York's famous parade ring for the first time as an owner.

Mary knew exactly where to stand, as she wanted to be as visible as possible; she took up a position on the grass right in front of the winners' podium. This consisted of a raised plinth with steps, under a large white pergola. Facing the four small viewing gantries at this end of the parade ring, she soon spotted Sarah and Audrey who had reached their pre-arranged vantage points. She gave them both a quick nod and waited.

More owners started to enter the ring and she was beginning to feel a little exposed when Danny rounded the pergola.

'Sorry,' he began, rolling his eyes in apology, 'The er... preparation took a bit longer than I expected. I've not missed anything have I?'

'No, they're not here yet although...'

Over Danny's shoulder Mary spotted Eddie stepping over the horse walkway and onto the parade ring grass. He was waiting for Vincent, but he'd been stopped at the gate.

Danny watched as Mary set her jaw and strode over to the entrance to the parade ring.

'Vincent can't come in, Eddie. Only you have an owners' badge,' Mary stated, loud enough so Vincent and the gate attendant could both hear, immediately halting his argument with the elderly man. Eddie seemed to accept that further argument would be futile, so nodded curtly to his lieutenant and Vincent slunk back into the growing crowd of people on the parade ring rails.

'I hope you made good use of the lunch with your owners' badge,' Mary added sweetly, 'Come on Mr Romano, we're over here.'

Eddie was about to fire something sarcastic back at the woman, but became aware he had a row of people at the rails only a yard or two away, all listening intently to what was being said. He bit his tongue, following her into the centre of the parade ring, where a nervous young man he pegged as being in his early twenties was waiting for them. He was all elbows and knees and Eddie immediately decided he posed him little threat, despite his height.

'This is Danny Carter, the trainer of my horse, Lucky Jake,' Mary said breezily.

Eddie sniffed, ignoring the introduction and turned his back to the crowd, 'Just give me the bloody Stone, Woman,' he growled quietly.

Mary arched her eyebrows before adopting a benign expression which she hoped Eddie would interpret as deeply patronising, 'I think you must be a little confused Eddie. I told Vincent this was your opportunity to *acquire* the Stone. What did you expect; that I would just hand it over?

After all, I've discovered Emily is in no danger, and you're not the only interested party.'

Her timing could not have been better, as at that moment Yousef Amari appeared around the side of the Pergola. She called him over and gave him a similarly effusive welcome during which Eddie stood bristling in the background. Introducing them proved superfluous, as Eddie stepped forward and cut her short.

'I know this piece of sh...'

'Ah, gentlemen,' Mary broke back in, delighted with the effect Amari's arrival had had on Eddie, 'Let's keep this well-mannered. After all, we not only have an audience, we also have television cameras here to record everything.'

Mary gestured to the cameraman and Racing Channel host who were currently roving around the ring conducting interviews with some of the trainers and owners.

Most of the horses were now being led around the parade ring and the crowd had quickly tripled in size. All four of the small gantries in front of them were full and the paddock rails were three deep in places.

'Are you here with your brother?' Mary asked Yousef.

'It's good to see you again, Mary,' Yousef replied, ignoring her query and offering his hand instead. Mary shook it uncertainly, although she was pleased to note Yousef was exhibiting no lasting effects from the beating he'd taken at the yard.

'His brother won't be coming,' said Eddie contemptuously, 'Will he *Yousef*?'

Yousef's cheeks coloured, yet his eyes stayed as cold as ice, as he glared at Eddie. Finally, he turned to Mary, 'You weren't to know. My brother died a number of years ago... at the hands of Eddie Romano.'

Eddie sniffed, shrugged, and looked away into the crowd.

Mary swallowed hard and tried to free herself of the boggling set of entirely new questions that were now whirling around her mind.

After a pause, Eddie leant in to Mary, 'What the hell are you playing at, you stupid woman?'

He spoke in a low, urgent manner; demanding attention although he was concentrating his gaze elsewhere. Mary examined him close up. If she wasn't mistaken, Eddie had applied foundation to his face. A line of grey demarcation ran around his jaw where the application finished. There was an overpowering aroma of lemons and other citrus fruits, Mary presumed from his aftershave.

'Give me the Stone now or face the consequences,' Eddie continued, his threat making his lip curl.

Mary took a step back and looked Eddie up and down with a theatricality that would have delighted a pantomime dame. Once again, he was immaculately turned out and if it wasn't for his facial features, betraying him as an arrogant man consumed by his own self importance, he could have been categorised as handsome.

'I've heard this all before from you, Eddie,' she snapped, 'In fact, three or four times, and yet here I still am.'

Mary threw her arms up to advertise the fact she was very much still alive. Danny slanted her a worried glance and she dialled her act down. He was right, she had to keep her cool with Eddie. For now.

'You will have your opportunity to acquire the Stone very soon Eddie,' she continued in a lower, less animated fashion, ensuring Yousef could also hear her. 'Besides, we're still waiting for other parties from Newcastle to arrive.'

Eddie narrowed his eyes and was about to speak, but Yousef cut in first.

'No, I'm afraid there won't be anyone else joining us. It will just be the two of us, my dear,' said Yousef with a sad shake of his head, 'Myself and the loathsome Mr Romano here will be your only audience today.'

Eddie scowled. Danny edged away from him and gave Yousef a questioning look. Yousef remained silent, flashing a beatific smile at Danny before turning to engage Mary, only to find her staring at him in open-mouthed, horrified confusion.

Mary flicked between Yousef and Eddie, but not really focussing on either of them, desperately trying to work out what was going on. The momentum she had garnered from Eddie's arrival was now quashed, Yousef had seen to that. She was desperately trying to determine what this meant to the rest of her plan.

The horses continued to parade, all seventeen runners filing past, but the three male connections with Lucky Jake were oblivious to what was going on around them. They were waiting for Mary. Danny made to say something in order to come to Mary's aid, but Yousef silenced him with a flat palm.

'Henry was protecting you from him,' Yousef said quietly, 'We couldn't let you face this piece of detritus alone.'

'We?' Mary echoed.

'Adam and I.'

Realisation spread across Eddie's face and upon examination of Mary's blank expression he started to chuckle.

'You and the peacock, working together...'

Only vaguely aware of Eddie's descent into laughter, Mary's eyes twitched as she allowed Adam East's name to filter through her mind. His list of names, the criminal gangs... had been a lie. A moment later she closely scrutinised Yousef, an accusing look in her eye.

'Right!' Mary growled, 'My patience is wearing thin so this all ends here, right now.'

Eddie, still grinning, said, 'Wonderful, so if you'll just hand the...'

'If either of you want the Stone, you'll shut up,' broke in Mary, no longer frightened. She'd had enough of their lies and was using her anger to dominate the men around her.

'The Stone is in this parade ring and can become yours for as little as fourteen thousand pounds. It's been in here for the last five minutes.'

'Fine!' Eddie snorted, looking Mary and Danny up and down for evidence it was on their person, 'Cheque or cash?'

Mary gave him a lingering look of contempt before continuing, 'In order to acquire the Stone of Shiazzano you will have to acquire my horse, Lucky Jake. That way, there will be a bona-fide transaction and all the interested parties now and forever more, will know I no longer have anything to do with the Stone.'

Eddie and Yousef stared blankly at Mary. Keeping her tone flat and low, she began to explain. The two men stepped closer, and Danny moved aside, still keeping a close eye on Eddie.

'This is a Selling Race, in fact, it's the season's top two-year-old selling race. That means that after the race has been run, you can become the owner of any of the competing horses if you wish.'

Mary checked with both men before continuing, 'There are two ways you can acquire the Stone. If Lucky Jake runs and finishes in second place, or any further down the field, you will be able to claim him for the claimable price printed in your racecard, which is fourteen thousand pounds. The claim will have to be made by a person registered with Weatherby's.'

'This is ridiculous,' Eddie complained, 'What happens when we both claim him?'

'Then it becomes a random decision made by Weatherby's. You'll both go into a hat and the winning claim is drawn out. You have to take your chance and you'll be informed by the racecourse afterwards.'

'Who the hell are Weatherby's?' Eddie demanded. He was becoming agitated again and his antics were attracting attention in the viewing galleries.

'They're like the civil servants of racing,' Yousef retorted, 'Don't you know anything?'

Eddie gave him a black look, 'Unlike you, I don't fritter away my money on such a pointless inconsequence.'

'Okay, that's enough,' said Mary sternly, 'The other possibility is that Lucky Jake wins. In that case he will be auctioned in this ring after the race. If you have the winning bid, he's your horse.'

'So, you'll swap the horse for the Stone?' Yousef queried.

Mary smiled inwardly, 'No. Lucky Jake has the Stone. Once you own him, you can retrieve it.'

Both men reacted with confusion and began to question, and in Eddie's case, to berate Mary. She held up a hand until they fell under her spell once more.

'Take a look at him. He's been walking around the parade ring for the last ten minutes and the Stone has been on open view to the public.'

Mary waited a few seconds for this information to sink in, checking where Lucky Jake and Graham were in the ring.

'Here he comes now,' she told them. Then, with a tone laden with sarcasm, she added, 'That's horse number nine, Eddie.'

Yousef and Eddie waited for Lucky Jake to pass by. Graham had Jake close to him, leading him on the horse's left hand side, giving anyone on the inside of the parade ring a complete side-on view of him striding out. The horse was wearing a thin blue sweat rug over him which rippled as he walked. Mary watched him go by and found herself swelling with pride.

'What the hell,' Eddie spluttered as the gelding headed away from them again, 'Are you telling me you've made him swallow the Stone and I've got to cut it out of him?'

'You really are a total ignoramus,' scoffed Yousef. Turning to eye Mary he added, 'Very clever my dear. I assume it can be popped out afterwards?'

Danny stepped in to explain, 'The horse isn't even aware it's there, as the whole area doesn't have nerve-endings. It's very firmly held in his Prophet's Thumbprint, but we also used soluble glue in there too, just to be sure. It will take a few minutes to remove after the race.'

Eddie was fizzing. He should have known better; his brother had been an insufferably clever show-off and Mary was just the same. Eddie liked things simple. Both in his working and personal life, he kept things straightforward. That was why he was a rich man. There was nothing complex about running a debt recovery business. You just kept shaking them harder and harder, until they paid up. He didn't have a wife and children for the same reason; far too much complexity. When he taxed his mind his eyesight would jump around and the dull headache would start. Then the feeling of inadequacy would strike... and he reacted strangely when he was in that sort of mood.

'Where is the Stone, woman?' Eddie asked menacingly, stepping up to invade Mary's personal space.

Mary stared up at Eddie, 'Lucky Jake has what's known as a Prophet's Thumbprint. In his case, it's an indentation surrounded by a rosette of skin at the base of his neck, close to his shoulder. It's just perfect for a circular brooch with a valuable stone at its centre to be slotted into. Look...'

Lucky Jake was coming back up the opposite side of the parade ring now and Eddie picked him out by the number nine on his saddlecloth. He peered at the animal's neck. It wasn't obvious, you really had to look hard, but Eddie caught a glimpse of something glinting red that was rhythmically poking out from under the horse's rug. Every time the horse strode forward and extended his front right leg the Stone of Shiazzano was uncovered for a fraction of a second. Eddie licked his lips, and stepped toward the animal, but common sense halted any rush to the Stone.

'What's stopping me just taking the Stone?' he asked suspiciously.

Mary gritted her teeth, but it was Danny who answered, 'Be my guest Mr Romano! Go ahead and try. You'll probably be thrown out of the racecourse for attempting to tamper with a horse. That's if you can handle being bitten and kicked by the gelding for the five minutes it will take you to get the Stone out of him. Lucky Jake's not too good with strangers.'

'The only way either of you are getting that Stone is by claiming him, or buying him at the auction, if he wins. Either way, I'll be rid of both of you,' stated Mary in conclusion.

The men fell into silent contemplation, both watching the gelding continue his perambulation around the ring.

Presently, Yousef asked, 'Can he win, Danny?'

Danny glanced at Mary and after receiving an affirming nod, he answered, 'If he gets out of the stalls cleanly, I think he'll go well.'

'So we're done here,' Mary stated in conclusion, 'I'll see you both after the race, if you decide to put in a claim or bid for him.'

Mary took Danny by the arm and directed him around the islands of owners and trainers to the other end of the parade ring. When they were well out of earshot, Mary tugged on his arm, bringing him down to her level.

'Do we need to protect Jake?'

Danny shook his head, 'Nope, he'll be fine. Believe me, if either of them or anyone goes anywhere near him, Graham knows what to do.'

'What do you mean?'

'His ears!' Danny said conspiratorially, 'He still hates anyone touching them. We have a devil of a job getting his head collar on some days. If anyone goes near, Graham only has to touch his ears and Jake will take a chunk out of anyone close by! Would serve them right too, I did warn them.'

Mary considered this for a moment, enjoying the mental image of Eddie being bitten by her horse. However, she was smartly brought back to the present by Ewan, dressed in her silks and whip in hand, arriving at her side.

'How did it go?' he asked excitedly.

Danny sighed, Mary shrugged and Ewan's face fell.

'It looks like Henry's best friend lied to us. There's only two people here trying to get the Stone. I think it was always just the two of them. They've been competing with each other for the last eight months and also making our lives a bloody misery.'

'And now one of them will go home with your Stone and Jake,' Danny said sourly.

They all went quiet for a few seconds. It was Ewan who attempted to disperse the air of despondency.

'I'll have to make sure I win on him; at least it would mean they have to pay a proper price.'

Forty-Four

With Ewan and Lucky Jake on their way to the start Mary, Graham, and Danny remained in the parade ring to watch the race on the big screen. Yousef and Eddie were nowhere to be seen.

'I should be down there at the start, making sure Jake doesn't get worked up,' Danny muttered as a view from behind the stalls was displayed.

On the screen, Mary counted four horses still to load.

'He'll be fine,' she replied, sounding like she was trying to convince herself.

'I can't believe he's nine to one. Have either of you had a bet on him?' Graham asked.

On the big screen Lucky Jake and Ewan started to be led forward.

'No,' replied Mary succinctly.

Danny rolled his eyes for Graham's benefit, 'You don't talk much when you're nervous, do you, Mary?'

Lucky Jake paused halfway into his stall.

'Errr...'

Ewan urged the gelding from his saddle and he stepped forward, the gates closing behind him.

'..No,' Mary breathed in relief.

'If he comes out on terms with the rest of them he'll win, you know. He's better than this lot,' Danny stated confidently, 'And he's got the sheepskin cheek-pieces on him today to make sure he concentrates.

Despite four stalls handlers' coaxing and pushing, the last horse to load planted its legs. It was spun around and a blindfold was applied. Mary's became aware of her elevated heartbeat. The horse was introduced to the stalls once more and this time was bundled in. The camera angle altered to show the seventeen pristine stalls lined up at the six furlong start.

'Come on, Ewan, get him out,' Graham whispered.

Beside Mary, Danny started to hum. Annoyingly, Mary knew the tune; it was *Flight Of The Valkyries*. It began to rotate around her mind. She was about to make a remark about the melody, then realised Danny was going to watch the race with her. He never watched a race with his owners. At that moment he darted a nervous glance her way and broke into a tight, hopeful smile. He's watching the race whilst watching over me, she realised.

Ewan was poised, ready to push. The call came from the starter... and Jake anticipated the start, bouncing forward against the closed wings of the gate, head-butting the padded metal. The gelding snorted, threw his head up and jinked back. Holding tight to the horse's reins, momentum tipped Ewan forwards and up the gelding's neck. Scrabbling to find his irons, Ewan expected the stall gate to open and he would be catapulted over Lucky Jake's shoulder. To his relief, calls of 'No!' went up from a couple of jockeys at the other end of the line. The stall gates remained closed.

Pushing off Lucky Jake's mane, Ewan's backside found his paper thin saddle and he quickly dug his toes back into his stirrups. Jake was stamping his foot and Ewan wondered whether he had time to settle the gelding. He didn't have the opportunity to answer his own question as the call of, 'Jockeys!' went up for a second time and Lucky Jake shot forward. Ewan, already perspiring and holding his breath, crouched low in the saddle, relieved that on this occasion the gelding had waited until the gates were at least on their way to opening before he went forward.

It took a few strides for Ewan to register just how well Jake had got away. All the sound from the other runners was coming from behind him. Ewan looked across to his left, and then his right. The gelding had accelerated up to galloping pace so quickly he was leading, and already had a few of his competitors towards the rear pushing their mounts to stay in touch with the generous pace he was setting. The thought of taking a pull in order to conserve the gelding's energy flashed through his mind, but Danny's instructions to allow the gelding to go his own pace and let him bowl along hardened Ewan's resolve to maintain a decent gallop.

Mary was torn. Initially delighted to see her colours leading the charge in the opening few strides, concern overcame her as Ewan and Jake passed the four furlong pole leading by three lengths.

'He's going far too quickly, he'll never get home at that pace,' she ventured.

Danny tore his gaze from the screen to assess Mary. There was something a little... wrong with the way she'd phrased her comment. Was that relief he detected?

Mary sensed Danny's inspection of her, due in main to his curtailment of the humming, and concentrated steadfastly on the big screen. Graham was engrossed in the television pictures and racecourse commentary, and eventually Danny turned back to the big screen, resuming his hum of the same tune as earlier, only louder. She wondered whether he'd sensed her confusion.

Ewan stole another look around at the three furlong marker. Being on his own, the gelding was edging toward the inside rail, so a glance to his right allowed him to estimate he was five lengths clear. If he's going to fold, then it will happen soon Ewan decided. Five lengths though...

Ewan eased his fingers up the reins. He hadn't planned to do it, he didn't make a conscious decision, it just felt right. For eight strides Lucky Jake was instructed from the saddle to slow down, and accordingly, the rest of the field closed him down to reduce his lead to only a length.

Mary hated this. She swallowed and tried to become objective. The fact was, if Jake was beaten it would make things easier, her plan revolved around him being claimed. Yes, it would be a neater solution she told herself. Yet she didn't want her horse to fail, she was *desperate* for him to win.

'You need him to lose, don't you?'

She raised her eyes and discovered Danny with his head tilted down toward her. He was still. Composed. Not the way her trainer was supposed to act in the middle of a race, and especially not a race of this importance. There was no need for her to provide an answer. She'd probably transmitted her response; she recognised the disappointment in his eyes.

'I understand why. It's because it becomes a lottery as to who ends up owning him. But why didn't you tell me?'

'I couldn't tell you or Ewan not to try your best,' she replied apologetically.

Audrey had told her to come clean the night before, but Mary couldn't do it. She couldn't tell her trainer to throw the race. Mary had registered all three of her friends as owners in the unraced filly, which made them authorised to put in a claim by telephone call after the race. She had hoped that with three separate claims, all under names not known to Eddie, they might retain the horse, and the Stone. They may have had to deal with a very angry Eddie afterwards, but the Stone would no longer be associated with Mary Romano.

A sustained roar went up from the grandstand as the favourite moved into second place over a furlong and a half out, rendering any further conversation impracticable.

Danny returned his attention to the big screen and watched Lucky Jake and the favourite cover the remaining distance to the final furlong pole. He crossed his arms and shouted.

'I'm sorry, Mary!'

'Why?' she yelled back.

'Your horse is going to win.'

Juliet, standing with Charlie on the verge of the pursuit lane, a little way before the furlong pole, saw it too. Lucky Jake flew past her, only a few yards away, hugging the rail, Ewan motionless in his saddle.

Lucky Jake continued to charge down the Knavesmire, breathing rhythmically, stretching out over the ground. Having filled his lungs for over a furlong, the gelding was bristling with captive energy. Ewan let out two inches of his reins as he passed the furlong marker, gave Jake a single deft flick of his whip and began to push. Jake eagerly grabbed the ground and primed himself to pull the winning post to him.

The response felt immediate from the saddle. In the space of three strides Ewan knew Jake had the race put to bed. Easing down two strides before the line, Lucky Jake passed the winning post three and a half lengths ahead of his nearest rival, his head in his chest.

Forty-Five

From the moment Danny had said the words '...going to win', Mary had forgotten her plan. She had cast all thoughts of Eddie, Yousef, and the Stone away, replacing them with a single, all consuming wish to see her beautiful big horse win his race.

At the furlong pole, she screamed encouragement. When Ewan asked Jake for his final effort she grabbed Danny's arm, and as he crossed the finishing line, Mary hugged her trainer's chest before wildly bouncing up and down and waving her hands around. Graham shot off to retrieve and lead in Jake and Ewan. Taken aback, and somewhat confused, Danny gave in and joined in Mary's celebration, only halting when one of the first four horses home started to come back into the parade ring and head for the winners' enclosure.

'I've screwed up your claiming plan, so come on, we've got to get to the winners' enclosure and see what happens at the auction,' he told Mary after they'd got their breath back.

Mary had a faraway look in her eye, 'I'll meet you there. I need to make a call first.'

'More plans?' Danny queried with narrowing eyes.

Mary shrugged, 'Maybe.'

At that moment, Ewan and Lucky Jake exited the racecourse chute. The jockey was grinning from ear to ear.

'Got to go,' Danny told her, 'Don't miss the auction!' and he jogged away to catch up with his winning horse.

Mary found her phone, called the number and was mightily relieved when a man's voice answered. She spoke for a minute and then dashed to the other end of the parade ring to meet with her friends in the winners' enclosure.

Danny, Audrey, Maisie and Sarah were there, crowded around Ewan, while Graham was dealing with Lucky Jake. He'd already thrown the gelding's sweat rug over him and Mary spotted the faintest glint of the Stone peeping out from under it, secure in its little pocket of skin.

A large crowd had gathered at the end of the parade ring and the gantries were close to capacity, all there to watch the winner's return, and the auction. A little way off, there were two small groups standing well apart and eyeing each other with undisguised hatred. The first consisted of Eddie, Vincent, and another man behind them. When Mary looked again, she wasn't too surprised to discover the third man was Adrian Fitzpatrick. They're about right for each other, she reasoned.

The second group consisted of only two men, Yousef Amari and to her horror, Adam East. Mary glared at Adam, oblivious to the fact he was returning her stare. She realised it made perfect sense. Adam had lied to her because he was in league with Amari. Yousef had tried to put her off retrieving the Stone... because Adam had the letter and was in the process of cracking the code himself.... the dreadful truth came like a punch to her gut; they must have been responsible for the two thugs at Cullercoats.

Mary felt a rush of rage toward the man. Eddie and Vincent might be despicable, but at least they were up front about it. Adam was talking with Yousef, sharing a private word with him. Mary was incensed. Adam had been Henry's friend for thirty years, yet he was there, as bold as brass, willing to commit crimes and sell out his life-long friend for a red bauble.

Maisie caught sight of Mary and joyfully pulled her across to join their little crowd. Ewan was completing his story of the race, given to a rapt audience.

'I felt he was strong, so I let him take a breather, and bang! He went away from them like a really good horse.'

The young jockey locked eyes with Mary, 'Try and keep him if you can, Mrs Romano, there's a lot more to come. He really responded to the cheek-pieces. They kept him honest.'

'That's enough thanks, Ewan,' Danny said lightly, 'Get going and don't forget to weigh in.'

It was something Danny always told every jockey, whether they were a professional, or as in this case, an apprentice. He pondered his words for a moment as Ewan departed, thanking the group of ladies one more time. If he weighed in light, or not at all, Lucky Jake would lose the race...

'Mary...' Danny spun round and Mary was right there, staring up at him with an air of expectancy.

'As soon as you said it, I thought the same thing,' she said with a slow shake of her head, 'A nice thought, but you, Ewan and Jake deserve this. I don't want to take it away from any of you, not now, and especially after Beverley.'

'Well you better find a new option quickly, the auction is about to start,' Danny replied, indicating a tall man standing at a lectern on the winners' podium, 'That's the auctioneer.'

He was young for an auctioneer. Mary didn't know why, but every auctioneer she'd seen to date had been middle aged with a slightly dishevelled appearance. This young man was well turned out, had a shock of upright black hair and grasped his microphone confidently.

The placed horses were ordered away over the public address system and Lucky Jake was left in front of the winners' pergola, being led in slow, ponderous circles by Graham. Eddie hungrily watched the gelding pass him, licking his lips when he caught a faint red tinge under the gelding's sweat rug.

'Ladies and gentlemen, I am authorised under rule...' the

auctioneer began, running through the standard rules and regulations, 'This gelding is a son of a Grade One winning miler, his sister has won, and the mare is the daughter of a graded winner in Italy. He's a big, rangy sort and he won today in tremendous style and is obviously capable of contesting races of a much higher quality. Given the crowd around the ring, I anticipate there will be plenty of interest in him. So who'll give me six thousand pounds to start me off?'

Adrian Fitzpatrick tried to catch the auctioneer's eye, but, he was already accepting a bid from outside the ring. Danny looked across to the gantry and recognised one of the leading Northern trainers waving his racecard.

'Thank you, Sir. I have six thousand.'

'Seven on my left,' the auctioneer accepted, waving his small wooden gavel in the direction of Fitzpatrick's little group.

'Here we go,' Danny muttered sadly, 'He won too easily.'

Mary sidled up close to him, 'What's Jake worth?' she whispered.

'The way he won that, I'd say anything between twenty and forty thousand.'

Close by, Sarah leaned in, hovering over their shoulders for a few seconds before speaking, 'Surely the question is not what Lucky Jake is worth, but how much the Stone is worth?'

The bidding had quickly grown to twenty-six thousand pounds, rising in two-thousand pounds increments, when the trainer outside the ring shook his head and dropped out. The auctioneer toured the ring twice with his gavel, asking for any other interested parties. He was about to start his final round with the words, 'For the last time...' when a voice in the far left gantry cried, 'Over here!' in a soft Irish accent.

'New bidder!' exclaimed the auctioneer in delight, 'I have twenty-eight thousand pounds.'

Mary noticed Eddie scowl when the bid was registered. Screwing his neck round to identify the new bidder, he was soon prodding Fitzpatrick into action. A minute passed, during which the crowd around the ring started to hush, enthralled as the gelding's bidding reached fifty thousand, then jumping up in fives, topped eighty-five thousand pounds, Fitzpatrick and the mild-mannered Irishman sparring with each other.

Eddie leaned into Vincent and said something which prompted his sidekick to make a phone call. Meanwhile the bidding rose to one-hundred and twenty thousand pounds.

When one hundred and fifty thousand pounds was reached, Mary allowed herself the luxury of taking her eyes from Eddie and she glanced around the ring and over to the far end of the enclosure. The bidding war was being piped through the public address system and there were people on balconies, peering over them into the ring, in some cases, two or three deep. On the champagne lawn there were racegoers standing on chairs to get a view of the unfolding drama.

'At least, it's all very public.'

'You can say that again,' Danny agreed, 'Look over there.'

He swivelled his eyes to his far right where a television camera was pointed at Eddie's little group, then panning up to the right to catch the next counter bid.

'Do you think Eddie realises what's happening?' Danny asked behind his hand.

'I doubt it.'

'How high have you told Rory to go?'

'Two hundred and fifty thousand pounds,' Mary replied calmly.

Danny gave her an impressed look, 'I assume you know how much this is costing you?'

'I checked with Weatherby's yesterday. As the current owner, buying him back will cost me ten percent of the winning bid. I've got about fifty thousand pounds left out of my Premium Bond win, so added to the winnings from today, I can go up to a quarter of a million and still have enough to keep him in training until the end of the year.'

'I think it's time you stopped this little charade,' said an easily identifiable man's voice behind her. Mary shivered and balled her fists before she turned to face Vincent, wondering how much of her conversation had been overheard.

'You really are a terribly annoying sneak,' she told him. It wasn't a rebuke she was proud of, and it had little effect on Vincent. He drew close to her.

'I know that's your boyfriend.'

'I have no idea what you're talking...'

'Please stop, Mary,' he said sarcastically, 'I don't have time to waste listening to you. Get him to stop bidding. Now. Otherwise Eddie will stop, you'll be left with the Stone, and he'll get it from your Irish friend by other means. Physical means.'

He finished his little speech with his eyebrows raised expectantly. Mary rolled her lips around ruefully, spun around and cast her gaze into the far gantry.

By the time she caught Rory's attention the bidding had reached a hundred and seventy thousand pounds and was rising in ten thousand pounds increments. Silently drawing a line across her throat with her hand brought Rory's bidding to a halt. Vincent mouthed a sarcastic, 'Thank you', and slipped away.

The auctioneer tried to coax another bid from Rory, but a firm shake of his head confirmed he was finished.

'Well, ladies and gentlemen, this gelding has certainly proved to be popular. This is the highest value two-year-old ever sold after a Selling race. He's going to the gentleman to my left in the parade ring once, twice...'

'A quarter of a million pounds,' called Yousef Amari.

There were gasps from around the ring, and indeed, around the racecourse. The auctioneer, his gavel raised and mouth open, stared over to the two men standing in the parade ring to his right. He came to his senses quickly, giving a little smile to cover his shock.

'Sir, am I correct, you wish to bid two-hundred and fifty thousand pounds?'

'I do,' Yousef confirmed in a clear voice. He was standing with his chest out, glaring over at Eddie. Adam was at his side, looking slightly amused.

Transferring his attention to his original bidder, the auctioneer asked with incredulity, 'Do I hear two-hundred and seventy-five thousand pounds for this exceptional winner of the Rous Selling Stakes?'

Adrian Fitzpatrick bent his head toward Eddie. All the signals coming from his hand gestures and body language told Mary he was advising his client to refrain from bidding further. A small argument ensued and Fitzpatrick shook his head.

The auctioneer had reached his final round of the ring when Eddie stepped forward, shouting, 'Three hundred thousand,'

'Thank you for taking charge, Sir,' the auctioneer said with a hint of sarcasm. He had been party to Fitzpatrick's antics and had done his best to string out his wrapping up of the bidding in order to elicit another increase in his percentage. However, Mary sensed he was beginning to question the veracity of his two bidders, eyeing them suspiciously one by one before asking for his next bid. Yousef must have felt it too, as he now called out, 'Half a million.'

Eddie was aware of his lip curling upwards, it was only the presence of the television camera and the amphitheatre of people pressing in on him that stopped it becoming a snarl. He and the Amari brothers had history stretching back twenty-five years. He'd pushed them hard for that debt, but extracted payment eventually... Eddie gazed over at him, confident he could beat the man again.

Eddie transferred his attention to Adam East. He'd been a thorn in his side since he and Henry started building their business. Adam had always been influential in the local business community, however times changed... He allowed his mind to fill with an image of Henry... this whole situation had been manufactured by his brother. It was his fault.

He'd not even known Henry had married his little casino bunny girl until Vincent had tracked him to that tiny cottage she lived in; he'd assumed she'd left him after her father died. For a couple of years he'd assumed *he* was the only blood relative left, but no, Henry had married her and then kept her safely out of the way... out of *his* way for all those years.

Eddie snapped out of his reminiscing; he wasn't finished yet. A quick call to Forrester before the race had given him the confirmation he needed. He knew how much Adam East and Yousef Amari had in liquid assets, both privately and available in their businesses. He made it his business to know how well his enemies were doing. It was useful to know what would break a man; the sum of money it would take to bring his business, and his life, crashing down around him.

He'd done it enough times; pushing people into bankruptcy. That's how he'd broken the Amaris'. It was no concern of his that, as a consequence, the eldest brother decided to commit suicide. East and Amari combined couldn't match his wealth, and besides, they were both weak men. They rarely got their hands dirty. Neither of them would risk what was left of their combined worth to acquire the Stone, they probably didn't even possess the contacts to conduct a proper sale in order to realise the ruby's true value.

Eddie knew to the penny his own net worth, and the Stone was worth up to twenty million... well worth a punt. He'd waited for thirty years to get it back from his thieving brother, and there it was, glinting at him from the shoulder of a bloody racehorse only a few yards in front of him. He wasn't going to be denied.

Eddie wiped the sheen of sweat from his forehead and flicked the residue from his fingers. The auctioneer locked a pair of expectant, impatient eyes on him and Eddie morphed his snarl into a smile before delivering a bid he knew his challengers for the Stone Of Shiazzano would be unable to match.

'I bid nine-hundred and fifty-thousand pounds.'

Forty-Six

'He wasn't interested in Lucky Jake,' Graham informed his audience around the farmhouse's kitchen table, 'Not after Jake took a chunk out of his back and ripped his suit jacket!'

It was the morning after York, and Mary had called the staff into the farmhouse to treat them to bacon sandwiches for breakfast. Danny, Juliet, and Graham were there, along with a trio of work riders.

The story of how Vincent had attempted to recover the Stone from Lucky Jake's Prophet's Thumbprint on the way back to the racecourse stables was entering its third telling, yet still producing generous laughter from the stable staff around the table.

'His face was a picture when I went up to Jake and just popped it out,' Danny added, 'He must have realised there was no glue or anything like that. As if I'd use super glue on one of my horses, for heaven's sake!'

'Can you believe the vicious little sod was threatening to cut it out of Jake's shoulder with a knife at one stage?' asked Graham, shaking his head, 'I told him. You'll have to cut through me to get to him!'

Mary clapped her hand down onto Graham's shoulder, 'You did very well, I'm proud of you.'

Graham beamed heroically around the table.

'We still lost him though,' said Danny with a grimace, 'I just hope Fitzpatrick will look after him. He took him away once Eddie got his hands on the Stone.'

'Will Eddie pay you, do you think?' asked Juliet seriously, 'It's such a lot of money.'

Mary bit her lip thoughtfully, 'The course officials were all over him once the bidding had finished. And if he doesn't, then Weatherby's will pursue him for the money on my behalf. The racecourse will also be due to get ninety-five thousand pounds of it, so I imagine they will want to take it seriously if his funds aren't forthcoming.'

'I love it when you talk accountancy,' Danny joked.

'To be honest, I'm not too bothered about the money. I've managed to get rid of that damn Stone, and very publicly. On the flip side, we've lost Jake. It'll be a bonus if we get paid. I'm just relieved no-one got hurt and I can put all of this behind me.'

'The papers and internet are full of it today. Even the Sun and Daily Mail have a report. I bet Eddie didn't reckon on being featured in the newspapers!'

'What happened to the under-bidders? You know, the Asian chap that owns a few with us?' Graham asked, helping himself to a second bacon sandwich and a top up of tea from the pot.

'I guess Eddie's pockets were too deep for them,' Mary replied with a shrug. She was still trying to piece together what the relationship between Yousef, Adam, and Eddie could be. Being lied to by Adam had stung. But if they hadn't become involved, Eddie would not have been forced into parting with the best part of a million pounds for Lucky Jake. Perhaps they had been successful in what they had set out to achieve; Eddie paying through the nose to recover his father's gemstone.

Mary continued, 'Yousef stormed off once the bidding had finished. Adam came up to me afterwards, apologised if they'd caused me any problems and told me he was happy with how things had turned out. He credited themselves with driving the price up for me.'

'That's a bit rich,' Danny pointed out, 'The only way Amari could have got hold of Henry's letter was if he sent those two blokes to bash your car.'

'I asked him about the letter,' Mary confirmed, 'Adam mumbled something about Yousef knowing the right people.'

'That's lame. Do you believe both of them were blameless in all of this?'

Mary paused in thought, 'That's what I can't work out.'

The conversation moved on, leaving Mary continuing to consider how the day at York had turned out. Eventually she was distracted when Juliet brought up the subject of Gentle Jill. Her filly was due to start racing in the next week or two after having completed a very decent piece of work that morning.

'You may have lost a nice horse, but at least you got a fantastic price for him. Now you have another nice one to look forward to, and you can relax because the Stone isn't your problem anymore,' stated Danny firmly.

'That's just it,' Mary stated dolefully, 'I have an awful feeling I may have left a few stones unturned.'

Forty-Seven

'How long until they get here?' demanded Eddie for the third time that morning.

Forrester patiently consulted his mobile phone again.

'Five minutes.'

Eddie checked his watch. It was an automatic reaction; he hadn't actually registered the time. He was too busy rerunning his pitch through his mind for what would be the most important negotiation and biggest payout of his life. Forced to wait three weeks for this meeting, he was keen to see the profit from his investment after paying the racing authorities for the woman's horse. Forrester had warned it would bring them further unnecessary attention if he didn't.

He was shocked by the interest shown by the media. His purchase had been widely reported. Even the local *Evening Chronicle* had picked up on his bidding war at York and sent reporters to his office. Still, they knew nothing of the ruby. However, it grated that he'd had to pay out; that woman didn't deserve to get anything. He had no intention of keeping the filthy animal and was considering telling the trainer to just shoot the bloody thing.

Vincent drummed his fingers nervously on the arm of the leather sofa upon which he and Eddie were lounging. Forrester sat facing them, checking his phone once more. Forrester had chosen it for its position in the corner of the hotel coffee shop. Facing the entrance, it meant Eddie was provided with a clear view of foot traffic in and out and it also gave a modicum of privacy, being spaced a little apart from the other coffee tables.

Eddie inspected the room again with a feeling of dissatisfaction. Although it wasn't full, there were enough customers to ensure that conversations conducted any louder than in a whisper had the possibility of half a dozen people overhearing.

'Why did you agree to this place?' he quizzed Forrester, with unconcealed irritation, 'It's full of people.'

'I think you've answered your own question,' Forrester replied in a disinterested tone, concentrating his gaze on his phone.

Vincent slid to the edge of the sofa, leaned forward and gave his colleague a black look, 'I don't like it either. It's too public.'

Forrester swung his head round and engaged Vincent. They shared a mutually disdainful stare.

In a sarcastic voice he reserved specifically for berating Vincent, Forrester replied, 'So, you'd prefer to sell a stolen ruby in a swanky hotel room, or perhaps a dark alley somewhere. I know, why don't we meet on the roof of an empty multi-story car park at midnight, would that satisfy your thirst for stupidity?'

'Alright you two, keep it down,' Eddie intervened curtly, but not without a little amusement.

'I chose this hotel exactly because there are people around,' continued Forrester in an urgent whisper, 'We've never met these contacts before and they know we are carrying a ruby worth millions. If there are plenty of witnesses around, our buyers are less likely to try anything.'

'He's got a point,' Eddie admitted, before silently encouraging Vincent to calm down with a wave of his hand.

Forrester returned to monitoring the coffee shop entrance and his phone, but not before smirking at Vincent.

An electronic alert on Forrester's phone made all three men tense.

'It's him. Max Schmidt. He's arrived,' he informed them as he read the text message, 'As arranged, he's sending his jeweller in here first to examine the stone.'

Two minutes later a small, neat man with thinning hair combed flat to his head and a wispy beard appeared at the door of the cafe. He was carrying a small leather case and peered around the room over a pair of thin wire spectacles. Forrester beckoned him over once the jeweller's gaze rested on the corner of the room.

'Gentlemen,' the jeweller said in greeting, sitting down in the only remaining armchair. He made himself comfortable, placed his bag on the coffee table and opened it before giving the three men an expectant look.

'The stone?' he enquired. Vincent thought he detected the hint of a Germanic accent.

Forrester nodded at Eddie, who obediently dipped his hand into the inside pocket of his cashmere jacket and placed a thin wooden box onto the coffee table. The jeweller took the lid off the box and examined its contents. Satisfied, he removed a pair of latex gloves from his case and carefully put them on before returning for a small pair of pliers and a magnifying eyeglass.

'This will take a few minutes. I need to remove the stone from the brooch,' he told the three men watching him hawk-like, 'Perhaps I could have a cup of tea?'

Forrester checked with Eddie, who shrugged. Forrester got up and went to the serving counter.

Vincent and Eddie watched as the jeweller slowly prised the ruby from its setting. He placed it onto a square of cloth and put the magnifier to his eye. Picking the ruby up, he held it between two fingers and turned it slowly. With an 'Umm..' he took a tiny torch from his case and repeated his examination with the small, bright light behind the ruby.

'Ah!' he said, removing the magnifier and locking eyes with Eddie, 'You have a very nice fake, gentlemen.'

Eddie's eyes bulged and his mouth dropped open. He snatched the ruby from the man's hand and peered at it desperately, quietly cursing under his breath.

'That can't be right,' protested Vincent, 'Check it again.'

The jeweller stayed quite still, weighing up the two men, 'If you insist, I will demonstrate.'

He took out a small square glass plate from his leather case and placed it onto the coffee table, then held out his open palm to Eddie, who dutifully returned the ruby.

Forrester loomed up behind the jeweller with a cup of tea in his hand, 'What's wrong?'

Eddie and Vincent both raised their heads and Forrester was greeted with a combination of consternation and anger. He quickly took his seat and watched as the jeweller took the ruby and gently scraped it across the top of the plate of glass.

'This is a colour test. A real ruby would leave no colour when I scratch it over the glass.'

The three men bent over the coffee table, transfixed by the jeweller's thin fingers as he gripped the Stone Of Shiazzano. Eddie felt sweat starting to bubble up under his arms and across his forehead as a steady streak of red was drawn across the surface of the glass.

Forty-Eight

To everyone's surprise, and Mary's amazement, her Weatherby's bank account had been credited with eight hundred and fifty-five thousand pounds in the first week of July. As a thank you, Mary hired a private box for all her friends, including a special invitation for Rory, back at York for their York Stakes day at the end of July. Stories of Lucky Jake's win abounded all day long, there was laughter and merriment, and she even allowed Rory to convince her to attend a race meeting with him at The Curragh in September.

The day out at York had drawn a neat line under the subject of the Stone of Shiazzano, and gradually the yard settled back into normality. Gentle Jill ran her first race over six furlongs in a Maiden at Chester and finished a very creditable third. Danny entered her only a week later at Redcar and she stormed home by two lengths, looking like a really nice prospect. The filly was a worthy distraction, but she wasn't Lucky Jake. Mary missed her gelding. It wasn't just the association with her dad; he'd been her first winner.

Mary remained living at the farmhouse, managing the accounts and acting as the stable's racing secretary. She also turned her hand to sorting out staff issues, liaising with owners and suppliers, as well as cooking breakfast. Neither she nor Danny brought up the subject of her moving out. However, the complete absence of Eddie and Vincent in their lives made Mary eventually decide she had no good reason to remain at the farmhouse.

Mary chose an evening in late August to broach the subject with Danny. All the stable staff had gone home for the day and he'd disappeared twenty minutes previously to the paddocks saying he was going to check on a couple of horses he'd turned out. It was a cool evening and, as Mary opened the farmhouse door and whistled to Charlie and Milo, the breeze whirled in and gave her the sense autumn was on its way. The dogs jumped up from the kitchen floor and followed her out into the yard and across the horseshoe of stables. When she reached the top of the paddocks Mary paused, shading her eyes from the low sun, and spotted Danny's familiar gawky shape in the very bottom paddock.

She smiled to herself when a very faint humming came lilting across to her on the breeze. She bent between the bars of the gate and started to make her way down over the grass that was sparse, dusty and dry through lack of recent rain.

Charlie and Milo followed her into the paddock, the youngster wanting to play with his older pal. Mary ignored the first growl, assuming Charlie was fed up with the younger dog's attention, but it came again, low and sustained. She looked around, intending to smooth the argument,

'Now come on you two...'

Eddie and Vincent were only ten yards away, leaning against the paddock fence. Neither spoke. Both men were grimly scrutinising her with dull, dead eyes. A shiver of vulnerability ran through Mary as she realised they must have followed her through the yard. To be as near as they were now, they had to have hidden, or closely tracked her.

They were different, and Mary couldn't work out why at first. Then she realised; they were both wearing unflattering overalls. Eddie appeared positively ordinary. He looked smaller, non-descript. As Charlie maintained his low, menacing growl, Mary broke the silence.

'Really boys, you shouldn't have bothered getting all dressed up for me.'

Eddie sneered, and he and Vincent dipped through the horizontal bar of the fence together, 'Always ready with the sarcastic remark or the snide put down. You were the same when you were eighteen, you and my brother, thinking you're so clever. I keep things simple, that way you don't get things wrong by trying to be *too clever*. Can you think of anything you've done recently that might fall under the category of being *too clever*?'

Vincent turned his sombre eyes on his boss for a moment, as if sizing him up, remaining a half step behind him. Mary decided his manner was different too. If she wasn't mistaken, there was dead-eyed seriousness about him; he'd lost the veneer of wryness that almost made his presence palatable.

Mary stood her ground, 'What do you want, Eddie?'

He gave a sly chuckle and shared his amusement with Vincent by sliding him a glance and a raised eyebrow.

'She doesn't know what we want,' he pondered, 'The scheming bitch steals the Stone and is still playing games with me.'

'You need to give it to Eddie, Mary,' said Vincent coldly, 'We'll take what is ours and leave you alone.'

Eddie grinned at Mary, his eyes were dancing.

Mary crossed her arms, 'I have no idea what you're talking about. You got the Stone at the races, don't tell me you've lost it!'

'We never had it to lose,' Vincent replied, watching Mary's face intently. He looked disappointed, and then a little anxious when she returned nothing but a bemused stare.

'The Stone in the horse was a fake, but you already know that,' said Eddie, wandering a few feet to Mary's left, widening the gap with Vincent, so she had to constantly turn her head if she wished to keep an eye on both men.

'Hey, Vincent!' Eddie exclaimed, 'Do you think this woman knows what day it is today?'

Vincent didn't reply, instead he addressed Mary, 'When we had the Stone tested for carat quality it came back as a fake. The brooch was gold, but the ruby was worthless. Give us the real one and we'll go.'

Mary furrowed her brow, 'I didn't take it. I never even touched it. No one did until it was put into Jake.'

For the few days the Stone was in her possession, Sarah and Maisie had looked after it. When it arrived in the post, Danny had made sure it would be safe to place the brooch into Lucky Jake's Prophet's Thumbprint. They'd been lucky, it was an almost perfect fit; not too large to be noticeable, not so small it couldn't lodge in the rosette of bunched up skin. Lucky Jake hadn't been aware it was there.

Mary considered the day of the race. Danny took the Stone to the races, hidden in the horsebox, she didn't even know where, but it might have been something to do with that new flat cap he'd been wearing. Juliet and Charlie had carried it over the Knavesmire, and Sarah finally handed it over to Danny before the race. She considered all those people trusted friends. Could they have stolen the ruby and replaced it with a perfect replica? She dismissed the idea immediately.

'This is bullshit,' she countered defensively, becoming aware Eddie had stopped moving and was facing her.

'Oh, quite the contrary,' Eddie said lightly, 'I am *dead* serious. You embarrassed me you see. There we were with a foreign client about to purchase the Stone, only to be informed the ruby is just coloured glass. We've had it tested three times.'

As he spoke, Eddie pulled a pair of thin latex gloves from the trouser pocket of his overalls and carefully slipped them over each hand. He put great effort into wiggling every digit until they filled the appropriate finger hole, and throughout he smiled wretchedly at her.

Reading Mary's heightened state of nervousness, Vincent asked again, a pleading quality entering his voice, 'Tell Eddie where it is and there won't be any unpleasantness.'

Mary almost laughed, this was ridiculous. What did Eddie think he was going to do with those gloves? He was just intimidating her. It's what he did; it was his job.

'I don't have the Stone!' she insisted, glancing quickly behind her, hopeful Danny had become aware of the unexpected visitors and was on his way up the hill. Her hopes were dashed; he was still at the bottom of the paddocks. She thought of shouting for help, but the breeze was behind her, he probably wouldn't hear. Besides, it might set Eddie off on whatever sick game he had in mind for her.

'Please, Mary,' Vincent urged.

She turned to him, her arms open, fingers splayed, 'I don't have it. Henry must have replaced it years ago. I thought it was real!'

'You never answered my question,' Eddie stated in a dangerously low tone, 'What do you think is special about today?'

Mary shuddered and Vincent stared at his boss and swallowed hard. Vincent was worried things might go too far. Eddie had been impossible to work with since the sale of the Stone went sour ten days ago. Both he and Forester had been treading on eggshells for a day or two afterwards, and then Forrester had disappeared, leaving him to cope with Eddie's increasingly psychotic behaviour alone.

Eddie responded to Mary's blank look by fixing his eyes on the parched ground at her feet and hugging himself.

'You killed my father on this day thirty-three years ago.'

He disengaged one of his arms from his chest and lifted a latex finger to his chin, tapping it thoughtfully wearing a glazed expression. Mary gawked at him in dismay.

'I *saved* him, Eddie. If I hadn't scared those two muggers off him, Joe would have died right there in the street.'

'That should have been my job,' he replied in a faraway voice, '*I* was supposed to find him, bravely send the muggers on their way, and earn the respect I was due from Pa. But he would insist on fighting back, and it only took one stray punch to burst his heart...'

'The muggers were sent... by you?'

Mary could hardly get the words out. She was back in summer 1986, screaming at the two men. Then in the gutter, cradling Joe's head in her hands... until Eddie stumbled across the two of them. He'd been angry, so very angry.

'Eddie...?' Vincent queried anxiously, only to be answered with a sullen scowl.

'Henry was Pa's golden boy. My brother was the son with the business ideas, the girl, and the future,' Eddie continued bitterly, 'All Pa's money was going Henry's way. When I told him my business idea, he told me I wasn't *clever* enough, I wasn't good with people, that I should go to work with Henry in his new venture....'

'You blamed me!' blasted Mary. The years of torment she'd suffered believing she had been the catalyst in Joe's death were now cast aside, 'I didn't kill Pa, *you did!*'

'Oh no, you killed him sure enough. They were my men, but your actions killed him,' Eddie blustered, lifting his cool brown eyes and fixing them on Mary, 'You, running around Grey Street looking for him. I had to wait for you to get out of the way. It meant I got to Pa too late. Even worse, you got there before me. Not only did you steal my thunder, you ensured they gave my Pa too many punches, waiting for my entrance. You killed Pa as surely as if you'd stuck a knife in his heart and twisted the blade.'

Eddie opened his mouth and tenderly slid his tongue around the side of his lips, as if he wished to savour the taste of the moment. Vincent took a step toward him, but Eddie's raised flat palm halted him. Mary couldn't take her eyes off Eddie, watching in morbid fascination as a hint of madness caught hold of the man.

'That's why I killed your father,' he said with a shrug.

It took a few seconds for Mary to feel the impact of Eddie's statement. Speechless and horrified, Mary's whole body sagged as she contemplated Eddie's words. Out of her range of sight, Vincent groaned, yet she couldn't tear her eyes from Eddie.

Pleased with the impact of his statement, he was smirking back at her, enjoying her incomprehension.

'No. He died of a heart attack,' she rebuffed sternly.

Her mouth was dry and the words seemed to stick at the back of her throat. She swallowed, and again, readied herself to counter Eddie's hateful lie, but he spoke first.

'Yes he did,' confirmed Eddie, the glint in his eye matched by a lascivious smile, 'I watched him die.'

He paused to see what effect this revelation would have on Mary, delighting in the pain in the woman's eyes, revelling in how her shoulders sagged, her mouth dropped open and tears started to race down her cheeks.

'I think it was two days before you were due to get married, wasn't it?' Eddie asked rhetorically, 'I found him in that sad little tin hut of his down at the quayside at two in the morning and I literally scared the living daylights out of him! Bashed his shed and told him I was going to toss him into the Tyne, but there was no need. He came out and dropped dead...'

'Eddie! This isn't helping,' Vincent cut in, 'We're here for the Stone.'

'Ah, yes, the Stone. Clever Henry worked out Pa's last words didn't he, just like he worked out I was responsible for your father's death. Never spoke to me again, and hid you away. He kept me from you so I couldn't keep my promise... until Henry became ill and you ceased to have his protection.'

Mary suddenly felt a surge of realisation as the roots of Eddie's revelations sank into her mind and proliferated. Henry had known Eddie was responsible for her father's death. Henry had shielded her from the truth. Henry had protected her from Eddie. And he'd lied to her.

Eddie suddenly strode forward, ignoring the immediate growling and yapping that came from the two dogs. He aimed a half-hearted kick at Charlie, but the pointer was far too quick and nimble, always staying just out of range. But Eddie had no interest in the dogs. He was set on closing the gap with Mary, bearing down on her.

'Don't come any closer!' she warned, backing away from the

advancing man. Eddie ignored her, striding the last few yards. Caught out by his injection of pace, Eddie's nose came so close it touched her forehead, his pallid face contorting with anger. He pushed her shoulders firmly. Still backing away, she lost her balance and Mary stumbled, falling backwards, raising a cloud of dust as she landed awkwardly on the flat of her back, her neck whipping backwards on impact. Eddie was on her immediately and she screamed for Danny.

'Tell me where the Stone is you bitch,' Eddie snarled, ignoring Mary's protests and her feeble attempts to push him away. Vincent peered down the paddocks as Eddie grabbed a large handful of blonde hair and dragged Mary up to a sitting position. Charlie and Milo both went nuts, nipping at Eddie's heels. He batted them away with his free hand.

Vincent continued to watch with bulging eyes as Eddie maintained his grip on Mary's hair and moved behind her as she clawed at his hands and protested with squeals and shouts. He'd seen Eddie perform this ritual a number of times. It was a practised technique, placing the sitter in a position where they couldn't see their captor, and every movement of their head became scalp burning agony.

Behind Eddie, Vincent spotted a running figure, over six hundred yards away, 'The trainer is on his way; he'll be here in about a minute or so. Mary, tell us where you've put the Stone, please, we don't want to hurt you.'

Eddie examined his colleague, confusion written in the deep furrows of his frown. He had every intention of hurting her, even if she told him where she'd hidden the Stone. Still holding onto a fistful of Mary's hair he unzipped the top of his overall and dipped inside, removing a hand gun.

'Your dog's getting on my nerves,' Eddie told Mary, extending his arm until it was straight. He took aim and shot Charlie.

Forty-Nine

Danny had heard the scream, spotted Mary with the men and, forgetting his inspection of the mare in the bottom paddock, started on a dead run up the hill. When the gunshot cracked through the air, he was dipping through the last paddock fence and was charging toward the two men, his lungs burning.

The gunshot served to spur him on. It wasn't until he was almost at the scene that he questioned what he could possibly achieve when faced with an armed man more than willing to use his weapon. He slowed as he approached, recognising Eddie and Vincent. They were facing each other, engrossed in an argument. Milo, who had been cowering behind an oddly shaped mound, sought sanctuary around Danny's heels. When he looked again, Danny realised the mound was Charlie's quivering body.

'Don't come any closer,' Vincent warned, holding a flat hand up to Danny, returning his attention to his colleague.

'Eddie, this wasn't a part of the deal,' Vincent insisted loudly, the gunshot having temporarily deafened him.

Waving the pistol around in Mary's face, Eddie ignored Vincent's plea and demanded from her the details of where the Stone had been hidden.

'She doesn't know, Eddie.'

'Of course she does,' he spat back, dragging Mary up to her knees. He bent down to bellow in her ear, 'She's clever, aren't you! Very clever to make me pay for my own Stone in public, clever to get East and Amari to bid me up. I had half a mind to kill you months ago in your cottage but decided to still go ahead with my little bit of subterfuge.'

'Yeah, and that worked like a charm!' Mary shouted back defiantly.

She tried to ignore the pain, but squealed as Eddie gritted his teeth and lurched side-ways, dragging her in a semi-circle on her knees so he had a clear view of the trainer.

'Eddie, I can't do this... my Emily,' Vincent whined, 'You've always said no guns. I've never... I mean, we don't kill people.'

Eddie cocked his head toward his colleague, '*You* don't kill people,' he said. His gaze lingered on Vincent for a few seconds, waiting for a reaction. The overriding emotion he read in his partner's face was fear. Disappointed, he soon transferred his attention back to the small woman hunched over in front of him.

'One last chance. Where's the Stone?' thundered Eddie, lifting the pistol and holding it at arm's length once more, this time pointing the barrel toward Danny.

Mary considered lying. Telling him the Stone was at her cottage, in the farmhouse; anything to get Eddie away from them. But what was the best option, which tale would he believe? Eddie tightened his grip on her hair and her scalp radiated fiery pain down her cheeks and neck. Gritting her teeth, she tried desperately to conjure up a statement, something that would make sense to Eddie.

'I don't know where it is and neither does Mary,' Danny shouted, responding quickly to having a pistol pointed at him and automatically raising his hands above his head.

Eddie, cackling with laughter, pulled back on Mary's head, forcing her to look up into his leering face. There's nothing I can say, she realised. He's lost. Betrayal and rage has consumed him. He is set on a course that can have only one outcome.

'Shall I shoot your young trainer?' Eddie asked in a hiss, his spittle spraying over her forehead and eyes.

'Okay, you've got five seconds and if you haven't told me where the ruby is by then you'll have his blood on your hands as well as Pa's... One, two, three...'

A light fizzing sound cut through the breeze, followed by a small crack from behind Danny, and Eddie stopped his countdown.

Feeling blessed relief as Eddie's hand softened its grip on her hair, Mary fell forward from her kneeling position and scrabbled away on her hands and knees, desperate to put distance between Eddie and herself.

Vincent stared at his boss, with a mixture of relief and fascination. Eddie was drunkenly staggering from side to side, trying to maintain his balance, his pistol still gripped in his hand. He extended his arm and tried to speak, but could only produce garbled nonsense. Vincent watched in horrified wonder as Eddie's face seemed to solidify, and although his eyes were darting around, his eyelids seemed be under someone else's control, jerkily opening and closing.

Another crack of gunfire from Eddie's pistol deafened everyone again before he collapsed forward onto the ground, sending a puff of dust into the breeze.

Vincent noticed a small gurgling fountain of blood start to colour Eddie's back from under his shoulder blade. At its centre was a small black dart. Suddenly aware of his own mortality, he threw himself crablike to the ground, his eyes wild with fear. Danny, initially confused by the two men dropping, now strode over and kicked the pistol from Eddie's limp hand, then carefully pocketed it.

Mary was still on the ground, a few yards away, lying on her back, eyes closed.

'Mary, we've got to call the police,' he urged.

Mary's head was still ringing from the latest gunshot. Danny's call was distorted and distant. She opened her eyes and immediately felt discomfort in her lower back; so no change here then. She lay flat on the warm earth and blinked a few times before being able to focus on the candyfloss clouds that were scudding over her, rushing to reach the east coast. She was experiencing a warm, fuzzy feeling, like she was tingling all over.

She wanted to sleep, but was dimly aware Danny wanted her to do something. It was a struggle to push upward but she managed to prop herself up on her elbows on the second attempt; it seemed her stomach muscles were too tight to get her all the way to sitting. Bending her chin to her chest, Mary blinked a few more times in order to focus on her legs. They didn't seem to want to move. She peered around. Vincent was on the ground about two yards away. He looked nervously over at her and said something, but she couldn't make out what it was. Beside Vincent, Eddie was lying motionless, face down. She shivered and screwed her head further round and saw Danny on his knees. He was bent over something... she couldn't quite make it out. He looked up and spoke to her, but the singing in her ears was too loud. Whatever it was, he wasn't happy, judging by his expression. He narrowed his eyes, and strode over to her, kneeling at her back and supporting her.

She realised she was panting slightly and straightened with Danny's help, which made her breathing much easier. She decided to take stock and was annoyed when her eyes misted and she became a little dizzy when attempting to look down at herself again. So she closed her eyes and waited for the feeling to pass, safe in the knowledge that Danny was with her.

She couldn't make out how long it had been, but when she opened her eyes again and looked down, her blouse had changed colour near her stomach and her new jeans had developed a patch of black at her hip. Before she could investigate further, something blurry moved in the middle distance. Mary blinked away the floaters and sure enough, a figure was coming up the paddocks. A man was striding at pace straight towards her but there was no definition; he was just a dark blur.

She watched him dip under the paddock fence and close in on the final thirty yards with short, quick strides. Mary screwed her eyes up and tried to concentrate. With every yard he moved closer she felt sure there was something very familiar about him. He was wearing a Breton Cap with a brim that shaded his eyes.

He stood over her and was talking with Danny and Vincent, but it was muffled. She watched his lips, trying to read the words; they looked like orders. Mary stared into his shadowy face for a few seconds before her head became heavy and her chin lolled onto her chest, making her cough. Her eyes wanted to close, but she fought it. A hand gently rolled her head back and Mary thought it best to accept the help and allowed her eyes to close. She eased herself back onto Danny's warm chest.

Mary embraced the blackness thinking about the man. He'd been standing, looking down at her and she'd been sure she recognised that face. Before she lost consciousness, a name popped into her head. Mary decided she had to be mistaken.

Fifty

Tubes. Lots of them. And the smell of plastic and antiseptic. Mary half opened one eye and a sharp, blinding light caused searing pain to penetrate her eyeball and work its way to the back of her head. She slammed her eye shut and waited for her brain to stop fizzing.

She heard a voice. Female, light, and it was beckoning her. The effervescing bubbles started to subside a little and she commanded her eyes to open. It was darker this time and the features of a shiny young woman smiled down on her. Mary tried to say, 'Where am...' but there was something in her throat; she gargled.

The young woman, no more than a girl really Mary decided, placed a gloved finger to where her lips would be under her facemask. Her face darkened, then dissolved under Mary's closing eyelids. Mary wanted to stay awake. She fought her tiredness for a moment until the downward spiral took her and she slid away into the blackness.

***

She'd woken in stages. Each time she opened her eyes it seemed she was in a different place, a new environment with a new set of concerned faces. Dreamless sleep came upon her quickly and regularly.

Those first few weeks in York General Hospital were lost on Mary. She had been in an induced coma for most of it, and subsequently drugged up to her eyeballs for a period of which she had no memory. When she finally emerged from the various states of unconsciousness long enough to question her carers, Mary discovered she'd been shot.

Eddie's bullet had entered her lower abdomen, robbing her of several pints of blood and making a mess of her bladder and a few other organs which it had nicked on its way into her and out the other side. She'd become aware of the full extent of the damage halfway through the third week, when the morphine was no longer enough to stem a tide of pain in her hip and the staff had realised she was haemorrhaging. She was whipped into theatre and lost another few days in intensive care.

Once consciousness was restored, Mary greeted the news that she might lose the use of her right leg with stoicism, followed by a few private tears when the consultant had departed. However, it seemed her luck was holding out. The nerves, whilst badly damaged, were slowly repairing. They jangled like crazy in her leg when her muscles were at rest, but on the twenty-second day of her recovery she'd woken and was delighted to discover the toes on her right foot responding to her command to waggle.

The police had been the first at her bedside and had returned three times before they were satisfied with her version of events. Mary had been purposefully vague during their first visit but decided on reflection that it wouldn't hurt anyone to tell them everything; well, almost everything. Having run through her story, she subsequently discovered Danny had already furnished a carbon copy account of their path to the confrontation with Vincent and Eddie in the paddocks.

The inspector, a brash, ruddy faced chap in his late thirties introduced himself as Max Harrison. He had wanted details of Eddie's assault and had been appalled with her decision not to involve the authorities earlier. Mary accepted his reprimand, although it soon became obvious Harrison's real area of interest was in discovering who had fired a tranquilising dart into Eddie Romano's back.

'There was enough sedative in that dart to fell a charging rhino,' the inspector had rumbled.

'I've no idea who it was Inspector. My guardian angel?'

'Apparently so,' he agreed grimly, 'Although I'd categorise his actions as a vigilante, Mrs Romano. I don't like men running around the Wolds carrying powerful hunting rifles, even if he did make sure you made it here with a fighting chance.'

The vigilante had called in an air ambulance, shown expertise when nursing Mary until professional help arrived, and then managed to vanish without a trace in the ensuing confusion. He had introduced himself simply as 'a friend' and neither Danny nor Vincent had been able to shed any light on the mystery man, despite rigorous questioning. The inspector had also left Mary's bedside disappointed in this regard. The answer had seared itself into Mary's memory, but she omitted that nugget of information from her account.

Mary legitimised her decision by telling herself she could have been mistaken. Her eyesight had been blurry. The shock had possibly affected her judgement. Perhaps she had seen what she *thought* was a familiar face and her addled brain had done a poor job of recognition, jumping to the wrong conclusion...

For now, her guardian angel's identity would remain open, pending further inquiry.

Fifty-One

Six weeks into her stay in hospital Mary was beginning to feel like her old self. She turned another page of her newspaper and tried to ignore the sounds of her fellow patients on the ward that were presently invading her concentration. Whilst she was pleased to be out of the high dependency ward, the lack of privacy and constant traffic of beds, people, visitors and medical staff was beginning to test her patience.

Her copy of the *Racing Post* reminded her of how much she was missing. Danny had two runners at Thirsk today, and a glance out of the window confirmed it was the sort of weather that would have made it a perfect day for a mid-week jaunt to the races in North Yorkshire. Danny and Juliet had been regular visitors for the last fortnight, something Mary always looked forward to, but with a runner in the last race on the card, there would be no such visit today.

Instead, Mary was picking apart the form.

'Mary! You poor thing.'

She glanced over the top of her paper and saw Adam East approaching her bed with his arms held out in benediction. Trying to hide her disappointment, she quickly checked and adjusted her covers and pushed herself up into a more erect position before he arrived at her bedside. His shoes squeaked with each pace he took towards her bed.

He began to bend over with the intention of planting a kiss on her cheek, but Mary halted him with an open palm.

'Please, Adam, save your kisses and platitudes. What do you want?'

Adam recoiled, looking a little hurt, but soon regained his composure, 'I'm sorry, Mary, Yousef and I should have done a better job of protecting you from Eddie. It's entirely our fault you're in here. I just wanted to come and say sorry.'

Mary took care in folding her *Racing Post*, placing it on her lap, and frowned up at the man standing over her with hunched shoulders. He really does do the naughty schoolboy routine incredibly well, she thought.

'You've been trying to protect me?'

'Yes, of course. It's what Henry asked me to do,' he beamed, Yousef Amari and I have been working hard over the last few months to keep Eddie and the others away from you.

Mary screwed her face up, 'You have a funny way of going about it, Adam. Does smashing my car with baseball bats whilst I'm still inside constitute looking after me?'

Adam's smile drooped.

'And don't tell me you were acting in my best interests at York races. You wanted that ruby for yourselves. You just couldn't afford it.'

'No, really Mary, you have it all wrong...'

'Here's what I think,' said Mary, halting Adam's plea with another flat palm, 'You couldn't work it out, could you? Henry's cipher was too difficult. You needed me to find it for you. Those names of the people seeking the ruby were complete fantasy apart from Yousef's.'

Mary was starting to enjoy herself. Adam was flicking his eyes around the beds in the vicinity, worried who was listening.

'Please, Mary, keep your voice down.'

'That first name you gave me, Elizabeth Weatherstone, who supposedly financed a loan on the Stone. She works for you! She's a manager in your training department. For heaven's sake Adam, did you not think I would Google the names? There's a photo and profile of her on your company website. I assumed you'd added her to keep your eye on me, but the entire list was false.'

Mary paused. Adam's warm and confident persona had crumbled and he was staring forlornly down the ward. Mary instructed him to sit down in the plastic chair beside her bed.

'Tell me what happened,' Mary said. Her words were softer, but injected with enough irritation to warn Adam her patience would wear thin if she thought he was lying.

'I didn't want to... hurt anyone,' he moaned, 'But since Henry left the company three years ago, things have been... difficult. We've lost important clients Henry worked with and we're running out of cash reserves. I've had to re-mortgage my house and Yousef is the same - he's facing bankruptcy. When Henry died we got talking and reckoned the Stone would stay hidden and forgotten, so there was no harm if we...'

'...found it and kept it for yourselves?' Mary said wearily.

Adam wouldn't meet her gaze, preferring to continue staring mournfully across the ward.

'I didn't realise Yousef was so obsessed with Henry's brother. It all got out of hand. Henry told me he'd left a letter for you or Eddie, way back in the eighties when we got our first loan on the ruby. He said he'd left a mind teaser, just in case.'

'And when the two of you couldn't solve the puzzle, you decided to threaten a little girl?'

Adam looked close to breaking down. He bent forward in his chair, placed his elbows on his knees and put his head in his hands, staring at the slick linoleum floor.

'Yousef liked the idea of getting Eddie to do all the work for him, so asked me to send a copy of Henry's letter to Eddie's house with a few threats.'

'Did you try and kidnap Vincent's daughter?'

Adam shook his head vigorously, 'We never did anything like

247

that. We just sent the letter. I don't think Eddie would have given the Stone to us anyway, he didn't care about the kid.'

'Did Vincent attack Yousef at Danny's stables?'

Adam nodded, 'There was no warning, Vincent pulled him into a stable and started to lay into him. Said he knew about the blackmail and why Yousef was getting involved in the yard. Told him Eddie had done for his brother and would see him in the same place if he didn't back off.'

Adam's eyes dropped to the floor and he continued in a bitter tone, 'It only made Yousef want to get back at Eddie even more. Yousef reckoned he was lucky. Some chap intervened and warned Vincent off. Bit strange though, the chap took him to a stable, or a pen of some sort, and said he'd be safe there until he could get help. But no one came back. After a few minutes he started shouting and that's when you found him.'

It occurred to Mary that she may not have been the only person with a guardian angel.

'So what's the real reason for your visit? I'm sure you didn't come here just to bare your soul and seek forgiveness.'

Returning to an upright sitting position and looking anywhere except into Mary's eyes, Adam asked, 'Have I been forgiven?'

Mary almost laughed. She cast incredulous eyes over the desperate man and slowly shook her head.

'Tell me why you're here,' she insisted.

Adam shut his eyes, paused, then fired them open again and forced himself to lock eyes with Mary.

'It's coming up to the anniversary of Henry's death. I wanted to speak to you beforehand,' he said carefully, 'Henry told me he would wait a year before letting you know about the Stone. He thought after a year Eddie would have forgotten about it because you'd be back at work, and maybe even moved on.'

'Even if that's so, why would you be interested in that?'

Adam breathed in deeply, 'I want you to know I'm totally focused on my business. I'm going to build it back up and make it a success.'

He waited, his eyes shifting around Mary's face, eager for a response.

'Right,' Mary answered, a little nonplussed, 'Well, thank you, I think, for coming. But I'm a little...'

'Of course,' Adam interrupted hurriedly, 'I'll leave you. You must be... tired. Just remember, it's a good business, and worth... er... keeping. Goodbye then.'

He got to his feet, took a few steps to the edge of Mary's curtained area and spun around. He was wringing his hands.

'I really am desperately sorry about... this,' he muttered, his eyes flitting around the room. He paused for a moment, as if contemplating adding something else before thinking better of it. Mary listened to the squeak of Adam's shoes fading as he disappeared down the corridor.

*****

Two days later, on the anniversary of Henry's death, as Adam predicted, another visitor dropped in to see Mary. He was waiting for her by her bedside when she returned from a physiotherapy session.

Markus Warcup introduced himself and explained that he was her husband's solicitor, and had travelled down from Northumberland to fulfil a number of requests her husband had insisted were dealt with exactly a year after he died.

'I was sorry to learn of your ill-health. However, I believe I may have news that will aid your recovery. You may not be aware, but your husband had a variety interests,' began the solicitor.

Mary's mouth dropped open and she remained in perpetual astonishment for the next ten minutes as the solicitor ran through the terms of a will Henry had lodged with him just after his terminal illness had been diagnosed. It transpired that a stolen ruby wasn't the only item Henry had been hiding from her.

Fifty-Two

'You should have died before you arrived here in the helicopter. Whoever he was, he had to be a trained medic because he saved your life.'

'I know, I've been reminded of that several times. It's a shame too, I've always fancied a go in a helicopter but managed to remain unconscious throughout the entire journey.'

The consultant lifted his eyes from Mary's notes and regarded his patient. She sat on the side of her bed, swinging her legs like an impatient schoolgirl.

'Getting a bit stir crazy are we?' he queried with a single raised eyebrow. Mary returned a look she hoped telegraphed a sarcastic, 'Do you think so?'

'I'll have been in here two months on Friday,' she replied irritably, idly swinging her legs. It helped stem the jangling of the nerves in her leg.

This particular consultant was an amiable Asian man with a round, happy face. Mary almost felt sorry for inflicting her sarcasm on him. She had witnessed a procession of medical men and women as the days and weeks had ticked by, and although they had done a terrific job of putting her back together again, she'd had enough of the regime that characterised hospital life.

The consultant flicked over another page of Mary's medical notes and she rolled her eyes at Danny, who was sitting quietly in the chair beside her bed.

'So you can get around?'

'I've a set of sticks,' Mary replied, slanting a look to the crutches leaning against her bedside drawers, 'The physiotherapist says I'll be running by Christmas.'

'And there's someone to look after you at home?'

Mary hesitated.

'Yes,' stated Danny firmly, 'I'll be looking after her. When I'm not around there's up to another six people who will be on the premises to put up with her incessant demands and sarcastic putdowns.'

The consultant's smile deepened and he murmured something to himself as he continued to read. Mary rolled her eyes at Danny and received a stern, silent 'Stop it!' mouthed in return.

She had pitched up here, in this private recovery room at the back of the hospital, the day after Henry's solicitor had visited her. He'd arranged for her to go private after witnessing the comings and goings on the general ward and insisted he did something for her. Mary wasn't used to this sort of treatment, but hadn't complained; it was wonderful to have silence back again.

The room overlooked the York to Scarborough railway line. Twice a day Mary would rise from her bed and hobble to the window, waiting for the steam train to chug past. The East Coast line boasted its own steam train, taking day trippers, holidaymakers and railway enthusiasts to Whitby and back. It was a ritual that helped to mark the passage of her day. She'd decided to try the train journey for herself once she was released from hospital.

Released. Yes, that's what it felt like. She'd been sentenced, served her term, and depending on what this funny little consultant decided, she was about to taste freedom again. Danny was ready to take her back to Malton for a period of further recuperation at his yard. That's if she got the all clear from this parole interview.

Presently, the consultant put his clipboard down, asked a few more questions, investigated the entrance and exit wounds at the base of her abdomen and, to Mary's relief, pronounced her fit to return home as an outpatient.

With Danny's assistance, Mary slowly made her way to the ground floor and after peg-legging across the car park, she was greeted by her trusty old Volvo.

'I thought we'd travel back to Malton in style,' Danny said with his tongue in his cheek, 'I've had the windscreen replaced and the dents on the roof have been straightened out.'

He was about to turn the ignition key when Mary asked him to wait.

'You don't have to say thank you, or apologise again,' Danny insisted.

'Well I am grateful, and I should be thanking you again, but it's not that. I wondered if we could call in at my cottage in Northallerton?'

***

Despite being uninhabited for several months, the cottage looked a picture. The hollyhocks and dahlias were still in bloom and although the grass was a little long, someone had mowed it recently. Mary inspected the cottage and found herself experiencing the strangest emotions; it felt like it was no longer her house.

Once she was inside, they made straight for the kitchen. Danny led the way, pushing the door open leading from the hall. Mary peered over his shoulder, half expecting someone to be waiting for them, however the kitchen was bare and thankfully lacking in unwelcome visitors.

'What was it you wanted to pick up?'

'Nothing really, I just had a feeling...'

Danny followed Mary's gaze and discovered what had grabbed

her attention. The kitchen table was empty apart from two items at its centre; a small tin box and a folded card propped up on its lid.

'Would you?'

Danny plucked the card from the top of the tin, straightened the thick paper out and read the message, 'Yours, I believe.'

Mary was quiet for a few seconds, then wheeled around on her crutches and hobbled into the hall, calling over her shoulder as she went, 'Come on, bring the tin.'

Danny stared uncomprehendingly after Mary for a few moments before following her out with the tin rattling in his hand.

Outside, Mary wasn't struggling to fold herself into the car as he had expected, she was at her garden fence, speaking with her neighbour. They shared a short conversation and she joined Danny in the Volvo half a minute later.

'Let's get going, please,' Mary said as soon as she'd stowed her two elbow crutches in the footwell. Danny frowned, but did as he was asked.

They travelled in silence for two minutes until Mary asked him to pull over into a small lay-by beside a mature wood. The tree branches arched over the parking place, forcing the car into shadow. Danny turned the engine off and pulled out the tin box.

'Not yet,' Mary said quietly. Danny placed the tin on the dashboard and waited, not sure what was going on, but willing to be patient.

Mary began speaking. She spoke for ten minutes and finished by turning to Danny and asking, 'What do you think?'

'I think it's a wonderful idea!'

'Which one?'

'Both of them.'

'Good, that's settled then,' Mary said, beaming at her new business partner.

Fifty-Three

It was mid-afternoon when the Volvo pulled into Cordike Stables. Mary was pleased to see the yard had continued to make progress in her absence. The entrance to the yard had been widened and the car park was notably lacking in potholes. The stabling blocks had been painted and there was the tang of creosote in the air. It also appeared that all the stable doors had horse's heads inquisitively poking over them.

Danny opened the door to the farmhouse and people poured out. Mary's friends flooded into the courtyard to welcome her home with Maisie, Sarah, and Audrey leading the charge. The yard outside the farmhouse soon became a joyous huddle of people intent on congratulating Mary on her recovery. From around the yard other faces emerged, Graham joined them and a number of stable lads and lasses, old and new. There were even a few owners Mary had got to know over the previous months, plus one or two lads from George Lilley's yard, including the man himself.

Mary began shaking hands and hugging people, and when Rory dipped in and gave her a peck on her cheek, she added shocked delight to the mixture of emotions she was experiencing.

Once the initial excitement had died down, drinks had been passed around, and a chair found for Mary, Danny made a short speech and finished by announcing that Mary would not only be staying at the yard to recover, she would be a fixture at the yard for the longer term as an owner, racing secretary and as of earlier today, Danny's business partner. This was received with universal positivity from the little gathering.

'We have a couple of your friends that haven't welcomed you home yet,' Danny said in closing.

He walked to the farmhouse door, disappeared inside for a few seconds and when it reopened, Milo shot out and bounded into the yard, closely followed by a black and tan pointer with three legs.

'Charlie!' squealed Mary excitedly.

Charlie skidded to a halt, his good ear pricking and the ragged one twitching. Mary called again and the dog bounded in ungainly fashion towards his seated mistress and launched himself straight onto her lap.

'He was at the vet's for two weeks,' Juliet told her as Mary was covered in his frenetic licking, 'They couldn't save his leg, and he's a bit slower than he was, but otherwise he's fine.'

'And we have a surprise for you,' Danny called above the kerfuffle caused by Charlie's entrance. He and George Lilley crossed over to the lunging pen, went inside and closed the door behind them.

Audrey was finding it difficult to contain herself, giggling uncontrollably, which set off a few people around her who were in on the subterfuge. Mary eyed them all suspiciously. Two minutes ticked by before Maisie hunkered down beside her and said, 'Close your eyes.'

When commanded by Danny to open them thirty seconds later, Mary was greeted by the sight of George holding a liver chestnut horse with a Prophet's Thumbprint.

'I said I owed you and Danny one,' he told her.

Mary could feel the beginnings of a tear start to well in the corner of her eye, but fought it back; she'd done enough crying.

'It's Jake,' she said softly.

'I got him off Adrian Fitzpatrick. That chap who bought him out of the Seller at York never paid him for any keep, so he was put up for sale. I got him for twenty-five thousand pounds. I wondered if you'd like to buy him off me?'

Mary struggled up from her chair and with a helping hand, gave Lucky Jake a pat on his neck. The gelding held his head up high and snorted.

'He's not run since the Rous,' Danny said, 'We've had him here for a couple of weeks, and he'll be good to go to Haydock in a fortnight.'

Mary moved to shake George's hand and gently pulled him closer to her as she did.

'How about thirty thousand for Jake, and I'll make sure you get a share of any prizemoney and any sale value we get from Gentle Jill, that filly I, er...'

'You nicked from me?' George rumbled.

The two of them locked eyes, sharing a moment of understanding.

'You know she's won again since you went to hospital?' George asked.

'Danny did mention it.'

'In that case, I think that's a very fair deal,' George declared quietly.

The party broke up twenty minutes later as the owners started to say their goodbyes, and Danny and his staff filtered away to finish their work. Rory restated his offer of a weekend at the Curragh, which Mary agreed to before he headed off to the airport.

With the rest of the welcome party departed, Mary retired to the farmhouse for a coffee with her friends from Northallerton. They were bursting with questions regarding Danny's announcement, so Mary filled them in with their plans to go into partnership and her decision to move to Malton and at least for the short term, live at the farmhouse.

'Danny is going to build up this yard, and as soon as he gets close to full, which by the look of it, won't be long, we're going to find a bigger place I can buy. I love being involved in the yard, and we get on well, so I'm going to use the money I got for Lucky Jake to set us both up.'

This received unequivocal approval around the table.

'I hope you'll still visit us for our card nights!' exclaimed Audrey.

'Oh yes, I wouldn't miss them. Once I'm fit again, I hope to have plenty more outings to the races with all of you!'

In a rather more subdued tone, Mary told her friends there were a few other bits of information she felt she needed to impart.

'It turns out I'm a fairly rich widow,' Mary stated flatly.

'Isn't that a good thing?' asked Audrey, getting the distinct impression she was missing something.

'I guess so; you see Henry made a second will. It had a personal letter attached. Henry explained why he'd hidden me from Eddie for so many years,' said Mary, 'He instructed his solicitor to enact the second will a year after his death.'

'Why wait so long?' asked Maisie.

'Henry thought that if I didn't attend his funeral and I was forced to go back out to work to pay the rent on the cottage, Eddie would realise the Stone was lost and leave me alone. Unfortunately I did the exact opposite. By buying a racehorse I actually advertised the fact I was cash rich, which only stoked the flames of Eddie's obsession with getting his hands on the Stone.'

Mary went on to explain that Henry had been protecting her from Eddie for a long time and never let on, for fear it would ruin their marriage. He had led a double life, including downplaying how successful his career had been, so as not to draw Eddie's attention. In his letter he explained how he owned fifty percent of Adam's business and had invested most of his wages and profits from the business into property. He had also warned Mary to be wary of Adam, who was basically a figurehead for the company, but had a tendency to make ill-judged business decisions. Henry had still been advising him, even when he lost his speech, writing instructions to him on notes from his death bed.

'We paid rent on our little cottage for thirty years,' Mary said, 'In fact, for the last fifteen years we were actually paying ourselves. Henry bought the entire row of houses... so I'm now a landlord. I'm apparently the owner of properties dotted all around the North East.'

'What about your share in Adam's business?' prompted Audrey.

'Adam came to see me in hospital, wanting forgiveness, but I've instructed my solicitor to sell Henry's share to Adam at whatever rate the business can afford. I don't want to be in business with Adam East. It was a difficult decision though. In his letter, Henry said he got the idea to go into training security people after speaking at length with my dad, which makes the business a little special. But I've decided I could never trust Adam.'

Sarah produced an impressed whistle, 'Your Henry certainly led a complicated life.'

'You can look at all of this two ways,' Mary said with a shrug, 'I was either married to an extremely controlling, deceitful man, or you could argue Henry was willing to go to extraordinary lengths in order to protect me.'

Audrey took Mary's hand, 'I imagine it was a bit of both. You always struck me as being happy with him.'

Mary gave a sad little smile.

'I was twenty when Eddie threatened me for the first time, and I did take it pretty badly. Months later my father died and I took it badly. I can only think Henry saw how I reacted and decided he would insulate me from any further contact with his brother.'

Sarah stroked her chin thoughtfully, 'Henry may have been protecting his brother too. If he knew about Eddie and your father, maybe Henry also knew the truth about who attacked his own father.'

This brought silence to the table.

'I hadn't considered that,' admitted Mary, 'In his letter, Henry apologised at length for keeping his working life from me. He said once we'd moved to Northallerton keeping up the pretence became second nature. Eddie found me within a few years, but Henry distracted his brother enough to keep him away from me, but of course that all changed when he became ill. When he received his terminal diagnosis, Eddie saw his chance, and... well, you know the rest.

'What's happened to Eddie and that chap who was following you?'

'Eddie's on remand. He's been charged with attempted murder, but Vinny is out on bail on a much lesser charge. I'm sort of okay with that. He may be a bit of a thug, but Vinny never struck me as a killer.'

Maisie asked, 'Do the police have any leads on the man who tranquilised Eddie?'

'I don't think so.'

Sarah leaned back in her chair and crossed her legs, maintaining her focus on Mary.

'You know more about him than you're letting on.'

Mary surveyed the kitchen table to ensure she didn't catch any of her friend's eyes, and took a sip of her coffee. A lengthy pause in the conversation developed. The three ladies waited, sharing knowing glances.

Eventually Mary answered, 'Let's just say... I have my suspicions, but I'm not going to voice them, or act upon them.'

Her friends all started to complain at the same time.

Mary ignored their protests and shook her head, refusing to be drawn on the subject, but eventually relented a little.

'In Henry's letter, he told me he'd hidden the Stone and given me instructions to find it. He also said he'd done something similar a long time ago, for fun really, just in case I'd worked out what his father had meant the day he died, but he thought that letter would have been lost many years ago. He also advised to only go and recover it if I was desperate, as the Stone had only ever brought him trouble.'

'He was right there!' quipped Audrey.

'Henry also said he had put in place some protection for me, which would last as long as I needed it. He said they were true friends and he was ashamed I'd never been introduced to them.'

'So, there was more than just the man who shot Eddie?'

'Yes, I think so.'

'You're not going to share with us who that might be?' Maisie asked.

'I owe him, or perhaps them, my life, so I think they deserve to have their anonymity preserved,' Mary said with a touch of finality.

The four ladies lost themselves in introspection for a few seconds.

'So here's the big question,' said Sarah finally, eyeing each lady around the table and taking a deep, dramatic breath, 'What happened to the real Stone of Shiazzano?'

Three sets of eager eyes swivelled to rest on Mary.

She looked around each of them for a moment and then produced a coy smile, 'I think the Stone is more trouble than it's worth. But I'm guessing it'll turn up again, sooner or later.'

Fifty-Four

He settled into his padded leather seat. He was the first one there; he usually was. The rectangular pitch glowed an unnaturally fluorescent green under the floodlights, but was empty apart from the odd groundsman, so he took the time to cast his gaze around the ground.

Die-hard fans who enjoyed watching the player warm-ups were starting to cause small specs of colour to invade the racks of dark grey upturned seats. As the grandstands filled with fans, the sound of team announcements and promotional messages interspersed with middle of the road hits from over ten years ago bounced around the stadium. Bert's eyes completed their tour of the Newcastle United ground and came to rest on the two vacant seats beside him. He couldn't help imagining Henry still sitting in one of them, pontificating on the merits of the club's latest multi-million pounds signing, considering the manager's team choice, and complaining about the club's owner. It was difficult to accept his seat would remain empty.

Forrester emerged from the entrance to the stand and spotted the back of Bert's head. The familiar Breton Cap made him easy to pick out. He noted with satisfaction that the stand was currently largely empty; perfect for what he had in mind. He dropped down the steps until he was one row above Bert, then silently made his way across until he was standing directly behind him. He bent down, so he was only inches away from his target.

'I thought I might beat you here tonight!' he boomed into Bert's ear, 'I should know better, you're always where you're supposed to be.'

Bert looked up, initially shocked but immediately recognised his best friend and his face lit up in greeting.

'Kevin! Bloody good to see you, it's been a while!'

The two men shook hands firmly and quickly embraced, after which Bert Heck and Kevin Forrester sat down in the same match-day seats they had occupied for the last thirty years. They exchanged some small-talk. Bert enquired after Kevin's family and he reciprocated, but their conversation soon took a more serious turn.

'So we're done,' Kevin said.

'Yeah. I left the cottage in Northallerton a fortnight ago. Someone else was in there within a few days. I even cut both lawns before I left,' he added thoughtfully.

'Ever the professional,' Kevin joked, 'I spoke with Vincent for the last time a week ago to wrap things up. Told him I'd had a better offer and to find my replacement.'

'He'll probably be glad to be rid of you. I assume he never guessed your real allegiance?'

'Not a chance. He was blinded by his devotion to Eddie. As long as he thought I was trying to usurp him by sucking up to Eddie, I was safe.'

'How's he coping without his boss?' Bert enquired.

'Like a lost lamb. He won't be able to cope. He was a foot soldier, not a leader. That business will wither and die without Eddie; besides, there's still a chance Vincent will be joining Eddie in prison if the police have their way,' Forrester noted.

The two men fell silent as they stood up in unison to allow two other fans to slide past them and take their seats further along the row.

'Did you get the Stone to Mary?' Forrester asked once they'd retaken their seats.

'I watched her go into her house and find it,' Bert replied, displaying a warm expression of remembrance.

'Henry really was nothing like his brother,' Forrester marvelled, 'I still can't believe how easy it was for me to switch the two Stones. And Eddie fell for you being a jewellery expert hook, line and sinker.'

Bert smiled his agreement but didn't reply.

Forrester pushed his glasses up his nose and adjusted his twenty-year-old Newcastle Brown sponsored 'Toon' bobble hat to keep the September breeze from cooling his bald head.

'My final payment from Henry's solicitor came through a few days ago. I don't have to work again if I don't want to.'

Bert turned and caught his friend's eye, 'Strange, isn't it. It's been the longest security job of my life, the most lucrative, and in doing it for Henry, my most fulfilling. I thought I'd feel relieved, but I actually miss it already.'

Forrester chuckled, 'I don't miss working for that swine Eddie, or having to spar with Vincent, but it was three years well spent for Henry and my bank balance.'

'Yep,' agreed Bert, 'I reckon Henry would have been satisfied with the way things worked out. Although, I still smart at the thought of Mary being shot on my watch...'

'We couldn't have known he'd go to Malton with a pistol, or that he'd be stupid enough to use it. I got no indication he kept a gun around the place,' Forrester pointed out.

'She recognised me,' Bert said quietly, 'I'm sure of it. She was lying there, bleeding out, and didn't take her eyes off me before she lost consciousness.'

'If she did see your face, she can't have told anyone,' suggested Forrester.

'Maybe she realised there's no need for people like us in her life anymore,' Bert said stiffly, 'Henry made it crystal clear not to become involved unless we had to.'

'Still, you took a chance allowing Eddie into her cottage,' Kevin admitted, 'I watched my phone for messages all night expecting the worst.'

Bert grimaced, 'Mary needed to know beyond any doubt that Eddie was a serious threat. I thought it was an opportunity and managed the risk. She was never in any real danger.'

'Do you think Mary ever cottoned on that you were monitoring the cottage and could move between the two houses at will?'

'No,' Bert replied with a shake of his head, 'And Eddie had no idea I was watching him from only a few yards away. Henry's idea to allow me access through the loft came in really handy. It was a calculated risk to allow Eddie to slip in behind her. Mind you, I expected her to report him to the police, not grill him, share a video call to Newcastle and then embarrass him in front of the terrace!'

The two men met each other's gaze and shared a moment of amusement.

'How is she by the way?' asked Forrester, 'Did you get to see her in the hospital?'

'I made sure she was asleep when I popped in. They did a decent job of putting her back together. She was lucky,' ruminated Bert, 'Still, it was a mistake to underestimate Eddie's propensity for hatred. Henry wouldn't have made that sort of error. I got lucky.'

Keen to change the subject, Kevin said, 'She'll recover. She's tougher than Henry gave her credit. He thought the world of that woman. The way she played East, Amari, and Eddie off against each other at York races, I get the feeling she'll be just fine on her own.'

Bert brightened a little, 'You're right. Mary Romano *will* be fine. She's a fine woman.'

The players took to the pitch to a smattering of applause and the two men watched the warm-up and spoke no more of their three-year-long contract to protect Mary Romano. The seats around them filled, and half an hour later the match started. Beside the two men, the seat reserved for season ticket holder, Mr Henry Romano, remained empty.

Fifty-Five

Eddie Romano crossed his cell, found the remote control, flicked the television on, and channel hopped until he caught the local news.

He scowled at having missed the main body of the broadcast; the presenter was finishing with that bit of frivolous news supposed to leave you on an upbeat note.

'Finally, a cancer charity worker in York had the shock of her life earlier this week,' reported the female anchor.

Over pictures of a young woman holding up a ruby the size of a large marble, the anchor continued, 'A small tin box deposited anonymously with their charity was found to contain an incredibly valuable gemstone. The Burmese ruby has been valued at fifteen million pounds. The charity, that supports cancer care in the York and District area, said it was the biggest single donation they have ever received and wanted to publically thank their mystery benefactor.'

A shot of the studio returned and the presenter paused to smile into the camera, 'Whoever and wherever you are, a huge thank you...'

Eddie planted his foot into the screen, bringing the news report, and the working life of his television, to an end.

Enjoyed this book?

I do hope you have enjoyed reading this horseracing story. If you have, I'd *really* appreciate it if you would visit the Amazon website and leave a rating and perhaps a short review. Your ratings and reviews help readers find my books, which in turn means I can dedicate more time to writing.

Go to: https://www.amazon.co.uk/Richard-Laws/e/B07J1HYTR5/ or simply visit **www.amazon.co.uk** and search for 'Richard Laws'.

Many thanks,

Richard Laws
June 2020

Printed in Great Britain
by Amazon